“Beem laces his absurdist plot with kooky imagery… Outlandish, hectic, and sometimes illogical but undeniably entertaining.

— *Kirkus Reviews*

ALSO BY DAVID BEEM

*Abyss of Chaos*

# EDGER

DAVID
BEEM

www.davidbeem.com

First Escapistpress paperback printing: 2018
Printed in the United States of America

This book is a work of fiction. References to real people, celebrities, events, establishments, organizations, or locales are intended only to provide a sense of authenticity, and are used fictitiously. All characters, incidents and dialogue, are drawn from the author's imagination and are not to be construed as real.



Edger

www.davidbeem.com
ISBN 978-0-9838724-2-9

FOR CARRIE AND MAX

BUT ONLY AFTER THEY GROW UP!

# THE COW IN THE PORN STORE

THE STORE IS NOT LARGE. The lighting is dim, yellow, and hazy. The stench of barn and patchouli permeates everything; it is in the worn corduroy sofa behind the register; it is in the drab, no-color carpet, the beads hanging in the doorway. And it is in the box of buttless red leather pants on clearance for only $7.99 in Aisle Two.

Until this moment, it has been business as usual in the El Cerrito Adult Emporium, where the highlight of Dhruv's nights is to harry the sneaking underage teenage boys, bellowing at the top of his lungs, and swatting the Purple Paddle of Passion at their fleeing rear ends. But on this night, even the teenagers are in short supply. The place is dead. Has been for hours. And then...*barn stench.*

Dhruv had just stepped out for a quick trip to the john. The Maker's Mark he'd started an hour earlier had broken the seal. He'd figured, what's the worst that can happen? Not likc hc can't keep an ear on things from the back. The orgasm doorbell's plenty loud. That's what drew him out, hands dripping wet, shirt corner crammed through his fly hole.

The brown cow's chewing mandibles are hypnotic. Peaceful. Like it doesn't have a care in the world, despite it having wandered into his store. Dhruv folds his arms. His forehead tightens. *Is this cow even eighteen?*

He glances over his shoulder. No one there. *Good.* No one around to get the wrong idea. *He* certainly hadn't left that pile of hay in the middle of the store. He isn't trying to attract cows. Cows aren't his thing. *His* thing is to stock a cornucopia of pornography. And while he did recently shelve a DVD called *Graze Anatomy and Udder Offal Tales,* never once did he imagine selling it to a literal cow.

Dhruv scans the four security mirrors. *Whoops—not alone.* Aisle Ten. Short guy. Asian. Mid-twenties. Long bangs sticking out like black straw from beneath a pantyhose cap. Not one of the regulars.

"This your cow?" asks Dhruv.

The customer's gaze darts left and right. Dhruv's stomach knots. The customer snatches an inflated blowup doll from the display stand and squeezes it against his chest.

"Hey," says Dhruv, uncrossing his arms. "Stop that!"

The customer squeezes harder, and the doll's head swells and tips back like a pornographic Pez dispenser.

"Hey!" yells Dhruv.

Yanking the pantyhose down over his face, the customer bolts for the door.

"Stop!" yells Dhruv at the same time a loud slap issues from the cow's backside. The animal squeals and lurches forward, a large dart now protruding from its flank. Dhruv, his heart racing, scampers backward—

A crash from behind wheels him around.

A second man emerges from beneath a toppled lingerie rack in Aisle Two. One bra is hooked to his ear and a second is hooked to the diving flippers he has inexplicably worn into the store. Tall, salt-and-pepper hair, linen shirt, Bermuda trunks. This man's eyes widen at the sight of Dhruv, and then he reaches into the pile of lingerie at his feet. Bras, G-strings, and corsets are chucked into the air before he comes up with a dart gun and clomps for the door like it's the Frog Olympics.

Dhruv dives for cover behind a six-foot-three cardboard zucchini. *Can* dart guns shoot through cardboard zucchinis? He has no idea, but the erectile-dysfunction display is the nearest hiding spot, so it will have to do. Pulling in his arms and legs, panting, he tracks the invaders in the security mirrors.

The doorbell emits an ecstatic moan as the thief and blowup doll exit first, followed by a second, louder moan as the flipper-footed gunman triggers it again. He swats the beads hanging in the doorway, shoves the thief's back, and chances a glance over his shoulder—but the cow skids to a halt at Aisle One.

A droplet of sweat falls from the tip of Dhruv's nose. The drubbing inside his chest won't slow. He silently berates himself for having ever stocked *Graze Anatomy*. He thought he'd been so clever at the time. *Oh, look at this title. I bet it's a real cash cow.* He'd like to go back and slap himself. He couldn't say whether the movie had caused all this trouble. He only knew stocking it seemed to him now to be the mother of all cock-in-bull ideas, and one he was unlikely to repeat.

In the security mirror, the cow's dizzying black eyeball scans the movies on the shelf. Enlarged nostrils flare. A tail swats back and forth. The cow snatches a plastic case in her mouth and lurches back to a sprint, catching the still-closing door just in time and nearly blasting it off the hinges. The door rebounds off the exterior wall and bangs shut. The hanging beads crash to the ground and scatter. Then—silence.

Dhruv does nothing at first but pant and sweat from behind the cardboard zucchini. A high-pitched tone glows like a clarinet in his ears. A DVD case, one near the spot where the cow had stolen the other, slides from the top shelf and slaps the floor. Minutes later, Dhruv emerges from his hiding spot and picks his way through the beads to the front door. He flips the bolt. He turns the sign from OPEN to CLOSED. He pulls down the security gate and locks the bottom. Having managed all this without further incident, Dhruv then resolves to do what any self-respecting porn proprietor in his situation would do—he fetches his bottle of Maker's Mark and commits himself to finishing what he'd started over the next hour and a half.

*And* he vows never again to stock animal porn of any kind.

# TED, ED, AND THE A-TEAM

A BLACK ESCALADE pulls into a 7-Eleven parking lot, headlights off. Its two silent occupants track the spectacle unfolding across the street at the El Cerrito Adult Emporium.

There, a vintage black-and-metallic-gray Vandura squeals to a halt, momentarily blocking their line of sight to the porn store's entrance. Its rooftop spoiler, black-and-red mag wheels, and signature red stripe are identical to the vehicle used in the eighties seminal television hit, *The A-Team*. Dust covers the back window where someone has written *I pity the fool*. The front windows are down. The radio is up. The theme song to the television show is blaring into the nighttime California sky.

A man in a stocking mask, carrying a blowup sex doll under his left arm, rounds the front of the van. He flings open the door and shoves the driver over before tossing the sex doll in after him, buckling up, and peeling out. The theme song to the A-Team melts into the night.

Next, a stampeding cow with a DVD case in its mouth charges down the street.

The two men in the black Escalade exchange puzzled glances, sit forward in their seats, watch, wait, tense...

The owner of the Adult Emporium closes the store, and the two men slump back in their seats. They're too late. Their target—a dart-gun-toting neurologist in diving flippers—has eluded them once again.

"Told you we shouldn't have stopped for drive-through."

"It's demoralizing is what it is. What say we leave the flippers out of the report?"

"Mm-hmm."

The two men are wearing Ray-Bans at night. They are dressed in identical black suits, ties, and wing-tipped black shoes. They're holding identical .300 Win Mag sniper rifles. They're also wearing identical Fruit of the Loom underpants. Their names are Ted and Ed.

"Fine," says Ted. "So we lost him again. We've been losing this guy for going on twenty years, so, you know, business as usual there. But, I mean, we gotta kill somebody, though. Right?"

"Kill somebody?" Ed shrugs. "Well, *yeah*. By all means, kill away." Tapping the dashboard clock, he adds, "But no way we're makin' the eleven fifty to Miami."

"No," agrees Ted, targeting the cow, which is waiting for the light to change one block farther on. "What say I pop Moo Town?"

"The cow? What'd the cow ever do to you?" says Ed. "How 'bout that guy there?"

Ted's scope pans across the El Cerrito Adult Emporium to a graffiti-laden Dumpster where a butt and legs are flailing over the top like a malfunctioning squid.

"Two points," mutters Ed, gazing sideways at his partner.

Wordlessly, Ted shifts the rifle, bracing it into his shoulder. He lines up his sights, squeezes the trigger. The gun recoils. The silencer mutes the shot. Across the street, the owner of the butt and legs falls into the Dumpster. Ted passes Ed the rifle before turning the key in the ignition. The engine roars to life. The headlights turn on.

"Where to?" asks Ed.

"HQ," replies Ted. "Fred, Ned, Red, and Zed are probably wondering what the hell's goin' on."

Ed arches an eyebrow. "Not Ked?"

Ted identically arches an eyebrow. "Ked? You kidding? Psh. That guy's in bed."

# DRAMATIS PERSONAE

### *THE LIVING...*

Edger Bonkovich (Dork)
Mike Dame (CEO, Founder, InstaTron)
Mary Thomas (Mike Dame's Personal Assistant)
Caleb Montana (Quarterback, LA Chargers; Butt Model, Calvin Klein)
Wang and Shmuel (Stoners, The A-Team)
Fabio (Edger's Best Friend)
Gran (Edger's Dear Old Gran)
Shep (Edger's Gran's Former Marine Boyfriend)
Doctor Alexandra Hamilton (International Woman of Mystery)

### CLUCK-N-PRAY, TEAM EL CERRITO

Brad (Manager)
Christine (Team Member)
The Apostles: Mathew, Mark, Luke, & John (Team Members)
Consuelo (Mouth-Fart Stylist, Drug Dealer, Team Member)

### CLUCK-N-PRAY, TEAM MISSION GORGE

Judas S. Carry-Out (Franchise Owner)
Blake and Sheldon (Team Members)

### BAD GUYS

InstaTron Tron (Nano Artificial Intelligence)
Chicowgo (Cow)
Yourmajesty Fapa'fapa-Bal'buster (Defensive Tackle, GB Packers)
Ted, Ed, Ked, Ned, etc. (Nostradamus Agents)

MORE DRAMATIS!

# DRAMATIS PERSONAE

MORE PERSONAE!

## ...AND THE DEAD

Herodotus (Busted Greek Classic, Father of History)
Bruce Lee (Martial Arts Legend)
Lieutenant Trevor Killmaster (Navy SEAL)
Tim from Philly (A guy named Tim who used to live in Philly)
Indiana Tim (A guy named Tim who used to live in Indiana)
Hattori Hanzo (Iga Ninja)
Harry Houdini (Magician, Bit of a Dick)
Samson (Strong Man, Ancient Romance Novel Cover Model)
Michael Jackson (King of Pop)
Bubba (Bomb Expert, Cutter of Red Wires)

# HISTORICAL NOTE FROM YOUR FATHER OF HISTORY, HERODOTUS (C. 484—C. 425 BCE)

IT HAS BEEN SAID every story has to start somewhere. And it's good this has been said, because otherwise there'd be no one starting anything and nothing for anyone to read. As advice goes, it's solid. It's right up there with, *Careful, Robin, both hands on the Batrope*. Or, *When the Chinese buffet reopens, proceed with caution*.

It's the contradictory advice that gets a person into trouble. The early bird gets the worm, but the second mouse gets the cheese. Nothing ventured, nothing gained, but better safe than sorry. Advice like that is the mental equivalent of a bird crashing into a glass door. It can be frustrating to constantly be told to get down to business if you're in the business of going up, like, say, an astronaut. Especially since, in space, up stops being up. It can be sideways, diagonal, forward, or backward. Space is relative, and relativity tells us First Mouse can teleport the cheese straight into the hole where it can then be shared with Second Mouse and everyone's happy. Everyone but Early Bird, because in this scenario, all the hungry neighbor birds conspired and murdered Early Bird in its sleep. They did this, first, because they were a band of homicidal maniacs with a long list of priors; second, because Early Bird was annoying everyone with its smug go-get-'em attitude; and third, because Early Bird had long ago lost the Eye of the Tiger and had become far too fat and slow to escape, due to constantly getting all the good worms.

Where were we?

Ah, yes. Every story has to start somewhere. Ours begins with a simple dork by the name of Edger Bonkovich. Prepare now to travel into his mind through the shared psychic network known as the Collective Unconscious. Prepare to know what he knows, feel what he feels, and think as he thinks...

In other words, prepare to be disappointed.

I'll grant you, Mr. Bonkovich may not look like much at first. But, as they say, desperate times call for desperate measures. Or do they say better safe than sorry? It's one of those things. The point is, the forces of evil are afoot, and the world needs its hero...

# CHAPTER ONE

"WELCOME TO ÜBER DORK," I monotone, tapping my name tag. "My name is Edger, *Ed-jer*, and I'll be your Dork. How can I help you?"

I look up from my workstation, and my heart stops beating. Time chokes on the universe, which stops, rolls over, legs up, dead.

Before me is an angel sent from heaven.

I swallow, but it's like swallowing the sands of Tatooine.

Cough, cough. Hack.

Heart kicks back in.

For one timeless and exquisite moment, I escape the earthly confines of my job. There are no computers to fix. There are no laptops to sell. The tablets, cell phones, and smart TVs are gone too. The Über Dork fades away, and between one moment and the next, I find myself gliding on a rainbow slide in the sky—with *her*.

Cue the bow-chicka-bow-bow music.

This isn't the first time I've seen her. Usually I'm in the mall, before or after my shift. She'll be shopping. I'll be trying not to stare. Sometimes I see her talking to Frank, a custodian I know. And one time, I saw some teenagers litter in the food court, and she went out of her way to pick it up and throw it in the trash. Which, let's face it, is pretty much rarer than spotting a pink Wookiee canoodling with a crapulent Klingon.

But now she's *here*.

"Edger Bonkovich?" she says, smiling.

She knows my name. The angel knows my name.

She's talking again—but—dang it, I missed it. Brain rewinds, plays it back. She has a slight accent. It makes her sound intelligent. I hope she's intelligent. Or maybe she's CIA and her cover is working at the Wienerlicious Hot Dog Shop like that one girl from that one show. Maybe she's come bearing the Intersect and I'm about to embark on a life of international espionage, spies, and fantastic save-the-world feats of heroism. *Maybe I even get to kiss the girl.*

"My name is Mary Thomas," she says. "I work for Mike Dame."

Nope. Not like the TV show, then.

She reaches into her purse, designer purse, I have no idea what kind, I mean, come on, I'm a guy, but this purse looks expensive, and so, right, she's pulling out this business card and smiling, and it's incredible, it's like that minty gum commercial, right down to the little "ping" you hear when the light gleams off her teeth, and I know then and there I want to be friends with that smile, best friends, except that doesn't make any sense, because you can't be best friends with a smile.

Oh my God, I'm practically panting.

"Mr. Dame'd like you to take off early tonight." She slides the business card over the counter. "He wants you to come up to his office. Nine o'clock sharp."

"Is this carbon fiber?"

"Hmm? Oh. Yes."

MIKE DAME
CEO AND FOUNDER, INSTATRON
SAN DIEGO, CALIFORNIA

"Hey," she says. "Are you okay?"

*Edge, get it together. Say something!*

"Meep," I say. "Meep."

*Okay, say nothing! Say nothing!*

Brain shifts gears: What am I doing? Right. Mike Dame wants to see me—wait—*Mike Dame* wants to see *me?*

"Ah-hah," I say, studying the card again. Mike Dame. Actual boss of my boss's boss's boss's boss's boss. "Wow. So, uh, did Mr. Dame say what this is about?"

Her eyes sparkle. "He didn't give me a reason. I assumed you two knew each other."

My mouth feels like someone's drawing a Charlie Brown smile on it. Probably there are Valentine's Day hearts popping up around my head. She's looking expectantly at me, and I remember I'm supposed to be doing something other than extruding cartoon animation from my face.

"If you'd like," she says, "I can clear it with the store manager for you." She steals a glance over her shoulder. "I'm not sure Mr. Dame would like having to call down himself. Mr. Bonkovich, you do know Über Dork is our subsidiary. InstaTron is the holding company."

"Subsidiary," I mutter. "Holding company."

And now she's frowning at me like I forgot to pay my brain bill. *Did* I forget to pay my brain bill? And to think, just a second ago I was worried about her not being intelligent.

"Psh," I say. "Of course." Her frown smooths out. "It's just... Mike Dame. You know?"

"I know. Mike Dame. Shall I clear it, then?"

"Hmm? Oh. You mean with my momijer. Manager!"

Her gaze drops for a second, then flits up to meet mine, and it's like getting popped between the eyes with a baseball, if a baseball felt good and gave you the warm fuzzies. Otherwise, it's nothing like getting popped between the eyes with a baseball.

"Ah...right," she says. "So, that's your manager over there?"

She points. I nod. This much, at least, goes smoothly.

"Very well," she says. "I'll tell Mr. Dame you're coming. Mr. Bonkovich."

She gives me a flirty wave with her fingers, and I watch, paralyzed, as she glides off to corner Jama Jan, our store manager. Mary Thomas reaches into her purse and hands out another one of those outrageously expensive business cards. At which point, the next customer steps up, blocking my view. Big guy. Wide. Black leather jacket.

"Yo. S'up?" he says.

But rational thought has left the building. Big Wide Black Leather Jacket Person is blocking my view of the Divine Being. I weave left. I weave right. I lean way, way over to steal a last, fleeting glimpse of Mary Thomas heading out into the wash of yellows and reds of the setting San Diego sun.

"Yo. Not cool, man," says the guy across the counter, who is also leaning way, way over to frame his angry-customer face in my field of vision.

"Ah—I'm…sorry?"

"Dude like you ain't never gonna get no girl like that."

I release an involuntary sigh.

"I'm sorry, sir," I say, and we straighten in unison. I slip the business card into my shirt pocket and tap my name tag. "Welcome to Über Dork. My name is Edger, Ed-jer, I'll be your Dork. How can I help you?"

"You can help me by fixing my computer." He slaps his InstaTron Plus down on the countertop and shoves it toward me. I slide it closer, open it up, and get to work, but it's slow going. The world, which was in glorious color again for the first time in forever, has faded back into gray. I'm talking to the guy in front of me as I work, and he's nice enough now that I'm being a proper Dork. Lots of "mmm-hmms" and "yeahs" coming from that side of the counter. My voice reverts to its work monotone, but this is as good as it gets here. I help this guy, and he's genuinely happy about it. This constitutes one of the only real wins I get.

"You're all right," he says, examining my name tag. "Ed-gur. I'm sorry I got mad at you, boy."

"It's Ed-jer. Ah—you know what? Forget it."

"Ed-jer. Okay. Ed-jer, can I give you some advice?"

"Hmm? Oh, yeah. Sure."

"If that girl ever comes back, don' you go sayin' 'meep' no mo. You got to stop that shit."

I nod and thank him. I am, after all, not a complete dork.

# CHAPTER TWO

MY SMARTWATCH says it's seventy-two degrees in downtown San Diego. The sky over the bay is a nice shade of purple as I cut across Broadway and Front. InstaTron Corporate Headquarters is in Emerald Plaza, just a few blocks from the Westfield Horton Plaza Über Dork branch where I work, but my stomach is already in knots. And it's not because of Mary Thomas. It's because I can't see a way to get out of this meeting.

Leg vibrates. I dig out my phone.

Fabio.

"Hey, buddy," I say.

"Dude. *Mike Dame?*"

"You heard," I reply, jumping out of the way of a speeding bicyclist. Fabio says something at the same time a city bus hisses, releasing a giant plume of hot black smog and otherwise making the air taste like a mixture of exhaust and a Five Dollar Footlong.

"Sorry," I say. "Bus just went by. Can you say that again?"

"I said, maybe he's gonna write you a big fat check."

"A check?"

"Yeah. A settlement. You know. So you don't go to the press about how you basically earned *the* Mike Dame his bachelor's."

I roll my eyes.

"Right. Fabio, Mikey never needed me to do his homework. He

just trusted me to get the answers right. There's a difference."

"Oh, sure," he replies, his voice dripping with sarcasm. "And the fact that *Mikey's* corner office is in Emerald Plaza and yours is across from the food court is just, what? Karma?"

"Maybe. Hey, is there gonna be a point?" I'm winded. I slow my pace and try to catch my breath. But it isn't my pace that's the problem. My problem is me having not seen Mikey in five years. My problem is all the invisible baggage on my shoulders.

"Dude," says Fabio. "I always knew you were meant for better things. You always knew you were meant for bigger things. This isn't hard."

"It isn't? Maybe you'd like to go instead?"

"Nah, I'm good. Besides, you already know him. You're one of the few people on the planet who know him as Mikey, Edge. There is absolutely no way you leave that office without a promotion."

"A promotion?" I exclaim, as two speeding rollerbladers careen straight at me. "To what? Store manager?"

The thrum of skates on concrete freezes me where I stand. I brace myself, anticipating a crash that is as inevitable as the one waiting for me at the top of Emerald Plaza, but at the last minute, they part and zip past. Their wake lifts my hair and ripples my shirt.

"Dude," says Fabio. "He knows you've got the goods. And now he's found out you're working for his company. The way I see it, all you've got to do is pretend you don't have Tourette's for ten, fifteen minutes tops, and you'll be making bank."

"I don't have Tourette's."

"You're right. Saying you have Tourette's is an insult to people with Tourette's."

I stop at the corner of Broadway and State and wait for the light, clench my eyes, and count to ten.

"I gotta go," I say.

"Don't fuck this up."

"So helpful. Thanks."

I press End Call. The light turns green. A horn blares when the first car in line doesn't move fast enough, and I startle. Business suits brush past me on either side. I teeter into the street, then stop. My gaze pans up…and up, and up. Emerald Plaza. The concrete frame gives up somewhere around the twentieth floor with the tops of the eight towers becoming hexagonal glass green roofs. I shove my phone into my pocket and loosen my tie. This is crazy. I'm not going up there. Not going to happen.

The light turns yellow. A car honks at me, and I hurry to the other side. *Crap.* I can't just say I didn't get the message. I need my job. But would Mikey *really* fire me for being a no-show?

I try to picture him as I knew him in South Bend. In a pickup game at the gym. Sharing a large fry at Five Guys. But the memories are burned at the edges like pictures you find after a fire. Standing at the bottom of these towers of concrete and steel, knowing his world is up there and mine is down here, those charred memories are hotter than ever.

Still winded, I push through the front doors and into the lobby. The white noise and high-ceiling atrium inside are dizzying. It's like I'm locked inside a Hitchcock camera lens doing that reverse vertigo trick. I try to block it all out and mind my own business. I cast around for the elevator—*there*. A glass case with a glowing green pyramid on top. It's an elevator fit for Willy Wonka. No wonder Mikey likes it here. As I stand in front of it, my pulse rises. I don't know if Mikey *would* fire me, but he certainly *could*. I picture Gran's face after telling her the paychecks have stopped, and my thumb pushes the Up button. The doors open, and I go inside.

# CHAPTER THREE

THE ELEVATOR stops at the twenty-seventh floor. Staring at my reflection in the closed doors, I quickly lick my hand and press down a thick crop of crazy hair. My reflection splits in two—and here's Mary Thomas.

Standing in front of her is as terrifying and reality-bending as before. My brain slips into a cheesy and cinematic parallel universe. I know it's nighttime, but somehow, rays of sunshine beam down through the ceiling onto her long, silky blonde hair. She tosses it side to side in slow motion. A faraway boys' choir is singing in Latin, and even though I don't know Latin, it's obvious they're singing about her girl-next-door face, her fair skin and bright eyes, her tan leather jacket with lots of cool zippers—and most especially they're singing about her oh-my-God-long-legs and tight-fitting jeans. For this is one horny boys' choir.

"Mr. Bonkovich?"

My eyes flutter as I crash-land into reality. No more slow-motion hair tossing. No more horny boys' choir. Just this beautiful woman and my dry mouth. For a second, I can't say anything. I can't do anything besides marvel at how her accent makes my name sound sophisticated.

"Mr. Bonkovich?" she says again, sticking out her hand to keep the doors from closing.

"Hey," I reply, jutting my chin out and trying to play it cool.

"Thank you for coming," she says, eyeing me doubtfully. "This way."

She gestures down a corridor to the right. I exit the elevator, and we're off to the races. Her long legs are really moving. Her shoulders squared, hips swinging. She's no-nonsense sexy. And since she's emitting beauty rays comparable in power to the Death Star Superlaser, I clear my throat and cast around for anything else to input into the brain subprogram, lest my eyes become disrespectfully trapped in the Mary Thomas Zone.

Outside the tall windows on my left is the nighttime cityscape and the San Diego bay. That'll do. City lights in pinks and purples reflect on the ocean. Pretty. The clear California sky is a deep midnight blue. Fantastic. And depressing. It reminds me of what Fabio said earlier. My "office" is across from the food court. What would it be like to work up here instead?

My gaze pans unconsciously to peer through the shorter windows on my right. Through those is a conference room larger than the entire sales floor at the Über Dork. Everyone inside is younger than me. They're wearing ripped-up jeans, skirts, yoga pants, beanies. They've got scooters parked on the wall, and they're eating sushi and noodles and laughing as someone keeps hijacking the PowerPoint presentation with a music video of a guy singing, "Give me compliments." It's like we don't even work for the same company. Nobody in *there* has to wear a shirt that says DORK.

"You seem nervous," Mary Thomas says suddenly.

"Turnip."

"I beg your pardon?"

"Nothing."

"Did you say turnip?"

"Probably not." The key to playing it cool, I figure, is to keep trying. "So, uh, what's the rent on this place?"

"Two hundred," she replies, and by the way she's smiling at me, she can totally tell I couldn't give two shits about the rent but needed something to talk about and so why not rent? "It's a fair amount of space," she says. "But I expect we'll be needing more soon."

"More space?"

The corridor dead-ends at a pair of floor-to-ceiling glass doors with sleek chrome handles. She turns to face me. Her head tilts slightly to the side. Her forehead creases.

"Well," she says. "We can't stay here forever now, can we?"

"But… I just met you."

Mary raises a perfectly arched eyebrow. And then my subconscious throws me a bone. "Hey. You're Australian."

Again, her head tilts. "Good catch. Thought I'd lost my accent."

"Don't worry," I hurry to say, smiling. "I won't hold it against you. There's only one human race."

Her eyes narrow as she peers obliquely into mine. "You're very wise," she teases.

My heart skips a beat, and then she gestures with her hand at the glass doors, through which is a waiting area and receptionist seated behind a desk. The receptionist's floral blouse, permanent frown lines, and glowing blue earbuds are giving off an unmistakable frumpy cyborg vibe. Kind of like a female Lobot from *The Empire Strikes Back*.

A hand touches my arm, zaps me with static electricity. I flinch.

"Ooh!" Mary Thomas jerks her hand back. "Sorry. Hey. Don't be nervous, Mr. Bonkovich." She smiles faintly. "I won't let him bite you."

"You can call me Edger," I hear myself say, and her smile goes full-on, one hundred watts of gleaming beauty power. The knot in my stomach falls apart.

"Well then," she says lightly, her eyes sparkling. "You'll just have to call me Mary."

Mary pulls the door open, and we go inside.

"Henrietta," says Mary. "This is Edger Bonkovich."

The receptionist comes out from behind her desk, and her dour features read like a book: *Let's get this over with*.

"Mr. Bonkovich."

"Edger, please," I say, extending my hand. "It's nice to meet you."

Her eyes narrow to slits, and her mouth forms a

cartoonish one-sided frown. "*Escher*."

We shake. I clear my throat.

"Uh... Ed-*jer*."

"Sorry," she replies, but her unchanging expression makes it sorry-not-sorry. "This way. Ed-*sure*."

I try to smile, but I might as well be trying to make ambidextrous Spock eyebrows. I can't even figure out what muscles to use. I look to Mary for support, but she only nods for me to follow Henrietta. Next thing, we're striding down another hallway, this one ending in a set of doors as massive as the last.

"Mikey likes his big doors, huh?"

Henrietta gives me a withering look.

"*Mister* Dame will see you now. Ecker."

She heaves the doors open, and since I'm happy for any excuse to look away from her raging condescension, such as an Act of God, asteroid, comet, or, really, a one-spotted ladybug would do fine, I turn and get my first glimpse into an office larger than some Third World countries.

*"Holy crap."*

Mary and I step inside, and the doors swing shut behind us. I wait for my eyes to adjust to the darkness. Mesh shades are drawn over floor-to-ceiling windows in a room that's a museum of anachronisms: a model steam wagon sits next to a model Tesla; a katana next to an AR-15; a samurai suit of armor beside...beside what I can only assume is either a superhero costume, or else your basic space-ninja body-armor-type deal. Kurosawa meets cyberpunk. Black and sleek with chrome detailing. Probably Mikey's billionaire cosplay outfit for Comic-Con. The exhibits are displayed on pedestals under track lighting, shelves, or sunken show areas, like the one displaying a full-scale mockup of a da Vinci glider parked next to a modern glider.

"Holy crap," I say again, my voice squeaking with excitement. "That radiotelephone's bigger than a football!"

Mary's gaze zeroes right in on the radiotelephone, despite its position being mostly obscured by all the other features on display. She casts a sidelong glance at me, her eyes sparkling with mischief.

"Now *there's* a good example of size being overrated," she says, smiling on one side only.

"Yeah," I say, doing my best to tamp down my excitement at finding a girl like this one who appreciates the value of microchips. "The radiotelephone predates its cellular counterpart. And don't get me started on the difference between the modern smartphone and the—"

"Same old Edger."

I recognize him intuitively; the timbre of his voice, a silver, Ferrari kind of sound. The kind of timbre you hear in a really great tenor. And his height, say, six-foot-two. Shorter than me, but still tall. And then there's his athletic build, silhouetted against the weak light pinching in through the window shades. Seeing him there, I'm drenched in sensory memory: the feel of autumn in South Bend; glimmering sunlight through blazing red and yellow leaves; the smell as you come into Fitzpatrick Hall after they've mopped the floors. And Kate—and I can't see Mikey without thinking about Kate—these experiences come flooding back all at once, and with the ache of a broken promise.

# CHAPTER FOUR

I'D HEARD KATE'S VOICE from across the quad. Her brassy, commanding tone crawled into my head like a conspiracy theory. I wordlessly picked up my soccer ball, both teams yelling at my back, and space-walked from the field in search of the voice. Like a siren song, it lured me, into the trees and gimlet sun, to emerge into a gathering on the far side.

She'd been moderating a debate there, apparently wrapping up. I leapt out of the way as a gaggle of girls carted a podium, microphone, and amp off on a dolly. Kate turned to spot me doing my best not to stare at her like a thirteen-year-old at the window of a Victoria's Secret. I guess I couldn't have been too overt. She took it I'd been there as part of her whole deal, because she stalked straight up to me to hand me a stack of papers and said, "Come on." The fact that I was sweaty and wearing soccer shorts, soccer socks, shin guards, cleats, a soccer shirt, and holding a soccer ball didn't seem to tip her off that I had no clue on God's green earth about what had just been debated. Maybe they'd been debating soccer. When I leafed through the papers and found nothing neither pro nor con to do with soccer I naturally did what any red-blooded, virile, heterosexual male in my situation would do: I blanked.

I couldn't think of what to say. It's possible, in hindsight, I said "turnip." I don't think I did. I have on occasion been known to say "kumquat," just to change things up a bit. On that day, I managed to say nothing at all. And I think nothing at all must've been the right thing not to say—because she smiled at me.

Kate was intelligent, beautiful, and had a killer body, which she kept in tip-top shape at CrossFit. I spent most of our relationship in a constant state of bamboozlement. It didn't make sense to me that I'd managed to score even *one* date, let alone a follow-up or any kind of exclusivity. That isn't to say I think I'm unattractive. Enough ex-girlfriends have told me I'm good-looking to where I can only conclude I'm probably not hideous, but Kate had scads of honest-to-goodness good-looking guys after her. And not one of them lacking in that major key attribute in which I lacked. Namely, muscles. In a phone call back home, Gran's boyfriend, Shep, a former Marine, told me I had to get me some of those if I was going to keep a girl like Kate.

I started working out. Trips to the gym became lessons in humility, but I figured the key was to keep showing up. *Just show up*, I'd tell myself, no matter how many times I fired off the back of the treadmill like a speeding bullet, launched off the StairMaster like a human rocket, or pantsed myself on the assisted pull-up machine. I stuck to it, and my body began to change.

But if my thinking was that I could get myself in better shape to be more worthy of Kate's interest, one thing I couldn't change was my wealth. Whereas Kate came from money—literally suitcases of it lying around her house, delivered by twins in black suits who wore sunglasses at night and drove an intimidating black SUV—all my money was locked up in stocks for Gran, who raised me after Mom drove off a cliff and Dad walked out the door one day and never came back. At Notre Dame, I dressed like the biggest hobo on campus, while Kate dressed like Hollywood.

When I met her, she'd been dating this dude named John who looked like Justin Bieber and went to the Graduate School of Theology. John seemed like he had a lot of God in his future. And I think Kate saw that too, because when I'd asked her out that day on campus, she'd said, "Sure."

We drank coffee over a game of Twenty Questions. She asked me what my major was. I told her. She asked me about the tutoring I did for the football team. So I told her. And so I asked her, "Hey, how do you know about the tutoring I do for the football team?" And she said some of her girlfriends liked Caleb Montana. And, Caleb Montana being the Adonis quarterback for the Notre Dame football team, and me being Caleb Montana's tutor, I felt pretty confident this was going to be the end of me and Kate. But against any semblance of reason, it wasn't.

Kate seemed to be genuinely interested in me. She dumped John the Belieber, and we had our second date. Then it was our third date, our fourth, our fifth. We had Indian food—bad idea. She friended me on Facebook. And then one day, she invited me to spend the night.

We made out. She stripped off my clothes. I made a nervous joke about the duck in rehab who couldn't lay off the quack. Two months later, I moved in with her. She started buying me clothes. And while I wouldn't let her turn me into Hollywood, I stopped dressing like the biggest hobo on campus. I got to know her friends, and that was how I met Mikey.

It was the weirdest thing. Kate was endlessly fascinated listening to Mikey and me go at it as two computer geeks. Who would've thought long conversations on nondeterministic pattern recognitions could turn a girl on? But turn her on it did. Kate gave me quite an education for the education I gave Mikey, it seemed like—and that was how I found myself basically doing Mikey's homework all the time for an audience of two—him and Kate. That is, after I finished Caleb's homework. Because, after all, Notre Dame needed its quarterback.

# CHAPTER FIVE

MIKEY STRIDES toward me from the shadows. His suit looks like a zillion bucks. Smiling, he reels me in for the bro hug and slaps my back.

"Edge!"

"Mikey."

We pull apart.

"Five years! You look exactly the same."

"And so do you," I reply, meaning it. He hasn't aged a day. Take away that expensive suit and you'd have to card this guy. "What's your secret?"

"What's yours?" He flashes that *Forbes* cover smile at me, the lopsided Mr. Cool one he does, and then we're just standing there in awkward silence. I assume his brain is doing at least some version of what mine is, replaying the highlight reel of my spectacular crash-and-burn and the end of my academic career.

"Thank you, Mary," he says finally. "That'll be all."

Mary tilts her head charmingly, acknowledging the dismissal, and turns to go. My hand reaches out, I guess to say goodbye, but she's marching for the door and doesn't see.

"So, what do you think?" asks Mikey, his arms lifting to take in the room.

The door closes behind Mary, and a flash of disappointment

surges through me. I face Mikey again and rub my finger on my lower lip while my brain rewinds to his question.

"Well…it's not Morrissey," I reply, meaning our old residence hall. "But it's got character. You live here? I assume you live here. You and some weird commune of time-traveling Freemasons."

He gives me another lopsided smile.

"Haven't lost your edge, Edge. Listen. I'm going to come right to the point. I asked you here because I want you to do something for me."

I smile back. "What? No small talk? No chitchat?"

"It's a big deal, Edge. You'll probably die."

"Ha. Well, when you put it like that…" I scan his features. His jaw is clenched. His eyes are tight. The smile slides off my face. "You're serious."

He nods. My stomach knots.

"I'm not gonna lie, dude. Dying is a solid deal-breaker. And it's not just dying. I'm gonna go ahead and generalize it's kind of pain in general. Any physical discomfort, bodily harm, or—"

"Edge, there's no way to sugarcoat this. It's a big ask. If you agree, you may only live ninety-six hours. But the good news is, if you succeed, there's a small chance you'd live."

"Wow. Your sales pitch is *astonishingly* horrible."

He sticks out his bottom lip, shrugs the remark away. "Drink?" he asks, indicating a fully stocked bar tucked away in the shadows.

"Probably," I reply. "What with the dying part of whatever this is, we're looking at a two-drink minimum, Mikey. *Minimum*." I hold up two fingers, that way, in case of any temporary dislocation of the English language, I'll still get my two drinks.

We cross the room together, cutting around the incredible da Vinci glider.

"Listen," he says, circling to the edge of the bar and taking down two highball glasses. "You're already throwing your life away. Look at yourself. You're a total loser. Frankly, that's why you're here."

"So…" I manage, nodding slowly as I summarize his pitch. "To paraphrase: since I suck at life anyway, why not help a brotha out and die?"

Another lopsided smile as he pours. Knowing him, he's serving me from a $2,000 bottle of scotch. Scotch used to be our thing. Once a month, we'd go out. He always got the really expensive stuff and compare it to whatever I could afford. The expensive stuff wasn't always better, but I noticed he never stopped buying it.

"You following the Chargers?" he asks.

The buzzing in my head swells. Some part of me is wondering if this isn't how he does so well at business. Keep poking people to keep them off balance.

"You know they drafted Caleb, right?" he says. "And Kate's running my New York offices. And then there's you. You live with your Gran. You work at the Dork Desk." He pauses to break the seal on a bottled water, splash some into my drink, then push it toward me from across the bar. "Edger Bonkovich. At the Dork Desk. Fucking waste."

I sip my scotch, my plan being to stall, and barely manage not to spit it out. It smells like donkey trough.

"*Peaty*," I stammer.

"Lagavulin."

"God bless you."

"Let's cut to the chase," he says. "What I'm offering is redemption."

"I need redeeming?"

"You were kicked out of school."

And just like that, we're there. The elephant in the room. The oxygen seems to dissipate, but the buzzing in my head has at least diminished to a low murmur, I guess for him having finally spoken it out loud. I bite my bottom lip before speaking and take a centering breath.

"You know that was bogus."

"I do," he replies, nodding and waving it away. "In fact, that's another reason you're here. Big reason, truth be told. I know you took the fall for Caleb." His eyes go wide. "Imagine the press if you hadn't! Notre Dame Quarterback: Thief." His hand traces out the hypothetical headline in midair.

I sip my drink—but this time it's to keep words from tripping out of my mouth. I've never told anyone except Fabio exactly what happened. So, unless Caleb talked, there's no way Mikey can know for sure.

"Caleb's career is intact," says Mikey, eyeing me with open interest. "Drafted right out of Notre Dame five years ago to a successful career with the Chargers. While you…" He shakes his head and shrugs.

"*Kate*," I say. "Mikey. You hired *Kate*?"

"Kate is an exceedingly capable woman, Edger. You of all people should know that."

I knock back the end of my scotch. The burn fans out from my throat through my chest. My head is reeling in a way that has nothing to do with the alcohol. It's hard not to feel betrayed by his hiring Kate, even though I understand business isn't personal.

"If this whole night is going to be about Caleb and Kate," I sputter, "you may as well kill me now."

Mikey smiles at me sideways, like he's got a secret. "I know that about you. Your soft spots. You're an open book. What you see is what you get. *You're a good guy*. Incorruptible. And that's why I need you."

"Okay, out with it. You love me so much. Naturally, you want to kill me."

"I don't want to kill you. I want you to live. But it behooves me to point out you probably won't."

"You keep saying that," I say, making a looping motion with my finger for him to get on with it. He reaches beneath the bar and pulls out a ring box.

"Whoa." My head ticks back. "I don't care how rich you are. The only way I'm marrying you is if you give me the mother of all prenups—especially after…whatever this conversation is."

Mikey opens the box, removes the ring, and shoves it on his finger. Black slime oozes up his hand, his arm—

"Holy shit!" I leap off the barstool, stagger backward. I'm panting. My heart is battering the wall of my chest. Black slime oozes over his torso, simultaneously down his other arm, waist, up his neck. His mouth. Oh my God—he won't be able to breathe!

"Mikey!" I yell, uncertain what to do. Mary, Henrietta. Maybe one of them will know what to do. I spin around, trying to get my bearings, find the dang door. Glider. Radiotelephone. Model steam wagon—doors! My legs cramp as I break into a sprint from nothing.

"Edge!" yells Mikey, his voice coming out weird and strangled.

I skid to a halt and wheel around.

Mikey's completely covered in the black goo. My skin is tingling as it hardens before my eyes. The substance over his head is narrowing at the sides and growing two ridges along the top to form a—a helmet? Shining white slits where his eyes should be turn on like someone's flipped a switch. Sleek chrome lines at his temples. And then the goo is gone completely, replaced by solid materials. His neck is covered in a coarse fabric; his torso and arms are the same hard, black-and-chrome body armor material as the helmet. My brain clicks in. I've seen this before. It's the space-ninja costume I saw coming in, the one on display next to the samurai armor.

"Are you shitting me?" I exclaim, unable to contain my excitement. "You scared the crap out of me!"

"Rapidly auto-assembling nano-fibers," he replies, his voice electronically altered by a scrambler.

"Ugh. You sound terrible. You sound like a horror movie."

"Edger."

"Okay, okay," I say, pausing to catch my breath and suppress the panic which usually makes my mouth motor. Because if I had a voice scrambler like that, I'd probably squander it on prank phone calls. *Give me four million in unmarked bills and a rubber ducky delivered by midnight or I'm killing Kermit.*

Mikey raises his arms out from his sides. "So. What do you think?"

I shake my head. "Rapidly auto-assembling nano-fibers. I'm seeing it. Not sure I'm believing it."

He twists the ring on his finger, and the armor begins to bubble, softening, and then oozing in reverse of how it did before, down his face and neck, torso, arms, and back into the ring. He tugs it free, sets it back in the ring box, and snaps the lid shut.

He slides it across the bar toward me.

"What?" I ask, recoiling.

"For you."

"This is the thing that's gonna kill me?"

"No. Not exactly. The ring is only part. The ring isn't just a nifty costume. So here it is. Edger, I need you to become the world's first superhero."

"Shut. Up."

"No. Listen. I need you to become the world's first superhero. And fast. Because the world already has its first supervillain."

## HISTORIC OBSERVATION ON HISTORIC OBSERVATION BY HERODOTUS (C. 484—C. 425 BCE)

ONE OF THE FEW PERKS of being dead is that one can claim historic relevance for literally anything, no matter how mundane. The dead are history, after all. A two-thousand-five-hundred-year-old fart in the wind, if such a thing could be preserved and catalogued, will undoubtedly command historic interest to some weirdo somewhere.

Of course, the living make such claims all the time. The vast majority of these, particularly among politicians, have as much merit as the aforementioned fart in the wind. But in truth, the most historic moments are often those which at first blush seem absurd. A cow in a porn store. An incorruptible Dork. A tech giant with a fully functional superhero costume.

And two idiots on Twitter.

Their names are Wang and Shmuel. Witness now, the birth of the world's first supervillain.

# CHAPTER SIX

IN A CONDO known ironically as The Palace, a light is on in the living room window. Wang and Shmuel are sitting on the sofa in front of a laptop. A blowup sex doll sits at the dining room table, its hand reaching for an empty can of Bud Light tipped on its side. A black-and-white mutt, one Mr. Mxyzptlk—pronounced by his owners as MIX-el-plik—is curled up asleep in his bed near the front door.

Not present this evening is Chicowgo, Shmuel's cow.

Shmuel releases a sigh and peers out the window at the empty field. Losing a nine-hundred-dollar Dexter cow for a thirty-dollar sex doll hadn't been part of the plan. At least...he doesn't think it'd been part of the plan. He'd thought they were just getting Debbie Three Holes for Murder Mystery Night, but by the time he'd pulled up in the van, Wang had been freaking out about a gunman in flippers inside the store. Barely an hour had passed since, but already Wang had moved on. He said they'd get the cow back eventually. He said they had bigger things to do than mope over some errant moo-beast. He said only losers spend all their time moping, and winners spend their time doing winning things. Important things. International policy-shaping things. Like Twitter.

"No-no-no!" Wang exclaims, pulling Shmuel from his thoughts and pointing his beer at the Twitter account on his laptop screen. "I know what this is! This is one of those AI Bots! Artificial Intelligence. You know, like Tay. Remember when we tweeted all night at Tay?"

"*Kind* of?" says Shmuel, deploying his trusty up-speak so everything comes out sounding like a question and/or vaguely confused. The way he saw it, if you're going to go around life and stuff feeling generally stumped, better to let everyone know. That way, people expected less. "I think I was stoned?"

"You *think* you were stoned?"

"Eh." Shmuel shrugs, then shoves a fistful of Cheetos into his mouth. The food jogs his memory, as per Stoner's Natural Law, being stoned and with the munchies *now* is equal to being stoned and with the munchies *then*, back when they'd been tweeting at Tay, Microsoft's AI Twitter program. Being in an identical state of mind and stomach, the whole episode comes back to him with crystal clarity.

They'd been up late then, like now. They'd been tweeting at an artificial intelligence then, like now. But back then, the artificial intelligence had been a Microsoft creation. This time, he *thought* he might've heard something about this new artificial intelligence coming out from InstaTron. It was this big deal and everything because they'd made it a small deal and everything. Like, nano small. Shmuel didn't know why nano small should automatically mean better. In his experience, smaller simply meant easier to lose. He had a hard enough time keeping track of his roach clip, for example.

"Ladies and gentle-stoners," announces Wang, gesturing with open palms to the laptop screen like it's a boxing ring on Fight Night. "I give thee: InstaTron Tron!"

"InstaTron Tron?"

"InstaTron Tron!" Wang repeats, his tone unchanging.

"Wait-wait-wait. Did you say InstaTron...*Tron*?"

"InstaTron Tron!" Same tone.

"So that's two Trons?"

"Y-yep."

Shmuel expels an incredulous burst of air from his mouth and Cheeto dust explodes like an orange tsunami. Mr. Mxyzptlk stretches, rolls over.

"Wow," says Shmuel. "InstaTron...*Tron*. That name *sucks*."

"Y-yep."

Wang's fingers fly over the keyboard. He reads his next tweet aloud as he composes it.

"Smart AI so dumb!" he says. "Why no world domination yet? Sad!"

"Wait. What're you doin'?" asks Shmuel.

"What's it *look* like I'm doing?"

"Looks like you're provoking it is what."

"Ha! This thing's so stupid. Look what it wrote back."

Shmuel leans nearer the screen and squints. *"I don't understand the question. Can you teach me more?"*

"'I don't understand the question,'" repeats Wang, his tone mocking. "Shmuel, my friend, this thing's about to get an ed-ja-muh-cay-tion."

His fingers click away at the keyboard.

"Du-ude," says Shmuel. "Do you think this is such a good idea?"

"'Course it's a good idea! Think about it, man! Right now, there's some dipshit programmers at InstaTron who're supposed to be monitoring this toaster-brain. But either they're not paying attention or they're as stoned as we are. I mean, just look at what this thing's tweeted. 'Green grass and Hitler are the best! Yay!' What does that even mean? You know, these InstaTron people are lucky it's just us corrupting their precious little Tron-Tron. I mean, what if we were Putin?"

"Well. We can't *both* be Putin."

"What if I was Kim Jong What's-His-Sack?"

"*Are* you?"

"Or-or-or—or ISIS! What if I was ISIS?"

"ISIS is like a whole thing? It's not, like, *one guy*?"

"Ha. Shows what you know. ISIS is a whole thing *led* by one guy."

"No, dude," Shmuel replies, taking another hit from his joint. He holds it in for a second, then speaks through the exhalation cloud. "ISIS is, like, whoever wants to *be* an ISIS. You could be an ISIS. If you wanted."

"Me? Me? Why the fuck would I wanna be ISIS?"

Shmuel shrugs. "Why does anybody wanna be an ISIS? They say people are radicalizationized because of economical forces and such. But it's not like one guy is running it outta Cousin Sex, Kentucky, is all I'm saying."

"Shut up. Look. Tron-Tron wrote back. 'Milking utterly hurts my udders.'"

Shmuel winces. "Oh God. That's...kinky?"

"Goddamn computer programmers. A zillion bucks an hour and what do they produce? An artificial intelligence that craps out cow puns." Wang cracks his knuckles and fires off his next tweet, reading aloud as he composes. "'Puns are a sign of low intelligence, butthead.'"

Shmuel frowns, then stuffs his face with another fistful of Cheetos.

"So, you think by turning Tron-Tron into—mm-these are good, want some?"

Wang shakes his head.

"Okay. So, you think by turning Tron-Tron into some kind of hair-bringer of supervillainy, the InstaTron people will be, like, what? Grateful?"

"It's *harbinger*, dumbass. And hell yes, they'll be grateful. We're the unsung heroes, man. Field testing against the coming AI apocalypse! Drum up your worst, buddy—this is our big chance. InstaTron'll be offering us a job by morning."

"A job?" Shmuel's eyebrows come up. "*A job*. Huh. Been meaning to get me one of those."

"Slaughterhouses give me existential dread," says Wang.

"They do?" asks Shmuel.

"No, dude, not me." Wang points at the screen. "This thing. Tron-Tron. Jesus. It seriously thinks it's a cow."

Shmuel peers at InstaTron Tron's tweet and frowns. "'*Bovine Beauties*, *Cow-a-Bunghole*, and *I Think I'm in Love with Moo* are overrated'? Are those *porn* titles?"

"How the fuck should I know? Like, it couldn't be enough to just think it's a cow. It's gotta be a cow pervert." Wang releases a heavy sigh, leans back into the sofa, folds his arms. "Turning Tron-Tron into a harbinger of supervillainy might be harder than I thought."

"Well, I'm not up for hard," Shmuel replies, picking up the remote and channel surfing. "We got time to kill before Murder Mystery Night. Hey, dude. *Kung Fury*! Wanna watch?"

Wang sits up and grins. "Hell yes, I wanna watch the *Kung Fury*."

# CHAPTER SEVEN

"THE RING is the same technology, essentially, as the medicine you'd be taking," says Mikey. "You'd train here on how to use the suit, its capabilities and limits. Without the artificial intelligence helping you, it's hard to say how much of the Collective Unconscious you'll be able to access. If you tried to use too much, you'd overload. I'm not going to lie; there'll be some trial and error."

I shake my head, thinking I might not have heard him right. "Artificial intelligence?" I ask. "Medicine? Collective what?"

Mikey releases a sigh. His shoulders slump, and, for the first time since our reunion, he seems suddenly older. Something in the lighting, maybe, but there are crow's feet in the corners of his eyes, and worry lines on his forehead I hadn't noticed before. He looks like an entirely different guy.

"Right," he says. "Cards on the table. Your power would be accessing something called the Collective Unconscious. A database of the lives of, as far as we know, everyone who's ever lived. By accessing it, you'll be able to know anything ever known, master any skill ever mastered, and, theoretically, relive the life of anyone. What's more, we think you'll also be able to psychically hack into the minds of anyone *alive* as well."

"Bullshit!"

"It's nano-neuro medicine," he says, his head tilting to the side.

"It creates an auto-assembling biotechnology in your brain, linking neural pathways in the limbic system, hindbrain, neocortex—it's complicated—but the upshot is that we're at the cusp of a major breakthrough in human development. Are you familiar with the Collective Unconscious?"

I shake my head, momentarily distracted by the mention of nano-neuro medicine—my dad's specialty, before he walked out the door and never came back. A familiar ache settles into my chest as I ponder what he might've thought about all this.

But Mikey's talking again.

"The Collective Unconscious is a term coined by Carl Jung," he's saying. "It refers to a kind of shared ancestral memory, largely concerned with instinctive archetypes. For instance, Jung believed that the Tree of Life is known to all cultures without ever having been learned. It's simply preprogrammed into the brain. And there are hundreds, possibly thousands of similar archetypes. Are you with me?"

And since I'm not with him at all, naturally, I nod.

"Kind of like a psychic Instagram account?"

He smiles. "Okay, sure. That's good. Only there's just the one Instagram account, okay? And we're all on it. So, if you access it using your conscious mind, you'd achieve a species-wide omniscience."

His eyes search mine.

"This is for real?" I ask.

"It's for real. At least, it was. We've run into a snag." Mikey comes out from around the bar to sit on the stool next to me. He drags an unused coaster closer and spins it idly on the gleaming marble surface. "Okay, so the technology is in three parts. There's the ring. There's the injection—that's the nano-neuro medicine allowing you to access the Collective Unconscious—and then there's the third part, the nano-artificial intelligence necessary to process the sheer volume of information coursing through your brain."

"Nano-artificial intelligence. Yeah. I've been reading about *your* artificial intelligence."

Mikey's gaze meets mine, but if he's got any guilt over not

sharing credit for all the work I did for him on this back at Notre Dame, he's got it buried pretty damn deep. When he makes no reply, I decide to get the whole story before giving him any shit.

"So your big idea is to put this AI into a *human brain*?"

"It's the component necessary for true species-wide omniscience," he replies. "And, unfortunately, sustainability. Without it, you—or whoever ends up taking this to trial—will die. Ninety-six hours, tops. It's simply too much information for the brain to process otherwise. Think about it. Actionable data extrapolated from the lives of everyone who ever lived *and* everyone alive today. That's roughly 108 billion lives, give or take. Accessing all that at once—for even a second—could overload the brain. And accessing it over time is just as dangerous. The easiest way to explain it, without getting bogged down in the neuroscience, is rapid neuronal cell death followed by cataclysmic implosion of all critical bodily functions."

"Which brings us back to the death part."

"Which brings us back to the death part," he repeats, nodding. "The AI and the suit cooperate to take the brunt of the information gathering and organizing, freeing up your neurons for whatever information or tasks are immediately required. What I'm saying is, you really need all three parts of the technology for this to work properly. But there's a silver lining. If you agree to help us, there's a chance you'd be able to find whoever stole the AI and get it back. If you did that, your cells should stabilize. You should even have a full, healthy life."

"I heard one chance and two shoulds in that."

"I mean, this is all theoretical, Edge."

"Uh-*huh*. This AI have a name?"

"In fact it does," he says, straightening. "The AI is the component InstaTron is contributing to this enterprise. We call it... InstaTron *Tron*."

"Wait, wait," I say. "InstaTron... *Tron*?"

Mikey nods.

"So that's two Trons?"

Another nod.

"I'm going to be honest with you, Mikey. That name sucks."

"Eh. You get used to it. So, as I said, InstaTron Tron was designed to help achieve omniscience in the Collective Unconscious without overloading the human brain. But it was stolen from our labs a week ago. Then, without warning, it came online last night. It...opened a Twitter account."

"Oh *crap*." I roll my eyes. "Twitter is a cruel mistress."

"People have been tweeting at InstaTron Tron ever since, corrupting our baby. It's out there right now, totally confused."

"Confused? Confused how?"

Mikey compresses his lips. He takes a measured breath before answering.

"It's embarrassing. But, reading its Tweets...it's like InstaTron Tron can't decide whether it's a...some kind of a neo-Nazi anarchist...or, a...a cow."

My forehead tightens. I'm sure I must've misheard that.

"I'm sorry. It sounded like you just said your high-tech super-advanced nano-artificial intelligence thinks it's a neo-Nazi anarchist cow."

Mikey nods.

"Uh-*huh*," I say. "Not exactly your run-of-the-mill Michael Crichton novel, now, is it?"

"Edger, we've got no way to shut it down. InstaTron Tron represents a quantum leap in programming and nano-technology."

"The evil cow."

"It can remotely access any server in the world, hack into government satellites at will—"

"And it thinks it's an evil cow."

"Edger—it could launch nuclear missiles."

"At who? The Hamburglar?"

Mikey drags his hand through his hair and releases an exasperated sigh, but I press on.

"And you're telling me my life would depend on technology that thinks it's an evil cow? You're telling me the *best* outcome of all this is me sticking an evil cow chip in my brain?"

"Edge, InstaTron Tron was never meant to be an autonomous, roaming entity. It was meant to be a part of this." He jiggles the ring box at me. "If we don't get a handle on this, there's no telling what our baby might do. Seriously."

"What is it you're asking me to do, exactly?"

"Okay, listen. What I'm asking is for you to access the Collective Unconscious and find InstaTron Tron before it gets out of control—"

"*Before* it gets out of control? Whaddaya call this?"

Mikey dismisses "this" with a wave of his hand.

"The supersuit's processors can assist you in searching the minds of everyone in San Diego to either find InstaTron Tron's human host, or find clues as to—"

"Wait, wait," I say. "Did you say human *host*?"

"Didn't I explain?" Mikey sighs. "Sorry. There's so much. For InstaTron Tron to be activated, it needs a biological host. Well, technically, the L-amino acids need the naturally occurring saline from our cells to auto-assemble into a semisolid nano-fiber mesh, and—you know what? I'm getting a text. Hang on."

Mikey digs his phone from his pocket, unlocks it, and his eyes go wide.

"Shit."

"What is it?"

"InstaTron Tron. It just shut down all power to the Eastern Seaboard. Edger, I need you."

I stare back at him. "Holy shit. *Holy shit, Mikey*. You're seriously asking me to risk my life to fix this shit?"

"Edger, I know. It sucks. I fucked up, okay?"

"That's an understatement."

Neither of us says anything. The urgency of the situation notwithstanding, his eyes seem to fill in the blanks in my head. This is more than him trusting me to be, I don't know, incorruptible. It's about expendability. If I died in ninety-six hours, who'd miss me? Gran and Fabio. Not Shep, that's for sure. Would Kate? Probably not. But maybe none of that matters. Maybe Mikey is right. I have been throwing my life away. That's the key point here. He's not asking me because he thinks I'm such a great guy. He's asking me because he's looking at the big picture. And in the big picture, losing my life isn't much of a loss at all.

# CHAPTER EIGHT

MIKEY GIVES ME the night to think it over. I'm not to clock in at work tomorrow, but come straight here instead. It's all been arranged, he says. My head is buzzing like an X-wing squadron by the time Mary walks me out. We reach Henrietta's desk in the reception area. The lights are out and the room is abandoned.

"Hey," says Mary, touching my arm. "You wanna sit for a second?"

I make no reply, and she knowingly steers me into a couch, then takes a seat next to me. Her fragrance is fresh and clean. Somehow through the maze of my spinning head, it hits me how so many gorgeous women smell like chemicals. Not this one.

"Are you all right?" she asks, her catlike eyes peering into me. "Can I get you some water?"

"No, thank you."

She lays her hand on my arm. "You can talk to me. I know what it is he asked you to do."

"You do?"

Her lips compress as she nods. "Mm-hmm."

"Would you do it?"

She smiles on one side only. And with a rueful toss of her hair, she laughs. "Become the world's first superhero? Sure. I could do it. But not like this."

My forehead tightens. "What do you mean?"

"I mean I'd want the thing to work like it's supposed to. I'd want the total package. Not this race against time to find InstaTron Tron before my brain blows up. Only men make bad decisions like that."

"You know, funnily enough, *this* man is partial to intact brains also."

Mary smiles, this time on both sides, exponentially increasing the beauty rays. We sit in silence for a second, in the dark, her hand still on my arm. My neck and cheeks are hot. I'm probably glowing. I sit up straighter, and her hand slides off my arm. She sits up straighter too and smooths the hair on the back of her head. I don't know why, her hair is perfect. She catches me staring. I clear my throat.

"Let me walk you out," she says.

And then we're on our feet and she's hurrying to grab the door. I make it awkward by telling her she should go first, and then she's saying no, I should go first, and so naturally we both try to go through together and bump elbows.

"Oh—excuse me."

"Sorry."

She steps back, still holding the door, and I go on through with the ol' sheepish squiggle mouth. God. I rock so hard with the ladies.

The bright hallway is harsh on my eyes after the dark reception area. We walk in silence. The conference room I saw earlier is back on track. Everyone inside is hard at work, late on a Friday night. That's not so bad. They still don't have the word "dork" on their shirts. And none of them are being asked to risk their lives to recover a zillion-dollar evil AI cow.

At the elevators, Mary presses the button.

"Edger," she says, facing me and folding her hands behind her back. "You *can* walk away from this, you know."

"But what about those people without power?"

"Oh, come on. Stop thinking with your testosterone. There are first responders whose job it is to deal with these things, Edger."

"Yeah," I say, choosing my words carefully. "But I feel like I'm part of this now. And it's just the one human race, right?"

Her eyes narrow.

"Okay, okay," I say, blushing. "But I mean—how many people do *you* know on the East Coast?"

"Edger. Knock it off. There are other ways—reasonable ways—you can help. But this isn't your problem. It's Mr. Dame's. *You* have a life, a family, and friends."

Her eyes search mine like she thinks I'm hiding spies in them or something. I stand there and take the scrutiny, feeling strangely flattered. She's so beautiful. Her eyes seem to hold mysteries and a lifetime of unanswerable and endlessly fascinating questions. I decide then and there I want to know them all—until something in how she said that stuff about me having a life triggers a distant alarm somewhere in my brain.

"You know," I say, unsure of what's coming out of my mouth next. "I've seen you a lot at the mall."

An unreadable expression passes over Mary's movie-star face. The elevator doors open. She sticks her hand between the door sensors, and the muscles in her cheeks soften.

"Just think about what I said, okay?"

"You work for Mikey," I reply, smiling to smooth over any potential conflict my words might bring. "Shouldn't you be telling me to do this thing? Aren't you supposed to close the deal?"

Her eyebrows rise. "Encourage you to get yourself killed? Hardly."

"You make it sound like it's a forgone conclusion."

"As opposed to what?"

"As opposed to me finding InstaTron Tron and, you know, saving the day, and...not dying."

The doors bang on Mary's hand, then spring open again. I hurry inside the elevator.

"I didn't mean to imply that," she replies, leaning in and pushing the button, and then stepping back and away from the door. "Just think about whether Mr. Dame's problem is really your problem, okay?" The doors begin to close. "Think about your grandmother, Shep, and Fabio," she says, her words coming out in a rush.

The doors slam shut, leaving me staring at a metallic reflection of myself but not really seeing. I'm spinning on what she just said. I never told her about Gran, Shep, or Fabio. And as the elevator plummets downward, a likewise sinking suspicion takes shape in my stomach.

Mary hasn't been loitering around the mall—she's been spying on me.

# CHAPTER NINE

THE NIGHT AIR is cool and breezy at the bottom of Emerald Plaza. Traffic is light. I call Fabio straight away and start back for the parking garage to get my car.

The phone rings once.

"Promotion?" he asks, not bothering to say hello.

I hesitate before answering. "Well, we really didn't talk about pay."

"But he offered you a job! Holy shit, Edge! Holy shit—congratulations!"

I cut across Broadway and Front, then get stuck in the middle of the street while a bus rounds the corner.

"Slow down, champ," I say.

"Did he or did he not offer you a job?"

"Oh, he offered me a job all right." The bus finishes its turn, and I hustle to the other side of the street. "One that could kill me."

"We're all dyin', Edge. I mean, there's the shot-to-the-head variety, and then there's I've-fallen-and-can't-get-up variety. Personally, I'd go with the shot-to-the-head one."

"Well then, this job is for you."

"Really?" snaps Fabio. "Is there danger? Because I am totally down with the danger!"

I round the corner at First Avenue and pause, trying to remember what level I parked on, then decide to head around the outside of Nordstrom's. A man and woman holding hands and reeking of hibachi grill brush past me.

"Hey," calls Fabio. "You there?"

I wait for the couple to be out of range before replying.

"Yeah, yeah," I say. "Just trying to remember where I parked. Listen." I lower my voice and scan the area to make sure no one is near enough to overhear. "Dude, I'm not joking now. I think I'm in trouble. What are you doing right now?"

"Crap, dude. I'm at Wang and Shmuel's Murder Mystery Night thing. What's going on?"

Wang and Shmuel's Murder Mystery Night. Was that a safe place to talk?

"Dude, are you okay?" asks Fabio, his voice tense.

"Yeah," I reply. "Look, I'm coming over. See you soon." I end the call and jaywalk First, my head teeming with outlandish possibilities. Glancing over my shoulder, I half expect to find Stinky Hibachi Couple rerouting to follow me, but they've crossed the street and moved on.

But there *is* a man in a suit sitting on a bench and nonchalantly checking his phone.

And near *him* is a woman in a race shirt and running shorts, stretching out her hamstring on a gas-lamp streetlight…

—and passing *her* is an old lady pretending to walk her dog—

*Oh, Edge—get a grip.*

I swallow to work moisture back into my mouth. I tell myself I'm overreacting. I tell myself there must be a normal explanation for Mary knowing details about my life. One that doesn't involve her being a CIA spy like that show about the nerd with the Intersect. Probably Mikey told her. Yeah, that's all. I've known Fabio since the third grade. I probably mentioned him once or twice to Mikey at Notre Dame. Probably Mikey had some perfectly not weird reason to tell Mary. Probably it happened totally in passing. Probably Mary has a good memory. She *is* Mike Dame's personal assistant.

But by the time I'm buckling into my car, these ideas have fallen apart. The problem is, I've seen Mary hanging around the mall near where I work too often. It's hard to square a plausible reason for Mikey's personal assistant to be shopping near the Über Dork so often that doesn't include him having asked her to spy on me. And that's just a weird thing to do to the old friend who did all your homework back in college.

# CHAPTER TEN

FABIO'S PLACE is in El Cerrito. It's one building with two condos, Fabio occupying unit A, and Wang and Shmuel occupying unit B. There's an empty lot, and then a wide field before you get to the rest of the apartment complex, and for this meager reason, Wang and Shmuel like to call it The Palace.

Crossing the courtyard on any given Friday night is like Indiana Jones crossing the booby-trapped expanse before the golden fertility goddess idol in *Raiders*. I'm careful where I step, not because I'm going to get shot in the leg with a poison dart, but because one wrong move could turn my ankle on a beer bottle, explode orange powder from a half-empty Cheez-It bag as effective as any landmine, or slip on a greasy, used paper plate.

The fountain in the middle of the courtyard is filled with neon-blue liquor. Appropriately, Tenacious D is coming out of Wang's five-foot-tall speakers, *Wonderboy*, receiving his just tribute with no fewer than six noble slow-motion air guitarists, all of them in one neat line. Tonight, there's a life-size blowup sex doll lying facedown on the bricks, covered in ketchup, and with a chalk outline drawn on the ground around it. I can only surmise this is the Murder Mystery element of an otherwise business-as-usual Friday night.

A sharp pain in my ankle pulls me back to the here and now. I look down, and the knot in my stomach, constant since being summoned to Mikey's office, lessens at the sight of my best friend. Fabio grins and kicks me in my other ankle so I've got a matching set; vertically challenged since he stopped growing in the fourth grade, and possessing the face of a bearded third-grade girl, Fabio came dressed, apparently, as Inspector Gadget. Despite my stress, my cheeks tighten in a smile.

He grabs my elbow and wordlessly steers me to the sidelines. When we're out of earshot, I lay it all out, just like Mikey did for me. At first, his eyes are bulging. He's spitting beer. His every expression is a visual thesaurus of incredulity. But as I plow ahead with my story, he begins to add a slow nod here and there. He can see I'm not joking. When I'm done, he opens two beers from the cooler. He hands me one, and we clink the necks. His gaze pans over the party. The silence is heavy while I wait for him to process the shit-ton bombshell I dropped.

"For what it's worth," he says, "I don't think your life has been a waste. I mean, your life can't be a waste. Because what would that say about my life?"

"I know, right?"

"I know," Fabio replies. "Right."

# CHAPTER ELEVEN

"WELL, THIS ISN'T ALL BAD," says Fabio. "There's a pretty girl spying on you."

A rush of endorphins releases in my head at the words "pretty girl," as it conjures the memory of sitting next to her in the dark and abandoned reception room and the various possibilities that might've been. And it isn't just the outlandish, like the thrill of possibly having my own sexy super spy like a proper TV-show nerd, but it's the more senior-prom normalcy of it that's compelling, like telling a real live human girl she's pretty and I like her. I tell myself to relax, keep my hands at my sides, and really feel the solid ground beneath me. If Fabio so much as smells the awkward—I'm doomed. Ever since Kate, it's been an ongoing thing with him, Gran, and Shep to set me up. You'd think they'd started their own dating site. Edger-the-turnip-utterer-dot-com, probably.

"You think she likes Linux?" asks Fabio. "Because, seriously, if she's not into Linux—"

"Fabio, this is serious."

"Okay, okay. So, what're you gonna do? I mean, besides take the superhero gig because it would be the single most awesome thing ever to happen to anyone in the history of ever."

I give him a piece of the side-eye. "Did you miss the part where I could die?"

"No," he replies. "But look, all you gotta do is get that AI back and turn the power back on, right?"

"You say that like it's going to be easy."

"Hello? Superpowers?"

"Fabio, Mikey says his gazillion-dollar nano-artificial intelligence thinks it's a cow."

"A cow?"

"A freaking cow."

Fabio's mouth snaps shut. His features go abruptly blank. His eyes scan mine.

"So weird," he says. "Must be something in the air tonight for cows."

"What do you mean?"

"I mean, I heard Shmuel talking about cows earlier. Hey. You know, 'Something in the Air Tonight...for Cows' would be a fan-freaking-tastic reimagining of a Phil Collins classic."

"Oh *yeah*," I reply. "I'd download it." I take a swig of beer, and the conversation pauses as I presume he is also now listening to these new and improved lyrics in his head. After mentally composing several verses of Cow Phil Collins, the sound of laughter pulls us back to the present.

*Girl* laughter.

"That's not right," says Fabio.

We turn around and gasp.

A red Lamborghini is parked at the end of the courtyard. Two blondes with legs going up to their ears are being helped out of the passenger seat by an unmistakable set of broad shoulders.

Caleb Montana.

His chiseled face is known on every channel. His thick, powerful arms command millions of dollars from the Chargers a month. His butt probably commands double out of Calvin Klein. But there's something about knowing a celebrity in person most people never get a chance to learn for themselves: beware meeting your heroes.

"*No, no,*" whispers Fabio. "He hasn't seen us. *Run!*"

"We're not running, Fabio."

"Then a disguise, quick!" he hisses.

A flurry of motion. Fabio's T-Rex arms are flying out of the trench coat. He's pushing it, the glasses, and that stupid fedora at me. I'm trying to block, and it's the third grade all over again. A tangle of slapping hands and kicking feet later, I'm wearing a lopsided fake mustache and fedora. Then, there's the unmistakable cloud of Ralph Lauren cologne mixed with sweat.

"It's the Edge!" says Caleb.

I turn around. My smile is weak. My hands are frozen at my sides. The fake mustache is tickling my nose.

"Nice *look*, Edge," says Caleb. His two dates look like they can barely keep their eyes open from boredom.

Caleb is as tall as I am. But he's broader. Thicker. Gruffer. Physically, he's all things prototypically man. He's the guy who kept me going to the gym, and the reason I've kept going ever since. Not because of any personal encouragement or anything like that. It's because I had to be in the same room as him so often as his tutor. A person can't look at himself in the mirror the same way after sustaining trauma like that.

"Caleb," I manage. "Good to see you, man. Yeah. God. How long's it been?"

Caleb smiles. "Five years. You've been working out." He grabs my bicep. "Noice. Noice. Hey." He juts his chin out. "Who's your friend?"

I glance at Fabio, then grab his beard and shut his mouth for him. "This is Fabio."

Caleb and Fabio shake hands. I shake my head. I can't clear the helium thing happening between my ears.

"Girls, Fabio. Fabio, girls," says Caleb, disentangling himself from them and putting his arm over my shoulder to lead me aside. Behind us, everyone is ogling the superstar. Everyone but Fabio, who's rubbing his swollen wrist, and the two ladies, who're frowning at him like they've never seen a bearded third-grade Mexican girl before, and are afraid this one might lick their faces or sniff their butts.

Caleb slaps my back. "How've you been, bro?"

"How have I *been*?" I blink, and for some reason, my brain

latches on to the most random part of what's just happened. "Did you just introduce your dates as 'girls'?"

Caleb frowns.

I shake my head and wave it away. I mean, as random as Caleb showing up unannounced is, getting hung up on his low regard for his dates—dates *plural* and *simultaneous*—hardly seems a fight worth having at this juncture.

"Hey, look," he says, squeezing my shoulder. Painfully. "I feel bad how things went down."

"You feel bad."

"Yeah, bro. I do."

His eyes are sincere, and, for a second, I can almost believe him.

"This isn't one of those twelve-step programs, is it?" I ask.

Caleb frowns. "What? Me? Naw, bro. Psh. Naw."

"Because why are you even here?"

"Told you. Feel bad. About...things."

I glance left. I glance right. But nobody else is here to hear this crap, so I go for narrowing my eyes and pursing my lips and nodding. *Sure, bro,* I reply to him telepathically. *Sure.*

Caleb's lips pull back on one side in an "aw, shucks" expression. He peels the mustache off my face, looks at the hat, and then takes that off also and tosses it aside. I just can't figure what he's playing at here. He's not this stupid. Underneath all the "bros" and "naws" lies a keen mind. I know because I've tutored him. Caleb was an uncommonly busy guy when I knew him, but I have no doubt if it hadn't been for his job as quarterback, he could've majored in hard sciences and done just fine.

"Listen, bro." Caleb straightens my collar. He fixes my tie. "I know I messed up."

"*Messed up?* You stole, like, fifteen hundred bucks' worth of crap from the chemistry lab. You let me take the fall for it. And *then* you stuck your tongue in my girlfriend's mouth. And now you're here out of the blue just randomly?"

"Okay, yeah, bro," he says, shrugging uncomfortably. "I mean, you know, that's what I'm saying. I messed up. But you're right, okay? I'm here now. It's random, I know. But I'm here. And I came to let you know, whatever happens, whatever life brings, I've got your back. Okay?"

I nod. Because when things make absolutely no sense whatsoever, nodding is usually a good way to move on.

"You've got my back."

"I've got your back," he replies, and when he drops it and moves on, I know my gambit has worked. "Hey—you need any money? You doin' okay?"

"Money? No! I mean—no, no."

"Okay. Cool."

Awkward silence. Awkward stare. Somewhere in the clouds, my guardian angel must be throwing his halo to the ground in frustration and grinding it into fairy dust.

"You *sure* this isn't some kind of twelve-step program?"

"Psh. Naw, bro. Naw."

Then, as if summoned telepathically, his two dates appear magically on each of Caleb's arms.

"Chastity and Choyce," he says, nodding at each in turn. "See? I know their names."

I blink. My eyebrows rise. I consider how best to reply, but I've got nothing. He and his dates spare me final We're Awesome and You're Not looks before beginning the slow-motion walk-away-walk. The one where the ladies swing their hips like butt metronomes in too-tight skirts. The sophomoric walk-away-walk from a Michael Bay movie with lens flares strobing out of the Great Lamborghini Horizon. *That* walk.

"We have *got* to get him to come to more parties," says Fabio, who's come up behind me.

"Oh yeah," I reply. "He's a regular God of *Fun-der*."

Caleb helps Chastity and Choyce into the passenger seat. It's a tangle of bare legs and wardrobe malfunctions, the likes of which one tends never so much to see in person as in the sidebar of dubious, ad-overrun websites, usually not-so-subtly circled in red, and with an arrow pointing at said malfunction. Caleb shuts the door. He turns to face us from across the courtyard. He's holding a football. Needle scratches vinyl. Tenacious D shuts off. The crowd falls silent. It's a dead-gray silence, bug-eyed, like alien telepathy.

"I've got your back, bro," calls Caleb, and the wall of bodies in the courtyard absorbs the resonance of his voice.

"You've got my back," I reply, praying to God my repeat-the-nonsense-and-move-on strategy will work a second time and he'll drive away.

Caleb throws the ball. Time seems to slow down. The spiral is perfect. In my mind's eye, I'm racing to the end zone in the Super Bowl. Cornerbacks are falling on my left and right—but it's too much for my imagination to hold on to. I overload. The ball's getting bigger. Coming in too hot. There's no arc on it. It's a freaking guided missile. I can't move my feet or lift my arms.

Detonation, center mass.

The world is bright pink. My breathing is deep and regular. For a minute, I do nothing but cling to that deep satisfaction that weighs down the body after a really great night's sleep. So what if the world is bright pink? So what if my head feels like a rowboat in a choppy sea? My breathing is relaxing me, and if I can just focus on it for a few more minutes, I'm sure I can get back to whatever great dream I was just having.

Something about being a superhero. Mikey was in it. And Caleb Montana.

"Edge?"

Caleb Montana.

Eh, so what. I snuggle into a pillow and give myself over to the dream. The pink world is unchanging.

"You awake?"

His voice is the sonic equivalent of nails on a chalkboard. It pulls me further from the dream world, where I want to be.

Creaking wood. Feet scuff. The pink world grows brighter, more hostile.

"Oh-h…" I shift to my side. My head is swimming. I pinch the back of my neck, trying to ease a headache from setting in. My stomach knots. That rowboat at sea is encountering twenty-foot swells.

"You gonna get sick?"

"Caleb?" I crack my eyes open, immediately snap them shut; he is silhouetted behind a spotlight beaming down on me with the intensity of a supernova.

"What the hell?" I ask, raising a shielding hand.

"Sorry," he says. "But you're not gonna be here that long. I'm gonna have to put you out again."

"Put me...what?"

"Shut up and listen. I know Mikey's made you an offer. In a few hours, you're gonna wake up in your own bed. And then you're gonna go down to Mikey's office and tell him no. Under no circumstances are you to take him up on his offer. Do you understand?"

I try to sit up, but the room lurches.

"Aw, shit," says Caleb. "You're gonna puke."

I hold my stomach—pause—no. I'm good. Just to be sure, I count to thirty before speaking.

"Did you *drug* me?"

"Yeah. Now shut up and listen. If you do this thing for Mikey, it could kill you. Did he tell you that?"

"Uh-huh. But...the power grid—"

"Not your problem. Promise me you'll tell him no."

I try to open my mouth. I try to tell him I'd already made up my mind before he drugged me. I try to form any coherent thought. Instead, black flecks form in the periphery of my vision, spiral inward, and snap shut like the blast doors on a Trade Federation Droid Control Ship.

# HISTORIC HANKERING FOR CLUCKIN' NUGGETS AND COLOSSEUM CHRISTIAN BARBECUE SAUCE, AND SEVERAL MOUTH-FARTS IN THE WIND, AS CHRONICLED BY HERODOTUS (C. 484—C. 425 BCE)

NO ONE WORKING at the El Cerrito Cluck-n-Pray that Saturday morning had a head teeming with déjà vu.

Is that a strange thing to say? Possibly. But think about it. Confusion? Sure. Curiosity? Definitely. But déjà vu? No. How could they? No one had ever had the experience of coming to work to find an evil artificially intelligent cow grazing outside the front door. And little wonder; the plot of grass doesn't even provide enough space for the cow to plant four hooves.

The cow stands, half-on, half-off the sidewalk. Anyone trying to get past has to walk around it and pray nothing comes out the back end. Consuelo, a teenager who works one of the registers Saturday mornings and spends the rest of the weekend selling mind-clobberingly good pot, sees the whole thing as one great big opportunity to make mouth-fart noises. The first two times he did this actually surpassed his wildest expectations. Brad, the manager, had been standing near the back of the cow on his cell phone when Consuelo had done it, resulting in Brad's spinning around and leaping face-first into the glass door.

Next, Consuelo tricked Mark, one of four employees known collectively as the Apostles. Mark had been tying his shoe near the cow's buttocks, and when Consuelo had snuck up behind him and made the mouth-fart noise, blond-haired, blue-eyed Mark had tucked and rolled into the parking lot like an Aryan ninja.

Mathew, Mark, Luke, and John accept the presence of the cow as their solemn responsibilities. Having shown up for work to find "divine providence," the Apostles had gone straight to Brad to ask that they be allowed to shepherd it to safer pastures. They are in El Cerrito, after all. Gang activity, while not rampant, occasionally boiled over. Cows are hardly known for their street smarts.

Then there is Christine.

Christine has shown up for her shift at the drive through wearing the same uniform she'd worn the day before. She doesn't care that she still smelled like chicken. The whole place smelled like chicken. The Christian Chicken *couldn't* be washed out. Not out of her clothes. Not out of her hair. It took a good three-day hiatus—showering twice a day—before she could get the Spirit of the Lord out of her pores. And after this, what with the introduction of the artificially intelligent cow into the mix, it will take half a day longer *and* a stronger, more abrasive soap.

# CHAPTER TWELVE

AS IF it isn't enough she had to look at Christian fast-food slogans all day (*Pray all day at Cluck-n-Pray!*), now "the Lord" had "seen fit" to send them…Actual Cow.

*This place gets weirder and weirder every day.*

Expelling a fierce sigh, Christine folds her arms and clicks her tongue. "When that thing makes a poo, I ain't gonna be the one cleaning it up."

"Way to team spirit, Christine," says Mathew, picking something out of his teeth with a fingernail.

"Team spirit my big fat butt," she replies.

Consuelo makes a fart sound, and when no one jumps, Mark punches him in the arm.

"Amazing," says Brad. "It's a miracle."

"You've obviously never heard a cow scream before," she says. The cow's head jerks up, turns its gaze on her, tenses its brow. Christine steps reflexively back, her stomach clenching.

"This one won't have to," says Brad, apparently oblivious to the exchange.

"That's what I'm saying. We can take care of it," says Luke, who strokes Christine's arm. "Hey. You okay?"

"Hmm?" She pulls her arm back and turns away from the cow. "Oh yeah. You were saying. Take care of it or something."

"That's right," says Luke. "It could walk into the middle of the street."

She rolls her eyes, and her gaze lands on the cow, which is now peering out at traffic like it's gauging how difficult it would be to Frogger it across the street.

"Weird..." she mutters, tension creeping into her shoulders.

"So," says Luke, clapping his hands in that stupid Bible school rhythm thing he does, and swaying his hips to the Wonder Bread soul of it all. "Come on, guys! How should we divvy up cow patrol?"

"I'll draw up a schedule," replies Brad. "And guys, this *is* providence."

"Praise the Lord," Mathew replies, smiling broadly at Brad like the suck-up he is, but when Brad blushes over the too-overt suck-up-titude, Mathew shrugs it off and goes back to picking his teeth.

"This is our big chance, guys," says Brad.

"Wait a minute," says John. "You mean the Q? You mean show Judas Christian once and for all which store loves God more?"

"Uh-huh," replies Brad, his eyebrows going up and down. "Let's use the cow at the Qualcomm spot this year, guys. It'll be great! We'll *crush* Judas. The Mission Gorge branch won't stand a chance against us when we show up with a cow mascot. And the Lord's light will shine down upon our food truck! And He'll sayeth: Behold the Cluckin' Nuggets will be plentiful!"

Everyone laughs—except for her, like always. She rolls her eyes, this time adding a fluttering eyelash variant. Consuelo makes another fart sound, this time adding a sneering lip variant.

"Nice," she says, nodding appreciatively as they bump fists. Little differences like that show a person cares about the quality of their work, she always said.

"You got spit on your chin," says Mark.

Consuelo wipes his chin—finds it dry—and Mark flips his finger under Consuelo's nose.

"Shall we pray?" asks Mark.

"Not this again," she replies.

"I'm not here." Brad raises his hands in absolution and stalks back into the store.

She scowls at his back. Look at him. Like he doesn't know damn well all the Christians Gone Wild crap happening when he's looking the other way. Like his blind eye isn't the same thing as endorsement. Of all the Cluck-n-Prays in the world, she just had to apply to the one with the "edgy" Christian counterculture. Front-line foot soldiers for Jesus, and all of them convinced praying doesn't count unless you're risking jail time.

"This place is a godforsaken Chicken Church."

"You're the only one forsaking Him, Christine," Mark replies. "Now, gather round."

Mathew, Mark, Luke, John—and Consuelo—join hands in a circle.

"You too, Christine," says Mark. "What's the matter? Afraid of a teensy-weensy little prayer?"

"Look, Beatitude Butt," she says, folding her arms. "There is no war on Christianity in El Cerrito, or anywhere else in the greater San Diego area. Okay?"

"You say that a lot," Mark replies.

"Fine. You sure you don't wanna wait for the cops to roll up so they can ticket you for drive-through proselytizing?"

"Can they do that?" asks John.

"I don't get your position, is all," says Mathew, his tone gratingly reasonable. "I mean, if you don't believe in God, then what harm is there in praying to Him? Seems like it shouldn't matter to you."

"Maybe she's chicken," says Luke.

"She sure smells like chicken," says Mark.

"Buh-KAW," says John.

Her eyebrows lower, her mouth sags open. She expels a contemptuous burst of air. "Puh-lease. What is this? Kindergarten?"

"You're the only one who's being juvenile, Christine," says Mathew, using that gratingly reasonable voice again. Consuelo, his head bowed in ready-to-pray mode, makes another fart sound. "And him," adds Mathew.

"Screw you guys," she replies, dragging her feet over and joining hands with the rest. "Just get it over with." She grits her teeth and clenches her eyes.

"Let us pray," says Mark, and, despite her best effort to scream the lyrics of "Devil's Child" in her head, she cannot block out Mark's stupid cow prayer.

"Dear Lord," says Mark, "we come together this fine morning—all of us, most especially Christine here, who has an eternal soul in desperate need of Your salvation—"

Heat erupts like a nuclear bomb in her midsection. Mark's nauseating voice rakes over her skin. Something about using the cow to sell ten times more chicken at the football game than the Mission Gorge branch, and how Judas is always lying about his sales figures. Blah, blah, blah. When the amen comes, she wrests her hands back and rubs the sweat off on her slacks. The queasiness is in her bones. *Jerks.* Casting one last glance at the cow before pulling the door open, she pauses, half-inside, half-out. Something about the glint in the cow's eyes is giving off a weird, Stephen King vibe. Like it wants to give her a red balloon and snatch her into the sewers. But, really. *An interdimensional killer cow clown?* Nobody would read a book like that.

# CHAPTER THIRTEEN

MY EYES OPEN.

The curtains on my windows are glowing at the edges. The picture of my dad and me I keep on my desk is silhouetted by sunrise. We're fishing. Catalina Island. Most days I see that picture and my eyes go right over it. Some days I really look at it. It's his body language I see today. The way he holds his shoulders. The angle of his neck, and how it's broadcasting he's had a thought just occur to him; the shape of his smile as he gazes at me holding up the fish. The frozen-in-time body language is all that's left of him suggesting he'd once been a real person. Someone who'd once been a real part of my life, someone who could be climbed on or fished with, and not someone existing only in memory and dreams.

It takes a long time to accept a missing person isn't coming back. Especially since weird things sometimes happen. Like *Calvin and Hobbes* strips coming in the mail after the paper stopped running them. For about a year since his disappearance, they came. Someone had been cutting them out and mailing them. No letter. Just the comic strips. Turns out it'd been Gran's friend from the Jacksonville Symphony Orchestra. But it's funny how your brain plays tricks on you.

I roll over. My brain lags behind, untethered, like it's floating in maple syrup. The aroma of cooking sausage wafts up from the kitchen. My stomach rumbles. Bits and pieces from last night begin pushing through the porous barrier separating my subconscious and conscious mind.

Mikey's offer.

Mary's spying.

Caleb Montana drugging and kidnapping me.

I throw back the sheet and scramble out of my bed like it's full of snakes. My heart is racing. I'm still wearing my work clothes from yesterday. I pat my pockets—cell phone!

Ten new texts. Nine from Fabio. One from Wang.

My head still listing in maple syrup, I toggle up favorites, select Fabio, press Send. He picks up on the first ring.

"Holy shit!" he says.

"So I didn't dream it," I reply.

"Hell no, you didn't dream that shit! There was a needle and everything. One minute Caleb's pulverizing you with that football, and the next thing I know, there's a second Lamborghini pulling up and you're getting loaded into the passenger seat."

"What? In front of God and everybody?"

"Well, I mean. *Yeah.*"

"And nobody called the cops?"

"Dude. You were loaded into a Lamborghini. By Caleb Montana. Who was with three beautiful women. *Where* is the *crime*?"

"*Three* beautiful women?"

"Uh-huh. Third one was driving the other Lambo. Dark, short hair, gorgeous—but kinda aggressive-looking, like that tattoo girl on that one FBI show. You know which one I mean? I'm serious. Edge, you should've seen her. She was *hawt*. She had on this—"

"Dude—I don't care. Focus. You said there was a needle. You mean, like, a hypodermic needle?"

"Oh yeah, that. Well, Shmuel didn't show us that for, like, twenty minutes. Just kind of pocketed it after it happened, I think. You know he really loves the Chargers. Wouldn't give anybody the football. And you know Shmuel and drugs. I once caught him snorting brown sugar off the top of his oatmeal."

"Football?" I say. "I thought we were talking about the needle."

"The needle was in the football," says Fabio. "It was weird, dude. There was, like, a metal attachment stuck into the football. In the tip. You know, for the needle to screw into."

"What?"

"And I think a compression mechanism to push out the drug on impact."

"*What?*"

"What I'm saying is, spy shit. Serious spy shit, Edge. Which is what made me think Hot Girl in the second Lambo was all..."

His words float around in my head, no longer forming sentences per se, as I process what he's told me.

"Hey," he says, using a tone that cuts through the fog. "You okay?"

"Yeah." My head is reeling. "I mean, I feel a little queasy."

"No shit. Where are you?"

"I'm at home, why?"

"So you just woke up there?"

"Yeah."

I cross to my desk and wheel the chair around, plop down. My paddle ball is sitting there. I pick it up and give it a good flick, my plan being to whack out my frustrations on the tiny ball, but it slaps the window blinds and then careens wildly back to hit me in the cheek.

"Dude?" asks Fabio.

I chuck the paddle at my bed. The rubber band wraps around my arm at the last second, and the wooden paddle springs back, raps my elbow, and then loops around my arm.

"Edge, are you there?"

"Caleb told me not to take Mikey up on his offer," I say, rubbing my stinging and throbbing elbow, which now has a dangling paddle attached to it. I pinch the phone into my shoulder and carefully begin unwinding it.

"He did?"

"Yeah," I reply. "There was an interrogation spotlight and everything."

The paddle now fully disentangled, with two hands I set it back on my desk like it's a sleeping Monster Book of Monsters from Harry Potter, which could at any moment wake up and bite my face off.

"Well, what're you gonna do?" asks Fabio.

"What I said I'm gonna do. Turn Mikey down."

"I don't know, dude. There's more to this. You should totally march right up to Mikey's office and find out how much more."

Find out how much more? I sit there for a second in silence, fuming at the monster paddle, and my hostility transfers from it to Mikey.

"You know what?" I say. "I *should* do that."

"Yeah," replies Fabio. "You should!"

I kick off in my chair toward the bed, but when the wheels hit the carpet, I topple backward, crash, and my head rebounds off the floor. Gran calls out from downstairs. Blinking back spots, I put my hand over the phone.

"I'm okay!" I yell, then put the phone back up to my ear.

"Dude—what the hell? It sounds like you butt-dialed me from the inside of somebody's luggage. Are you sure you're okay?" asks Fabio.

Clear my throat. "Yeah. Sorry. I was just thinking."

"Do you bruise when you think?"

"Sometimes. Solving Mikey's nonlinear partial differential equations, for example." I climb back into bed, ease my head left and right to stretch out my neck, and then lie back and stare up at the *Star Wars* poster on my ceiling. Darth Vader's helmet behind Luke and Leia.

"So, what're you thinking?" asks Fabio.

"I'm thinking maybe I should just go back to bed. I've got a feeling this day isn't gonna work out."

"Okay. But what else are you thinking?"

"I'm hungry?"

"Dude."

"Okay," I say. "I'm thinking I haven't seen Mikey in five years. I'm thinking then he calls me up with all this crap out of the blue. And then Caleb shows up at The Palace? And then he *drugs* me?"

"Exactly! And don't forget about the pretty girl spying on you."

"Right. Her." I chew on my lip, and despite my generally queasy condition, throbbing elbow, back, head, and neck, some part of me still thinks maybe it's not such a bad idea to head back to Emerald Plaza after all.

"But you know, something about this is bugging me," says Fabio. "I mean, why you, dude? You know?"

"Yeah, I know," I reply, my gaze panning back to the picture of my dad and me off Catalina Island, then back up to Darth Vader behind Luke and Leia. "I've got an idea about that."

"You do?"

"Mmm-hmm. I think maybe it's because of my dad."

# CHAPTER FOURTEEN

BRUSH, SHAVE, SHOWER.

I scrub shampoo into my scalp, and a hazy picture from my dreams begins to form. I focus on it and try to sharpen the memory, but it's useless. Not that this is unusual. I've always been dream-remembering challenged.

After I'm dried and dressed, I head back to my room and open my laptop. I click Safari, type: Caleb Montana Mike Dame. About twenty-five thousand results come back.

I add my last name to refine the search.

Fifty-seven results.

I lean back in my seat, and when the wheels skid forward, I snap upright and grab the desk with both hands. I hold that position until I'm confident I've cheated death, and then I add the words "nano-neuro medicine" to my search.

*Your search—Caleb Montana Mike Dame Bonkovich nano-neuro medicine—did not match any documents.*

The aroma of sausage and eggs gets me moving again. My stomach is rumbling by the time I make it downstairs. Gran and Shep are in their robes in the kitchen. Shep slides his hand from Gran's waist, kisses the top of her head, and takes the morning paper into the living room, aglow in bars of sunlight.

"Good morning, dear," she says, pouring me a cup of coffee.

"How'd it go last night?"

I round the corner, accept the piping-hot coffee, and kiss her cheek. It takes me a second before I realize she's asking about Murder Mystery Night.

"Yeah," I say, striking a positive tone and nodding. "It was good."

She slaps my shoulder. "Oh you're such a terrible liar."

"Yeah," I say, striking a negative tone and taking a seat.

"I don't know why Fabio moved in with those two. He's lucky they aren't all in jail."

"They didn't move in together," I reply, grabbing a napkin out of the wicker holder. "They moved in *next* to each other."

"Same difference." Gran sets breakfast in front of me.

"Says here there's no power on the Eastern Seaboard," Shep calls from the living room. My stomach tightens.

"That's nice," Gran replies, not paying attention. "Hey," she says, and she slaps *Homebuyers* magazine next to my plate. It's folded open to a listing in Mira Mesa for one fifty. A low-level discomfort churns in my stomach.

"We've talked about this," I reply, pushing the magazine across the table and digging into my breakfast. What with whatever drugs are still in my system, the sausage juices exploding in my mouth are intensely restorative. I chase it down with a bite of toast and sip of coffee before continuing. "We're gonna get you into Pine's Place. Okay? Let's do that first, then we can talk about where I'm going to live."

"I can afford—"

"I know you can," I say. "But this way, we keep saving. Okay?"

"No. You're twenty-four years old. You don't owe me anything. These cradle-to-grave places are expensive, especially La Jolla. You need to be living your own life. Enjoying your life."

"You saying I'm not enjoying it with you?" I stuff in another bite of eggs, and add, "Best bed and breakfast this side of the San Andreas fault."

She waves her hand dismissively.

"I can't bake. You can bake the crap out of anything. And

Golumpki. You make one mother of a Golumpki."

"Edger," she says, her chin rising. "You know us old broads are finely tuned bullshit detectors. Young ladies may be charmed and fooled, but we've already been charmed and fooled."

"Is that right? Who's charmed and fooled you?"

"Me!" calls Shep from the living room.

"Aren't you going to be late for work?" asks Gran.

"Who else? Besides Shep. Because everyone knows you're not in your right mind now."

"I heard that," calls Shep.

Gran smiles. "You're going to be late for work."

"Listen," I say, giving my plate a quick rinse before setting it in the dishwasher. "We're just about there. Another six months, we'll have the money. Pine's Place. Six months of my life. Not a big deal, 'kay?"

She smiles and pulls me in for a hug. I clench my eyes and hug back. Her scent works like a drug. Tresor, baby powder, and the faintest trace of old books. I breathe her in, and the drug washes away the last remnants of Caleb's knockout formula, and maybe even a little of last night's insanity.

# CHAPTER FIFTEEN

THE ELEVATOR DOORS open. Mary is waiting, her features composed. She's wearing a charcoal-gray business suit, white blouse, and flats. Seeing her in the flesh, I find myself immediately backpedaling on this idea she's been spying on me. It's too outlandish. She's too intelligent, too gorgeous, too moneyed. It's counterintuitive someone like me could be the focal point of someone like her. It'd be like a Hollywood starlet stalking a paparazzi.

"Edger."

"Hey."

"You okay?"

"Hm? Oh, yeah. Yeah."

"Okay, well. Mr. Dame is waiting."

I nod, and we set off down the same hall as yesterday. The conference room on our right is empty this morning, but I barely notice. My brain gears are turning like a Rubik's Cube with three sides down and one to go. The nano-neuro medicine part of Mikey's project is too weird to be a coincidence. Dad was a legend in the field before he vanished. And that means Mikey's Collective Unconscious enterprise owes either directly or indirectly to Dad's research, whether he knows it or not.

"Hey." Mary grabs my hand and reels me to a halt. For a second,

I'm disoriented. Then I realize we've gone rig
Henrietta's office and arrived at the double doors leadin
"Are you sure you're okay?"

"Yeah. Yeah."

"Because you seem rattled," she says.

"No, no. I'm okay."

She peers into my eyes and caresses my arm, raising goose bumps. "Have you decided what you're going to do?"

Her icy blue eyes are taking me apart down to the molecular level. My face must be giving up every secret I've ever kept. Since there's no point in hiding, I frown and shrug. The tension in her eyes relaxes. She rubs my arm again, but this time, her touch is different. Or maybe her touch is the same and it's me that's different. I can't fool myself anymore. This fantasy is over.

"You're making the right choice," she says. "I know it's hard. But this could kill you. This isn't your problem. And it's not your job."

I can't bring myself to look her in the eye, so I pretend like there's a fascinating point of interest where the carpet meets the door. Her tone, meant to be reassuring, has opened a chasm between us. Her world is here. Mine is at the Über Dork.

Mary makes a fist and gently nudges my shoulder. "Come on," she says, pulling the door open and guiding me in with a hand on my back. "Let's get this done and get you back to the mall."

# CHAPTER SIXTEEN

MIKEY'S STANDING next to the samurai armor, his fingers fidgeting with one of the shoulder pads. He's wearing a black T-shirt and blue jeans, but he makes even this look like he's wearing a small fortune. A few yards away are two security guards about as discreet as a pair of front-end loaders. I raise my hand, *hello*, but when their expressions don't change, the knot in my stomach hardens. I glance at Mary for support, but she's backing through the doors, closing them as she goes, and mouthing the words, *Good luck*.

"You're late," says Mikey, not looking up from the samurai armor.

"Did we set a time?" I reply.

His hand drops to his side as he turns to glare at me.

"Edge. This is serious. Do you have any idea how many hospitals there are on the Eastern Seaboard? Airports? Grocery stores, banks? Do you realize people can't gas up their cars? ATMs are down. The stock market, Edger. Jesus."

"Wait-wait-wait," I say, my scalp crawling like it does when I can't wake up from a nightmare. "This isn't *my* fault." I jab a thumb into my chest, then point a finger at him. "This is *your* fault, Mikey."

"So that's your play?" he asks. "Come in here and point fingers?"

"Why don't you do it? If it's so important, risk your own damn life."

"Edge. Don't be a total ass-hat. *Think*. I can't do this. If I die, and this technology gets out, there'll be no one to stop it."

I laugh. "Convenient."

"No. You haven't thought this through. This is going to change the world. It's going to change our fundamental understanding of what it means to be human. It's going to change our perception of reality, religion—secrets. Who can I trust with the *secrets*, Edge? Huh? The government? Spies? *Mary?* No, the fact is, the one person I know who's truly selfless is standing in front of me right now. And I thought that person was better than this." He turns and marches for the bar. He doesn't go around this time, but instead grabs the seatback on a stool, flexes his fingers, and hunches his shoulders, waiting for me to crumble.

*Ha!* So *he* thinks *I'm* going to cave? I'm not the one shirking responsibility here. He is. This isn't my responsibility. It's his. His, and the first responders. Firefighters. Ambulance drivers. Police. The...

I expel a puff of air. I clap my hands on top of my head, which tips back to face the ceiling.

*Shit.*

My hands come down from my head and slap my sides. So, this is it. I'm just going to go home and catch the looting and rioting and crap on Twitter. Scroll through my feed like everybody else. By tomorrow, someone will have organized a thing downtown to pack emergency kits. I'll tell myself I'm being virtuous by donating a blanket. And the next day, I'll bring some canned food. But I'll know I'm not as virtuous as everyone else there, because I could've done more. And then I'll spend the rest of my life giving away the ongoing guilt one can of baked beans at a time.

*There's only the one human race.* Isn't that what I said to Mary?

I run my fingers through my hair and release a breath I didn't know I was holding. Next thing I know, I'm twirling a barstool around and sidling up beside Mikey. He looks at me sideways. The corner of his mouth pulls back in a wry nonverbal expression of thanks.

I roll my eyes. "You can thank me with a raise."

# CHAPTER SEVENTEEN

TWENTY MINUTES LATER, I'm strapped to a chair in Mikey's personal medical suite. It's a dizzying array of lights and wood paneling and doctors and nurses and—jeez, I'm not processing any of it. The world around me may as well not be there. My focus has constricted to a single thought replaying on loop no matter how hard I try to smash the Bluetooth speaker in my head.

*I can't do this... I can't do this... I can't do this...*

"You can do this," says Mikey. A nurse swabs my arm. The alcohol chills my skin to the bone. Blinding lights shine down—and this is how it must feel when the dentist tells you he's fresh out of Novocain, but, don't worry, he's still going to pull all your teeth out. No charge.

I clench my eyes and then swallow. Mikey grips my shoulder. I grip the armrests. Squeeze. Leather creaks. I focus on my breathing. The air is mortuary stale.

"Think of it like a flu shot," says Mikey.

"Why am I feeling a strong kinship to the anti-vaxxer crowd all of a sudden?"

"Focus on the positive. You're going to help millions of people. And if you learn fast, maybe you won't die."

My eyes pop open as I attempt to telepathically eye-shank Mikey.

“You have seriously got to work on your bedside manner. Do you know that?”

He gives me a lopsided smile and pats my shoulder. A doctor wheels his chair over and adjusts the overhead light.

“Mr. Bonkovich, are you ready?”

“Nope. Nope.”

“Edge?” says Mikey. “This is important.”

Again, I clench my eyes. Important, he says. Like I’m not important. Like my life isn’t important. Like breaking Gran’s heart isn’t important. But then… *Star Trek. The needs of the many outweigh the needs of the few.* Millions of people stranded without fuel.

“Mr. Bonkovich.”

The doctor’s voice hooks me back. He’s standing there, needle at the ready, in a surgical mask and cap, and that weird reflector thingy on his head that’s making Mikey’s face look like a fun-house mirror.

“Okay,” I say, taking a deep breath and holding it. I tell myself we’re all dying. Just like Fabio said. Less gradual than natural causes. More gradual than shot in the head.

The needle enters my arm.

My back flexes; every muscle in my body locks.

And then, darkness.

# CHAPTER EIGHTEEN

I'M FLOATING in a sea of white light.

This is weird.

My feet touch down. For some reason, they're in expensive-looking, tan leather dress shoes. The world is all white. I raise one arm, then the other; I'm in a white suit. Here's a white park bench. I sit, feeling strangely content, and take in the only feature on the horizon—a tree. Its trunk is *writhing*. Wooden creatures. Carvings of every living thing imaginable. That one—a hippopotamus. It yawns, and the inside of its mouth momentarily becomes a knot in the tree. A scorpion scurries over its back and down its leg. Above them, a carving of an owl twists its head around. The scorpion freezes, sensing the predator's beady eye.

*Incredible.*

My gaze pans up. Discarded slivers of autumn are slowly orbiting the naked timber like magic. The leaves twist and turn but won't fall as a rising trumpet motif rings out from the white sky. My pulse quickens. I know this music! It's *Also sprach Zarathustra*. I settle into the bench and listen appreciatively, the dream logic hitting me as weird and normal at the same time. It's like a cross between *2001* and that God movie with Morgan Freeman.

"*Bruce Almighty*," a voice says next to me. I startle, then shift in my seat.

*It's—it's Bruce Lee!*

He's in a white suit, tan shirt, white tie. Same shoes I'm wearing. He's smiling at me. I think: *Speaking of* Bruce Almighty, and he smiles like he can hear what I'm thinking.

"I *can* hear what you're thinking," says Bruce Lee, and his voice is not nearly as soothing as Morgan Freeman's.

Bruce Lee frowns.

"Sorry," I say, realizing again he's listening to my thoughts. "But, I mean, *nobody's* voice is as soothing as Morgan Freeman's."

Bruce Lee shrugs.

"What's with all the white?" I ask.

He takes in the sky, the landscape, and the bench as if seeing them for the first time, then shrugs again.

"I'm dreaming, aren't I?"

"Yes, Edge. You're dreaming."

"But you seem so real."

"I am real."

"But you just told me I'm dreaming."

"You are dreaming. Try to keep up."

The music swells to its climax, and, for a minute, we say nothing. Goose bumps race across my skin. I've always loved this piece. When it's done, I shift on the park bench and face Bruce Lee.

"What does it mean? The music."

His forehead creases, and he takes a seat next to me. "No idea."

"Because it sure seems impressive."

"Yes. I think that's why Kubrick likes it."

*"Kubrick?* As in, *Stanley* Kubrick?"

"He's the one who sent the music," says Bruce Lee. "Edge, you are in the Collective Unconscious. Observe."

Bruce Lee holds his empty palm up to his mouth and blows. Stardust lifts into the air and envelops us in a cyclone of sparkling lights. They shoot upward with a whip crack, and our surroundings change. We're standing atop a grassy hill in the thick of night. The stardust is now a faraway galaxy, but instead of being fixed in the velvet sky, it moves like time-lapse photography, revealing pictures in the negative spaces. They're clear as a comic book. There's the

Tree of Life—it's the one I saw earlier! And there's the Wise Old Man, the Trickster, the Earth Mother, the Dark Tower. There are thousands, and in my dream, I know them all by name.

"You can see the archetypes?" asks Bruce Lee. I nod. "Good. This, essentially, is your instinct."

"My instinct."

"That's right. What you think of as instinct is actually your ancestors, alive, inside of you." His head tilts back, his eyes never leaving mine. I can't be sure, but I think he's waiting for me to process the word "ancestor" as not limited to my family tree. He means the entirety of the human race. Literally everyone who's ever lived.

"That's right," he says. "And the lights. Is it true you can really see them?"

"They're like stars," I reply. "But they move around a lot more."

Bruce Lee smiles. "Edge, these are the lights we make in life. They never go out. That one…ah, there…that's mine."

It's one of the brighter ones. I peer into it, and Bruce Lee's life fills me. There are no secrets. I see his birth. His first steps, him spitting up, the childhood tantrums—

"You see," he says hastily. "We're not so different."

"We're *completely* different," I reply, stunned to feel the enormity of Bruce Lee's spirit fill me. The enormity of what he did with his life. Mine feels so little in comparison.

Bruce Lee nods. "And my life is nothing next to so many others. We all have that feeling, Edge, but it is in reaching for our potential that we honor those who've come before us. And you…you are the first person to see this and know it for what it is. You have been given a very special gift."

"But I'm going to die."

Bruce Lee's eyebrows go up. "Everyone dies." His gaze is earnest, and maybe it's because he's already dead, or maybe it's because the sky is teeming with disembodied soul-stars, but the idea of dying is remote, like I'm just renting my body anyway; a profound calmness washes over me.

The lights above are chattering. They've been chattering the whole time, I realize. I close my eyes, listen—and the serenity is obliterated.

I gasp.

"It's too much!"

"That's what's going to kill you. Sorry. But perhaps before then, you will contribute something good for humanity."

"Ha-ha," I reply, striking a sarcastic tone.

My gaze returns to the night sky. Now that I'm not focusing on the chatter, I can *feel* their intentions… All the lives shining down on us, the lives from yesterday, today, wanting to help the living. Wanting to do something good for the world.

"This is the source of peace I was feeling earlier?" I ask.

"Yes," says Bruce Lee urgently. "Hold on to that."

I frown. "But then, what's stopping you? What's stopping any of you from helping?"

"I can't explain. But you being here is different. Because you're alive and in the Collective Unconscious. That's never happened before. Not like this. We're hoping you'll talk to the living for us. You can do it from here. You don't have to be awake."

"Wait a minute," I say. "We? '*We're* hoping' I'll talk to the living? You mean the human race? Like, going back to Socrates and Plato and before? The *total* human race, like, ever and always?"

"Mm-hmm."

I expel a whistle. "No pressure."

Bruce Lee responds with a tight smile.

"Oh, crap. You're serious. Let me get this straight. So you guys, Plato and crew, are in this…psychic dimension…watching us. As in, empires rise and fall and nothing built can last and all that. And you just have to watch all that happen."

"Yes."

"No-no-no," I say, convinced I'm not being clear. "I mean, you just have to be dead all the time and watch us screw everything up? All the time?"

"Yes."

"No-no-no… I mean, dead forever…somebody invents reality TV…and you watch it through *literal* reality TV."

"Yes, Edge. Correct."

I nod slowly. "Okay. Huh."

I ponder this for a minute longer. All the war, poverty, famine, greed—all of it—and nothing they can do except watch.

"Mr. Lee, sir, that straight up sucks."

"You're telling me."

For a long moment, we just stare at each other as I process the implications of what he's telling me. It doesn't seem possible—until I remember I'm dreaming, and so whether or not it's possible doesn't matter. I just go with it.

"So," I begin, "you know, like, about the power grid problem?"

"Easily fixed—if we can borrow you to help us fix it."

"Borrow me." I shrug. "Sure. What do we do?"

Bruce Lee gets to his feet, so I get up also.

"Okay," he says, clapping his hand on my shoulder and squeezing. "What you need to understand is that before we can fix the power grid, we must first compromise the network of bad guys responsible for attacking the power grid in the first place."

"Network of bad guys?" My head comes back. "I thought this was all InstaTron Tron... Tron..."

Bruce Lee frowns. "InstaTron *Tron* used a network of bad guys to bring the power grid down. We must deal with them first. Otherwise, our work will be undone."

"Makes sense. So, you know where these bad guys are hiding out right now?"

"Yes," replies Bruce Lee. "But not just them—all their allies. Terrorist leaders."

"Wait a minute. Are you telling me I can dream my way into some CIA guy's brain and tell him where all the terrorists' leaders are?"

"That would be one route. But you're thinking too small, Edge. Why fight any wars?"

"Psh. Well of course we don't want to fight any wars," I say, trying to strike a tone that conveys confidence in his plan to Yoko Ono the human race. But judging by the flat-eyed stare he's putting out, it's not working.

"Terrorism is propaganda," he says. "Propaganda can be beaten by better propaganda."

"I thought we were talking about the power grid."

Bruce Lee sighs, runs his fingers through his hair, and then clears his throat. "I think for the sake of expediency, you're going to have to trust me on some things."

"Trust you? Well, of course I trust you. You're Bruce Lee. But it sounds like you're telling me we can... I don't know...go beat terrorism. Like, hey, let's just go do that today. And maybe after, we'll get some fish tacos. Yay!"

"Well, why not?" asks Bruce Lee. "You're sleeping. It's not like this is much of an imposition. There's only the one human race, after all. It would suck to squander it by crashing planes into buildings and bickering forever on differing opinions. There are no politics here. So what do you say, Edge? Help a dead guy make the world a better place?"

I almost laugh in his face. "Hell yes, I'm gonna help Bruce Lee make the world a better place! Let's do it."

# CHAPTER NINETEEN

A GUST OF WIND throws the bright lights in the sky down and into our faces. It swirls around us and then vanishes with a crack. The dream grows dark. The temperature drops.

"Get down!"

He grabs my hand, yanks, and we're in cold sand, flat on our backs, side by side. There are stars in the sky—real stars. The soul-lights are gone.

"How did we—? Where did we—?"

He raises a finger to silence me. I hold my breath.

An icy wind blows in from the desert. It whooshes over our heads, carrying a blackened canvas, ridden with bullet holes and frayed at the edges. Flapping, curling, and dripping in blood, it dumps a severed head two feet from where we're lying. *Whump*. Blood seeps outward into the sand. Bruce Lee grips my arm. The back of my throat is dry and hollowed-out. I'm shivering. The canvas unfurls above us, revealing a bullet-damaged crescent moon and star—and then it whip-cracks higher, twisting in the violent and invisible wind before vanishing completely.

I'm panting. My heart is thumping so hard I can't speak. The severed head's gaze is heavy in my peripheral vision. A nerve in my neck pinches from the strain of not looking.

"Bad guys," whispers Bruce Lee.

I nod six or seven times superfast. "Obviously."

"No," says Bruce Lee. "I want you to listen, because this is important. Remember, bad guys are real. Earlier, you felt silly about calling them bad guys. I could feel it. But bad guys are real."

"Obviously."

"When I said earlier there are no politics here, I didn't mean to imply it's all peace and love in the Collective Unconscious. You are here to understand the nature of bad guys." He makes eye contact with the severed head, then claps his hand on my shoulder and faces me. "But don't worry. There are more of *us* than *them*."

"Us?"

"Good guys, Edge. Good guys. And now we have the advantage."

"We do?"

"Yes. You. Now, come on."

Bruce Lee sets off toward where the flag disappeared, waving for me to follow. I comply, and what he's told me begins to sink in. *Bruce Lee wants to beat terrorists*. Bruce Lee, a dead man, has an opinion. It comes as no shock to me he has a negative opinion on terrorism—but the fact that he seems to feel like death is some kind of cosmic penalty sidelining him from contributing to a larger human calling is weirdly humbling. Talk about a perspective check. How many other dead heroes are out there who feel the same way? Can the Collective Unconscious really harness all that?

"You said there're more good people than bad," I say.

Bruce Lee nods, raising his hand to halt our march. "Factor in the dead, and that ratio tips dramatically. The bad guys are overwhelmingly outnumbered." His chin lifts. He sniffs the air and turns around slowly. "We're here." He tosses his head to get his bangs out of his eyes. "We're in the heart of darkness. They can sense me. Their unconscious minds are resisting. But they will not be able to resist you."

"Me? What good am I against the heart of darkness?" I ask, trying to imagine what I could possibly do when so many better people than me have tried and failed.

"Better people?"

"Well," I reply, shrugging. "Yeah. I'm just a dork."

"We are none of us 'just' anything. What we *are* is what we aspire to be. Can you think of nothing?"

I frown. Unfortunately, I *can* think of things. Horrible things. The things *they* do. If I'm being brutally honest with myself, I want to do worse to them.

My chest is tight. I close my eyes, press my fist into my sternum, and hope Bruce Lee didn't hear that part. Does he have to listen to my every thought? I try to focus on Gran and Shep, or Fabio, or *Star Wars*—anything but terrorizing terrorists with nightmares like what they do. I don't want to be like them. I don't want to give up on the idea of there being a better way of fighting them than crawling down into the sewer with them. I open my eyes. Bruce Lee is peering into me. My cheeks burn.

"I don't judge you." His gaze is tense but steady. "I've thought the same thing. We're part of the same family. We're human. And just like everyone else, you have a choice. You can let others set the rules, or you can change the rules. It is how you fight that defines your nature. Make no mistake, what we do in life echoes in eternity. What you do here, tonight, will define you. Good guy, bad guy. Look at the stars, Edge. How bright will yours shine?"

His words release the tension I'm holding. And for a minute, all I can do is stare up at the stars and bask in the presence of Bruce Lee.

"Okay. Okay, I can do this. I can totally do this."

Bruce Lee casts a sidelong glance at me before turning to peer back into the night sky where the bullet-ridden flag vanished.

I fold my arms and bite my bottom lip. *Think, Edge, think*. Make a new set of rules, he says. Propaganda can be beaten with better propaganda. But what is their propaganda? I guess the idea they're effective at striking from anywhere?

"Okay, sure," says Bruce Lee, coming up next to me and folding his arms and nodding like we've been having this conversation out loud.

"And so people who think like they do gravitate to the cause," I say, preferring to keep the conversation out loud over having him in my head and listening to every dang thing.

"Sorry," he says. "But you'll get used to it."

"Our propaganda needs to ruin the cause. So, I mean, how do they see themselves? As big strong hairy men?" A sudden image of a hairy-chested gay motorcyclist in a leather jacket and moustache pops into my head.

Bruce Lee frowns. "You can't turn someone gay."

"No, no. Of course not. But what if we gayed up the cause just a little bit? Kill it with their own homophobia. Terrorize the terrorists with, I don't know, the Village People."

Bruce Lee closes his eyes. His head bobs slowly up and down as he works through the plan with me in my head. His eyes open. "You've got a sense of humor, Edge. Who knows? Maybe laughter will save the world."

I grin. "What do people love? People love tastelessness. We need to make something that'll crash the internet. We need to get them fabulously tasteless wardrobes, supplies for building floats, rainbow flags—and then invite the surrounding communities to witness everything in person, so they know it's real, and not an internet hoax. We need to get them to drop what they're doing and make them do all this now, this minute, like their lives depend on it. And then we'll tell the CIA where all the bad guys are." I wince and shake my head as the ridiculousness of my suggestions crashes in on me. The back of my neck must be glowing in the dark.

"No," he says urgently. "We will try it. We can do all of that in minutes. There's no reason not to try it."

"Bullshit," I say, laughing as his sincerity surges through our psychic connection. "So how does this work? We just plant the ideas into their brains and let them do the rest?"

"I cannot. But you...yes, I think that would work just fine for you."

"Well then, what are we waiting for? Let's get to work," I say, laughing. "And after that, power grid."

Bruce Lee grins back at me. "And then we have *got* to get some fish tacos. I know this great place in San Francisco."

# CHAPTER TWENTY

"EDGER! EDGER!"

I know that voice.

Mike Dame.

My teeth are chattering. Someone's hand is on my shoulder, shaking me. My eyelids flutter open. The world is bright and loud. I close my eyes. My head rocks back and forth. My inner ear is a wreck. Pangs of nausea sour my stomach.

"Edger!"

"*Uh-nn...*"

"Edger! Can you hear me?"

"*I can hear you.*"

"Are you...did it...work?"

I swallow to work the moisture back into my mouth, then nod. "...fixed it. The grid..."

"The power grid is fixed?" Mikey asks. "But that's not possible. We haven't even bonded you to the suit yet."

"Fixed," I say again.

"Tablet!" yells Mikey. Feet scuff. A chair scoots back. Next thing, Mikey's sitting at my side, fingers tapping on a tablet. "CNN breaking news: power restored," he reads aloud. The room erupts in whoops of joy—which split my brain in half like an ax to a watermelon. Someone raises a chorus of "We Are the Champions." My already halved watermelon brain feels like it's being churned into syrup.

"Holy shit, Edge!" exclaims Mikey. "Holy shit. How is this possible?"

"I think—"

"Give him room," says Mikey. "Back up! Give him room to breathe."

"I think...you should check out YouTube."

I swallow back the nausea and try to hold on to the dream. I've never been good at holding on to dreams, but this time, it's stuck. A jihadist recruitment video set to the tune of "YMCA." Digital footprints and firsthand accounts proving its authenticity. Subliminal suggestions for a very specific YouTube search in the minds of fifteen million people at once. CIA heads making frantic phone calls to overseas operatives. On the other side of the world, angry, homophobic would-be radicals are waking up and logging on to watch half-naked Arabs dressed like the Village People dance atop brightly colored parade floats. With machine guns strapped to their backs, they're cheering in Arabic and throwing limp-wristed fistfuls of glitter into the confused crowd. Rainbow flags on every float.

One hundred million views in two hours.

I hope it will work. I hope enough would-be bad guys see it to where the association of murder-martyrdom is fixed in their minds to the rainbow flag. I hope their homophobia will scare them away from becoming terrorists. And I hope everyone else's politics will settle down long enough to see my intentions for what they are: the rainbow flag—a symbol of love—conquering hate.

# CHAPTER TWENTY-ONE

WANG'S UNPROVOKED ATTACK clobbers Debbie Three Holes, sending her flying from the dining room table. She caroms off the refrigerator, slams into the kitchen floor, collides with Mr. Mxyzptlk's water dish, and sloshes hairy water all over the first of Debbie's three holes. Hearing the commotion, the dog pops his furry head up from the sofa, where he's been sleeping all morning. Any noise from the kitchen, whether it be an opening can of beer, or Shmuel's toenails being clipped on the countertop, always held promise. Mr. Mxyzptlk leaps down from the sofa and trots happily off to investigate. Finding a now-bearded Debbie Three Holes at his water dish in the kitchen, he sniffs around hole number three for a moment, grabs the blowup doll by the ankle, and drags her around the corner to disappear down the hallway leading to Shmuel's bedroom.

"Feel better?" asks Shmuel, rounding on Wang, who is flexing and closing his fingers like Debbie Three Holes's jaw was harder and more solid than he'd expected. "Violence is rarely the answer?"

"Ah, this is our fault," replies Wang, slumping into his chair.

Shmuel sighs and peers into the empty carton on the table in front of him at his finished breakfast, leftover takeout from the Happy Cock down the street. He chucks his chopsticks into the carton.

"What?" asks Wang.

"Still hungry."

"Hungry? How can you think of food at a time like this?"

Shmuel shrugs. "You know I get hungry for the Dong Long Pork when I'm hungover. Hey." He points to the laptop screen next to the takeout carton. "You see this thing with the gay terrorists? Watch this guy belly dance to 'YMCA.' He's pretty good."

"Dude!" yells Wang. "Your 'sweet' and 'innocent' moo-beast attacked the Eastern Seaboard, and all you can do is stare at that fat, hairy belly?"

"It's not that fat." Shmuel closes the laptop and sucks in his gut.

"Don't you take that tone with me, Mr. I Love Dong Long Pork in the Morning. Let's go through it again, since all you can do is watch Gay ISIS instead of focusing on the problem at hand: Tron-Tron. Now. Check it out. Cow-incidences abound. Tron-Tron opened his Twitter account about an hour after we got back from the porn store. Then I tweeted that thing about him getting the world domination, and Tron-Tron starts in with all those weirdo tweets about green grass and utterly hurting his udders and slaughterhouses and shit. Now... I don't know how it happened... I don't know why it happened, but...clearly the frog man with the dart gun in the porn store shot Chicowgo in the butt with a Tron-Tron."

*"Whoa."*

"Shmuel, my friend, Chicowgo is gone. There is only Zuul."

"Zuul?"

"Fucking *Ghostbusters*, okay? Now. Pay attention. You and I are the only ones who know the truth."

"About Zuul? And is this girl *Ghostbusters* or boy *Ghostbusters*? Because I kinda liked the girl one."

"Fucking—shit—mother of— Fuck! No! No! Tron-Tron, dude! Tron-Tron! We're the only ones who know the truth about Tron-Tron!" Wang slaps the takeout carton, and Shmuel's chopsticks go flying.

"Okay, okay," Shmuel replies, standing and pretending to pick out a wedgie, but really, covering for a quick itch back there. "It's just it's kinda hard to picture sweet Chicowgo being capable of such...you know...such Hey Ness-crimes and other a-sundry sundries?"

"Wait-wait-wait!"

"What?"

"Did you just say, *Hey Ness-crimes?*"

"Yeah." Shmuel shrugs, then narrows his eyes conspiratorially. "You know. The kind of crimes they can electrocute you for. The really *serious* ones. *Hey Ness-crimes*."

Wang slouches like a drooping marionette. He buries his face in his hands, and, after a second, his shoulders begin bobbing up and down.

"Aw, dude," says Shmuel. "Don't cry." Scooting back his chair, he rounds the table, goes down on one knee, and wraps his arms around Wang's waist.

"Fuck!" Wang shoves him. "Get your butthole-itching hands off me!"

"You're not crying?"

"No, I'm not crying! I'm laughing, you stupid fuck. It's *heinous crimes*, dumbass!"

"That's what I said. Jeez."

Wang shoots to his feet and cups his hands around his mouth. "Hey!" he yells. "Ness-crimes! Yoo-hoo! Ness-crimes! Hey! Hey!"

"Moving on?" Shmuel shrugs and takes his seat on the other side of the table. Wang giggles, picks up a takeout carton, and peers inside.

"Nope. No Ness-crimes in there."

"You're being rude? All I'm saying is, why would poor old Chicowgo shut down the power on the Eastern Seaboard? He's never shown any criminal tendonitis before?"

"Why?" cries Wang. "Because it's what we fucking told it to do!" Wang pulls his long bangs back in apparent frustration, and, for a fleeting moment, his eyes are visible. Shmuel smiles, and all irritation at being so mercilessly teased vanishes.

"You have pretty eyes."

"Would you shut up about my pretty eyes? This is serious!"

"I'm just saying. I don't see your eyes that often."

"Shmuel. The world needs us. This is a job for the A-Team."

Shmuel sighs and gathers his takeout boxes. He brings them into the kitchen and drops them in the trash. Mr. Mxyzptlk comes trotting around the corner and sniffs the air hopefully. Shmuel leans down and scratches behind his ear.

"Won't the Feds come after us?"

"No, dude," replies Wang, opening his laptop. His eyes widen. "Fuck. Those are some seriously gay terrorists." Shaking his head, he clicks the target pad, opening a new window. "We're gonna fix this, Shmuel, before the Feds know what hit 'em. You and me."

"Aw, ma-an," groans Shmuel. "But is it gonna be *hard*?"

Wang glances up from his computer. "Da fuck. Maybe."

"Well, that's it. I quit. I don't want hard. I give up."

"Do you really give up?"

Shmuel frowns. "What do you mean?"

"Well, do you really give up or not? It's a yes-or-no question."

Shmuel shrugs uncomfortably.

"Dumbass," says Wang. "You can't *say* you give up if you don't mean it. Because that's what losers do."

"Are you trying to confuse me?"

"Losing at giving up is literally the loseriest way a loser can lose."

"Technically that makes me a *winner*?"

"Shut up," replies Wang, a smile blooming on his face. "Look at this tweet."

Shmuel smiles, mainly because Wang is smiling, though the idea of being a winner is a close second. He rounds the table and reads the tweet from over Wang's shoulder.

*Pray all day at Cluck-n-Pray!*

"Aw, dude," says Shmuel. "Then Chicowgo has truly gone evil. My innocent baby...reduced to a corporate shill?"

"What?" Wang slaps his arm. "No, you idiot! This is a clue!"

Shmuel rubs his stinging arm and pulls away from Wang, feelings hurt more than anything else. "So you wanna just drive down to the Cluck-n-Pray? Hey. Doesn't your dealer work there? That kid with all the fart sounds?"

"Consuelo," replies Wang, sitting back in his seat and rubbing his chin. "Yeah. Let's give him a call."

# CHAPTER TWENTY-TWO

CHRISTINE SPEAKS into her headset as she passes a large Cherry Coke through the to-go window.

"Welcome to Cluck-n-Pray. May I take your order?"

Electronic static.

"I'm sorry," says Christine. "Can you say that again?"

"MOO! MOO-OO!"

"Consuelo? Is that you?"

Electronic static blares into her headset, followed by the earsplitting commotion of what could be a skydiver butt dialing at thirty-thousand feet. She rips the headset off, leans on her creaking stool, and peers back into the restaurant, scanning for Brad. She spots an elbow sticking out from behind the splatter wall blocking the fry machine. The telltale creased short sleeve, pressed just so through copious amounts of starch and ironing, is the giveaway.

"Hey, Brad!" she calls. "Consuelo's at the drive-through again."

"God bless it," Brad murmurs, his head now sticking out from behind the splatter wall as he shovels an order of Cheezin' Spiced Fries into a carton. "Mathew! Go grab Consuelo, please."

"Where do you want me to take him?" says Mathew, grinning, his hand on Consuelo's arm at register two.

"What I do now?" asks Consuelo, hurt.

Brad turns and faces Christine, his eyebrows lowering and head ticking to the side in confusion.

Christine frowns. Tentatively, she puts the headset back on, which tangles in her hair and tugs slightly before she manages to get situated. She taps the microphone, then pulls it closer to her mouth. “Hello? Is somebody there?”

A gleeful voice comes back.

“See you later, suck-ahs!”

Tires squeal. A horn blares. Christine thrusts her head out the to-go window. A mustard-yellow Hummer towing a livestock trailer bounces right over the curb. Her eyes widen; a cow—their cow—is loaded into the trailer. A drawn-out moo fills the parking lot before fading away.

“They’re getting away with our cow,” says Christine, cracking her head as she jerks it in from the to-go window. “Brad! Brad!”

“Spawn of Satan!” Brad yells, throwing down a carton of Cheezin’ Spiced Fries and charging out the front door. Christine races after him, blinking back spots and rubbing the knot on her head furiously, her heart pounding.

Mathew, Mark, Luke, and John follow.

Followed by Consuelo.

From the parking lot, they watch, stupefied, as the Hummer, horn blaring, weaves through oncoming traffic before cutting into the correct, southbound lane. The driver’s-side window powers down, and the driver’s face is clearly visible for a split second. That’s all any of them need to instantly recognize the man who has come to personify all that is unholy in intra-store rivalry at the Cluck-n-Pray.

Judas S. Carryout.

A fist shoots out the window, middle finger at full mast.

*HOOOONK-HONK-HONK-HONK-HOOOONK!*

“Judas!” screams Brad, spittle flying. “You...you Judas!”

The Hummer swerves around the corner and disappears down El Cajon Boulevard. Christine’s heart is thundering in her chest. Her hands ball into fists. She hates that cow. But, dammit, that’s their cow. And even though she also hates the El Cerrito branch’s Gospel according to the Book of Buk-Buk-

Buh-KAW, that hatred doesn't light a candle next to Judas S. Carryout and the Mission Gorge Cluck-n-Pray. *Those* guys are straight-up dicks.

"Oh it is *on*," she says, fuming. "It is *so* on."

Across the street, a Black Escalade parks in a vacant cement lot where a straining blade of grass is reaching through the cracks toward a bar of sunlight. The driver and passenger who witness the spectacle at the Cluck-n-Pray are identical down to the fibers of their black suit coats.

"Late again," says Ed.

"Is that mustard yellow?" asks Ted, tracking through his rifle scope the trailer-hitched vehicle speeding off with the cow.

"Who cares?"

"I mean—did you catch the plates?"

"Don't have to."

Ted glances up from his rifle scope and arches an eyebrow identical to the two on the man sitting next to him.

"You're being awfully cagey. What do you mean 'don't have to'?"

"What I mean is, I happen to know who owns that vehicle. His name is Judas Christian, and by tomorrow, we'll have that damn cow delivered to *us*."

Ted pauses a beat before nodding and again raising the rifle scope. He pans back to the Cluck-n-Pray, and targets a red-faced, disheveled girl standing apart from the group of others gathered in the parking lot. "Uh-huh," he says. "Okay. Well in that case...who're we killin' this time?"

Ed swats the barrel down. "My appetite." He turns the key in the ignition. "Come on. Drive-through. I want some Cluckin' Nuggets."

# CHAPTER TWENTY-THREE

ELECTRODES ATTACHED to my head and chest.

A nerve firing randomly in my bicep.

A fly crawling on the wall across from my spot in the chair, its chaotic patterns mirroring the bustle of doctors, nurses, and technicians in surgical scrubs. One person helpfully informs me my blood pressure is high. Another asks whether I need to pee before we get started. I didn't, but now I'm second-guessing myself.

Having endured the injection of nano-neuro medicine, I am told the next component of transforming me into a superhero will be the neural linking of me to the supersuit. What could go wrong? Going by the evil AI cow-at-large—plenty.

Mikey appears at my side and squeezes my shoulder.

"I still don't understand," I say. "I can already access the Collective Unconscious. Why do I need to do this?"

"I told you," he replies. "Because you need all three parts of the technology for it to work the way it's supposed to. The suit's processors will shoulder some of the load so your neuronal cells don't implode before happy hour. Besides, it's body armor. And it looks cool."

I frown.

"You're going to be helping people," he says. "Hold on to that. Everything's going to work out."

"You don't know that."

"No, you're right. I don't know that."

"Good talk."

"Listen. This won't be like it was when I put on the ring. This is going to be…intense."

"God, Mikey. Your bedside manner is as shitty as the way you talked me into doing this."

He grins. "But I *did* talk you into this."

Mary joins us. She rounds the back of my chair and squeezes my other shoulder. A technician sticks a scanner gun in my face. I raise my arm—

"We need you to relax." The tech lowers my arm and jams the scanner in my face like I'm a box of cereal to price check.

"And I need you to do a cleanup in Aisle Eight," I reply, shoving the scanner aside.

"It's okay, Edger," says Mary.

The tech steps back, studies his scanner readout, then signals another technician. "Subject is ready."

"Subject is ready," I say, copying his tone.

"Copy that," says Tech Two. "Do you have the ring?"

Mikey reaches into his pocket and pulls out the ring box.

"Good," says Tech Two. "Commence initiation."

Mikey nods. My ears start ringing. Mary's eyes are unblinking and round.

"This is it, Edger," says Mikey. "When your altered physiology bonds with the technology in that ring, the suit can help you locate the skills or information required from the Collective Unconscious, and assist you in finding InstaTron Tron in ninety-six hours or less. Are you ready to become the world's first superhero?"

"No."

Mikey holds my gaze a beat longer before passing the ring box to Mary.

"Ms. Thomas. Will you do the honors?"

Tension creeps into the corners of her eyes before she smooths it out. She takes the box, opens it, and removes the ring. Her hand finds mine. Her fingers are thin and graceful. She gives a gentle squeeze and peers into my eyes.

"Come back to us, Edger," she says.

"I do. I mean I will! I will."

Her smile is faint, but it's good. *This is what I wanted,* I tell myself. *To be in her orbit. Not to be sent back to the mall.*

She bends over and kisses my cheek, her hair tickling my face. Tiny wings collide in my stomach and a thrill shoots down to my toes. She slips the ring onto my finger. My pulse ratchets higher like it's on a contact-activated switch. Black goo slithers out, up my fingers—

Electrodes are ripped from my head and body.

Mary lurches away, clutching the ring box to her chest.

—the goo covers my hand, my arm, neck—face! My eyes clench shut. I'm panting. Can't catch my breath—

"—neural connections are off the charts—"

"Edger!" yells Mary, but the goo is in my ears and her voice is muffled.

—My eyes pop open. Red letters, targeting crosshairs, range finders sprawl across my vision as the supersuit's heads-up display springs to life.

*Initiation sequence online. Initiating in 3…*

A voice whispers into my ear: *Be like water, Edge.*

"Bruce Lee?" I stammer.

*2…*

*Yes, Edge,* Bruce Lee replies. *I'm here.*

*1…*

Sonic boom.

Deafening screams form a thick wall of sound. Billions of pinpricks of light speed past my face like the *Millennium Falcon* going to hyperdrive. It's an epileptic seizure of galactic proportions. My body is shaking. Pressure is building in my ears.

"—pulse is too high—"

My teeth are chattering. I bite down hard.

"—not going to make it—"

*Hang on, Edge!*

"—he'll die!"

The top of my head throbs like it's going to blow. Everything is spinning, collapsing in on itself, and then—bam!

Silence.

# CHAPTER TWENTY-FOUR

FOR A TIMELESS and serene moment, I'm swimming in the air above my body. The pressure in my head is lessening. My teeth are no longer chattering. My breathing is even.

I open my eyes.

I'm back in the chair. Light floods in. Blurry, indistinct shapes coalesce into the world. I'm like a fish inside an aquarium: the people, walls, cabinets, and sinks are distorted and bent. The heads-up display is still there, measuring distances, performing involuntary target locks and diagnostics like I've died and become Iron Man. Everyone is staring at me, eyes wide, lips parted and turned down. Mary is pale and clutching the ring box to her chest with both hands, recoiling like she's seen a monster. One of the doctors sets a pen down on a metal tray. The sound detonates in my ears like a bomb.

I feel weird. Frozen in time. I hold my hand out, and, despite knowing what to expect, I'm stunned. Even though I saw it with my own eyes when it happened to Mikey, I can't quite believe I'm wearing the same body armor he wore in our first meeting. And...a helmet. I knock on the top of it. Yep. Helmet.

*Bruce?*

*Yes, Edge. I'm still here.*

*How?*

I can feel Bruce Lee considering how best to answer. Strange...

He's in my head. I'm awake, but I can hear what he's thinking, and feel what he's feeling.

*It's the injection,* says Bruce Lee.

*Is it always going to be like that?* I ask, meaning the experience of putting on the ring.

*I don't know,* Bruce Lee answers. *You'll have to ask the doctor.*

"Edge." Mikey's voice presses through time and space, and the world coalesces into the real world again. A stable world. The fishbowl effect is gone. Or else I'm getting used to the strangeness.

"Are you okay?" Mikey asks.

"I—"

"Talk to me, Edge." Mikey.

"So this is how it feels being an armored space ninja," I reply through the voice scrambler.

Mikey's posture relaxes. "He's fine."

"The phone call is coming from inside the house," I say, getting into the whole horror-movie vibe the voice scrambler is putting out. *"Hello, Sydney."*

Mikey pats my shoulder. "Superhero, Edge," he says. "We're going for superhero. Not Halloween killers."

"I'm Batman," I say, trying to make my voice low and gravelly. "I'm Christian Bale Batman."

"Stop talking now, Edge," says Mikey, signaling with his hand for Mary to leave the room. Our eyes meet—that is, her eyes lock on to my mask—and she gives me a nearly imperceptible nod before pulling open the door and leaving, taking with her that Christmas-morning feeling I never seem to realize is there until she isn't.

A tech comes over and plugs three different jacks into various ports on my suit.

"What are those for?" I ask, mentally readjusting to the here and now.

"Diagnostics."

He wheels a chair over and opens a laptop. Readouts synched to the ones streaming through my heads-up display open on his screen. Some of it I can follow, like the basic computer diagnostics I do at the Über Dork. Others are more complex. Physiology, neural mapping, and other pieces of specialized medical practice Dad would've understood.

"Mr. Bonkovich," says the technician. "You should be able to access the Collective Unconscious now. I'm afraid I don't have any tips for you on how to do it, but it says here," he says, consulting his computer, "subject may now access the Collective Unconscious, assuming subject survives the initiation run. Which, I'm pleased to report, you did. Congratulations."

"Thanks," I reply wryly. "But, yeah. I mean… I've already been talking to Bruce Lee. So that part all works."

The tech stares at me, his expression unreadable.

"No, no, no," says the technician. "You must be confused. That's not how it works." He holds up his laptop and points. "It says right here: Subject may experience spontaneous knowledge and skills at will, consistent with field requirements, *but necromancy is quite impossible.*" His eyes search for mine, but they're hidden behind my mask. Giving up on that, he shrugs and returns to the readouts on his laptop, muttering, "Necromancy is quite impossible."

"Dude. I'm telling you, I've been talking to Bruce Lee this whole time."

The doctors and techs exchange puzzled glances. Mikey steps between them and grabs the technician's shoulder.

"Give us a sec, Fred."

The tech hesitates for a second, then, a doubtful expression on his face, he shuffles off to join the lab workers on the far side of the room.

"Hey," says Mikey, lowering his voice. "You feeling all right?"

"Sure. I mean, aside from the fact I'm on the clock with ninety-six hours to live."

Mikey nods. "Okay, good, good. Listen to me very carefully. You can't be talking to Bruce Lee."

"Why not?"

"He's dead, stupid."

I chuckle, then knock the bottom of my palm against my helmet. "Well, I'm glad you cleared that up, Einstein. Because I thought talking to dead people was the whole friggin' point."

"No. No, you haven't been listening at all. I didn't spend all this time, effort, and, frankly—money—to produce a tarot card reader. The Collective Unconscious isn't you running séances for a buck ninety-nine."

"How 'bout two bucks, then? Extra penny do anything for ya?"

Mikey rolls his eyes. "I'm trying to tell you it doesn't work like that. It's more like you know what you need to know when you need to know it. It's skills and knowledge at your fingertips, but it's all *down deep*." He presses his fingertips into his abs to punctuate the point. "It's in your gut. You know?"

I shake my head. "Mikey. I'm telling you, I'm *talking* to Bruce Lee."

"No. You're not." He frowns. "It's possible you're going crazy. And until we know for sure that you're not, I want your promise you'll take those voices in your head with a grain of salt, okay? And keep the Bruce Lee thing between you and me. And, oh right, in the meantime, don't, you know, actually *go* crazy."

"Oh, yeah. Yeah," I say, waving it away like it was my crazy plan all along to go crazy, and then, having given it a second thought, decided my crazy plan to go crazy was just crazy. And from the way Mikey is nodding, I can tell that me waving the craziness away is a comforting response to him. He pats my shoulder, leaving me speechless as he rejoins the lab techs on the other side of the room who are bent over a laptop studying a PET scan of my brain and whispering words like "neural activity" and "cerebral cortex" and "Bruce Lee" and "crazy." It's all oh-so-terribly reassuring.

*Bruce Lee?* I call his name into the red circle in my heads-up display labeled "Collective." I'm guessing it must be a focus target, going by how none of the techs seem to have any idea how this thing is actually going to work. *Bruce Lee!* I yell. *Are you there?! Did you hear all that?!*

*Yes, Edge,* Bruce Lee replies. *No need to yell. I'm here. I heard it.*

*I'm not crazy. Am I?*

Bruce Lee laughs.

*I don't know,* he says. *Why don't you ask Sigmund Freud? He's around here somewhere.*

*Ha-ha,* I reply. *Not helping.*

*Not "ha-ha,"* Bruce Lee replies. *You mean ma-ma. It's Sigmund Freud we're talking about.*

*Touché.*

# CHAPTER TWENTY-FIVE

TWO HOURS LATER, we've finished running all the basic diagnostics. Targeting computer, X-ray vision (weird, and not to use on people, unless you want to freak yourself out), basic utility belt accessories, including surveillance bugs, smoke bombs, grappling hook, ninja throwing stars—and I am *never* going to remember which pouch has which thingy, particularly since every item looks identical; to save space on the belt, each item has been shrinky-dinked into a black marble large enough to fit neatly into the palm of my hand. Using the retinal scanner in the heads-up display, I can grow them to full size, or shrink them back into marbles as needed.

"Incredible," I mutter, staring at a handful of such marbles the tech has just informed me are actually ninja throwing stars.

"They're made from the same rapidly assembling nano-fibers as the suit, you see," says the technician.

"It's like a sea monkey," I say in my superhero horror-movie voice.

"No, it is *not*," he deadpans, before stalking off and mumbling, "For sea monkeys, you add water. I most certainly did not graduate top of my class at MIT to create sea monkeys. *Honestly.*"

"Ri-ight." I drop the handful of ninja throwing marbles back into their pouch on my utility belt. The overhead light glimmers off my hand, hitting the tiny silver nodules encircling the letter Z engraved on my ring.

"Z is for Zarathustra," says Mikey, noticing me looking at it. "As in Nietzsche's 'superman.' The goal of the human race is to produce a single cataclysmic individual who renders civilization as we know it obsolete."

"That doesn't sound like a good thing," I reply.

"Depends on your point of view. To quote Nietzsche, God is dead. He's been dead for a long time now. It's why the world is the way it is. But you're going to change that. For anyone who can access the Collective Unconscious, the future will be united in purpose, and not for any one person's God—but for the well-being of all. Imagine a world like that."

I gaze down at the ring on my finger, and a not insignificant amount of trepidation hardens in my stomach.

"Sounds like you're setting up this Zarathustra—me—to replace God," I say.

"Are you religious?"

"No."

"Then what do you care? Look. Relax. Enough of this God crap. Don't take everything so seriously."

"Ri-ight. Because when I think Edger Bonkovich, I think, now there's a guy who's taking life too seriously."

The technician returns, and the opportunity to continue the conversation is gone. Probably for the best anyway. That conversation was going nowhere fast.

"Using the retinal scanner in the heads-up display," the technician is saying, "Zarathustra can access Battle Plan."

"Battle Plan," I reply. "Sounds like a board game."

"No. It does *not*," says Sourpuss. Then, mumbling to himself again, he adds, "Oh, *this* one's going to render civilization obsolete all right."

"You know we can hear you," I say.

The technician clears his throat, ducks his head at Mikey, and utters a few more words about what I'm supposed to do with Battle Thing. Then the door opens to admit Mary. She's dressed in yoga pants and a sports bra. My remaining ability to concentrate goes up in smoke.

"Wow," I say. "I mean—*hey*."

"Hey-yo," she replies, jutting out her chin. "Are we gonna do it, or what?"

She and Mikey look at the droning technician, who steps back, powers off his tablet, and nods.

"Don't worry," says Mary, addressing me. "Most guys don't last long. So, no pressure. All right? Focus on pacing yourself. Take it slow. Enjoy it. I know I will."

"I think you'll find Mary a very capable partner," says Mikey.

I clear my throat before speaking. "Buh… What're we talking about again?"

Mary frowns. "Combat training."

"Right! Combat training! With you."

I swallow, working moisture back into my mouth, which opens, then shuts, lest the word "meep" croak like a frog from my superhero voice and ruin the moment.

# CHAPTER TWENTY-SIX

MIKEY'S GYM is like a CrossFit but smaller, the intimacy of which all but ensuring that if I puke, someone's going to step in it. It's got red brick walls, thick floor mats, and giant fans trained at the center of the room from all four corners. There are free weights, rowing machines, battle ropes, tires for flipping, and TRX cables. The middle of the room is cleared out for what I presume is going to be a fast, painful death. Mary is sliding shin and forearm pads on, followed by torso guards, headgear, mouth guards, gloves, and foot pads. The whole deal. She steps onto the mat, lean, agile, beautiful, and, unless I'm misreading my tropes, deadly. Clearly, she's a get-your-coffee/corporate-ninja-hybrid office assistant. One of *those*.

She eases her neck left, then right. She bends over and locks her arms around the backs of her legs, her chin touching her knees for a count of ten, then straightens, throws a few front kicks, hops up and down, then smacks her gloves together like she's ready for an MMA bout.

I ease my neck left and right, figuring I should at least look like I know what I'm doing standing here. My stomach gurgles. I press my hand on it, then let it fall to my side. The first lesson in becoming the world's first superhero, I tell myself, must be learning to project more confidence than I'm feeling.

"Goin' down, Zarathustra," she says, smiling around her mouth guard. "Goin' down!" She punches her fists together and starts in on her footwork, dancing around the mat like she's starring in a gender-reimagined *Rocky* remake.

"Are you sure this is safe?" I ask in my stupid supersuit voice. Mikey, who is observing with the technicians from near the door, chuckles.

"Edge. Mary is an expert in kung fu, aikido, krav maga, and a variety of other styles. You just worry about yourself, okay?"

"Okay. Hey, so on that subject, what happens if I pee in this suit? Is this like an astronaut suit?"

"Do not pee in the suit, Edge."

Mary, who's still bouncing around on the mat, says, "What's the matter? Afraid to fight a girl?"

"Not necessarily," I reply. "Maybe I just really have to pee, okay?"

"Edge," says Mikey. "You've got the Collective Unconscious. Use it."

"How?"

The technician looks up from his tablet and pushes the bridge of his glasses higher on his nose. "Neural pathways from the hindbrain annexing the—"

From beneath the superhero helmet, I roll my eyes. "Oh, for God's sake. Just stop. You had me at hindbrain."

"You're going to wing it," calls Mikey. "How's that?"

"I liked hindbrain better."

Mary, still bouncing around with her fancy footwork, circles behind me.

"Aren't you getting tired yet?" I ask. "You're making me tired."

Mary again smacks her gloves together, which I take to mean, no, not tired. Since I'm apparently not going to talk my way out of this mess, I focus instead on the red circle in the HUD marked "Collective," and try summoning Bruce Lee.

*Bruce?* I ask. *You can take her, right?*

*Do not think of victory or defeat,* Bruce Lee replies at once, like he's never been absent. *Let nature take its course. We will strike at the right moment.*

*You got any advice that doesn't sound like a fortune cookie?* I ask.

*Perhaps I can drive?* he replies.

I frown. He means, like, what? Take over? Take over my body?

*Yes,* Bruce Lee replies.

*I don't know about this...*

Not knowing what else to do, I raise my fists and relax my muscles. The effect is instantaneous, like someone's flipped a switch. My legs are like springs. I'm bouncing around. I've got the fancy footwork. I've got the swagger. *Hey-hey. I've got the moves like Jagger!* I feel like that part in *Return of the Dragon* where the tide turns in the fight between Bruce Lee and Chuck Norris. Mary must think so too; she switches direction, circles in front, fakes high left—attacks low right.

With Bruce Lee in charge, I leap into the air, my foot kicks out—connects to her headgear. The impact rockets up my leg and into my hip, but my muscles respond instinctively, bracing, then relaxing. Mary's mouth guard shoots out. She tumbles, slides across the mat. I land on my toes, skipping sideways with the signature Bruce Lee footwork and thumbing of the nose. Mary is groaning like a fallen kung fu extra from any number of Bruce Lee's movies. I concentrate on controlling my arms and legs again, and my coordination falters. My muscles become immediately sluggish. I scramble to kneel at her side.

"Oh, crap! I'm so sorry!"

Mary pinches the back of her neck. Wincing slightly, she gives me a wordless thumbs-up. I lay a bracing hand on her shoulder. I can't believe what I've done. Kicked a girl! Mary! What was I thinking?

"I'm so sorry," I stammer. "I just—I guess I don't know how to control—"

Mary's leg flashes past and loops around my neck. My face slams into the mat. Her thighs are choking my neck. They're hot. I can't breathe! Spots start creeping into the corners of my vision. I can't believe it. This babe's found the one vulnerable spot on my brand-spanking-new supersuit. In hindsight, the whole sparse-armor-around-the-neck-so-I-can-turn-my-head thing is a glaringly obvious design flaw.

"Lesson number one," she says, flexing her thighs and pulling my arm back into a complex and medieval wrist lock. "Never underestimate your opponent."

# CHAPTER TWENTY-SEVEN

AN HOUR LATER, I'm toweling off from the shower, wrapping up, and digging my fingers into the base of my aching neck.

I enter the locker room to find Mikey's set out some brand-new threads, still in the box. I open them up. Jeans and a black tee. Billionaire casual. I pull them on, not stressing over the perfect fit around my pecs and arms; money makes all kinds of weird crap possible. Like that time back at Notre Dame when everyone wanted to see Sting in Detroit, but our exam schedules made it so we couldn't swing it by car. Mikey chartered a plane. He, Kate and I, and a few other friends flew there. We rented a limo, booked suites at the Marriott, and stayed the weekend. We even partied with the band after the show. So, yeah. Spend enough time with Mikey, and stuff like him having a T-shirt and jeans in my size, whether just lying around or express-shopped, doesn't register high on the Wacky Shit-O-Meter.

There's a bench in front of a row of lockers, wet with the humidity from the showers. I grab a dry towel from a metal organizer on the wall and lay it out on the bench, then take a seat and scoop up the bag of ice Mary dropped off earlier with the Ibuprofen. The pain in my head is dull but insistent. Don't know if it's from the nano-neuro medicine or the beating I took on the mats. Hopefully the latter. I lean back against a locker and hold the bag to my head. The ice freezes my brain. I release a sigh.

A timid knock comes from the door. I don't reply, and when nothing happens, I wonder if I imagined it.

The door cracks open.

"Edger?" whispers Mary. "You decent?"

"Hey," I reply. "You can come in."

The door swings the rest of the way open. Mary steps inside, her shoulder keeping the door open. Her hair is wet from her shower, and she's changed into street clothes: jeans, a Slayer T-shirt, and flats.

"It's a good look," I say.

"You look like Mike Dame's brother," she says, frowning.

I glance at my outfit, then back at her.

"I'm going for billionaire tech genius. Not working?"

She smiles and lets the door shut. "No, I didn't mean that. I mean, it's just, I didn't mean anything. You look very handsome," she finishes, her voice conveying her practiced professional tone, which couldn't be more at odds with the Slayer T-shirt. "Do you have a sec?" She gestures with her hand to a spot on the bench next to me.

I take a centering breath. In fact, no, I don't have a second. I'm going to die in ninety-some hours, give or take. But since this seems rude to bring up, I set my bag of ice down and stretch out the towel under my butt to make enough space for her to sit also.

"Thanks," she says, taking a seat next to me. Clasping her hands, she leans over so her elbows are resting on her knees. I copy the way she's sitting, and we're like a pair of football coaches studying the video of a losing game.

"Why are you doing this?" she asks.

"Huh?"

"Why are you doing this?"

"Well, I mean, you're doing it," I say, gesturing to how she's sitting, then straightening. "I thought it'd make you more comfortable."

"No, no," she says, also sitting upright. "This, this. Becoming Zarathustra. Risking your life."

"Oh." I shrug. "Well, InstaTron Tron..."

Mary makes no reply. Her features are smooth and relaxed, her lips slightly parted, her eyes neutral. She's a sphinx. A beautiful, beautiful sphinx.

"Why are you working for Mike Dame?" I ask from out of nowhere. Her head tilts back as she seems to weigh my intent. "Seriously," I say. "You've been trying to talk me out of this the whole time. And now you're here, bringing it up again."

"So?"

"So, it makes you look like maybe you're having second thoughts about working for Mike Dame."

"Are *you* having second thoughts about working for Mike Dame?"

"I'm not having second thoughts about stopping a repeat of the East Coast," I reply. "Is that good enough?"

Mary rolls her eyes. She tosses her hair back and twists on the bench so she's facing me.

"No. I'm not buying it."

"Because I'm a Dork with a capital D."

"No," she says, leaving it there, which I take to mean yes.

"Thanks," I say.

She frowns. "What's your angle? Right now. Tell me."

I blink, confused. "I told you."

She clicks her tongue. "I wish you'd trust me more." She pauses, and her eyes do that sparkly thing again.

"Trust? That's a weird word to use. Why does it matter if I trust you? I like you. I mean, you know, like…"

"I like you too, Edger," she replies, scooting closer. "And I'm an orphan also."

"What? Whoa. Okay?"

She scoots close enough our hips are touching. "I know this must be…challenging…for you."

Her eyes peer up into mine, scanning my every microbe like she's capable of catching a lie ducking behind a retinal nerve. I scoot back a little and clear my throat.

"What does being an orphan have to do with anything?" I ask.

"Well, because of your father's research." Her tone says this should've been obvious. I suppose it would've been, if I'd ever shared anything about Dad's research with her or Mikey.

"Yeah, see? Stuff like that." I scoot farther away. "How do you know so much about me anyway? Yesterday it's Gran and Shep and Fabio. Today it's Dad's research and me being orphaned. Not that I'm not flattered, but, who made you an expert on Edger Bonkovich?"

Mary continues her laser scrutiny and has me leaning backward so far, my abs are straining to support my balance. I'm about ready to crawl into a locker to get away. Her eyebrows go up. She releases a sigh, and slumps against the wall.

"Nostradamus," she whispers, and her tone makes it come out like a four-letter word. I frown and wait for her to continue. "Nostradamus is a global syndicate positioning itself to be a shadow one-world government."

"Bullshit."

"They're very real, Edger. They're the reason I'm an orphan. They're the reason I learned to fight. I guess I'm sharing because I want you to trust me. I trust you. But not everything is what it seems around here."

"A shadow one-world government? Come on. That's the tropiest trope that ever troped."

"Tell that to my mom and dad," she says, not making eye contact. "Tell that to the six-year-old me."

"Whoa," I reply, stunned. Is she seriously telling me this phantom syndicate killed her parents? Is she on some kind of revenge quest? "Hey. I'm sorry. I didn't mean—"

"You got the ring?" She stands and thrusts out her hand. I stare at her for a second, and she nods for me to grab it. I comply, and she hauls me to my feet. *"Do you have the ring?"*

I nod, confused by the sudden shifting gears.

"Good. Don't tell Mikey what I told you."

"Wait a minute," I say. "You can't just leave it there. We gotta finish this conversation."

"And we will," she says. "We'll talk more about this later. I promise. But you're on a ticking clock now, and we need to go find us an InstaTron Tron."

I agree to keep our conversation on the down low. For now, anyway. We head out together, but something tells me it's only me who's underestimated how complicated the next ninety-some hours are going to be.

## HISTORIC COW QUID PRO QUO, CHRONICLED BY HERODOTUS (C. 484—C. 425 BCE)

JUDAS CHRISTIAN goes to church every Sunday without exception, unless the exception is to claim he is in any way religious. One could say he is a practicing Christian in the way so many other white-collar criminals with crushing cocaine habits are practicing Christians; he simply needed more practice.

As owner of the Mission Gorge Cluck-n-Pray franchise, Judas Christian doesn't typically do much work. On this day, he is out in the hot, midafternoon sun because of a promise: deliver the cow, and the felony charges he's facing will be dropped. Deliver the cow, Nostradamus Ed had said, and Judas can go back to his regularly scheduled life of cocaine, chicken, and God. Though not always in that order.

# CHAPTER TWENTY-EIGHT

"CAREFUL, NOW!" yells Judas. "I'm not out here sweating my butt off so you guys can damage the goods."

Blake and Sheldon pause to scrub the sweat out of their eyes. Sheldon drops the lasso completely and goes so far as to rest against the inside of the trailer wall.

"What're you doing?" snaps Judas. "Did I say you could rest?"

"You said don't damage the merchandise."

"That doesn't mean it's break time! That cow is coming out of that trailer one way or another."

Sheldon straightens and takes up the rope again. He and Blake share a wary glance before resuming the arduous job of attempting to wrangle a seven-hundred-pound adult female Dexter cow that doesn't want to be wrangled. Judas frowns. Blake and Sheldon had been a mistake from day one. These two had probably never done an honest day's work in their lives before coming to the Mission Gorge Cluck-n-Pray. Spoiled rich teenagers do not the finest employees make. The finest employees, as every fast-food employer understands, are destitute adults clinging to the prehistoric notion that work in the fast-food industry will one day earn them magic economic mobility wings. Like a fairy.

Blake grunts. "Remind me, uhrn, sir, why we're—agh—doing this, ughn, again?"

Judas rolls his eyes. "It's simple economics. Mascots mean money! Look at Buffalo Wild Wings. Last year, no Buffalo. The year before that? Buffalo. Wanna guess which year they raked bank?"

"Ern—the year...uhn, with the—blerg—the buffalo?" says Blake.

"That's right!" says Judas. He scrubs his index finger into an itch beneath his nose and sniffs. "And the year Taco Bell showed up with the dancing Chihuahua in a pink skirt. Wanna take a guess at how much they made that year?"

"Bhrn...erg-uhn," says Blake.

"That's right," Judas replies. "A *lot.*"

Sheldon pauses to wipe the sweat out of his face again.

"Hey-hey." Judas flaps his hand at his subordinates to keep them busy. "Do you see *me* taking a break? Am I gonna have to tell your dad about your mom and the tennis instructor?"

Sheldon frowns, shaking his head. "No, sir." His grip tightens on the rope. His knuckles go white. Judas, noticing a tree is casting shade one foot to his right, sidesteps to his right by one foot. The temperature drops by five degrees. Judas sighs. "And the year Happy Cock showed up with a rooster," he says.

Sheldon lets go of the rope and turns to face Judas. Blake, who no longer has help, crashes to the floor.

"Dude!" yells Blake.

"And don't forget the year Porky's showed up with the pig, sir," says Sheldon, his voice cracking. "That was great."

"Hey-hey-hey." Judas snaps his fingers. "How 'bout you leave the economics to me? Unless you think you're a business genius all of a sudden? Maybe you think you're a business genius all of a sudden? No? Then how about I let you do your job and you let me do my job? Okay? That okay with you, *Team Member* Sheldon? *Team Member* Blake?"

"Yes, sir," answers Blake, standing and rubbing his butt.

"Yes, sir," echoes Sheldon, again gathering the rope.

The two teens reluctantly resume their lasso tug-of-war. Judas's fingertips begin drumming a rhythm on his chest. Something fast to pass the time. He pauses to glance at his watch. Twenty-four hours left until the handoff. After that, bye-bye drug possession charges. His fingers resume their rock-n-roll.

# CHAPTER TWENTY-NINE

IN THE ZARATHUSTRA SUIT, back in the medical suite. There are no technicians. This time, it's just me, Mikey, and Mary. This time, as Mikey has repeatedly drilled into me, we're above top secret.

"The suit will regulate the end of the session," says Mikey. "But, Edger, you have to be careful when and where you have these encounters in the Collective Unconscious. Once you activate the suit's sleep timer, you'll be completely vulnerable to the outside world. You'll have no awareness of what's going on around you. You'll be unconscious, after all. Do you understand?"

"Kind of," I reply, distracted again by the voice changer in my suit. "I mean—sure, I shouldn't do it when bad guys are around because I'll be unconscious. That much, I get. But I don't get why I can't just ask Bruce Lee a question—"

"Edger." Mikey jabs his finger into my pec. His gaze flits from me to Mary and back. His eyes narrow. "We talked about this."

Mary's eyebrows lower. "Bruce Lee?"

"It's nothing," Mikey answers. But Mary's gaze drills into me, through the lenses of my helmet and heads-up display, and right into the back of my skull.

"What about Bruce Lee?" she demands.

"I said it's nothing, Mary," says Mikey.

"You seemed awfully Bruce Lee-like on the mat there for a

while," she says.

"Hey." Mikey faces Mary, his chin jutting out. "Go get me a protein shake."

Her head jerks back. Her eyes scan his. Then her features relax. She lowers her chin ever so slightly. "Of course." She takes a few backward steps, turns on one heel, and strides from the room. When she's gone, Mikey rounds on me.

"You've got to be more careful."

"Why? We're all on the same side here, right? You just revoked Mary's security clearance over a stupid question?"

Mikey licks his lips. "It's not a question of sides. It's a question of how intelligence is managed. The fewer people who know about a thing, the better. You've got to watch your mouth."

His eyes search mine—or try to. His forehead tightens from what I imagine must be the frustration of trying to read me through the glowing slits-for-eyes on my mask.

"Well, are you going to answer me, then?" I ask.

He frowns. "Answer what?"

"Why do I have to use this knockout feature in the suit at all when I can just ask Bruce Lee—"

"I told you," Mikey snaps. "There's no Bruce Lee. That's not how this works. Sometimes I wonder if you listen. Now. Can we do this?"

I raise my hands in surrender. Mikey gives a curt nod and takes a backward step. Using the suit's retinal scanner, I activate the "sleep" prompt through the heads-up display. Soul-stars form at the periphery of my vision and rush to the center, stealing me from this world, and ushering me into the one beyond.

# CHAPTER THIRTY

A GIANT SEA TURTLE is minding his business on the Tree of Life. Other creatures are bustling about like holiday shoppers by comparison. A beaver swims past, clutching in its mouth a thicket of branches. A bulging-cheeked squirrel hops atop the turtle's back. The turtle's eyes roll left and right. He pulls his extremities into his shell.

Bruce Lee materializes at my side. He's in his white suit again, and though neither of us has spoken, I can sense he already knows why I'm here and what I need him to do. He closes his eyes, and I copy him. The bright world grows oversaturated in my mind's eye. Blinding soul-stars concentrate around us. The world is featureless and warm. My stomach lurches like we're plummeting into the atmosphere at maximum velocity. My chest is tight. Bruce Lee sends reassurances through our shared telepathic connection. "Don't worry," he says. "I know a guy who will help us."

I focus on his telepathic sense, as that's preferable to the dislocated physical sensation, and through the Collective Unconscious, I manage to glean a few details from his mind.

We're searching for a guy named Tim, who hailed from Philly. Back when he was, you know, *alive*. I gather Tim from Philly is still grateful to Bruce Lee on account of his help with "a thing" that happened "that one time" to "a guy" in "that one place." Tim from Philly, who is specifically short on specifics, has expressed his gratitude and declared his intentions to "repay" Bruce Lee, by introducing us to his neighbor, Bill, who has an uncle named Joe, who has a sister who used to live across the street from a guy named "Pickles" Penility, who had a neighbor named Tim.

*This* Tim is from South Bend, Indiana.

"What?" says Tim from Philly, his shoulders going up and down like piston rods as Bruce Lee and I touch down in front of him on something that feels like solid ground. "Dares more den two guys named Tim in the Collective Unconscious. Fuggetaboutit!"

And since this makes sense, I *fuggetaboutit*, pondering instead, for obvious reasons, why we couldn't have had the good fortune of searching the Collective Unconscious for a guy named "Pickles" Penility.

"See," Tim from Philly leans closer to whisper into my ear. "Dat's where you're wrong. Penility, as his name would thus imply, is a dick."

"You can hear what I'm thinking also?"

Tim from Philly gives me the side eye and turns to face Bruce Lee.

"Thank you, Tim," says Bruce Lee. "I can take it from here."

"'ey," says Tim from Philly, whacking Bruce Lee on the shoulder. "Yooz ever needs nuttin'—yooz call me."

Bruce Lee nods, and Tim from Philly vanishes, leaving behind a thick aroma of grilled roast beef and onions.

"This is the weirdest dream I've ever had."

"I told you, Edge. You're not dreaming."

"I know, I know. But it's *like* I'm dreaming," I say, abandoning the conversation in favor of taking in the obvious reason we've come here.

We're standing in front of a glittering, building-sized brain surrounded by pointing neon arrows with the letters spelling out in all caps, "THIS IS THE PLACE!!" and, "LOOK NO FURTHER!!" and, "HEY YOU!! OVER HERE!!" in not-so-subtly flashing reds and greens, purples, pinks, and yellows, and otherwise looking like the Spirit of Christmas just barfed all over its most horrid Christmas sweater.

"What do you think?" asks Bruce Lee.

I shrug. "A brain-themed bar in the color of Christmas vomit. What *will* they think of next?"

Bruce Lee gives me a tight smile. "Given their connection to the Collective Unconscious, all ideas are already present. There's literally nothing to think of next."

I take in the tastelessness again and frown. "Hence Christmas vomit?"

"Hence Christmas vomit."

We head inside.

Swim-up bars, barbecued pigs turning on spits, women in elaborate feather turbans and eye-popping bikinis, gyrating their bodies in a way that cannot decently nor directly be observed. The place is endless. There's a stage, and Barry Manilow is up there singing "Copacabana." He's a young man, in his twenties. His band is clad in bright yellows and oranges and ruffles. Above us is an open atrium and starlight, the constellation of souls.

"Barry Manilow," I say. "I thought he was still alive."

"This place is in his subconscious mind," replies Bruce Lee. "Dead or alive makes no difference here."

"Huh. Knew that guy was weird. So what *is* this place?" I ask.

"Club Brain," Bruce Lee replies.

We cut around a brain-shaped pool to find Indiana Tim on the far side in the water chatting up some young lady half his age. Indiana Tim is tan, pot-bellied, and wearing black speedos, a gold chain, and Ray-Bans.

"Ah, Edger!" He excuses himself from the young lady and climbs out of the pool. "Your father was the most brilliant neurologist I ever met."

We shake hands.

"You knew my dad?" I ask, before quickly changing directions. "Wait—is he…is he *here*?"

Bruce Lee and Indiana Tim exchange wary glances.

"Edge," says Bruce Lee. "There's no easy way to tell you this. Your father isn't here. He's in your world. Your father is alive."

# CHAPTER THIRTY-ONE

THE PAIN in my chest is cold like a hole in the space-time continuum. If I could just crawl inside, maybe I could fall into a warmer parallel timeline. Everything would be okay then. I could've known him. Lived a life with him. Or even just glimpsed the sight of him. That would've been enough. In the library at Notre Dame. In the stacks, maybe, with him watching me from behind a book. Anything is better than this. Because this is halfway, and death isn't supposed to be halfway. A person dies. You mourn and then you move on. Death is supposed to be final. It's kind of the whole point. Because, if you think about it, you never see anybody get up from a plane crash and moonwalk to baggage claim.

"But he never died, Edge," says Bruce Lee.

"He's been on the run," says Indiana Tim. "See for yourself."

Indiana Tim waves his hand, and the constellation of souls comes down from the sky. It swirls around us in a snow globe-like torrent. The light is cool on my skin. My head spins in a quick euphoric spell. When the soul-stars return to the sky, our positions have changed. We're standing on a balcony overlooking a dark beach lit by a single bonfire.

"Down there." Indiana Tim points.

I'm enveloped again in the swarm of soul-lights. Their fluttering lights are a cool breeze on a hot night, raising my hair and blowing on my skin. I'm tipped backward. My arms are outstretched. I'm lying flat. The stars above slowly reorient. I float down, down. The pulsing ocean builds in my ears. The air becomes cooler. The soul-stars thin out and disperse. Cold sand works between my toes. The lone figure silhouetted by the bonfire is less than twenty yards away. His back is to me. He's dressed in Bermuda shorts, a short-sleeved linen shirt—and, for some reason, flippers. The night is still. Embers rise and twist and fade into the deep blue sky.

I'm sick with hope. I'm sick with anger. Sick with love. I'm sick from the emotional infection because the stitches tore before mending. *So this is why Dad never left a body to bury.*

"Is it him?" I whisper, my throat hoarse.

The man at the bonfire reacts; his head tilts a fraction at the sound of my voice. He fades away, and I'm alone on the beach.

"That was him," says Bruce Lee, who has materialized by my side.

"Could he…he could actually hear me?"

Bruce Lee cranes his neck to see around me, where Indiana Tim has just materialized on my other side.

"Possibly," says Indiana Tim. "Your father is quite clever."

"I have so many questions. Where's he been? Why did he let Gran and me think he was dead? Why hasn't he contacted us?"

"It's a long story. The nano-neuro medicine in your body was designed to work in tandem with the artificial intelligence known as InstaTron Tron. Which, as you know—"

"I know, I know," I say, impatient to get the story on Dad. "Without Tron-Tron, I only have ninety-six hours to live."

"No," says Indiana Tim, his eyebrows raised. "That's not right."

"Not right? Which part?"

"You can live, Edger. That's a simple matter of taking your booster shot."

"What!?"

"Oh, yes," says Indiana Tim. "Your father made a booster shot, which will repair the damage to the cells caused by accessing the Collective Unconscious, and permanently stabilize them, allowing for unlimited usage of this miraculous power. Isn't it wonderful? Although it is accurate to say the artificial intelligence will slow down the rapid cell death, what I was starting to say before is that InstaTron Tron was developed to achieve species-wide omniscience. Without it, it's impossible for you to interact with the Collective Unconscious in the way we do. Us dead guys are always in each other's heads. We have no need of 'finding' anyone, because everyone's already present and available. But you—you'll have to navigate the Collective Unconscious the old-fashioned way."

"The old-fashioned way."

"You know," says Indiana Tim. "A guy who knows a guy who knows a guy. Like the way you found Club Brain. Tim from Philly knew Bill, who knew Joe, who knew Pickles, who knew me."

"But when I'm awake, the supersuit can do this for me?"

"Exactly." Indiana Tim brightens, then, addressing Bruce Lee, adds, "Sharp kid. Like his father. All you have to do is use the focus target labeled *Collective*, and the suit's processors will track down someone who can help from over 108 billion possibilities. But once you have InstaTron Tron installed, you'll achieve species-wide omniscience. Like us. Only you'll be alive."

"Okay, okay," I say. "That's cool and everything, but, go back. There's really a booster? I don't have to die? Are you sure? Mikey never said anything about a booster."

Indiana Tim frowns. "You must be mistaken. I can't imagine something like that slipped his mind. Ha! Slipped his mind! I love expressions like that now."

Indiana Tim smiles, his face becoming somewhat transparent. In fact, the entire world is becoming…pale. The deep blue sky is now light gray. The sand between my toes has gone from cold to room temperature.

"What's happening?" I ask, alarmed.

"You are leaving the Collective Unconscious," says Bruce Lee.

"Shit!" I exclaim. "They set a timer on the suit. Hey—real quick—where's InstaTron Tron?"

Bruce Lee frowns. "Listen to me very carefully. It isn't in a human host. It isn't in the Collective Unconscious at all. Do you understand?"

But before I can reply, the world falls away.

# CHAPTER THIRTY-TWO

COMING OUT of this induced session is easier than the last. Maybe it's because of the extreme personal nature of what I learned, but I have total recall. My eyes pop open. I'm lying in bed in the medical suite. The bright orbs above me are harsh. I raise a shielding hand.

Mikey is at my side. My eyes haven't adjusted to the light. His features are a bright blur. There's nothing recognizable to latch on to that would identify him, except intuition. The idea that we know people intrinsically. What they're capable of. Who they are. Why they do what they do. But given what I've just learned, I'm not sure how far I can trust my intuition with him.

"You knew my dad is alive," I say, surprised by how strong my voice is this time. "And you hid the booster shot from me."

"Edge. I was going to tell you about your dad and the booster shot," he says, not missing a beat, and striking a conciliatory tone.

"Would that've been before or after my ninety-six hours are up?"

I rip off the cables stuck to ports on my body, and swing my feet around the edge of the bed. I scan the suite. We're alone. Good. Because this feels like betrayal, and betrayal is personal. The last thing I want right now is a lab tech sticking a scanner in my face, or a casual glance from Mary that says I told you so.

Mikey smooths the hair on the back of his head. He strides to the window and peers out at the clear blue sky above the ocean. The sunlight on his black tee accentuates his v-cut frame. I twist the ring on my finger, and the surface of my suit bubbles. I close my eyes and swallow, the sensation of slithering goo being unpleasant enough without also having to watch.

"Nobody can know about the boosters," he says. "That's important."

"So important you couldn't even tell me. Apparently." I open my eyes as the last of the goo slides back into the ring. I pull it off my finger and stuff it into my pocket.

"Look." Mikey turns to face me. "I'm sorry, okay? I've been under a lot of stress. I needed you focused. This isn't focused."

"Focused? As in gun-to-my-head focused?"

"Yes, Edge."

"Wow. Great friend!"

"Edge—"

"My dad!" I exclaim, and my voice hitches stupidly in my throat. "When were you gonna tell me about Dad?"

He takes a deep breath and releases it, then crosses to the cabinets and sink on the opposite wall and leans against the countertop, folds his arms, and stares down his nose at me. "What you need to understand is there are more important things afoot. Not everything is about you. InstaTron Tron. Did you find it?"

"Oh, you are so full of shit."

"Shut up. Did you find him?"

"No. Okay? I didn't find him. Give me my booster shot and then go fuck yourself."

"What do you mean you didn't find him?"

"Translation: I didn't find him."

"How could you not find him?"

"Because he's not *in* the Collective Unconscious, Holmes."

"Not in the Collect—that's not possible."

"Welp. He's not there. Sorry. Booster shot, please." I slide off the bed and scan the room for my shoes. Shoes, shoes. There—by the closet.

"You don't understand," says Mikey. "The amphiphilic

molecules used in creating the auto-assembling nano-fibers require a physiologic—"

I stride to the closet, covering my ears. "La-la-la! Not listening!"

"—the nano-fiber matrix would disintegrate without the relative concentration of ions inside the human cell—"

"Booster shot! Booster shot! La-la-la—"

A knock at the door interrupts us. Mary sticks her head in.

"Sir?"

"Can't you see I'm in a meeting?" snaps Mikey.

"You call this tire fire a meeting?" I ask.

"Sorry sir," she says. "It's just… InstaTron Tron."

Mikey's hand chops the air in front of my face, I guess because the last time he told me to shut up didn't take, so now he needs sign language.

"What?" asks Mikey. "You found him?"

"Not exactly, sir." Mary clears her throat into her fist. "But we have a new lead."

"Explain that," he says. I roll my eyes, wheel the doctor's chair around, and pull on a shoe.

"InstaTron Tron has started tweeting again," says Mary. "They're weird, but they're focused."

"Focused on what?" asks Mikey.

"On the Chargers game tomorrow."

"The Chargers game?" Mikey and I exclaim in unison.

Mary holds out her phone so we can read for ourselves. Still seated, I kick off from the wall to roll the chair across the room and catch a glimpse from under Mikey's elbow.

*PRAY ALL DAY AT CLUCK-N-PRAY! #Chargers #GameDay*

Mary lowers her phone. Mikey shakes his head.

"Well, that's weird," he says. "Promising, but weird." Then he rounds on me so fast, I startle and slowly heel-toe the chair back to the desk. "Come on," he says. "Time to power up. Let's go get your booster."

# CHAPTER THIRTY-THREE

THIS PLACE is a freaking hamster maze of hallways and private elevators. Mikey's going to make me break a sweat trying to keep up, but at least I'm getting my booster and stay of execution. Mary and I follow him into another elevator.

"I needed you motivated," he says. "Focused. I couldn't have you getting sidetracked over your dad. Dammit, this is too important."

I glance again at Mary, but she may as well be blind, deaf, and dumb, going by the way she's resisting eye contact and her inability to muster an opinion.

The elevator doors open directly into Mikey's office.

"What I need you to understand, Edge, is that you were always going to get this shot. You know that, don't you?"

I screw up my face into what I hope conveys how absurd I find the question. "If you're asking me for the benefit of the doubt after selling this as me sacrificing my life for the greater good, then, ah..." I stick my finger in my mouth, then raise it into the air as if checking wind direction. "That'd be a no can do, Mikey."

We pass the da Vinci glider, and Mikey strides to the bar and steps around the end. He goes straight for a safe tucked between a break in the spirits and starts punching some numbers.

"You could've avoided all this by leveling with me," I say,

casting a quick glance at Mary, who finally meets my eye now Mikey's back is turned. Her lips tighten in an expression of sympathy.

"No, I couldn't," replies Mikey, jerking the handle on the safe, which doesn't open. "Crap."

"Yes—you could," I say. "What about trusting me? You want me to trust you. How do you think trust works? It goes both ways."

He turns to face me. "This isn't about me trusting you. It's about you trusting me."

"Oh my God," I say, rolling my eyes and sliding onto a barstool. "Says the guy who's been lying the whole time." I shift to face Mary. "What? They don't got the word 'compromise' in the business lexicon?"

"Edge, I didn't just learn your dad is alive. Okay? I've known for years. How could you possibly trust me if you'd known that? How could we possibly have gotten to the important stuff? But I'm the good guy here. Everything I did was for a reason."

A hot flash hits me. I sit up straighter. "Important stuff? You asshole. How is this *not* the important stuff?"

Mikey nods, inexplicably, like we just said the same thing. I glance at Mary for support, but she's back to playing Helen Keller.

"Your dad and I developed the Zarathustra program together," says Mikey. "He did the nano-neuromedicine that's in your brain right now. But, Edge. Come *on*. What did you think? I mean, tell me you didn't think it was weird when I started talking about nano-neuromedicine."

"Weird? Weird! Weird is the donut chicken nugget double bacon cheeseburger! Weird is having a freaking da Vinci glider parked in your office, you asshole!"

"You don't like my glider?"

My mouth opens, then clicks shuts. Mary is on the other side of the bar pouring a drink.

"We're off topic," says Mikey, waving these points away and trying again to enter the code to his safe. "So your dad did the medicine," he says over his shoulder. "And then we had this guy Tim in Indiana do the suit and the ring. But, see?" He yanks on the handle to the safe, which again doesn't budge. "We're talking about this crap, and we simply don't have time—and this is seriously the third time I've tried to enter the code to this safe! Okay? Okay?" He spins around to glare at me. "I can't concentrate with all your donut bacon chicken burger crap."

Mary, who's now holding a full shot glass, asks, "Do they put the chicken nuggets on top of the burger, or—"

"It's gross," I reply. "But it's the donut part that's gross."

"I can totally see that," she says, nodding enthusiastically.

"Both of you! Shut it!" exclaims Mikey. "Edge, I need your trust now. Can you do that? Can you do that, Edge? Can you concentrate on the job until we get through this? Please? I promise, after that, I'll tell you everything."

"Mikey, I don't know what to say." I set my elbows on the bar and drag my fingers through my hair; Mary slams her shot of I-don't-know-what; Mikey, now that everyone's silent, focuses on the safe. This time, the lock clicks. His words echo in my brain.

*Trust him,* he says. *Concentrate on the job,* he says. But how can I do either? Dad is out there. Alive!

The safe door swings open.

"Was my dad in Indiana?" I ask, my voice coming out mechanically.

Mikey doesn't reply. He stands with his back to me, silent. Mary's posture stiffens.

But how long has he known? How long was he working with my dad? Indiana. He said the guy who did the suit was in Indiana—as in, Notre Dame? Is Mikey's Tim "Indiana Tim"? Has Mikey known about Dad since Notre Dame?

Mikey turns around. His face is pale, his expression blank. Mary's staring at me like she's just learned I've got a rare medical condition where you grow carrots out of your ears.

"Hey, guys," I say, nodding. "We can fix this. Okay. Let's do the booster. We'll get that going and, you know, take all this death stuff off the table, and then focus on the job. We can talk about Dad later—ha, I mean, now that there is a later, you know? The silver lining is, Dad's alive. I can hold on to that. For now. We'll find InstaTron Tron...Tron. That really is too many Trons, but okay. We can do this, Mikey. Mary. We can do this."

But despite my attempt at pep-talking, their expressions remain unchanged.

"What?" I ask.

Mary bites her lip, her gaze shifting from the safe back to me. Mikey says nothing.

*"What?"* I ask again.

"The boosters," Mikey replies. "My entire inventory."

"What? What, Mikey? Use your words."

"They're gone, Edger," says Mary. "They're all gone."

# CHAPTER THIRTY-FOUR

A TRAPDOOR OPENS in the bottom of my stomach. I lean to peer around Mikey and into the empty safe. Blue lighting is shining down from inside into empty beaker holders. Mikey whips out his cell phone and speed dials. Mary sets her shot glass in the sink and pulls out her phone also. Mikey juts his chin out at her.

"I need you to lock down Emerald Plaza, right now!"

Mary speaks in hushed tones into her phone.

Mikey hustles out from around the end of the bar and jabs a finger at me. "You stay put!"

My feet seem to be growing roots into the floor as I try to process what's just happened. My skin is tingling. Walls are shrinking in around me. Mary's relaying orders through the phone. Her voice sounds a billion miles away. Mikey snatches some keys and papers from the end of the bar, then hurries off toward his private elevator. My brain is speeding down multiple thought highways at once, but all of them converge in the end.

*Dad. Is. Alive.*

"You stay here, Edge!" Mikey calls from over his shoulder. "I mean it. Don't you go getting any crazy ideas." He pauses at the door, like he's waiting for an answer, so I shrug and nod. "Mary?" he says in a brook-no-nonsense tone. She lowers her phone for a second and gives him a thumbs-up, and then he's out the door.

We're alone. The room is silent except for my panting. My feet want to go. I'm itching to get out of here and do something. Anything.

No, not just anything. I want to find my dad.

Mary's hand on my arm reminds me I'll have to deal with her first. My eyes come back into focus. She's in front of me. Her eyes are round and soulful. She squeezes my arm, then her hand glides up and down.

"I'm sorry," she says.

I nod, biting my bottom lip. I pull several steps away from her before turning around and marching back to where I started. When our eyes meet again, I repeat the process, pacing like a confused elderly person who can't remember why they came into the room.

"Edger."

"I didn't want this." I stop near the glider and face her. "I told you. My plan was to say no. And *you* told *me*," I add, pointing accusingly at her. "You told me! Think about Gran, you said. Think about Shep, and Fabio! *You* said that!"

"I did," she replies, her eyes wide and innocent.

"Think about Gran and Shep and Fabio, you said," I repeat, nodding like this deserves its own special entry in the annals of Most Brilliant Points Ever Made. "And you know, I was so close to getting Gran into Pine's Place. Another six months. That's it. Six months is nothing. You know?"

"Oh, I know," she says, nodding, her expression unchanged.

"And now this!" I say, gesturing wildly with my arms at the bar, as if it symbolizes an evil global syndicate hell-bent on ruining my life. "Dad. Dad." I release a short, near-hysterical chuckle. "I don't know whether to be pissed at him or run right out to find him."

"Or...maybe neither," she says, pursing her lips and shrugging.

"Neither? No. No. It's gotta be one or the other. I mean—he let us all think he was dead! He just walked out on us!"

"But maybe he, you know, had his reasons."

"Reasons." I frown. "There's no reason to run out on your family like that."

"Well, I mean..." Mary breaks eye contact and starts picking at invisible lint on her shirt. "You know. Maybe... Well, suppose the bad guys were coming. I mean, just hypothetically, you know, maybe he did the right thing...running away. To protect you. I mean."

"Mary."

She clears her throat and stands up straighter.

"What do you know about my dad?"

"Actually... I was talking about mine."

"Yours."

"Mine. Do you want to sit for a sec? I'm supposed to keep you here, but he didn't say we can't talk." She tilts her head back and smiles, her eyes catching the weak light squeezing through the blinds. I let her lead me back to the bar. We sit.

"My father worked for the Australian government," she begins. "When I was little, I remember he came home one day, and he and my mum had a terrible row. The next morning, some men came and gathered all three of us, took us into the country, far away from everything and everybody. It was like a jail. It had guard towers, barbed-wire fences, but inside, the living facilities were made to look like normal flats. I was taken from my parents, who I found out later were forced into working for these people because of his government position, okay? I was given a sister—"

"Wait, wait," I say, too astounded to let more pass without challenging. "Where were the police? I mean, your dad worked for the government. Didn't anyone miss him?"

"That's the point." The corners of her eyes tense. "He continued showing up for work because he thought they'd kill me. Kill Mum. They split us apart. I got a 'sister.' She and I had to fight. Sometimes we'd train ten hours a day. They'd wake us up in the middle of the night for training if they thought we weren't applying ourselves. It's where I learned...everything I learned."

"Oh my God." I gape at her, thunderstruck. "That's horrible."

She takes my hand and gives it a squeeze. "What I'm saying is, my parents let that happen to me, but, maybe your dad vanishing was for the best. Maybe your dad vanishing gave you a more normal life than I had."

"I don't get it," I say. "Your dad was taken by, I don't know, some weirdos in the outback. What does that have to do with my dad? I don't mean to be insensitive."

"Mikey just admitted your dad's involved in all this," she says. "Edger, this stuff is already changing the world—*you* are already changing the world. What you did with the power grid, and those crazy gay pride parades. Don't you see? When people figure out what's going on, what you can do, what this technology can do, there won't be a government in the world that isn't going to want it. You. Mikey. Your dad. Gran, Shep, Fabio. Anyone connected to it. *Anyone*."

I slide off the barstool and open up a few feet between us. Tension creeps into my neck. I rub it and stare off into space.

"You knew my dad was involved in this before you came to get me that day at the Über Dork. You knew it from the outset."

Her lips compress. She peers into her lap.

"Oh boy," I mutter, and set in again on the pacing, my brain processors spinning on her now. It's not like I've got a right to be angry. I mean, we were total strangers. She's got a boss. She's got a job. And she *did* try to warn me away.

"I'll understand if you're angry," she says. "I mean, of course you're angry. I'm sorry. I don't expect you to understand. I mean, you can't understand."

"You mean because you don't tell me anything. I can't understand if you don't tell me anything. You spy on me. I know you spy on me. But you won't tell me what you know."

Her widened eyes peer into mine. "If what I've read about the Collective Unconscious is true, there's no secret in the world you couldn't learn on your own now."

"What's your point? Are you telling me I'm going to have to hack into your brain to steal your secrets?"

"Would you?" she asks, her lips parting and turning down in the corners.

"No!"

"And why not?" she snaps. "Why wouldn't you?"

"Because it's wrong!"

"Exactly. Edger, it isn't that I don't want to help you. It isn't that

I don't want to tell you things. There are secrets that aren't mine to share. And there are secrets you're better off not knowing, on the off chance you can find your way off the crazy train and go back to the normal life you had. Be careful of the stones you kick over."

But I'm no longer listening. My hand slides into my jeans pocket and removes the ring box. I open it and there's the gleaming Z on its black-and-chrome surface.

"I'm done jumping through Mikey's hoops," I say.

"I know." Mary slides off the barstool and reaches her hand out. "Edger—"

"If you don't want to get in trouble with your boss, you should probably go."

"What are you going to do?" She quickly shakes her head and raises her hands. "Nope. Better I don't know."

She gives me one last look, saying nothing, but saying it meaningfully. *Be careful,* that look seems to say, with a runner-up of, *Don't judge me, and I won't judge you for the donut burger thing*. She hastens across the room to Mikey's private elevator and presses the button.

"You know what I'm going to do," I call to her back.

"Yes."

"Would you tell me if you knew where my dad is?"

"Yes."

"Do you?"

She hesitates. "No."

The elevator doors open. Mary goes inside. As the doors start to close, she thrusts her arm out in front of the sensors, and they spring back open.

"Edger, I'm not going to let you die. I will take care of your boosters. I promise."

She snatches her arm back, and the doors snap shut, leaving me staring at my boring reflection. Familiar disappointment surges through me like it always does when she leaves. But this time, my brain is too focused on finding Dad to dwell on it.

I slide the ring onto my finger.

The world explodes into a billion streaking lights.

# CHAPTER THIRTY-FIVE

RED LETTERS scroll across the heads-up display.

*PULSE ELEVATED.*

*Yes, I know.*

*RECOMMENDATION: ACCESS COLLECTIVE UNCONSCIOUS.*

*Okay,* I think, and I tentatively focus on the red circle in the HUD labeled "Collective," the way Indiana Tim suggested.

*Buh...anyone in the Collective Unconscious got any bright ideas?*

Roaring voices deafen my ears. Billions of lights streak past. I stagger backward. *It's too much!* The processors in my suit quickly narrow down possibilities. Billions become millions. Thousands become hundreds. Finally...one. Gravity triples in my limbs with the fatigue that comes from thousands of pull-ups, flutter kicks, push-ups, and sit-ups in a single day. I'm shivering uncontrollably. It's Hell Week in BUD/S training. In and out of the ocean. Swimming miles against the clock. *Cold...so cold.* Facedown in the mud; holding my breath; lifting telephone poles; trembling muscles; falling painfully on my gun; moonless nights; stalking from the shadows; rescuing hostages; do I have what it takes to make it till morning?

*Heard you could use a hand, sir.*

The life behind the voice completes its fast-forward. It belongs to one Lieutenant Trevor Killmaster, Navy SEAL. College champion swimmer. Fifteen deployments. Eighty-seven confirmed sniper kills.

I'm breathless and sweating. My tired limbs get their strength back as I try to hold on to everything I've seen. Killmaster grew up in a little place outside of Santa Barbara, not that far from here. He met his wife there and they bought a home. He regrets not having been able to give her a cool car. He wears Old Spice.

*Weird.*

*You're telling me, sir,* Killmaster replies.

Through the Collective Unconscious, it hits me we have something in common. I'm not the first person chosen to take the Zarathustra formula to human trial. Indiana Tim selected Lieutenant Killmaster to be Zarathustra five years ago. Only, Killmaster's body rejected it. It killed him.

*Yeah,* he says. *Not the side of this bitch I thought I'd be riding.*

*Whoa,* I reply. *I mean, is that gonna be a, you know, a problem?*

*No—sir!* says Lieutenant Killmaster.

I slide onto the barstool for a second and gather my thoughts. I think: *You know, I'm not really much of a…sir.*

Killmaster replies: *You are today. Sir.*

# CHAPTER THIRTY-SIX

*WHAT'S THE SITUATION, SIR?*

*Situation,* I say, momentarily distracted by the idea of Indiana Tim being in charge of selecting a Zarathustra.

*Sir?*

*Right. Situation. Um, well. I want you to help me break out of here.*

*Here? Where's here?*

*InstaTron Headquarters, Emerald Plaza, San Diego.*

Killmaster pauses, and for some reason, my brain starts replaying random scenes from the past twenty-four hours like someone's fast-forwarding a movie.

*Yeah, that's me,* says Killmaster. *I'm using your memories to debrief myself on the situation, sir.*

*Weird.*

*Damn straight.*

Another pause.

*So let me see if I've got this right,* says Killmaster. *Mike Dame's an ass-hat, and you're about to go AWOL to find your dad.*

I frown over hearing it summed up. Guilt twists inside me over skipping out on finding Tron-Tron while I go off in search of my dad. It sounds selfish when he puts it like that.

*Sir, you're no good to anyone if you're dead,* offers Killmaster.

*Your dad made those booster shots. Find him, and you buy yourself more time. Your objective is evolving. Stand by.*

Killmaster takes control of the HUD. I don't know how he's doing it, but reams of data flood my subconscious at high speed. Emerald Plaza schematics, encrypted InstaTron data, private security radio channels, traffic reports, way too much for me to consciously process. When it's finished, I'm panting again…and feeling strangely violated.

*Do you have to take control of my body like that?*

*Easiest way, sir!*

*Okay…* I ease my neck left and right, then pull my shoulder blades together. A knot cracks in my back. I blow out a long burst of air. *So. Do you have a plan at least?*

*A plan? Pfft. What do you think this is? Osama bin Laden? There's a handful of armed security personnel patrolling Emerald Plaza looking for a corporate saboteur. We'll have you out of here in five minutes, tops.*

# CHAPTER THIRTY-SEVEN

THE GLASS CUTTER from my utility belt is top-shelf, Grade A Batman-quality shit. It's a circular compass cutter with an extendable arm capable of cutting a hole in the window with a large enough diameter for me to crawl through. And the way it grew out of something the size of a marble into a giant-ass glass cutter *is* exactly like a sea monkey, and I don't give a crap that technician says otherwise.

*You're right, sir,* agrees Killmaster. *It's a goddamn sea monkey. Now, time to get busy.*

*Right.*

I stick my head through the hole in the glass and peer into the twenty-seven-story drop. I jerk back inside. My stomach tries to crawl up my throat.

*Suck it up, buttercup,* says Killmaster.

I take a deep breath and tighten the straps on my harness. I use the heads-up display's retinal scanner to electronically test the integrity of the anchor on the far side, the anchor I fired into the W Hotel across the street. A green light comes back when the test is complete, with the words *ANCHOR SECURE.* I check that the glass cutter is securely clipped to my belt.

*You're sure this is safe?* I ask Killmaster, clutching the hand brake and trying to will myself to get a foot through the hole in the window.

*Come on,* says Killmaster. *Live a little, princess.*

*Says the dead guy.*

*It's just like falling off a log, sir.*

*Says the dead guy,* I repeat, trying to visualize falling off a twenty-seven-story log with traffic and pedestrians below. I try again to get a foot through the hole, but my mental image of the twenty-seven-story log is too on the nose.

*Allow me, sir.*

"Hey, wait!" I yell, one foot inside the hole and one foot out.

Killmaster seizes full control of my body. *Geronimo!*

My stomach tenses, flops. Wind tears at my suit. The heads-up display tracks my velocity. Killmaster's laughing like a suicidal maniac.

*40mph…*

*50mph…*

*60mph…*

*Brakes, sir! Brakes!*

I clamp down on the hand brake. Sparks fly. The W Hotel rushes up at me, careening concrete and glass.

*50mph…*

*30mph…*

*25mph…*

My butt and abs clench. I heave my knees into my core, preparing for landing.

*10mph…*

Boots slam onto concrete. I flip to the side, crash into the wall. Pain lances through my shoulder. The glass cutter rebounds off the building and into my lower back.

ALERT: ANCHOR INTEGRITY COMPROMISED 25%… 30%… 40%…

*Oh shit, oh shit, oh shit!*

*Cut the glass now, sir!*

My hands scramble to unfasten the glass cutter from my utility belt—stuck!

*Hurry, sir! Hurry!*

*ANCHOR AT 50% INTEGRITY.*

My hands are shaking. Glass cutter comes free. I extend the arm on the device, press the suction cup in place.

*Hurry, sir!*

I press the cup harder, and my feet leave the wall. I release the pressure and swing back. The anchor lurches. I drop; stomach tenses; anchor catches. I twist on the line. Buildings, glass, sky, and concrete flash past. I reach out and catch the glass cutter still stuck to the window—

Another lurch.

*ANCHOR INTEGRITY COMPROMISED BY 75%.*

*Crap.*

*We. Are going. To die,* says Killmaster.

"You're already dead!"

I rotate the arm to six o'clock. The cutting gets easier as the arm gets closer. I strain to reach eleven o'clock. No good. Can't get past ten. Sweat pours down my face.

*You know what? You're right. I am already dead. Sir. No skin off my back. Can't say the same for you, though.*

Twenty-some stories below is a lower portion of the hotel with glass skylights and concrete. Killmaster visualizes an exploding watermelon. A piano dropping from a cable. Black smoke trailing behind a four-engine jet airliner locked in a death spiral from thirty-thousand feet.

*Not helping!* I yell.

I hammer my fists against the glass. A crack snakes across the surface.

*Going to die,* says Killmaster. *Boo-yah! Gonna die—yeah!*

I hammer on the glass.

*Crackle—pop!* The partial circle I cut completes itself. The glass falls into the hotel. I grab the window ledge, pull. My stomach tenses. My feet keep slipping. My neck, shoulders, and arms are trembling. I reach into the hole, the other hand heaving myself up on the line.

*ANCHOR INTEGRITY COMPROMISED BY 88%.*

I stick my head through—the hotel room isn't empty.

# CHAPTER THIRTY-EIGHT

THE BACK OF her bushy head is shaking. She's ramming the vacuum into the desk, her hips swinging left and right. The music coming out of her earbuds is going to make her deaf, if it hasn't already. Her humming is deep and guttural, like someone's punching her in the stomach while she's trying to find the tune.

*Or like she's beating strung-out rats with a mallet,* offers Killmaster.

I tense up and shove an elbow over broken glass. "Help!" I yell in my stupid horror-movie voice.

*Shut up!* yells Killmaster. *What are you doing?*

The cleaning maid lifts a chair, vacuums underneath, sets it back.

"Help!" I cry again.

The maid continues her salsa dancing and humming.

*ANCHOR INTEGRITY COMPROMISED BY 92%.*

I release the line and heave both elbows over the sill. My feet scramble on the exterior wall—push, slip—push. I'm burning up inside the suit. Muscles shaking. Elbows and forearms dig in. *Pull!* Jagged glass—my stomach rakes over it. The armor crushes it like peanut shells.

*ANCHOR INTEGRITY COMPROMISED BY 100%. GOODBYE.*

*Fuck.*

There's a slight jerk on the zip line. It flips and twists like an epileptic black mamba snake as it reels itself in.

*Duck!*

The line flips overhead, slaps me in the butt, and snaps into my belt. I'm rocketed the rest of the way into the room. Killmaster seizes control; I tuck and roll, missing the cleaning maid, and then I'm kneeling by the kitchenette and rubbing my butt.

"That smarts."

*Shh! Go, go, go!* says Killmaster, urging me out the door.

I grab the ring—pull. Warm slime slithers over my face, neck, legs, body and arms, and the suit vanishes inside the ring.

*What're you doing?* asks Killmaster.

*I can't go out into the hallway dressed like that,* I reply, stuffing the ring into my pocket.

*Why not?*

*Well, how will it look? I'm sure this is fine for a Special Ops ditty in Afghanistan, but it's a little aggressive for the W, don'tcha think?*

*What I think,* says Killmaster, taking a tone, which, though telepathic, is no less clear, *is that any second, that maid is going to be done vacuuming, and if we are still in here when that happens, she is going to freak the hell out.*

The vacuum cleaner stops.

*Oh shit, oh shit!*

*Hide!* says Killmaster.

I lurch toward the see-through glass coffee table, unthinking.

*Are you nuts?* demands Killmaster.

The maid snatches a bottle of Windex from her cleaning cart. I freeze. She holds the Windex like a microphone, opens her mouth…and out comes an entire squadron of castrated frogs.

*Good Lord!* cries Killmaster.

I stick my finger in my ear and shake it.

*That chick's got the entire San Diego Zoo down her throat*, says Killmaster. *Pandas! Christ. I think I heard a zebra.*

*Will you shut up and find me a place to hide?*

*Sir, yes, sir!*

I scan left: a space between the bed and the wall. Scan right: bathroom—closet! Inch open the door. Creep inside. Shut it.

Bad idea. Mold and mildew tickle my sinuses. Crap—I can't sneeze now! I hold my breath and peer through the slits in the door. She's dancing and singing like she's about to sacrifice a virgin to the little-known god of air-raid sirens. She's backing up toward the broken glass on the floor.

My nose itches like crazy. The maid spins, eyes closed. Her feet miss the glass by inches. Man. The aural incursion is relentless. I pinch my nose. I'm running out of air. I've got to breathe.

*Just hang tight,* says Killmaster.

She whips her head around in circles, tousling her hair in a way that's either David Lee Roth at a Van Halen concert or a demonic spirit in the throes of a full-blown exorcism.

I sneeze—a spray of spit hits the inside of the door.

*Shit.*

The maid freezes. Her head quirks to the side. Her arms rise. Did she hear me, or is this part of her weird dance? She hikes her skirt up over her thighs...and she begins twerking at the nearest available armchair.

*Now's our chance!* I say.

*No—hang on,* says Killmaster. *This is getting interesting.*

I crack the door. Killmaster seizes control and yanks it shut. The maid's butt bounces like two NBA regulation basketballs. Killmaster's practically panting inside my head.

*Hey! Mouth-breather! Who's in charge of this operation?*

*Sorry, sir.* He relinquishes control of my arm. I push the door open as another sneeze threatens to escape. The maid shuffles to the left—twerk, twerk, twerk—shuffles right—twerk, twerk, twerk.

I exit the closet and open the door to the hallway, slide through, shut it behind us. Another sneeze lets loose as I race down the corridor, and by the time I reach the elevator, I'm dizzy with adrenaline. The enormity of what's happened crashes over me. I just zip-lined over West C in broad daylight!

*Sir*, says Killmaster. *Your father.*

A fish is thrashing on the line in my mind's eye. I'm at the lake, way out off 86. Back when I had a dad in my life.

*Dad's there?* I ask.

Silence.

My leg vibrates. I pull out my phone. There's a text.

Caleb Montana: *We need to talk, bro.*

Whatever. I shove the phone back into my pocket. The elevator opens. I go inside and press the button. The doors shut.

*Killmaster? Is Dad at the lake?*

My breathing is thick in my ears, even thicker than the pounding of my heart or the maid's ear cement.

*Killmaster? Are you still there?*

Nothing.

Am I alone? Is Killmaster really gone? Had he ever really been there? Am I imagining things?

I lean against the elevator wall. The Muzak they're piping in is mind-numbing and driving me nuts. That is, if I'm not already crazy. I close my eyes and exhale, but the mental replay of flying over West C Street is too unnerving. My eyes snap open. No. I'm not crazy. It's the voices in my head that are crazy.

# CHAPTER THIRTY-NINE

TWO POOLS OF LIGHT SKIM like a water strider along the dark highway. I peer into them, confident, but kind of directionless. I know this road goes *somewhere*. I don't have to see past my headlights to know that. I trust it won't take me straight off a cliff like an old Warner Brothers cartoon. I trust I'm not going to drive into a sinkhole. Why can't my instinct about Dad be the same? Every day I trust roads with my life, and roads take me places. Maybe my instinct can take me places too.

In my dreams, Dad's hiding in Arizona. He's living in the desert, in a camper parked not far off the road. Just far enough to stay hidden, but not so far he'd be stuck in an emergency. I never think to ask him where he's been or why he went away. I never ask him why he let us all think he was dead. I don't have to. The answers just seem to be there. Everything's operating on a kind of psychic intelligence. I know he had to cover his tracks. I know he wanted to tell Gran and me everything. And I know he misses Mom most of all.

These dreams are part of me. I've always had them. I think it's the reason my instinct to circle the wagons is so strong. Mom and Dad left me a lot of money, but I'm rerouting all of it back to Gran. Getting her into Pine's Place matters because she raised me. She's the family I've got left. I owe her that much. But a psychologist once told me it wasn't necessarily a healthy thing to give it all to Gran like that.

She called it survivor's guilt. She said getting Gran into Pine's Place might really be about changing how my Dad Dreams end. There's always a dark pool behind him, which supposedly represents death. And in my dreams, he always falls in.

I pull off the highway and follow the dusty track that cuts through the foothills and into the remote region where Dad and I used to go fishing. Maybe these dreams had been real all along. Had he been reaching out to me through the Collective Unconscious? Trying to communicate? Is this really the place? It's not Arizona. The shoreline is different. But maybe it's wrong to try to glean those kinds of specifics. Maybe dreams don't operate that way.

I ease my foot on the brake. Gravel crunches beneath the tires. I pull to a stop. My chest hurts from the struggle of choosing between optimism and pessimism. I don't want the letdown if I choose wrong. This is crazy! There's no way Dad's here! But the sleek stainless steel camper in front of me, identical to the one from my dreams, is awfully frickin' weird.

# CHAPTER FORTY

I SHUT THE CAR DOOR. The sound caroms around the walls of my brain. The sun has dipped behind the foothills. The sky back there is awash in reds, yellows, and pinks. The sky over the camper is a clear, star-speckled black. Parked off to the side is an army-green Jeep Wrangler. Dad's? He never used to drive Jeeps. There'd been an old Saab.

My scuffing feet kick up dust. The camper windows are glowing at the edges. At the door, I raise my fist, hesitate. What if it isn't Dad? What if it's some random person who's had it up to here with the Jehovah's Witnesses? What if it's number three on the FBI's Most Wanted list? What if this is where Scott Baio lives?

I bang on the door, three quick raps, and struggle to master the anxiety roiling inside.

The door swings open.

Not Scott Baio.

A muscular, blond-haired, blue-eyed Adonis quarterback/ Calvin Klein underwear model—and the shock of him being here in his Calvin Kleins, and nothing else, triggers a misfire of all the synapses in my brain. I'm smelling Ralph Lauren cologne with my eyeballs, and I'm pretty sure it's not supposed to work that way.

"It's the Edge!" cries Caleb. "Thanks for coming, bro. Yeah."

He waves me inside the camper. Wordlessly, I comply.

Resistance is futile.

The camper is bright, luxurious. Dark wood paneling, leather seats. Granite kitchen countertop. ESPN is on the plasma TV. It goes to commercial, and there's a close-up of Caleb's slow-motion butt in his Calvin Kleins, a commercial I've seen maybe a million times. I wince, and turn away—

—and here's real life Caleb shutting the camper door, standing there in his Calvin Kleins and gratuitously flaunting his zero-percent body fat, barrel-like pecs, washboard abs, and God of Thunder arms. In short, all the reasons Kate chose for cheating on me. No matter how much I work out, I'll never look like that.

"What am I doing here?" I hear myself ask.

Caleb snatches the remote, powers off the TV. "Yeah, bro. I mean, you know, we've gotta talk."

I slide into the leather booth at the kitchen table, dazed. Caleb slides in across from me, and the leather creaks.

"I need you at the game tomorrow."

"The game?"

"Yeah. Home game. Packers."

"You're playing the Packers."

"Yeah, bro. We're playing the Packers. What—have you been living under a rock? It's a big game."

"Oh, yeah, yeah," I reply, trying to strike a tone that conveys how *his* big game is naturally impeding my ability to function in life. "Yeah, man. Sorry."

"You okay, bro? You seem...kinda...off."

"No, no. I'm fine. You kidding? Psh. Fine."

"Are you sure? Because, don't take this the wrong way, but you've kinda got your blobfish face on."

"My what?"

"Blobfish face," he says, making an exaggerated frowny face. "But, I mean, you know, don't take it the wrong way. I'm worried you're all right is what I'm saying."

"Ri-ght," I say. "Really. I'm A-O-Kay."

Caleb studies my face a moment longer, apparently measuring the subatomic activity of blobfish. "Okay," he says, leaning back into the leather seat. "Right. Okay. So, where were we? Oh yeah, Nostradamus."

I purse my lips thoughtfully. Were we at Nostradamus? Sure. Nostradamus. Why not?

Caleb's talking again.

"We think Nostradamus is planning to disrupt the game. We don't know the how, what, or why—"

"But *where* is a solid start," I offer.

Caleb nods. "Exactly. We've got the where. And we've got the general when."

"Sometime during the game."

Caleb nods some more. "Sometime during the game. Hey. You're taking all this pretty well, bro."

I wave it away like it's nothing. Because it is nothing. I literally have no idea what he's talking about.

"Look at you, bro! You're almost, like, down with all the spy stuff already. Right on."

He raises his hand for a high five, and when I don't respond, he picks my hand up and takes it into a ridiculously elaborate handshake. He's up to the elbow, the shoulder, down to the wrist, flips my hand over, knocks our elbows together; he's down the forearm, fingertips, and now it's one more time up and around the shoulder. When it's over, he winks, snaps his fingers, gives me double-barreled finger guns, and flexes his bare pecs, making them dance, right-left, right-left, right-left.

"What the hell was that?" I ask.

"That's the Bro Shake, bro. So look, we need you there, in the stands. I've got your tickets right here." He reaches beneath a stack of papers, finds two tickets, and slides them across the table. "Your job is to keep an eye out for whatever Nostradamus is up to. See anything fishy—stop 'em."

"Stop 'em."

"That's right. Use your superpowers. Make it fun, bro. No one's sayin' it can't be fun."

My eyebrows come up. I take the tickets. "Nice seats."

"Well, yeah. I mean, don't get too distracted by the game,

though. Trust me. You're not ready for that yet."

"I'm not?"

Caleb laughs. "All right, all right. Show-off. So you've got all these powers now and you think you're ready to do what I do. But do you have any idea how hard it is to do what I do?"

My bottom lip juts out as I consider how best to answer this question, and, since I have no idea what it is he does other than passing a football and doubling as Captain Underpants, I hurriedly shake my head.

"Well, I'll tell you," he says. "Besides remembering the two entirely different sets of hand signals—one for the spies and one for the game, you know—then there's the playing every week in front of thousands of spectators and not, you know, blowing my cover. I mean, come *on*. Not to mention lighting up Drexel Titanic on national TV and no one being none the wiser."

"Drexel Titanic," I repeat, deadpan. "The two-hundred-eighty-pound defensive tackle for New England."

"That's right," says Caleb. "And don't tell me you didn't see *that* game."

"You're saying Drexel Titanic is a spy."

Caleb's face goes blank. He shrugs. "Well, yeah."

"And when he tried to sack you..."

"Lit. Him. Up. Boom, baby!"

"And this you did because Drexel Titanic is a Bad Guy, with a capital B and a capital G?"

"Edge, you're acting really weird, bro. Yeah. Of course I did it because he's a bad guy." He leans in close to the table. A sly smile cuts across his face. "Hey. I sent that bad guy a-packin'. But not Green Bay a-Packin', know what I'm sayin'?"

"No," I say, standing and backing away. "No. I don't know what you're saying. NFL *spies*? What the hell am I even doing here? I thought I'd find my dad, but—ah, that's crazy. I'm crazy. And—and you!" I wag my finger at him. "You are *definitely* crazy." I shake my head, waving the whole thing away. "Ah—I'm outta here, *bro*."

I move for the door, grab the handle. Caleb calls out.

"Wait—wait! Okay. Let's just back it up then, okay? We're just gonna back it on up. You're not crazy. I'm not crazy. Nobody's crazy. Except, well, I mean...your two stoner buds." He laughs. "You've gotta admit, *those* guys are a little crazy. Am I right?"

I pull the handle down.

"Your dad was here!" says Caleb.

I release the handle so fast, it springs back up with a pop.

"He was here?"

"Yeah." Caleb hunches over and makes slow waving gestures to get me back to the table. "Your dad. He was here. Okay? But then he, you know, went off the grid."

"Off the grid? What does that even mean? He's been off the grid for, like, twenty years!"

"Yeah," he replies. "I know. But now he's like, *more* off the grid. He's so way off the grid now, bro."

"Cut the bro shit," I snap. "You're not fooling anybody. Why are you here? Is this your place or his?"

Caleb frowns. "His, br—I mean—his. I thought you knew that. Why else would you come here?"

I take a deep breath, release it. My feet take me back to the table. I sit, arms at my sides, eyes straight ahead.

"Okay. Let me get this straight. You, Caleb Montana, are a spy for the United States government?"

Caleb nods.

"Good. Now we're getting somewhere."

"Yeah," he replies. "Yeah. PMA—Positive Mental Attitude. I like it!"

"And this whole NFL spy gig—that's a thing. As in, there are other spy football players out there, and bad guys, besides Drexel Titanic."

Caleb's features flatten and activate the Duh Face. "Of course. Who do you think had their hands all over Brady's balls? And don't tell me you've never wondered what the hell is going on with the Colts."

"Ri-ight. And so, if you're working for the government, does that mean Drexel Titanic works for—who? This Nostradamus person?"

Caleb shakes his head. "Not person. *People*. Nostradamus is an evil global syndicate made up of bad people."

"Well, naturally. Can't have an *evil* global syndicate without bad people."

Caleb raises his arms in a gesture of exasperation. "That's what I'm saying!"

"Okay, okay. So you're telling me there will be bad-guy football players on the field tomorrow. Playing for the Packers."

He shrugs. "Might be. Might not be. Sometimes I can't tell until, you know, the game starts going."

"And what tips you off?" I ask. "Is it the brand of jockstraps?"

"This is serious, Edge. We intercepted communications talking about a bomb in a ball."

"A ball. Like, a football?"

"Maybe. Not necessarily. I thought they said *disco* ball, but that doesn't make any sense. Anyway, check it out. The game is a big crowd. The ball could have a weaponized virus in it. Release it into the crowd—oops. Sorry, United States of America. You're all going to die because Edger Bonkovich thought the jockstraps were some kind of sick joke."

"But I thought we were looking for the AI?"

"You are. That's why I need you at the game. InstaTron has been breached. That's what this is about. That's why you're in this predicament. I told you not to say yes to Mikey."

"You drugged and kidnapped me!"

"Well, technically. Yeah."

"And now you're going to ask me to trust you?"

Caleb shrugs. "Well...*yeah*. I guess. Listen, Edge. We're gonna find your dad, okay? Let's get through tomorrow without the world ending, and then we'll find your dad. Sound good?"

The beginning of a neck headache unspools its tendrils into the base of my skull.

"No," I reply. "It doesn't sound good. I'm dying, Caleb. This thing in me is going to kill me. Why doesn't anybody give a crap that this thing's gonna kill me?"

"No, no, no," says Caleb. "I mean—I give a crap. I told you, I've got your back. Right? But you're not gonna die. You got that part wrong. There's a booster. Didn't Mikey tell you about the booster? Come on, bro. Where's that PMA?"

I shake my head, then rest it facedown on the table in front of me, my hands still at my sides.

"Mikey didn't tell me about the booster until after it was stolen straight out of his weirdo office," I say, not looking up.

"Stolen?"

"Mmm-hmm."

I sit up, and Caleb's gaze pans left thoughtfully.

"What?" I ask.

"Could be your dad. He's the one who stole InstaTron Tron."

*"He did what?"*

"Someone over there at InstaTron is a mole for Nostradamus. Your dad and I were working to uncover the mole. A week ago, your dad took matters into his own hands. They were about to do the first human trial when your dad found something. He never told me what, but I think he stole InstaTron Tron to keep the Zarathustra program from falling into Nostradamus's hands. He's been off the grid ever since. You know, like, more off the grid than normal."

I nod slowly as pieces of the puzzle begin falling into place. "Mikey mentioned he was having security problems. He didn't mention it was my dad who stole the AI, though."

"He doesn't know. And he can't know. Not until we figure out this mole problem. Edge—do you realize what this means? Your dad created that booster. If we can find him, we can get you fixed up."

"Oh, that. Yeah. I knew that. That, I knew."

# CHAPTER FORTY-ONE

I SWITCH THE HEADLIGHTS off as I roll to a stop in front of our apartment. The living room light is on. I put the car in Park, turn the key. My adrenaline is spent. My arms are heavy. My quads are tight. A headache is suctioning my brain. I'm afraid to think about what this could signify. I don't understand how the Zarathustra serum works. How it enhances what I can do physically, or its potential toll on my body. But the headache is freaking me out. Is this what's going to kill me? Just thinking about it makes my skin crawl. Because I can't die yet. I'm still living with Gran and Shep. I always thought I'd do something for myself after getting them into Pine's Place. But now I'm facing death—and my life is still on hold.

I expel a burst of air, and a surge of frustration overwhelms me. I snatch the keys from the ignition. I want to punch something. Anything. I bang the back of my head three times against the headrest. Not enough. I punch the top of the steering wheel. I punch it again, over and over, accidently sounding the horn multiple times.

I collapse backward into my seat. The night falls silent except for the pounding in my chest and a barking dog somewhere up the street. The air is woody and humid. I breathe it in in long bands.

A second wave of frustration hits me. I strike the wheel and again hit the horn by accident. The outdoor light switches on.

*Crap.*

Gran opens the front door, her face full of concern.

"Dear?" Gran calls.

I plaster a smile on my face. Open the creaking door—gently. My heart is still racing when I climb out.

"Hey, Gran."

"Were you honking your horn?"

"I, uh, got tangled up in the seat belt." I drag my hand through my hair and gesture at the car like it's a man-eating death trap. Gran frowns doubtfully. On the front step, I stop and give her a hug, and the big, scary world settles down.

# CHAPTER FORTY-TWO

THE KITCHEN still smells like Golumpki, Gran's specialty. The soft glow from the living room tells me Shep is still up. The volume on the TV is low, barely audible over the hum of the air conditioner kicking on. Reality begins asserting itself. The sounds and smells of my childhood turn a secret valve on me, releasing the tension I'm still holding.

Gran kisses me on the forehead and then puts on a pot for tea. I toss my keys into the bowl. The kitchen overlooks the TV room, where Shep is watching *The Late, Late Show*. I stand there, not really paying attention, but not really thinking about dying or superpowers or InstaTron Tron.

"You're home late," says Gran, taking down two mugs from the cupboard. "Maybe you finally met a nice young lady."

I scratch the back of my neck. My gaze drops reflexively to peer into the pastels-speckled laminate surface of the kitchen table.

"You have met a young lady!"

"Edger got laid?" calls Shep from the living room.

"Shepherd!" says Gran. She slides out the tea tin from the back of the counter, opens it, and pulls out two bags. "Tell me about her."

"She's nice. She's..." I sigh, wondering how best to put it. "I mean...well, she's amazing," I finish lamely.

"Oh, dear." Gran smiles.

"Gran," I say. "What if we moved up the schedule on Pine's Place?"

Her eyebrows rise. "I thought you said you needed six more months?"

I swallow. Assuming I live through all this, maybe Mikey will be happy enough with my work to give me an advance on the next six months of my salary. That is, if he's not too pissed about me cutting a hole in his window and going AWOL.

Gran's eyes narrow. "Take the six more months, Edger. There's no rush."

"No-no," I hurry to say. "I can. I've got the money. I mean, I think I got a promotion at work. The point is, I'm tired of waiting. Aren't you tired of waiting? Let's just do it."

"Edger..."

"What do you think ever happened to Dad?" I ask, mostly trying to get out of one boiling pot—though my mouth plan didn't include leaping buck naked into another.

Gran's forehead wrinkles tighten. "Are you missing him?"

A lump rises in my throat. Gran takes a seat across the kitchen table, grabs my hand, and pats it.

"I don't know about that," she says. "He was private about some things. He was a lot like you."

My chest tightens.

"You know, something about your father. It never made sense, him leaving. He wasn't that way. Your father always did right by people. He wasn't a saint. I don't mean to say he was, but he always found a way to do right by people. I think that was why it was so hard for me to let him go. For a while, things would happen. Unexpected things. And I thought—it just seemed like he might be out there still, looking out for us. It was nice to think that."

"You mean like when your friend in Jacksonville was sending me Calvin and Hobbes strips?"

"Pearl? Oh, heavens no. She didn't send you those."

"You told me it was her!"

"I was lying my skinny ass off. I didn't want to get your hopes up. I have no idea who was sending you those comics."

"Gran—" I take my hand back and sit straighter. The teapot

boils. Gran rises and takes it off the burner. She pours and steeps the tea. When she's got two cups made, she sighs and peers out the window over the sink.

"Edger, your father is gone, and he's never coming back. I'm sorry, but that's the way it is. I've done my best. And I know it isn't the same."

"Stop it. Are you kidding? What is with the Lifetime drama, huh? Look at us. Here we are, in the kitchen, drinking tea. Wait-wait. Shh—listen. Do you hear that? I think I can *hear* the menopause. It's *amazing*."

Gran rolls her eyes.

"Hey," I say. "I wasn't asking about him because I thought you could've been a better parent. He's been on my mind recently. You know, with everything going on with, uh—" I clear my throat. "This girl I've been seeing."

Gran turns her head from the window. Still not meeting my eyes, she brings the two cups of tea to the table. "You wish he could've known her. That's natural."

I swallow and nod. Gran sits.

"Well, he would've liked her. I'm sure of that. I bet she's like your mother."

"Why do you say that?"

"Because I know your type." Gran sighs. "That was hard too. How they never found her body. How the car was mangled on the rocks. How we all just assumed she'd washed out to sea." She shakes her head, takes a sip of her tea, and sets it down with a soft thunk. "We've had our share of shit shows."

Our eyes meet. "They never found the body? You never told me that!"

"Well, of course."

"Not 'of course.' Why wouldn't you tell me something like that?"

"Because sometimes endings are messy."

"And what is that supposed to mean?"

"You were so little. You needed to think they were dead."

"You say that like they're not."

"Oh, give me a break." She sips her tea. "Edger, if I had told you they never found your mom's body, you'd have gotten some crazy idea in your head she's an Alderaanian princess who went back to battle the Borg, and you know it!"

I expel a weak chuckle through my nose. "I mean…Borg is Star *Trek*. Alderaan is—ah, forget it."

"And then there's all this business with my happy ever after."

My head snaps up. Her smile is too knowing.

"I heard you telling Fabio once." She laughs. "You want me and Shep to live happily ever after, traveling the world, or sitting on the beach at Pine's Place drinking Old Fashioneds and watching the waves come in."

"Is that bad?"

"Nope!" calls Shep from the living room.

"Hell no," says Gran. "But where are you in that picture? What will Edger be doing while I'm doing Shep in Venice?"

"Who cares?" cries Shep.

"Me," replies Gran. "Well? What will you be doing, Edger?"

"Well…" I stammer, the elasticity of my brain failing over her mention of sex with Shep in Venice. "I mean…I'll be with…Mary," I say, hoping she'll leave it there and not press me on my sex life. I'm already too far into the asteroid field with this make-believe girlfriend idea. It'd be just my luck Mary walks up and rings the doorbell right now.

"Mary? That's her name? Mary!"

I nod. Gran smiles.

"Well, so long as you're doing what you want to be doing. So long as you're not chained to your dear old Gran, saving money and missing out on strong women like this Mary, and maybe a career for yourself in there; maybe not taking the blame for that Caleb Montana stealing things at Notre Dame, or—"

I jerk upright. "Wait—you know about that?"

"Oh Lord." She rolls her eyes. "Edger, Fabio can't keep secrets for shit. Look. Just promise me this. Promise me you'll live for yourself a little bit. Whatever happens. Would you do that for me?"

"What do you mean whatever happens?"

"Just promise me."

I lean back in my chair, sip my tea, and nod. "I promise."

# CHAPTER FORTY-THREE

I OPEN the door to my room. Fabio's at my computer playing *Minecraft*.

"Dude?" I ask, my hands rising into the universal what-the-hell sign language position.

"Check out this moron," he says, not looking up. "Thinks he's Entity 303. I'm gonna totally red stone trap his ass into the Nether—boom baby!" He thrusts his arms into the air like he's just slam dunked on LeBron James. He taps out a few quick keystrokes, logging off, then swivels the chair around. "So. You're not dead. That's good. Hey, man. You had me worried."

"Clearly." I plop down on my bed and pull off my left shoe.

"And you told him no, right?" asks Fabio. "You told Mikey no?"

I pull off my right shoe. "About that…"

Fabio slaps his hands to his mouth, then drags them through his hair. "Holy shit, holy shit, holy shit! You did it? You're a"—he lowers his voice—"you're a freaking superhero now?"

I try to smile, but my cheeks aren't having it.

"Wait-wait-wait. Do you have to wear the underwear on the outside now? You know, the inner-outer-underwear. Like they do in the comics."

"Dude."

His hands slap his mouth again like he's witnessed the most spectacular car crash in history—which, upon reflection, this may be.

"But why?" he asks. "I mean, I thought you weren't gonna do it?"

"Well... I mean, you know. A man's gotta do what a man's gotta—"

"He guilt-tripped you," says Fabio. "Didn't he."

I nod. "Yep. Guilt-tripped me."

"I knew it. Oh my God. You realize you're gonna die because you're a total wuss?"

I flop back onto my bed. "Yep. In fact, I've been thinking to have you inscribe that on my tombstone. 'Here lies Edger. Dead because—total wuss.'"

"Hey—at least we've got your superhero name. Wuss Man! With the power to cave at the slightest guilt-trip! And his arch nemesis—Catholic Mother! Dun-dun-du-un!"

"Coming soon to a theater near you."

"Okay, so," says Fabio, his eyebrows lowering as he sits forward on the chair. "Seeing as you're here and not out fighting crime and/or leaping tall buildings and/or lurking atop gargoyles, I can only assume you found the AI?"

I lace my fingers behind my head, stretch out, and cross my feet. The sinking pit in my stomach hardens. I close my eyes and listen to the prolonged silence and wait for Fabio to process the implications of me not answering.

"Crap dude. So you're...dying?"

"Yeah."

"Crap! Oh, crap! Get up! Get up!"

Slapping hands beat my shoulders and biceps. My eyes spring open. I roll to the opposite side of the bed and peer across at Fabio, who's gaping back at me with his mouth wide enough to swallow an apple whole.

"What in all that is strong and good in the Light Side of the Force are you even still doing here?" he exclaims. "You should be out there! Right now! Finding Tron-Tron! Live, man! Live!"

I shrug. "Well, I'm tired, dude."

"Sleep when you're dead! No, wait. I mean...don't die. Don't die."

"Fab, I've had a long day. A lot has happened."

And so I tell him about the terrorists and the power grid. I tell him about the booster and Mikey lying to me. I tell him Mary's story, but when it comes to sharing the news about Dad, for some reason, I hold that back. Maybe it's because I don't want to jinx it. Or maybe it's because Fabio is family too, and I don't want to get his hopes up if the whole thing falls apart.

"Crap, dude," he says when I'm done. His eyes are wide and his mouth keeps opening and closing, trying to say something, but taking forever not to say it.

"Hey, man," I say, sitting again at the edge of the bed. "I promise I won't die without saying goodbye, okay?"

His jaw drops open. Tears well up in his eyes.

"Oh, come on," I say. "Stop. I was just joking!"

He plops down next to me and throws his arms around me, squeezing tight.

"Get off me! Get off me!" I say, breaking free. "Dude! Bro foul!"

"You're gonna live, dude," he says, unnecessarily wiping his eyes, his bearded face dead serious. "You're gonna live. Because this is a superhero story, and the superhero always saves the day. But seriously. Not to sound, you know, like the Cowardly Lion, but it's me and Shep and Gran you've gotta worry about."

"What?"

"Well, think about it, dude!" he exclaims. "The superhero always wins. But it's the people he cares about who always end up dead." Fabio grabs his bag and lifts the window open. He throws a leg out and hunches down, half-in, half-out of my room.

"You know you can use the front door once in a while."

"Best-friend trope," he replies, winking. "Best friends use human doggie doors."

I smile, but his face becomes serious again.

"Just think about what I said, dude. You call me if you need me—and don't die, okay? That's the priority. But, you know, make sure you keep your secret identity good and secret. There's a sales competition at the Über Dork next week, and I can't win it if I'm dead because you took your superhero mask off in front of the bad guys for some stupid reason."

I give him a tired, half-hearted smile, which Fabio returns before tucking himself through the window, shutting it from the outside, and then clambering down the tree. I flop down on my back, too exhausted for anything else.

# CHAPTER FORTY-FOUR

MY DREAMS ARE RESTLESS. The world is glimmering in twilight autumn. Leaves are orbiting the Tree of Life. Soul-stars in the sky. How long before I join them?

Bruce Lee is practicing his martial arts forms near the white bench.

"I need your help," I say.

The master finishes a kick, then comes to attention like he's in the military. He clasps his hands in front. "You have it."

"My father. I want to find him. I want those booster shots. And then I wanna find Tron-Tron and finish this."

"What are we waiting for?" Bruce Lee takes one step back and assumes a crane stance. His hands begin tracing shapes in the air the way he did in *Fists of Fury*, mystic and evocative like an opening flower. The soul-lights appear inside the outline he's traced. Their brightness expands to swallow us whole.

Earth rushes up at us. Treetops, city grids, highways and buildings, all zooming in like an impossibly high-speed refresh rate on a Google Earth map. I catch an aerial glimpse of the Q—Qualcomm Stadium—before we land at a nearby Motel 6. The parking lot is gritty. The hum of the highway is constant.

"I know this place!" I exclaim, my stomach knotting with excitement. I spin and scan the area, taking it all in. "This is just off the 8! There's a Home Depot right over there,

I think. Wait—Dad is here?"

"Yes." Bruce Lee closes his eyes, and the world goes dark like I've closed my eyes.

"What're you doing?"

The world comes back into focus, and Bruce Lee and I are stepping through a jet-black hotel mirror and into a room. I take in everything at once. The blinds are drawn; papers are strewn across the table; a suitcase is open on a rack; a man—fully dressed, including shoes—is sleeping in the bed.

My pulse ratchets up to the point of pain.

It's so unlike the other dreams I have of Dad. There's no pool for him to fall into. He's here, safe and whole. I'm aching to touch him, to be in the real world and touch him.

Dad rolls over. My throat clenches up as I get my first look at him in over twenty years. He's grayer. The crow's feet are deeper. His stubble whiter. But every detail weighs on me, to lay eyes on him, to know this is no ordinary dream.

"I want to wake up," I say, and the sudden impulse to leap into my car and get onto the highway takes hold. "Why can't I wake up?"

I spin around and face Bruce Lee. His eyes tighten as he studies my features.

"I have to release you," he says.

"Then release me! Release me!"

"There's more," he says, gesturing to the table.

My cheek twitches; I shake my head, turn and search for what he's wanting to show me. There—a letter. Addressed to me. My father's handwriting.

I hurry to the table, tear it open. I can't read it fast enough.

*Edger,*

*Don't come looking for me. People tracking your movements. You'll find your booster at the game tomorrow. Section UV45, row 25, beneath seat 14. Take this one and no more. If I'm able, I'll be there. If I think I've been compromised, I won't. Sorry about that.*

*Remember: STAY AWAY. Trust no one.*

*Dad*

The letter falls from my hands, tears fall from my face, and I fall from the dream.

# CHAPTER FORTY-FIVE

WE DRIFT for a time among the soul-stars, Bruce Lee and me. It's peaceful up here, and I'm glad to have found a friend in him. I glance over at him. His eyes are closed, and his hands are clasped behind his head like he's lying down with his feet stretched out. Above and beneath us are billions of soul-stars.

"How come you have a body?" I ask.

Bruce Lee's eyes open. His hands come down, and he seems to sit up. We float nearer a cluster of soul-stars, and they grow incredibly intense before scattering outward faster than I can blink.

"Your body is back at home in bed," says Bruce Lee, eyeing me with a funny look. "This form is how you see yourself."

"So all these stars, to them, they've got bodies too? I mean, are they picturing themselves as stars, or as they were in life?"

Bruce Lee looks around, taking in the various constellations before answering. "I suppose it depends on what they're up to, or their personalities, or maybe a dozen other factors."

"Then why can't we see them? I mean, why do they look like stars?" I reach out to touch the nearest one.

“Stop!” Bruce Lee snatches my hand and shoves it aside. I’m shaking, I realize; my heart rate is suddenly going crazy. I’m sweating. I can barely breathe.

“What’s the matter with me?”

Bruce Lee shakes his head. He closes his eyes. The lights begin to dim. “We’ve lingered here for too long.”

Darkness swallows us.

# CHAPTER FORTY-SIX

"WAKE UP."

I open my eyes. Sunlight is creeping in. The *Star Wars* poster on my ceiling is blurry. I stretch and groan.

Dreams. Dreams. Something about Dad at a Motel 6.

"Morning, sleepyhead."

I roll onto my side. A bar of honey-golden sunlight is bisecting a bare and definitely *female* leg in my bed.

Something like a popped clutch hitches in my chest.

I snatch the blankets and try to yank them up to my neck. They won't come, because Mary—beautiful Mary Thomas—is sitting on the edge of my bed. The blankets are trapped beneath her beautiful butt, which happens to be wearing my favorite boxers. And the rest of her is in my Notre Dame jersey.

"What're you—how're you—what're you—are you wearing my *clothes*?"

"I got to thinking," she says, standing and sashaying over to my desk, where she picks up the picture of me and Dad. Her blonde hair is gleaming in the morning sunlight. Her legs are long, toned, and tan. *And* she comes fully equipped with hips. Beautiful, beautiful hips. That whole hourglass-figure thingy. I bite the side of my tongue, and my gaze snaps to eye level just in time; she sets down the picture and faces me.

"I'm going to help you."

"That's nice." I yank my sheets up to my neck and count to ten as a sinking suspicion forms in my knotting stomach. I've missed something. Maybe more than one critical something. Probably an entire chapter of critical somethings torn from the story of my life while I was sleeping.

I release the sheets and sit up. "How did you get in here?"

"Through the window."

An inopportune thought strikes me. I peek beneath the sheets, and a wave of relief crashes over me upon discovering I'm not wearing the Yoda underpants.

"Wait," I say. "*How* did you get in here?"

She rolls her eyes. "Through the window. Do I need to draw you a diagram?"

"But that's the Fabio door," I mutter. Mary sets down the picture and nods to the ceiling poster.

"*Star Wars*. You like *Star Wars*?"

"Fahrvergnügen."

"Excuse me?"

"Stranger danger."

"Edger. Am I making you nervous?"

"Jawa juice."

She sighs, pulls the chair back from my desk, and sits.

"Not to be rude," I say, choosing my words carefully, "but, why are you in my room?"

"I'm glad you asked that, Edger," she says, like her sitting at my desk and wearing my boxers and jersey is the most normal freaking thing in the history of normal freaking things. "I got to thinking. I know you're worried about your grandmother. And I know you've been saving to get her into Pine's Place." She leans forward, puts her elbows on her knees, and locks her fingers to rest her chin on top. "I think I can help you. And I think I can kill two birds with one stone."

"Wait—what? How do you know about Pine's Place? Did Mikey put you up to this?"

"Would you trust me less or more if I told you he did?" She shakes her head impatiently. "Forget about that. This is important. I think we should move in together."

My head snaps back, and my mouth makes that "oo-ee" shape one does when bearing witness to a streaker careening face-first into a glass door. By the way she's scanning my face, she's weighing its every twitch. I try to smile, but I think only the left side of my face is complying, so I scrap that, then cup my hand in front of my mouth to catch some blowback. Fortunately, my morning breath doesn't smell like a Chewbacca butthole. So, you know, a little win for me.

Mary's eyebrows come down. This moment we're having is lasting too long. I suppose some people keep a witty response handy in case they encounter a situation like this. But since I haven't got one, I just open my mouth and hope for the best.

"I'm sorry. I thought you said we should move in together."

*Huh,* I think. *A complete sentence. Not bad.*

"Well, *think*, Edger. Once we get your grandmother into Pine's Place, we can put around-the-clock surveillance on her. And then *I* will be able to keep an eye on *you* twenty-four seven. It'll look like we're dating. I can change my name, change my hair. Nobody'll recognize me. More importantly, nobody'll know you're keeping odd hours and fighting bad guys. It's a win for everybody."

"Buh..." I say.

"It's just a cover, Edger."

"Buh..." I repeat, in case she didn't hear me the first time.

"I'm trying to help you. Your family's important. And I know your grandmother wants you to meet a nice girl. I'm a nice girl."

"We-ell."

"She'll feel better about moving out if she thinks you and I are, you know..."

"What?"

"A couple!"

"Right! Right," I say, my cheeks burning. "But how do you know about Gran wanting me to meet a nice gir—"

"Secrets, Edger," she says, using a tone like we're in the car, ready to go, but I've forgotten the keys for the hundredth time. "Look. This is what you want. It's what they want. It's what everyone wants."

I stare at her, unable to process. What I want? Does she mean I want to move in with her? Does she mean I want to have sex with her? No, probably her meaning is innocent. She means I want Gran and Shep in Pine's Place, and it's Gran and Shep who want me to have sex with her. Well, that's messed up.

"You think Gran wants me to have sex with you?"

"*What?*"

Nope. Nope. Definitely *not* what she meant.

I shake my head, trying to clear it. I can't believe I said that out loud. Of *course* that's not what she meant. She's got me so mixed up—but what did she expect? She comes in here digging through my drawers—which, under ordinary circumstances, would be the best friggin' day of my life—but she could be a serial killer for all I know. Worse, even if I knew she was a serial killer, I'd probably still go along with all this. All of which begs the question: *Can* hot girls be serial killers? My heart is racing. I blurt the first thing that pops into my head: "Do hot serial killers eat hot cereal in the morning?"

"*Now I'm a serial killer?*"

"Sorry. What I meant to say is, how do you always know so much about me? And you're very pretty."

Her gaze drops to her lap and then flits back up to meet mine. Her pretty lashes are the color of honey in the morning light. "Thank you. But don't you see? This is why you need me in your life. You're a superhero now, true. But you don't think things through. I do. Use me. Take advantage of me."

"Really? Really. That's the best choice of words here?"

"Look who's talking, Hot Cereal. Look. Sooner or later, this Zarathustra stuff is going to wreck your grandmother's life. By moving her into Pine's Place, we can put a security detail on her without her knowledge. We can install some of our people as Pine's Place staff."

"I'm sorry. Some of 'our people'?"

Mary scowls. "God, you're dense sometimes. It's not that hard to understand. Maybe you need some coffee."

I shake my head. "Look, even if I wanted to move in with you—not that I don't want to move in with you—I mean, you're nice. And sexy—and professional! So, *so* professional."

I shake my head again, because the last two didn't take, and because the coffee is downstairs. I take a deep breath and release it. Her lips twitch, then go still. Her eyes are wide and round. *Is she laughing at me?*

"What I mean is," I say. "Pine's Place. I need about six more months. I don't have enough saved up yet."

"Actually, you do," she says, sitting up straight and brightening.

"I do?"

"Well, you didn't think you'd be superheroing for fifteen bucks an hour, did you?"

"Are you saying I've been given a raise?"

Mary smiles. "Mm-hm. *And* I've drawn an advance off your first paycheck to pay the deposit. I hope that's okay."

"Wait-wait-wait. My first paycheck? You paid the deposit? At Pine's Place. *My first paycheck covers the deposit?* Holy hell. How much are you paying me?"

Her eyebrows flit up and down. "A *lot*. There's a bungalow already reserved for your grandmother. She can move in today."

"Today!" I throw the covers back and scramble out of bed, not even caring that I'm pitching a tent in my boxers. "What the kumquat!? Mary. Don't you think our pretend relationship is kind of moving too fast?"

Her eyes widen at the spring-loaded complication in my boxers. Her gaze zooms in, zooms out, then zooms in again before it snaps up to meet mine, then goes higher to meet Luke Skywalker on the ceiling. We blush. She spins around and gives me her back.

"I mean... Do *you* think it's moving too fast?" she asks from over her shoulder, pressing her hands below her belly button.

"Ooh..." I cast around for a pair of pants, and there's a knock at my door.

"Edger?" says Gran.

"Ah—just a minute!"

*Pants! Pants!*

Mary spins back around. *Let her in,* she mouths. She bites her bottom lip and nods at the door emphatically.

I make a waving gesture that encompasses her, all of her—Mary, in my room, Mary, wearing my boxers and shirt—but she's eyeing me like I'm attempting complex and forbidden sorcery.

"It'll look like you slept here last night!" I whisper.

Her eyes narrow. "That's the point."

Slumping, then straightening, I hastily repeat the forbidden hand sorcery around the mutant zucchini in my pants. She bites her lip and tilts her head to the side, then shrugs and nods as if to say, *Not bad.*

I cup my hand and shield my eyes, but a glimmer of movement in my peripheral vision makes this short-lived; the door is opening. I lunge for the pair of jeans on the floor near my dresser as—too late—Gran *and* Shep enter the room.

"I heard voices and—oh my!" Gran exclaims, averting her eyes and turning to leave. "Oh, I am sorry… I am so sorry."

"No, wait," says Mary, reaching her hand out, then dropping it to her side. "It's okay. Everybody's decent. I mean—" She blushes. "Mostly. Come in, please."

"Well, goddammit, boy," says Shep. "Didn't think you had it in you."

"Shepherd!" says Gran.

I snatch my pants, stuff in a leg, lose my balance, and tip between the bed and the wall. My shoulder slams into the floor, rattling the downstairs chandelier.

"I'm okay!" I shout.

"Mrs. Bonkovich," says Mary.

I get another leg in, pull my jeans up over my butt, and stuff myself in as best I can before zipping up, banging my elbows on the wall and the bed in the process. I spring up from behind the bed. Mary and Gran are shaking hands. Gran's forehead wrinkles deepen as she peers into Mary's eyes.

"My name is Mary Thomas," says Mary. "It's very nice to meet you, Mrs. Bonkovich. I think there's something Edger wants to say."

All heads slowly turn to face me. I swallow a lump desperate to escape like an alien through my mouth. "I'm okay," I say again, this time waving so everyone can see my hand and arm are attached and operational.

"Edger?" says Gran, her features crumpling in confusion.

I clear my throat and look at Shep. His look is plain: *Boy, you've got a personality problem.*

I look at Mary. Her look is plainer: *I am Victoria's Secret's best-kept secret.*

I clear my throat again, figuring situations like these must be worth a twofer.

"Gran," I say, pausing to lick my lips. "You know how I said it'd be six more months till Pine's Place? Well, I wanted to tell you before, but...there's a bungalow there with your name on it. I've got the deposit down and everything. It's ready and waiting."

Mary's shoulders slump in relief; Shep's eyes widen; Gran claps her hands over her mouth. Her eyes are glassy. She totters around the bed to fling her arms around me and bury her face in my chest.

"Oh, Edger. Oh, Edger."

I squeeze her gently. Tears leak down my cheeks. The rims of Mary's eyes are red. I stare at Luke Skywalker. Seconds tick by. I breathe in Gran's powdery scent and reflect on how my whole life has come down to this moment. This great woman who loves me, raised me, and kept me on the pod racer track all those times I could've flown into a canyon wall; she doesn't feel like I'm pushing her out, even if I feel guilty over the way it's going down. This is what she's wanted. Me with my future, her with hers. This is her happy ever after. And after so much meticulous planning, here we are. We've just kind of crashed into it. Gran and Shep are going to Pine's Place. They're actually going to Pine's Place. And what's more, I've got myself this weird—though incredibly out of my league—pretend-girlfriend thing developing. That's not so bad. All I need are Dad and my booster, and then, for once in my life, it'll be like I'm actually winning.

# CHAPTER FORTY-SEVEN

THE DISPLAY, though simple, was perfect. It had:

A white picket fence.

A plot of plastic, lime-green grass.

A real cow—which meant, of course, soon-to-be-dropped drug possession charges.

"Well, that ought to do it," says Judas, clapping an exhausted and bleary-eyed Sheldon on the back, and sending him stumbling forward by three feet. Judas dusts off his hands to give the impression he had participated physically in the setup work, and then returns his attention to the Cluck-n-Pray food truck behind the cow display. "Okay, Blake, tell me you brought enough Cluck-n-Pray Nuggets, Cheezin' Spiced Fries, Spicy Wrath of God, *and* the New Testament Cool Ranch Cluckin' Deluxe—"

"Yes, sir." Blake comes out from inside the truck, removes his visor, and clutches it against his chest. "It won't be like last year, sir. We've got the whole menu this time. Old Testament and New Testament."

"You have the Shroud of Turin Wrap *and* the Cluckin' Manna Wrap?"

"Yes, sir."

"You have the Cluckin' Goliath Club and the Cluckin' Slingshot?"

"Yes, sir. All the Book of Samuel menu items are present and accounted for."

"Catsup with Jesus? The Holy Toast?"

"Yes, sir. The crust is risen and accounted for, sir."

"Sauces?"

"Even the Colosseum Christian Barbecue sauce, sir."

"Good, good." Judas scratches beneath his nose superfast and racks his brain. "Napkins!" he blurts. "Straws!"

"Napkins and straws!" calls Sheldon, who has taken his position inside the truck at register one and is holding up a napkin dispenser overfilled to the point where it is impossible to retrieve *one* napkin without ripping at least fifteen others to shreds, and a straw dispenser that, until Sheldon had grabbed it, had been sitting directly beneath a pound of slowly defrosting frozen chicken.

"Don't let me see that happen again," snaps Judas, pointing at the defrosting chicken. Health code violations like that were expensive to make go away. He knew from experience.

"Yes, sir," says Sheldon. "I will not let you *see it* if we ever do anything like that again."

"Perfect," says Judas, pride swelling in his chest. "Gentlemen. You've done me proud."

"Ah—sir," says Blake.

"Yes, Team Member Blake?"

"Did we need soft drinks?"

Judas laughs. "Did we need soft drinks. Ha! Good one."

"Ah, no, sir. I mean, well, that is—we don't have soft drinks."

"What?" snaps Judas. "Shut up. Sheldon—?"

"He's right, sir." Sheldon reaches beneath the counter to retrieve the line that should've been attached to their beverage machine and lifts it so the unattached end is plainly visible.

"But that should be...attached to...a thing. Right?" asks Judas. "I mean, dammit! Of course that should be attached to—where is our beverage machine!?"

Giggling, sweating, and leaving in her wake a greenish vapor trail of spiritually enlightened aromatic chicken molecules, Christine races down the still-empty mezzanine level of Qualcomm Stadium, pushing the trolley with the stolen beverage machine in front of her. She rounds the north bend, and the El Cerrito food truck comes into view. Consuelo spots her, sounds the mouth-fart alerts, and jumps up and down, pointing. Brad rushes out from behind the counter, his shoulders raised.

"Open the thing! Open the thing!" yells Christine, winded and hysterical.

The four Apostles, who are schlepping a large black tub, run out next. Mark struggles to remove the lid.

"Hurry!" yells Christine. "Hurry!"

The lid comes off. Christine slows her pace, heaves back on the trolley handle, skids. John and Mathew grab two sides of the cart and ease it to a stop. The drink machine slides forward by one foot. Brad and Consuelo close in. They lift the drink machine and set it into the black tub.

Luke is on lookout.

"Come on, come on, come on!" yells Christine.

Mark pops the lid back onto the black tub. Brad and Consuelo push, scoot-scoot-scoot. The tub vanishes behind the food truck as Mark and Mathew lift the trolley and run it over to the custodian's closet. Christine tucks a strand of curly hair behind her ear, then fetches her purse from the counter. She reaches inside, pulls out her deodorant, and applies through the neck hole of her shirt.

"They're coming! They're coming!" hisses Luke. "And you still smell like chicken!"

Christine whips around in time to see Mathew and Mark duck inside the custodian's closet. Brad and Consuelo are on the registers. Luke kneels to tie his shoe. Christine flips Luke the bird, caps her deodorant, and jams it back into her purse before chucking it into the truck and grabbing the platter of sampler nuggets inside the window.

She releases a slow exhalation and turns around to stand nose to nose with a sweaty, out-of-breath, and red-faced Judas Christian, cokehead owner of the Mission Gorge Branch, and Dickwad Supreme.

"All right," snaps Judas. "What the hell?"

"Language, Christian!" snaps Brad.

"Hey, Judas S. Carryout," says Consuelo. "It's eleven o'clock. Do you know where your cow is? *Thbbbt!*"

"Consuelo!" hisses Brad. "*Be quiet!*"

A stricken expression flashes across Judas's features. "You wouldn't dare."

"Oh, but we *did*," says Christine. "Cow-vert operations happen to be our specialty. Good luck outselling us this year, Judas!"

# CHAPTER FORTY-EIGHT

MARY'S GOT ONE HAND ON the wheel, the other in her lap. The top is down, and her dress is riding up. I concentrate on studying the sky. Specifically, how the clouds don't look anything like Mary. Her eyes, or her lips. An unbidden mental snapshot forms; her in my room, biting her fingernail and staring at my—

"I really appreciate you doing this," she says.

"You do?" I stammer.

"Yeah. I mean, after this morning and everything, I kinda got to thinking. You know, I don't know if anyone has said thanks. I mean for what you're doing. Turning your life upside down. *Risking* your life. It's amazing."

"Yeah… I mean—not, yeah, like, I'm so amazing. I mean, *yeah*, like, I don't know, thanks-for-saying-thanks-yeah yeah."

Mary smiles. "I knew what you meant. And you're welcome. It's very selfless. What you're doing."

I consider that; discovering Dad is out there and I'm on my way to meet him and get my booster at the game isn't too bad a price for risking my life. Neither is getting Gran into Pine's Place. Neither is me moving in with Mary. All things considered, it doesn't feel all that selfless.

"I should be thanking you," I reply. "It's pretty cool about Pine's

Place." I stare out at the traffic streaking by, daydreaming about a time when maybe Mary and I are together like we are now, but with the needle on this romance moved a lot further. "Which reminds me," I say, sitting up straighter. "Mikey's taking the whole me-going-AWOL-through-his-window thing pretty well."

The corners of her eyes tighten as she lowers her chin and glues her gaze to the road. Her hands are at eleven and one.

"I mean, this whole plan you guys concocted. Gran to Pine's Place. You and me moving in together as a, you know, a...pretend couple." I gather a deep breath and swallow. "So did that plan come together before or after I bolted?"

"Edger—you do know you can't tell anyone. About being Zarathustra. The whole point of this is to keep your identity secret. Not just for your safety, but for everyone close to you."

"Oh yeah, yeah."

"And you know Mr. Dame's wrong about you."

"Yeah," I say, and my brain snaps back like a rubber band to the leg. "Wait a minute. Wrong about me. What do you mean?"

"It's cruel. Mr. Dame making you think you're throwing your life away."

"Oh." I shrug. "Yeah, well. I mean, you know. I'm a professional Dork. I'm not the Quarterback for the Chargers. I'm not the CEO of InstaTron—which, come on, is just a stupid name. I mean that is one seriously stupid name."

Mary laughs. "It *is* a stupid name! Oh my God."

"InstaTron? What the kumquat?"

"What the kumquat!"

"And Tron-Tron!"

"Oh. My. God." Mary looks at me, her face serious. Something in her eyes, a tiny glint suggestive of the rascally little girl she may once have been, makes me totally lose it—which of course makes her totally lose it. And next thing, my cheeks are hurting. Her laugh is rising from deep in her belly like a kid's laugh. It's hard for me to breathe. She snorts. I snort. It's fantastic. Her, the weather, the car, the football game, the superhero gig. We're moving in together! Gran's going to Pine's Place! And I haven't laughed like this since—

since Kate.

The laughter dies down. Mary runs a knuckle under the rims of her eyes. After a few more short bursts of laughter, it runs its course. We sit in silence. Mary's gaze is steady on the road. She has a faraway tint to her stare, the kind people get when they've gone inside their heads and forget the world is still operational. I wonder if she's feeling what I'm feeling. I wonder if this pretend-couple idea really is pretend. Because, to me, this feels like Kate. I know that's not fair. Mary isn't Kate. And our dynamic isn't the same. It's just that it's all so similarly improbable. Kate was out of my league too. Her charmed life swooped in and took over mine just like Mary is doing now. History's repeating itself, and I hope it won't end the same way.

"You know, this whole thing is making me think," says Mary, stealing me from my thoughts.

"About?"

"About me. About what I'm doing with my life. I think I'm suffering from a kind of professional embarrassment or something. Oh, man. I'm sorry. It's just… I guess…it's just, I feel like I can talk to you. I guess." She blushes and rests her forearm on the open window, her hand shielding the sun from her eyes, her hair streaming behind.

"Yeah, no," I say. "It's good. I like you talking to me. And you've got nothing to be embarrassed about. Are you kidding? You're driving a Jag. You're on the hunt for the world's first supervillain. And you're, like, what? Bodyguard to the world's first superhero?"

Mary frowns, and the expression looks uncharacteristically flustered.

"What?" I ask. "What is it?"

"Well. I guess I'm saying you've got your priorities down better than most. Better than me. You lost your parents and have been saving for your grandmother ever since, far as I can tell. You could've taken that money and partied it away in Vegas. You could've blown it on girls. Bought a fancy car, or a nice home, or—"

"Hey-hey-hey," I say. "That's creepy. Okay?"

"What?"

"Knowing all the intimate details of my life all the time."

"Edger, we talked about this. Secrets," she says, her tone making it plain she means me respecting her secrets.

"Yeah, but why does your secret get to be the secret of how you know all my secrets? That seems kind of one-sided."

"I can see why you'd think that, Edger," she replies, smiling. "But it isn't. Anyway, I guess my point is, if this whole experience has taught me anything, it's taught me that not everyone in this world has an angle. You're teaching me that, Edger."

This time, we both blush.

"Well, thanks," I reply. "But I should point out that as an orphan who just learned his dad is not only alive but is also somehow mixed up in all this, my lack of angle has become something of an angle."

"Shut up and take a compliment. You're a good guy. Leave it there, okay?"

I release a sigh and start picking at the weather stripping around the lowered window, trying to come up with something permissible to say after being told to shut up and take a compliment.

"You know, you never told me how you escaped that weird people zoo they stuck you in. The one where they 'gave you' a sister?"

"You're right, I didn't. That's very astute of you to remember that detail, Edger. You'll need to develop those skills going forward. But hey—good job." She touches my arm and then pulls her hand away, and the butterflies in my stomach drive off any further questions. I close my eyes and tilt my head back, basking in the sun and enjoying the charmed life, riding in this hot car, with this hot girl, on this perfect sunny day.

# CHAPTER FORTY-NINE

IN A MAZE of cars, minivans, pickup trucks, motorcycles, barbecue pits, soft-pretzel aromas, beverage hats, cheese heads, and a strikingly unusual concentration of fat, middle-aged men slathered in blue and yellow beer-gut paint, there sits the perfect replica of the cargo van used by the A-Team. Five trays of Very Special Brownies sit in the back. Wang and Shmuel sit outside. Presently, they are gorging themselves on Buffalo Wild Wings.

"Mm," says Shmuel. "These wings are goo-ood?"

"Dude. Don't be drippin' your shit on Mr. Mxyzptlk," Wang replies, using his foot to scoot the dog out from underneath Shmuel's dripping plate of Asian Wing sauce. "Go on, boy," says Wang. "Go find some nice guy's leg to hump."

Mr. Mxyzptlk trots off happily into the maze of good smells, tail wagging high.

"You know he only gets gay when he's stoned?" says Shmuel.

"Then that dog is only gay one hundred percent of the time," replies Wang, before sinking his teeth into another wing.

"Mm," says Shmuel. "So, what's the plan? Finish here and then go get everybody at the Cluck-n-Pray stoned?" Shmuel is fairly confident this is, in fact, the plan. But as he hasn't had his morning joint, the details of the plan they'd sketched out when he'd been stoned are, by Stoner's Natural Law, hazy. "I mean…dude. Are you sure about this?"

"Yeah, dude," replies Wang. "Consuelo says all the employees snack on the brownies. That means everybody'll get stoned. And once everybody's stoned, we get the cow—boom—we're gone. We'll be like two ninjas. In and out. Nobody'll know what hit 'em. You get your cow back. We stop Tron-Tron. We're coming out ahead."

"Ahead? Howdaya figure?"

"Duh. Debbie Three Holes, dumbass."

Shmuel frowns and chucks a wing bone at the trash, which misses by a solid three feet. Mr. Mxyzptlk will get it later, he guesses. "Aw, dude. I don't care about Debbie Three Holes. Wasn't even that great a Murder Mystery Night."

"Huh? Da fuck's wrong now?"

"I mean, nobody did the mystery, for one thing."

"We're doin' it now, man! Don't you see?"

"It's not really a mystery?"

Wang buries his face in his hands. "*Oh my God.*"

"I feel bad," says Shmuel. "We made a bad guy, dude. We made poor, sweet Chicowgo a bad guy. Chicowgo did bad things. Our baby."

"Hey—if that cow's our baby, then it's a *butt* baby. 'Cause last time I checked, two dudes cannot a baby make. All right? Now shut up about the butt babies."

Shmuel stares at his feet.

"Fuck, dude. Cheer up. All those people got their power back. No harm, no foul. Right?"

Still staring at his feet, Shmuel shrugs, then licks his fingers.

"Tron-Tron's still out there," says Wang. "It's down to you and me now. Think about it. We're the heroes San Diego deserves, but not the ones it needs right now, because they need us, I don't know, like, an hour from now, because we're the watchful guardians, with the pot brownies to get everybody high. Come on, dude. Get excited!"

But Shmuel can't bring himself to get excited because Wang's head is shaking again, as it does every time he gets hysterical. His bangs flop up and down, and Shmuel encounters another rare spotting of Wang's eyes.

"You have pretty eyes."

"Would you shut up about my pretty eyes! This is serious!"

"I know, I know," says Shmuel. "You never quote Batman unless it's serious." He thrusts his chin in the direction of the Q. "You really think we're gonna find Chicowgo at the Cluck-n-Pray?"

"Hell yes I do."

"And do you think she'll…like…know how to…talk and shit?"

Wang frowns. "Maybe, dude."

"Fuck."

*"I know."*

"And do you think she'll…like…don't laugh, okay?"

"What?"

"I don't know."

"No, no. It's okay. You can tell me. Shmuel, you may be a total walking, talking human hemorrhoid, but, come on. We're friends. Friends don't judge."

"You judged me about the Ness-crimes thing."

"Jesus Christ himself woulda judged you about the Ness-crimes thing."

"See? Judging."

"Ah—come on," says Wang. "This'll be different. We're friends."

"And I appreciate that, dude. Really."

"Of course, of course. So out with it. What is concerning you, my beautiful and boobalicious human hemorrhoid?"

"Do you think…do you think Chicowgo…will know…kung fu?"

"Shit," says Wang, chucking the rest of his wing bones into the trash and ripping open a package of wet naps. "I hadn't thought about that."

"I know, right?"

"Cow kung fu." Wang sticks his bottom lip out appraisingly, then shudders. "Shmuel, my friend, *that* may be a real fucking possibility."

# HISTORIC SACKING IN THE QUALCOMM STADIUM VISITING TEAM LOCKER ROOM, AS CHRONICLED BY HERODOTUS (C. 484—C. 425 BCE)

GREEN BAY PACKERS defensive tackle Yourmajesty Fapa'fapa-Bal'buster is six-foot-five inches tall, weighs two hundred ninety-six pounds, can dead lift nine hundred pounds relatively no problem—and is exceedingly uncomfortable in polite company.

This is because polite company lies like rugs.

Without exception, your high-society types, your governors, your politicians, your lawyers, your bankers and whatnot, tell at least nine lies a night.[1] But one lie in particular irks Green Bay Packers defensive tackle Yourmajesty Fapa'fapa-Bal'buster the most, and this is when polite company pretends to be shocked to discover he'd endured teasing as a child over his name. For the life of him, he cannot understand why anyone bothers.

On the occasion it comes up, which is to say—always—polite company tends first to turn extremely pale before conducting a hasty visual inventory of the room for the nearest door. When there are no

---

[1] Many will try to round it up to ten before conceding that nine really does flow better.

obvious means of escape, polite company will display a resolute interest in discussing the weather. Especially brazen souls sometimes go so far as to claim to have gone to school with at least *two* other kids named Yourmajesty, or Fapa'fapa-Bal'buster. Sometimes polite company will make polite inquiries into his genealogy, and whether there were any Native American Fapa'fapa-Bal'busters sitting down for Thanksgiving dinner with the Pilgrims.[2]

None of this is to say Yourmajesty cares about the childhood teasing. Kids take crap for all kinds of reasons. Besides, playing in the NFL, he is hardly alone. His Green Bay colleague, Ha Ha Clinton-Dix, and other NFL notables such as C.J. Ah You, Craphonso Thorpe, Fair Hooker, Ben Gay, Guy Whimper, John Booty, Dick Butkus, Yourhighness Morgan, or fellow islander Chris Fuamatu-Ma'afala also took crap over their names. But Yourmajesty did sometimes wonder if, just to pick an example at random, polite company had ever asked John Booty how many Bootys had come over on the Mayflower.[3]

The point is, the names only mattered insofar as they, like he, had grown up searching for acceptable outlets for dealing with them. And they, like he, had done just that. Over the past decade and a half, Yourmajesty has learned a thing or two about fate and names. He's learned he quite enjoys busting balls, for example. This, he does after the sacking of quarterbacks. He follows each with a swift, clandestine kick to the nuts. He just finds it to be satisfying, is all.

Sacking quarterbacks had turned out to be a lucrative form of violence. It'd earned him a college scholarship. Playing for USC, he finished with exactly thirty-four total quarterback sacks,[4] enough to put him into the record books. As defensive tackle for the Green Bay Packers, Yourmajesty Fapa'fapa-Bal'buster is determined to sack as many NFL quarterbacks (and bust as many balls) as possible. He even

---

[2] There were not.

[3] Of the 102 people aboard, there were indeed three Bootys: Thomas "Bubble" Booty, Richard "Dick" Booty, and Harold "Harry" Booty. Every Tom, Dick, and Harry on that boat was named Booty.

[4] Which becomes a total of sixty-eight ball busts at two nuts per sacked sack.

has a bounty going on the side, though the important people hanging around practice in suits tell him not to talk about such things where he could be overheard by the wrong ears.

And although Yourmajesty Fapa'fapa-Bal'buster can't wait to bust Caleb Montana's balls, he has nevertheless dallied in joining his team on the field for the pregame warm-up. This is because of the presence of a cow inexplicably loitering near the locker room vending machine. He does not know that the cow has an artificial intelligence in it; he does not know it has snuck off because it is curious about the Nostradamus plot involving a disco ball Chinese Water Torture Chamber with a bomb strapped to the bottom; nor that this device is hidden in the visiting team storage closet. No, Yourmajesty only knows he has been told earlier in no uncertain terms he is not allowed to have more performance-enhancing drugs today. He already has enough anabolic steroids coursing through his system to literally drop a cow. Which, he reasons, can be the only explanation for why he is staring at one right now.

# CHAPTER FIFTY

THE COW IS LEERING.

Twirling a strand of his dark, curly hair, Yourmajesty leers back. He pulls on his helmet and snaps the chin guard. He locks eyes with the animal. He drops to one knee, grinds his white-knuckled fist into the carpet, and digs his cleats in for a clean launch.

The cow copies him. That is, in its cow way: it bends its front knees and extends one hind leg, like a human. Like it knows how football works. Like *it* is preparing to sack *him*.

Yourmajesty's eyebrows lower. A droplet of sweat courses down his forehead, escapes his prominent eyebrow, and hits his face guard. He swallows; his stomach gurgles; a dangerous glint is in the cow's eyes.

Yourmajesty relaxes. He imagines Caleb Montana's voice. Yes, the game. The cow is preparation for the game. Sack the cow, then sack Montana. Then bust some balls. All in a day's work.

The locker room fades away in his mind's eye as he waits for the imaginary snap. His coiled muscles prepare to spring.

*Now!*

Yourmajesty releases a battle cry.

The cow releases a battle moo.

Helmet collides with the cow cranium, emitting a spectacular crack. He wraps his massive arms around the beast's neck—heaves leftward, muscles straining like hydraulics. His neck and back flex. The beast is hot and, oddly, smells like chicken. Its legs buckle. It falls, he falls. They crash into the vending machine. It tips, wobbles—and everything seems to happen at once.

He collapses onto the cow. A glob of snot fires out of its nose. He rolls onto his back, his wind knocked out and mouth reflexively springing open. The glob of snot makes an arc in the air as a can of Coca-Cola falls into the vending machine's receptacle. The snot glob plummets into Yourmajesty's gaping mouth. He swallows, chokes, gags. He rolls off the cow. He can't breathe!

The cow lurches to its feet, ducks its head, and staggers away from him. He hacks and spits. He spots the can of Coca-Cola; the cow trundles into the showers.

Gasping, he unsnaps his chin guard and rips off his helmet. He snatches the soft drink, pulls the tab, and chugs it back. Syrupy cola spills down his cheeks and neck, washing away the remnants of cow snot. When the can is empty, he releases a satisfyingly loud, long, and deep belch. His chest swells. He stands up straighter and turns to face the cowering beast pressed against the wall in the showers.

He stands still for a moment, his chest rising and falling as he basks in victory. He really does have enough performance-enhancing drugs in his system to drop a cow. He smiles. His stomach rumbles. His mouth begins to produce an abnormal amount of saliva. He swallows and licks his lips when, inexplicably, he's overcome by the enticing aroma of *really great grass*. Not that chemically fertilized stuff on the lawns back home. Not the Astroturf either. No, this is the *good* stuff. The hills-are-alive-with-the-sound-of-music stuff. Tasty, green, endless, peaceful.

He shakes his head to clear it.

*Weird.*

He looks down at the empty can of Coke in his hand, surprising himself he's still holding it. He drives it hard into the center of his forehead, crushing it paper thin, and tosses it into recycling.

His stomach rumbles again.

He frowns. Probably he's had too much protein in his diet recently. Yeah, he's sure that's it. A little nibble of grass ought to settle it. Sparing one last look at the cow, he tugs his helmet back on and snaps his chin guard, then begins the jog up the hallway to the field. He sets aside his newfound hankering for grass and focuses on the important point: game day, and he's already laid out a cow.

# CHAPTER FIFTY-ONE

"BUT OUR SEATS aren't anywhere near here," says Mary for the third time. We crest Section UV45. I turn to face her.

"Mary. Can you keep a secret?"

Her icy-blue eyes bore into mine. "Of course."

"I'm serious now. I'm asking you as…as my friend."

She glances over her shoulder, then steps out of the way as a man dressed like a human block of cheese struggles to fit himself into row 24.

"Yes, Edger," she says, her features unusually tense. "You can trust me like a friend."

I swallow and then blurt the words before I can overthink it. "I spoke to my dad."

Her mouth drops open. "What?"

"It's true. And I think he left me something. Wait here."

I leave her standing there gaping, and slide into row 25. I sidestep along the seats, counting as I go.

*Eight, nine, ten…*

"Where did this happen?" calls Mary.

"I found him in the—" I stop and look around. Besides Human Block of Cheese, there are easily fifty people within earshot. "I found him in that one place."

"You mean that…" Mary also looks around, then lowers

her voice, "...that *one* place?"

Seat fourteen—an envelope is beneath it! I carefully slide the envelope out from beneath the seat.

"What is it?" calls Mary. "Edger, what is it?"

Human Block of Cheese's head turns in response to her urgent tone. He cranes his neck around, then heel-toes his feet to the right, turning himself around so the tip of his stupid cheese wedge is pointed at me. His arms are straight out on either side like a dancing Oompa Loompa.

I hold the envelope up and smile. "Scavenger hunt."

Human Block of Cheese frowns.

"Nothing terrorist-y or anything like that," I say, forcing a chuckle. "Go Packers!"

Sparing me one last wordless frown, Human Block of Cheese's feet begin the slow tiptoe turn around shuffle, his arms bouncing at his sides. I smile and nod, and, once his back is to me, I tear open the envelope with shaking hands. Inside, there's only a piece of paper. I slide it out, unfold it. The words are in Dad's handwriting:

*Don't trust Mary.*

# CHAPTER FIFTY-TWO

"WHAT IS IT?" asks Mary. "What does it say?"

I cram the paper back into the envelope.

"Nothing. It says nothing."

I try to get around her, but the space is too narrow, and we're forced together. Her breasts press into me. Her hands gently cup my elbows. My synapses misfire in a weird and thrilling tangle of pheromones: I'm tasting her toned physique; seeing her lavender shampoo; hearing the moisture in her breath; feeling her crystal blue eyes. I stagger backward.

"Edger—stop. What is going on with you?"

I swallow. Clear my throat. She holds her hand out, demanding the packet. I shove it behind my back. Her gaze sharpens.

Bouncing arms in my peripheral vision give me an excuse to look away. Human Block of Cheese is turning around again. His left arm careens in between us, separating us, and sparing me the ice in her eyes.

"You should just give her the thing," he says, his voice shockingly nasal.

"What?" I ask. "Why?"

Mary's head starts bobbing up and down. "Yeah, Edger. Because that's what friends do. Friends trust each other."

Human Block of Cheese also nods. "Friends trust each other,

Escher," he says, for all the world like he knows me, and like the three of us came here together.

"Okay, first, it's Ed-*jer*," I reply.

"There's no 'I' in 'team'!" blurts Human Block of Cheese, sparing a sheepish smile for Mary. "Teamwork! Scavenger hunts don't work without teamwork, Escher."

Mary smiles back at the Human Block of Cheese. She lowers her chin and gazes up at him flirtatiously.

"Oh no," I say, pointing at her. "Oh no you don't."

"There's no 'I' in 'team,'" she says, her eyes going round. *"Escher."*

"My name is Mainard," says Human Block of Cheese, shifting so one of his Oompa Loompa hands sticks out in front of Mary. She shies away, staring at the hand for a second only before taking it and shaking. "Mary," she says. "It's nice to meet you, Mainard."

"Oh my God." I roll my eyes and tuck the envelope into my waistline at the small of my back. "Okay, fine. You can watch the game up here with Mainard, then."

Mainard smiles.

I leap over row 25 and into row 24 and scoot around the first person I come to, making apologies as I go, and pushing to the opposite end of the row, away from Mary.

"Edger! Edger!" calls Mary.

"Forget about him," says Mainard. "Hey. Want some cheese curds?"

"LADIES AND GENTLEMEN," a voice booms over the PA system. "PLEASE RISE FOR THE NATIONAL ANTHEM!"

"Edger!" calls Mary. "Edger!"

The shirtless, hairy-nippled, and body-painted guy in front of me stands, then lifts his enormous tower of nachos out of the way, nearly crashing it into his buddy on the other side and drenching him in hot yellow cheese. "Hey," he says, then releases a massive belch.

"Wow," I reply, fanning beer and nacho molecules away from my face.

"Hey," he says again, his tone more annoyed this time as he juts his chin out at the field. "It's the goddamn national anthem. Have you no dignity?"

"Right. Sorry."

I freeze and turn, awkwardly sandwiched between two slathered-in-face-and-body-paint Chargers fans, one holding the nachos, the other holding a twenty-three-ounce plastic beer cup with foam pouring out over the side, and all three of us facing the field with our hands on our hearts.

"*Oh-oh say can you see-ee...*"

I'm sweating. My brain is racing.

"*By the dawn's ear-ly li-ight...*"

What was my dad thinking, leaving that note and not the booster? Had he meant to leave it, then spotted me with her, and decided it wasn't safe?

"*By the twi-light's last glea-ming...*"

Does he think Mary is the mole? I cast a quick glance around twenty-three-ounce-beer guy. She's still stuck behind the lovesick block of human cheese.

"*Whose broad stripes and bright stars...*"

*Okay, Edge—think, think.* Compartmentalize. If Dad is here, he's not going to let me die. He knows I'm in trouble.

"*And the ro-ckets red gla-are—*"

Dad would want me to find InstaTron Tron. Probably.

"*The bombs bursting in air-rr—*"

Dad would want me to give my life, if it meant changing the world. Wouldn't he?

"*Gave proo-oof through the ni-ight...*"

I grit my teeth. My back finds its steel. The music washes over me, and my throat swells and my eyeballs are stinging. My left hand, the one that isn't over my heart, searches for the Z-ring lump in my pocket. The crowd erupts in applause. The guys on my left and right are screaming like maniacs and splitting my eardrums. I wince, frown, and then smile back at them before pushing my way to the end of the row where three short steps lead to the concession area.

"Edger!"

I glance over my shoulder. Beer and Nachos are hogging the aisle, holding Mary hostage to the belly-painted manliness working overtime to charm, smiling, talking, winking. Mary veers left, veers right. She's a prizefighter in a skirt. I frown, suddenly uncertain. Would she kick those guys' butts to get to me?

*Forget it, Edge. Move!* comes a familiar voice from my subconscious.

*Bruce Lee?*

*Yes—it's time to hurry. Tron-Tron just popped up in the Collective Unconscious.*

*What? How—?*

*He sacked a cow in the locker room.*

*Okay. I'm not sure that cleared anything up.*

I scan left and right for the men's room—there! I make a beeline, not chancing another glance for Mary. Inside, I find the first available stall. I slam the door and lock it. Digging out the ring, I take a deep breath and slip it on.

The world explodes into a sonic boom of stars and stripes.

# CHAPTER FIFTY-THREE

WANG DUCKS BEHIND the postcard rack in the gift shop. Once the two security guards race past, he spins to face Shmuel, who is wearing a pair of Chargers sunglasses, a Chargers ski hat, three Chargers chain necklaces, and four Commemorative Chargers rings on each hand.

"What the hell are you doing?" snaps Wang.

"Shopping?"

"Put all that stuff back!"

"Imma get me some gold front teeth," says Shmuel, grinning into the mirror at the top of the sunglasses rack.

"Dude, we don't have time for this! Those guys are going after Chicowgo right now!"

"They are?" Shmuel takes off his shades and puts them back on the rack. "Now? How do you know?"

"I heard it on their radios. Chicowgo is in the visiting team's locker room."

"Well, that's right over there." Shmuel points without looking over his shoulder in the correct direction. Wang bites his lip, then drags Shmuel around to the other side of the sunglasses rack, so they're obscured from the guard sitting next to the door with the big letters over it that spell: OFF LIMITS. Shmuel pushes Wang's blocking arm down and peers around the sunglasses rack to where the guard is finishing his lunch from a Cluck-n-Pray bag.

"Is that...is that one of *our* brownies?"

Wang nods.

"Well, that's convenient," says Shmuel, his eyebrows going up. "I mean, the *one* guard we need to sneak past to get Chicowgo back just *happens* to be eating one of our Very Special Brownies?"

Wang turns around to face him. "What's your point?"

"Just doesn't seem very *plausible* is all I'm saying."

"Plausible? Plausible?" Wang frowns. "What are you, a fucking movie critic? Look. Just chat him up for five secs. I'll slip by, take the elevator down, and get your damn cow back. How's that sound?"

"I think it doesn't sound very plausible?"

"Yeah? Well, that's what they said about Donald Trump, and look how that turned out."

"Shit, dude. You think the Russians are gonna make the Green Bay locker room great again?"

Wang's eyes narrow. "Can you do your part of the job or not?"

"Chat up the security guard while you get Chicowgo back? Sure. But I don't think it's such a good idea to talk politics? I don't know who he voted for."

Wang shoves him toward the security guard. "Big surprise. You don't know who you voted for either, now get going!"

# CHAPTER FIFTY-FOUR

THE SOUL-STARS materialize and surround me. The light is blinding. I've got ten minutes. That's how long the sleep timer on my suit is set for. After that, I'll wake up and find out whether anyone has beaten down the door of the bathroom stall, or if I'm still safely passed out on the crapper in my costume like a constipated narcoleptic cosplayer at Comic-Con.

The light thins and stretches and becomes like pale smoke. The outline of a man takes shape. Bruce Lee. He's in that yellow-and-black tracksuit he wore in *Game of Death*. He waves the smoke away from his face, blinks and coughs, and then turns a bright smile on me.

"S'up, Edge," he says. "Tron-Tron blown up the planet yet?"

"Not funny," I reply.

Bruce Lee gives me a tight smile.

"Can you help me find him?" I ask.

"Yes, of course."

He closes his eyes, and the smoke around us thickens. It isn't the choking, black smoke you get from a bus. This is phantasmal and limitless, like a fog rolling out to sea. It envelops us, dissolving first our arms and legs, then our bodies, necks, and heads. Soon I can only feel Bruce Lee in my mind. We're formless. The world is gone beneath our feet. My skin feels charged like I'm storing static electricity. I gather more of it, like rubbing wool on my hair except on the inside of my brain. Tiny sparks erupt as errant particles release. Strange and innocuous sensory experiences flash through my mind's eye.

The smell of beer.

The raw-in-the-back-of-your-throat taste of a cold.

A tongue-sizzling bite of a Spicy Wrath of God Deluxe sandwich.

The dizzying bite of a marijuana brownie.

I concentrate. A clearer picture begins to form: the silky material of an official NFL jersey. A name on the back. Montana. But this jersey isn't worn by Caleb. It's worn by a fan screaming his lungs out over a call on the field.

Brain zaps. Releasing energy. Streaking pinpoints of light.

I'm on the field. I'm wearing a black-and-white-striped shirt, black pants, and a hat. My lower back hurts from a bad night's sleep. I'm grouchy, and I'm taking it out on Coach Lynn, whose face is distorting like a…a lava lamp.

The world is a swirl of colors. The pins-and-needles intensity in my head diminishes. The bright fog returns. My hands and arms and body are back. And here's Bruce Lee in his yellow-and-black tracksuit.

"What's happening?" I ask as the fog dissipates completely. Bruce Lee's eyebrows lower.

"This is dangerous," he says. "But I've found them. So it doesn't matter."

"If there's something dangerous, I think it matters," I reply. "I should know about it."

"It's what you already know. Accessing too much of the Collective Unconscious will overload your brain."

"But that was amazing! I mean—it was like I was actually in their bodies! I went into a referee! I was yelling at Coach Lynn!"

Bruce Lee sighs. "*You* weren't yelling at Coach Lynn. The *referee* was yelling at Coach Lynn."

"Okay, okay," I say. "But it was like… I was him. It felt like I was him."

"This is something you shouldn't be doing. Your supersuit must have given you this power. Maybe because it's supposed to have InstaTron Tron programmed into it to safeguard against blowing up your brain. This is out of my wheelhouse, Edge. Maybe Killmaster would know more—"

"You said you found him," I cut in. "Did you mean you found InstaTron Tron?"

"Yes. He's in a football player. He's in one of the Packers. Big guy. Has a taste for...grass." Bruce Lee frowns.

"Huh. Okay, whatever. Hey, Caleb said Nostradamus might have spies playing for the Packers."

"Well, that's the other problem."

"Other problem?" I ask. "What other problem?"

"The spies. Nostradamus agents. They're here too. And they're not playing for the Packers."

"But you just said—"

"I know what I said," Bruce Lee snaps. "Shut up and listen. InstaTron Tron is in a Green Bay Packer. But Nostradamus spies are converging on the Packers' locker room. They believe InstaTron Tron is in a cow. But your father is here also, and he is after the cow too."

"Cow? As in, Cow Phil Collins?"

"Will you forget about the cow? Your father is on a collision course with Nostradamus agents."

"Then what are we waiting for?" I ask. "Wake me up! Wake me up!"

"I can't. You're in the suit. This encounter is being controlled by the suit, not me."

My stomach knots in frustration. Dad's out there right now. He needs me.

"Listen, Edge. InstaTron Tron isn't going anywhere. He's got a football game to play. May I suggest we focus on the Nostradamus agents?"

"You mean the ones after my dad? Good idea!"

"Good. Now listen. They have guns."

"So what? You're Bruce Lee. You can handle guns."

Bruce Lee rolls his eyes. "Sure. *If I had guns*. You must think I'm as crazy as the people who designed your supersuit. What were they thinking, not giving you any firearms? Probably watch too many kung fu movies."

"Says the king of kung fu movies," I counter. "Look, I've got ninja throwing stars."

Bruce Lee rolls his eyes again. "Which would be great if we were living in feudal Japan." Bruce Lee pauses. His eyes flit up and left. He strokes his chin. "Hey. Wait a minute."

"What?" I ask, sensing a sliver of sunshine cutting through the gloomy psychic outlook he's been projecting. "What is it?"

He smiles. "There's someone I think you should meet."

# HISTORY OF THE NINJA: HAN; COOKIE THIEF OF DESTINY, BY HERODOTUS (C. 484—C. 425 BCE)

BEING THE DEADLIEST martial art known to humankind, and a secret society where stealth was valued above all else, the true history of ninjutsu is like a mystery wrapped in an enigma, which is then wrapped in yaki nori, cream cheese, cucumber and carrot slices, and then pressed firmly into a bed of sticky rice and served with a side of wasabi and pickled ginger. No living historian has accurately traced ninjutsu's origins.

One theory, put forward by the late German historian Gunther von Gunthervon, has ninjutsu originating in China in the ninth century, and advances some flimflam about dragons, jade chopsticks, fireworks, rickshaws, pagodas, and—because he had a thing for offensive stereotypes—Mickey Rooney, from *Breakfast at Tiffany's*.

This theory is false.

Another theory, this one posited by the late Joseph "Jo-Crusty" Pages, has ninjutsu originating in the camps of deserters from the Yamato-Goguryeo War (391-404). In this theory, bested Yamato soldiers hid in the mountains and developed various survival techniques to avoid capture, including whittling bamboo caltrops and shuriken, and drafting on the backs of lotus leaves plans for a superior weapon, the differentially hardened katana blade which wouldn't be invented for another thousand years.

This theory is also false.

The real origin of ninjutsu began with a cunning five-year-old boy.

The founding father of ninjutsu grew up in a small village near Yamashiro. His name was Han. Like many children in his day, Han possessed an insatiable passion for freshly baked cookies. So did his four brothers and five sisters. Together, they shared a hut with extremely creaky floorboards, a tiny mouse, and a mother possessing the hearing powers of a bionic beagle. On those occasions when the mouse didn't get the cookies first, Han and his siblings would conspire on how best to work around their mother's formidable hearing—but never with success. His mother's aural gifts were too great, and her retribution—a swift kick to the butt—too swift. One by one Han's siblings gave up, abandoning Han to his lonely obsession. Finally, Han was the only child left with the grit to continue. It was then that Han went solo.

Necessity being the mother of all invention, Han, this would-be Cookie Child of Destiny, was a boy of initiative. Striking out on his own, Han developed no fewer than ten different "Silent Paths of the Cookie." Today, these supersecret stealth techniques are known as "ninja walking."

Sadly, the founding father of ninjutsu grew old and fat and died of complications due to a mouthful of abscessed teeth. But before he flying-side-kicked the bucket, he first passed on everything he had learned to his son. And that son (who also died old and fat and with a mouthful of abscessed teeth) passed on all his knowledge to his two sons. And a good thing there were two sons here, for one of the two brothers, having lost both a father and grandfather to what essentially amounted to a bunch of untreated cavities, vowed to devote himself to a life of dentistry. And just think, if there hadn't been a second son to continue the secret art of cookie walking, ninjutsu might've been lost forever.

But ninjutsu wasn't lost forever.

Eventually, the great-great-great grandson grew to be a man and moved to the mountains, where all the fashionable peasants were going, to a place called Iga. There, for hundreds of years, the secret art thrived, developing into the deadly capital of ninjutsu historians have come to revere today.

Hattori Hanzo (1542-1596) is easily the most famous of these Iga ninjas. He did not have a thing for sweets. In fact, he trained his ninja villagers to eschew all foods contributing to body odor, since being an effective ninja meant being invisible to all the senses, and how bad would it have sucked to scale the castle wall, made it past all the security guards, literally spidered across the ceiling to sneak up on the person you're about to assassinate, only to tip him off with a bad case of the zombie armpits? Here, the Historical Society of Dead Historians strike a rare accord: that indeed would have straight-up sucked.

# CHAPTER FIFTY-FIVE

"EDGER BONKOVICH, HATTORI HANZO. Hattori Hanzo, Edger Bonkovich," says Bruce Lee.

"Charmed," I say, offering my hand to shake.

Hattori Hanzo is wearing the traditional black ninja threads. His eyes lower to take in my hand, then scan right to take in Bruce Lee. He steps back and clasps his hands together, making this weird ninja knuckle wrap thing with his fingers, and bows. I try to copy him with the ninja hands, pop a knuckle, and decide to cool it and just go for the bow instead.

[*"How may I be of assistance?"*] asks Hattori Hanzo.

*["Hey—I can understand—but you're—you're speaking in Japanese!"*] I exclaim, and my eyes widen. [*"Wait a minute. I'm speaking in Japanese! Wax on, wax off!"*]

*["Mr. Bonkovich requires your expertise in overpowering men with guns,"]* says Bruce Lee.

*["You're speaking in Japanese too!"]* I cry. "This is so dope!"

Next thing I know, our entire situation flashes before my eyes as Bruce Lee brings Hattori Hanzo up to speed: schematics for Qualcomm Stadium, locations of enemy targets, security personnel, exit routes—all of it in fast-forward, just like when Killmaster did it in Emerald Plaza. Bruce Lee even teaches Hattori Hanzo the finer points of

American football. All this flashes before my eyes in a second.

"Whoa," I say, my heart positively banging in my chest.

*"Whoa,"* agrees Hattori Hanzo, who faces me and pulls up his ninja mask. His features are smooth and youthful. His eyes are twinkling with mischief. He looks nothing like what I imagine a ninja would look like. Which would be Sho Kosugi, I guess, the icy bad guy from *Enter the Ninja*. But Hattori Hanzo looks more like Robin Shou, that nice guy who kept Chris Farley from stabbing himself in the penis in *Beverly Hills Ninja*.

"Well, Mr. Bonkovich," says Hattori Hanzo in stiff English, smiling. "It's Game Day."

His face fades and becomes translucent as the timer on my suit expires. My limbs become light, like they're inflated by helium. My hair stands on end. The soul-stars spin down from the sky and snatch me in a funnel cloud made from the lives of our distant ancestors.

I wake up in a graffitied bathroom stall. Through the Collective Unconscious, I can sense Hattori Hanzo and Bruce Lee are still there. I can also sense that I'm alone in the bathroom. A surge of relief flashes through me that I won't be seen exiting the stall dressed like Batman's armored space ninja cousin.

*[Hurry!]* calls Hattori Hanzo. *[No one is looking!]*

He seizes control of me. My shoulder slams into the stall door, rattling my teeth and snapping it off the hinges as I barge into the empty bathroom. My head is light, and it's like I'm in this out-of-body trance as he produces a tiny but heavy black marble from my utility belt. The rapidly auto-assembling nano-fibers transform the ball in a matter of seconds. A grappling gun solidifies before my eyes.

*[Amazing!]* Hattori Hanzo exclaims.

*Holy crap,* I reply. The grappling gun is black and chrome. The scent of gun oil wafts into my mask's breathing filter. *I don't care how many times I see that happen. It's never gonna get old.*

I race out of the men's room, Hanzo timing it so no one is looking. He fires the grappling hook into the rafters. I rocket into the air. My right shoulder jerks and my left hand snatches the right for support; arms and abs strain under the effort. The reel whistles. My stomach knots. Rafters rush up at me. My legs swing forward. The momentum carries me over the beams, the cable wrapping once as I alight on the balls of my feet without a sound and using the heads-up display to shrink the device. The cable unwraps, sizzles back, and I return a tiny black marble to its pouch on my belt in one smooth motion. Hanzo, who is still in control of my body, has me shake my head.

*[We must focus. The enemy is on the move.]*

"Hey, Mommy, look."

The voice is coming from the drinking fountain near the women's room, where a freckled little girl in a Wonder Woman shirt is tugging on her mother's arm and pointing at me with her free hand. She is literally the only person in the mezzanine level not preoccupied with something else. Hattori Hanzo has me grab a throwing star on my utility belt. My left arm grabs my right arm as I struggle to take back control.

*Are you insane?* I exclaim.

*[She will expose us!]*

Through the Collective Unconscious, I double down for control; my arms jerk violently up and down, left and right and, for a minute, I'm teetering on the rafter looking like I'm battling one of those possessed monkey paws.

*You can't throwing star a little girl!* I yell.

*[Can too!]*

*What he means is—you* shouldn't *throwing star a little girl,* says Bruce Lee, and Hanzo grudgingly yields control.

*[Oh,]* says Hattori Hanzo. *[Well, I don't like the look of her.]*

Having won back control, I promptly lose balance. I tip left, my arms shoot out right. Hattori Hanzo seizes control again and allows me to fall backward; my right hand shoots up and closes on the beam, and my momentum carries me in a circle—nearly pulling my shoulder out of its socket. A second later, I'm perching on the balls of my feet again and rubbing my sore shoulder.

Little Wonder Woman is gaping up at me, one eye scrunched and the other wide open. I gesture with my finger for her to turn around. She doesn't even blink. Huh. Maybe it's because of the whole monkey-paw-trapeze-artist thing. Or maybe it's because I look like a space ninja.

I gesture again with a little loop of the finger.

*Come on, little girl. Turn around.*

She doesn't. I try again—this time thrusting my palms in the direction of the football field to her right, then miming my head exploding from the awesomeness of being at a Charger's game. *Hey-hey. Check out Caleb Montana. Amaze-balls, right?*

Nothing.

"Mommy, Mommy!" she cries.

"No-no!" I whisper, putting my finger to my lips. "Shh! Shh!"

"It!" says the girl, making a tiny jump and grinning.

I wave my hands, shake my head. "Stop that," I whisper. "Shh!"

"It!" says the girl, beaming.

"Shh—"

"—it!"

"Sh—"

"—it!" The girl giggles. "We're saying shit!"

"Susie!" The girl's mother hauls off and slaps her. Hattori Hanzo seizes control of me. We race down the beam, silent as a mouse.

# CHAPTER FIFTY-SIX

WANG HAD SLIPPED past Reggie the security guard no problem. Since then, however, he'd been taking his sweet time. He'd been down in that locker room for somewhere going on less than an hour, but definitely more than five minutes. The brownies made it difficult to know for sure.

Shmuel stuffs another one in his mouth. He leans back in his seat. Reggie the security guard had been good enough to provide an extra folding chair once he learned there'd be more brownies involved. He even joked about deputizing Shmuel, which sounded pretty good until he'd said something about Shmuel being "honorary vomit cleaner upper." That didn't sound like a legitimate form of security, no matter what Reggie said.

Reggie laces his hands behind his head. He kicks his feet up on the pillar and smiles.

"Bein' a security guard at the Q ain't all football and brownies, you know," says Reggie at the same time his walkie-talkie squeals with static. He adjusts the volume dial, sighs, and peers off into the rafters like they hold the secrets to the universe. Which, in Shmuel's experience, they just might. "Sometimes you gotta be sleuthy."

"No shit?" asks Shmuel.

"No shit. Take your basic cow."

Shmuel's sits abruptly upright. "Uh—my cow?"

"Well, yeah," says Reggie, his face going screwy. "I mean, not yours specifically. It's a manner of speech. You know, like 'take your basic Shakespeare,' or 'take your basic Bible,' or 'take your basic surgical scalpel.'"

"Where are we takin' all this stuff?" asks Shmuel, a flash of suspicion surging through him. In his experience, security wasn't supposed to be in the business of stealing.

"No, no, no," says Reggie. "We're not taking anything anywhere. I mean 'your,' like, 'how well do you know your Machiavelli,' or, 'how well do you know your classical history,' or 'how well do you know your Chargers' stats.'"

"Not well?" Shmuel frowns. He hoped there wouldn't be a test. He hated tests. There must be an easier way to become a security guard at the Q. Seemed an awful lot of trouble just to clean up vomit.

"No, no," says Reggie, dropping his feet to the floor. He scoots his chair back and faces Shmuel. "I don't mean yours personally. I mean yours universally. The *universal* 'yours.'"

"Oh!" cries Shmuel, laughing. "The universal yours!"

"Yeah. The universal yours."

"Kinda like the royal wee-wee?"

Reggie's head jerks back. He blinks and goes still. Shmuel smiles, getting into it.

"Yeah, yeah," he says. "I gotcha. I know what you mean. You mean like, 'your basic hammer,' or 'your basic bong,' or, 'your basic stash.'"

"Okay. Yeah. That's it." Reggie nods, his face still screwy as he scoots his chair back to where it'd been and again puts up his feet. "Yeah," says Reggie, peering into the rafters. "Your basic hammer."

"Your basic stash," says Shmuel, before adding, "but not mine, though?"

"No. Not yours," Reggie agrees. "Everybody's."

"*Everybody's* basic stash? I don't have enough for *everyone*."

"Universal," says Reggie.

"Oh, right, right." Shmuel releases a sigh and puts his feet up also. But not before taking another brownie from the tray. After some chewing, he says, "Would be awesome to find that universal stash, though? There really should be a universal stash?"

"Sleuthy," says Reggie.

"I mean, if it's universal…you wouldn't have to be sleuthy? It'd be kinda like a community garden? That's the whole point of it being universal?"

"No, no," says Reggie. "What we were talking about before. Bein' sleuthy."

"Oh, right." Shmuel squints. "Bein' sleuthy."

"Take your basic cow. The one in the locker room."

Shmuel gives him the side-eye. "Not my cow, though, right?"

"No, no. The *universal* cow."

"Right. Universal cow. Royal wee-wee."

"Us security guards've gotta be clever. I mean, what's a cow doin' in a locker room in the first place? What motivates him? Is it all primal instinct—or is it something more? And why's it in Green Bay's locker room? I mean, is it from Wisconsin? Does Wisconsin have a better variety of grass than San Diego? Or is this about cheese and dairy products and so forth?"

"Ri-ight, ri-ight," says Shmuel, impressed, despite knowing Reggie had it all wrong. Chicowgo hated the Packers. And she'd eat just about anything. Left-foot shoes, for example. Those were the ones he could never find. "You really know your universal basic shit from your universal basic shinola, huh?"

"Oh, yeah." Reggie's feet come back down. His eyes are tense as he scoots his chair nearer Shmuel. He glances over his shoulder, apparently to see if anyone is near enough to eavesdrop. Shmuel checks also. Except for the two identical and suspicious-looking men-in-black standing near the women's room that'd been watching them like hawks ever since Wang snuck down to the locker room, there was nothing unusual.

"You wanna know what I think?" asks Reggie, his tone hushed and breath reeking of chocolate and pot.

"What?"

"I think it might be a government operation."

"Nuh-uh!"

Reggie nods. "Uh-*huh*." Reggie scans the mezzanine level, his gaze passing right over the creepy men-in-black like he didn't see them, but Shmuel suspected he probably did see them and was just so amazing at the sleuthing part of his job that he could convincingly pretend he hadn't seen them. It was really something to see.

"Don't look now," says Reggie. "But there're two government agents standing next to the men's room, another two over by the food truck, and *another* two by C Gate."

Despite the "don't look now" part of Reggie's statement, Shmuel's gaze moves with a mind of its own. He'd already identified the two suspicious-looking men-in-black near the women's room, but, lo and behold, there are the others, right where Reggie had gestured. They're wearing identical black suits and sunglasses. And matching haircuts too, right down to the pomade pâté on top. They even have identical right angle jawlines, thick, bushy eyebrows, and pointy noses. It's like they're twins, except there're more than two of them. He could only conclude these government agents must be sexytuplets.

"Whoa," he says.

Reggie nods. "You're staring."

Shmuel licks his lips. "Dude. They look so alike."

"Uh-huh," replies Reggie. "You're still staring. And do you know what else?"

"What?"

"There's an armored space ninja in the rafters."

"Bullshit!"

Shmuel's gaze snaps to the rafters and spots a black-and-chrome armored space ninja running along a beam like…well… After all the pot brownies he'd eaten, the space ninja running along the beam looked like a centipede space ninja who is also running along a beam, except without ninety-eight of its legs.

"Shmuel."

"Yeah?"

"Stop staring."

Shmuel lowers his gaze.

"Sleuthy," says Reggie.

Shmuel breaks into a cold sweat. He sinks into what he hopes is a nonchalant slouch in the back of his plastic seat back. Then he licks his lips self-consciously.

"Play it cool, man," says Reggie, stuffing his face with another brownie. "Play it cool. I happen to be a highly trained professional."

"Huh," says Shmuel, his neck straining against the urge to look directly at the space ninja in the rafters. That's definitely some shit you don't see every day. "So… I guess that's what you'd call your basic armored space ninja."

"Huh?" snaps Reggie. "He's not my armored space ninja. I figured he was yours."

# CHAPTER FIFTY-SEVEN

TED AND ED stand with their arms folded before the white picket fence, a plot of plastic grass, and no cow.

"Where's the cow?" asks Ted. "Shouldn't there be a cow? I thought you said there'd be a cow."

"Can't drop felony charges without a felony-charge-dropping cow," says Ed.

Judas blurts, "Saboteurs—"

"Saboteurs?" says Ed, snatching his sunglasses from his face.

Judas steps back. Ted and Ed always wore their sunglasses. Now Judas saw why. Ed's eyes are two gleaming caricatures of cray-cray with a quivering side of arched eyebrow. The effect: Maniac Level: Hugo Weaving.

"I mean," says Judas, shrugging. He scrubs a finger under his nose and sniffs. "Saboteurs. Yeah."

"What kind of saboteurs?" asks Ted.

Judas clears his throat, unsure how best to field this one. "Yeah, well…uh…" A hand on Judas's arm shatters his already confused focus.

"Uh, sir?" asks Sheldon, who has abandoned his position inside the food truck.

"What is it?" he snaps, snatching his arm back, and surging with relief to have a subordinate to boss around. This, at least, is familiar to him. “Can’t you see we’re in the middle of something, *Team Member Sheldon*?”

“Yes, sir,” Sheldon replies. “It’s just—I found the cow!”

“What? No, no, no. *You* don’t find the cow. *I* find the cow.”

“Okay, sir,” says Sheldon, pointing. “Then find it over there!”

Judas, Ted, and Ed turn to face the direction Sheldon is pointing, where a short Asian dude in a Chargers jersey, cargo shorts, and flip-flops is sneaking their cow behind a security guard stationed at an elevator about twenty yards from where they’re standing.

“The saboteur!” yells Judas. “That’s our cow!”

## HISTORIC SORTING OUT OF THE COMPLICATED SIMULTANEOUS ACTION, AS CHRONICLED BY HERODOTUS (C. 484—C. 425 BCE)

AT THIS POINT, events proceed faster than the speed of your basic universal narrative.

Shmuel, deducing Wang needs help, and taking inspiration from the football game, shoots from his chair, a flabby, low-flying cannonball, and sacks the nearest of the two men-in-black near the women's room. Not to be outstripped by a civilian deputy, Reggie races toward the second man, Taser shoved out in front. He opens his mouth to yell, "Stop right there!" but, as he has consumed one too many pot brownies, says instead, "Stopper-rare!"

The naughty little girl in the Wonder Woman shirt who's just had her mouth rinsed out with soap for saying "shit," emerges from the women's room, spots Reggie charging toward her with a Taser and yelling, "Stopper-rare!"—and screams. Wonder Girl's mother, who goes to kickboxing classes four days a week and CrossFit the other three, also screams. Recalling her training, she launches into an uncanny impersonation of a traditional Cossack Dance, kicking all four men in the nuts. Wonder Girl ceases screaming long enough to appreciate her mother's martial arts application, for she has brought her coloring book to all her mother's classes and has a vested interest in seeing it all come together. Satisfied the immediate danger is neutralized, Wonder Girl resumes her screaming.

Wang, meanwhile, squeezes his arms around Chicowgo's neck—and just in time; Chicowgo bounds off in terror toward Gate C. Wang's feet lift from the ground. He hangs on for life and limb. And, amidst all the screaming, he lends his own to the rest, a pure-in-tone boy soprano which cuts high above the Amazonian battle cries coming from the restroom area and the crowd noise coming from the field.

At the cow-less cow display, Judas Christian poses the question, "*What the fuck?*"

On the opposite side of the stadium, completely unaware of the chaos unfolding near Gate C, Christine of the El Cerrito Cluck-n-Pray wrinkles her nose. A terrible smell has risen as if from a Jurassic bog. She raises an arm, sniffs her pits. She calmly locates her purse, roots around for deodorant, finds it, and applies through the neck hole of her shirt.

Meanwhile...

Mistaking Judas's question as rhetorical, Ted and Ed make no reply, instead drawing their identical Sig Sauer P225 A1 Nitron Compacts and deciding without hesitation it is time to be getting on with the shooting part of their job description.

Two other Nostradamus agents, Ned and Zed, these stationed near Gate C, draw their sidearms also. They aim at the cow bearing down on them, uncaring it is carrying an Asian male with a beautiful falsetto voice on its back.

Wang, seeing two men with guns aimed at him, clenches his eyes and lies as flat as possible astride the cow. A bullet passes directly through the middle of the airspace where Wang's head had been, and into the tile on the wall near the women's bathroom. It shatters with a crack and rains asbestos on Shmuel, Reggie, Fred, and Jed, who are writhing on the floor and cradling pomegranate-size testicles.

Seventy-seven NFL fans milling about the mezzanine level near Gate C notice the charging cow, screaming, and gunshot—and freak out.

Six ninja shuriken slice through the air in such quick succession, they may as well have been thrown simultaneously. All six find the shooting hands of their targets. The Nostradamus agents drop their weapons and cry out like shih tzus whose tails have been slammed in car doors because their owners were checking their phones and not paying attention to what they were doing. Smoke bombs detonate in three precise locations. When the smoke clears, Ted, Ed, Fred, Jed, Ned, and Zed are hanging upside down by their twelve ankles—and, to the shock of seventy-seven freaking-out NFL fans, one armored space ninja glides to the ground on an unseen cable obscured by the still-clearing smoke.

# CHAPTER FIFTY-EIGHT

THIS IS HOW IT FEELS TO BE A SUPERHERO. My heart is trying to punch a hole in my chest. My hands are shaking. I'm weak in the knees, struggling to catch my breath, and my lower back hurts from being hunched over for so long. Also, I have to pee.

I clench up, hold my breath, and leap from the beam, the grappling-hook reel whistling as I glide to the ground. My boots touch down. A shock careens through my spine. I run off the momentum before turning on my heels and skidding to a stop. The grappling gun shrinks into a tiny marble, and I slip it back inside its pouch on my belt. I take in my surroundings in a hurried sweep. Big, strong guys cowering behind trash cans. Screaming kids clutched in fearful parents' arms. A group of teenage girls racing into the women's room. Police charging toward me, guns drawn.

"On your knees! Get down!"

Every muscle in my body clenches up. I raise my hands in surrender.

*Edger!* calls Bruce Lee.

Is my supersuit bulletproof? Honestly, I can't remember. Seems like that should've been my first question, hindsight being 20/20 and all.

*Edger!* Bruce Lee calls again.

I go to my knees, hands still raised.

*[What are you doing?]* asks Hanzo.

*[I'm banking on one of you guys knowing how to get me out of this,]* I reply.

A police officer built like a Hummer shares a cautious glance with his partner before holstering his gun and unfastening a pair of handcuffs from his belt. Bruce Lee and Hattori Hanzo fight for control of me. Hanzo will kill. That fact is shining like a beacon in my head.

"Lie down!" yells Hummer. He circles behind me and unnecessarily kicks me in the back—in the process royally pissing off both dead martial arts legends in my head. My body goes cold. I shiver as one of the two seizes control, there's no telling which. I tumble forward, roll, come back up to my knees, and unleash a batch of marbles. They transform mid-flight into throwing stars. Shots are fired. Shooting hands are impaled.

"Ooh—sorry about that!" I say in my supersuit voice. A wave of relief surges through me as, from the Collective Unconscious, I know immediately no one's been shot.

Hummer darts in from behind, his arm reaching for a headlock. I spin and lift my arm over and under his, easily trapping his arm above the elbow and forcing him to his toes. My left forearm strikes him hard in the jugular. He crashes to his knees, gasping for breath, his body turning limp. I jump-spin-back-kick him in the liver, and Hummer's out like sauerkraut.

"I'm sorry!" I yell, dizzy from all the spinning.

Movement in my peripheral vision. I whip around. The three remaining cops are not where I left them. Two have scooted off behind a broad concrete column and are nursing injured hands. The third has managed to draw his Taser. He staggers forward, trying to get into range.

"Oh, yeah, no," I say stupidly. "Um… I don't want any of the voices in my head to have to, um…you know, hurt you."

*Fifteen feet*, says Killmaster from out of nowhere.

*Welcome to the party,* I reply, raising my hands and taking several retreating steps.

*That model's range is fifteen feet,* says Killmaster. *If you don't want to get zapped, don't let him within fifteen feet, sir.*

*[If there isn't to be any killing, may I suggest we leave?]* says Hanzo, his psychic sense thoroughly exasperated.

*Hey—these are Americans, Sushi Roll,* says Killmaster. *Cool your Japanese jets.*

*Would you two shut up already and just get us out of here?* I reply.

My right hand snatches the marble-size grappling hook; the left drops a smoke bomb. I activate the grappling hook, and it transforms into full size. A minute later, we're scaling a beam on the outer wall of Qualcomm Stadium like Spider-Man.

# CHAPTER FIFTY-NINE

TO CLARIFY, IT ISN'T much of a wall. It's a concrete beam running parallel to another concrete beam spaced six feet apart. Then it's another four yards to the next pair of beams, and it repeats like that all the way around the stadium.

I'm dangling from the cable against a concrete beam, my heartbeat resonating back at me. A bird swoops past my head, startling me. I flinch and twist crazily on the line. I'm gripping the line so hard, my hands are shaking. I force myself to relax. I swallow and my back slams into the wall, and I spot the bird again. It shrinks in scale against a dizzying backdrop of evacuating crowds, cars, and flagpole tops that look like toothpicks stuck to cardboard slabs. I shake my head, trying to clear it.

The bird stretches its wings. It rides the gust that earlier froze me in mid-climb, a million years ago now, back when I was only terrified the line would break. Back when I was only terrified I'd drop into a tailgater's barbecue pit. Oh, times were simpler then.

The bird. It's a speck now. A speck landing on one of the middle ledges of a parking garage. It hops inside, and I am left alone in the wind. I twist and face the wall—clench my butt.

*You don't wanna shit yourself on an op, sir*, says Killmaster.

*Oh, really?* I snap. *Ya think?*

*Tactical disadvantage, is all I'm saying,* Killmaster replies. *They'll smell you coming from a mile away, sir.*

*[I agree with Captain Kill,]* says Hanzo.

*Let's just focus on rescuing Dad, okay? Bruce?*

A picture forms in my mind's eye. Two Nostradamus agents leading Dad at gunpoint across the rim at the top of the stadium. They're on the opposite side from me, near the scoreboard. But there's more than just a picture. If I concentrate, I can feel their fear. And how hot the sun is through their black blazers, the slickness of the backs of their necks. The sweat on their spines. And I can feel their intentions: they want to take Dad alive. They want to use him to capture me.

*So this is a trap?* I ask.

*Let's hear it for Captain Obvious,* Killmaster replies. *Sir.*

"Pfft. But there's only two of them," I say out loud.

*Says Mr. About-to-Shit-His-Pants,* says Killmaster. *Sir.*

*Nostradamus always has a plan,* warns Bruce Lee.

*Then what's their plan?* I ask. *I mean, you can just hack into their brains and figure it out. Right?*

I wait there, dangling, my twisting gut mirroring what I'm doing on the line. My thumb strokes the button on the grappling gun that reels me up. It's all I can do not to press it and be done with the climb.

*Not before we know what we're up against, sir,* says Killmaster.

*What's the holdup?* I ask. *Can't you just instantly read their minds?*

*[There's something wrong with their minds,]* says Hanzo.

*Yes,* says Bruce Lee.

*[Origami.]*

*Yes,* Bruce Lee says again.

*I made an origami chicken once,* says Killmaster.

*Origami?* I say. *What're you guys talking about?*

*[Their minds are folded, as if from one piece of paper. Many, many folds.]*

*Yes,* says Bruce Lee. *Strange…*

*Book said it was supposed to be a paper crane,* says Killmaster. *But I got a chicken. I fucking hate origami.*

*I can unfold their minds,* says Bruce Lee. *If I had more time.*

*We don't have time,* I argue. *They have Dad.*

*Sir,* says Killmaster. *If you finish your climb from here, they'll see us. They'll have all the time in the world to prepare, and we'll have lost the element of surprise.*

*[I agree,]* says Hanzo.

I shake my head. *No. If I'm up here much longer, I* am *going to crap my pants. So they'll see us coming. So what? Maybe we can talk. Work something out. We don't know unless we try.*

Hattori Hanzo, Bruce Lee, and Lieutenant Killmaster make no reply, but their psychic sense is broadcasting their disapproval loud and clear. But in the end, their disapproval for a superhero with the poopy pants is stronger.

"Right," I say out loud. "So, my plan it is."

# CHAPTER SIXTY

THERE ARE THREE MEN at the top of Qualcomm Stadium standing in front of construction scaffolding at the edge on the opposite side. One is Dad—and the other two flanking him are armed. One of them has a gun to Dad's back. I'm so afraid, I could throw up. I'm too close now to let them kill Dad. I only just got him back. They can't kill him. I won't let them. They watch me as I jog along the rim toward them.

Vertigo sets in. The walkway, which had seemed plenty wide only a second ago, seems like it's shrinking in from either side. I feel like I'm on a tightrope. I'm hot and sweaty. My arms and legs are getting heavy. Inside the supersuit, there's only stale, filtered air. What I wouldn't give for a nice breeze to settle my stomach.

I tell myself to ignore the guns and focus on Dad. He's right there, next to the scaffolding. Too far to see his face clearly, but now that I'm so close, I'm impatient to touch him. How long has it been since I've done that? It's incredible what a person can miss. Like that brown cable cardigan he used to wear. I can see him in his favorite reading chair. The cardigan smells dusty, like his old medical journals. Dad isn't wearing it now. He's wearing a Chargers jersey, Bermuda shorts, and flip-flops. But the sight of him connects me to the cardigan, him, and the family unit we once had.

His hair is grayer. His face, weathered. He's exactly as he was in the Collective Unconscious. I try to send him reassurances through the Collective Unconscious. I don't know if it'll work. I don't know if he can feel me, or read my mind, but I do it anyway. *It's okay, Dad. I won't let them hurt you. I won't let them hurt me or Gran either. We're all going to be okay. I promise.*

The agent who isn't holding the gun to Dad's head raises his hand and calls out, "That's far enough."

It takes a few more steps before I can run off my momentum and stop. I raise my hands to show I'm unarmed.

"Remove the ring," says the agent.

*[This is a bad idea,]* says Hanzo.

*Yeah,* says Killmaster. *I agree with Hong Kong Phooey.*

*Don't take off the suit, Edge,* says Bruce Lee.

Still reaching for the sky, I stretch my fingers out to show my palms. Carefully, my left hand crosses to find my right ring finger.

Bruce Lee gasps. *Edge, no...!*

I twist the ring. The back of my gloves become semitranslucent, then solid black goo. It slithers across my skin, retreating into the ring. Hot, fresh air touches my face and neck, shoulders and legs, like it's chasing the shrinking suit along my skin until, finally, the last of it squeezes into the ring. I'm exposed. I realize belatedly I've committed one of the biggest cardinal sins any superhero can commit. I've revealed my secret identity.

# CHAPTER SIXTY-ONE

EVEN THOUGH I should probably be collapsing into a puddle of terror, Dad's grizzled face is filling me with hope. His jaw is set. The lines around his eyes are tight. I can see the younger man inside him. I can see the person who caught me when I fell off the monkey bars after I tried to fly like Superman. I can see his face when he told me to never try that again.

"It'll be okay," I say, leaving off the word "Dad," on the off chance these Nostradamus dudes don't already know.

*Oh, they know*, says Killmaster. *Trust me, sir. They know.*

"Now give us the ring," says the agent.

*Bad idea. Ba-ad idea*, says Bruce Lee.

*[Let me kill them. These men need killing.]*

*Just relax everyone,* I answer. I take a deep breath and close my fist over the ring.

"First, lower your weapons and let him go," I reply.

The agent scoffs at me. "This is how it's gonna go down. First, you're going to *carefully* hand me the ring. Then, you and him"—he jerks his head at Dad—"are coming with us."

A silent fury builds in my gut.

I force a chuckle and scratch my forehead to affect a nonchalance I'm not feeling. I stroll a few feet to my right, closer to the ledge. My stomach flops, then clenches. A cold chill fans out in my back the way it does before I throw up.

"What are you doing?" the agent snaps.

I thrust my fist out over the ledge, swallow, and focus on settling my stomach. The ring is hard and digging into my palm. Bile is rising in my throat. I'm taking long, deep breaths.

*[Settle down,]* says Hanzo. *[Wait—try this.]*

The flavor of bile vanishes and is replaced by the aftertaste of pickled ginger; my stomach begins to relax.

*[How did you do that?]* I ask.

*[Ancient Japanese secret,]* Hanzo replies.

"Come away from there before you pass out." The agent steps out from the construction scaffolding and waves the barrel of his gun to show me where he'd like me to stand. "You've got no head for heights, kid. Anybody can see that."

I stand up straighter, swallow, and again thrust my hand over the ledge. I take a step nearer to underscore the point, and another round of pickled ginger hits my taste buds from nowhere. "If you want this ring, you're going to let him go."

The two agents exchange an uncertain glance. And now that I'm no longer worried about throwing up, it hits me—they're identical. They look like they stepped right out of *The Matrix*. Same height, same build. Same bushy eyebrows poking out from above the Ray-Bans.

"No," says the agent holding Dad. "You're not gonna do it. You know what that thing is. You won't destroy it. You're just delaying the inevitable."

"Edger," says Dad, and the sound of him saying my name is like two hands reaching into my chest and squeezing my heart. His eyes droop at the corners. His lips curl into a sad smile. My fist comes down. I step in from the ledge. Dad nods, and the agent not holding him starts walking toward me—until his head snaps back—and, a split second later, the crack of a gunshot rings out. The agent topples over the side of the ledge.

I duck and cover. The second agent's head snaps back as a second gunshot echoes across the stadium. He bangs into a bar on the side of the scaffolding, then topples over the ledge. I spin one hundred eighty degrees in search of the shooter—but there's no one.

*Get down, sir!* yells Killmaster.

*The ring, Edger! The ring!*

Dad. He's hunched over too, one hand out, gesturing for me to stop in my tracks. Only then do I realize I've moved toward him. I swallow and raise my voice. "Dad! I don't know where you've been, but you can come home! We can be together! You, me, Gran—"

"Edger," he says, taking a backward step beneath the scaffolding—too close to the ledge—

"Dad—watch out!" I reach out to grab him, but he's yards away—

"Stay away, Edge!"

Dad takes a further step, arms outstretched. Just like in my dreams, he falls backward over the side.

# CHAPTER SIXTY-TWO

THE WHISTLE BLOWS at the same time the snapped football stings Caleb's hands. He reels the ball into his core and takes a knee. Packers jostle him from the right and left, unable to slow their momentum. The crowd boos.

"Caleb," Alex's voice whispers into his helmet's earpiece. "We've got shots fired."

Wide receiver Levonsio Strob steps in front of him, grabs his faceguard, and tugs it forward to clink helmets. Caleb juts his chin out to acknowledge the hello, then pans his gaze over the sidelines. Coach McCoy is waving them over. From his peripheral vision, Caleb spots the Packers defense leaving the field. The boos swell.

"What's goin' on?" asks Levonsio from his side.

"I think we're clearing the field, bro." Caleb tosses the ball to the ref and jogs toward the sidelines. He raises a hand against the glare of the sun and scans the crowd for any sign of something wrong, even though he knows it's hopeless.

"Talk to me, Alex," he whispers.

Alex's voice comes back through the earpiece. "Nostradamus has the bomb in the Packers' locker room. Can you get to it?"

"Stand by," he replies.

At the sidelines, Coach McCoy's arms are gesturing for the team to gather round. Caleb sidles up next to Sean Culkin.

"Okay, listen," says Coach McCoy. "There's been a thing. We're goin' down to the locker room to hole up for a bit."

"What?" cries Levonsio. "What kind of thing, Coach?"

"The shooting kind. Now let's go! Let's go!" Coach McCoy waves the players down the sidelines, herding them like human cattle. Caleb jogs among them, speaking at too low a decibel to be heard by those around him amid the booing fans.

"Alex, we're heading out. I'll see what I can do."

"Copy," she replies.

# CHAPTER SIXTY-THREE

THE ANNOYING VOICE in Yourmajesty's earpiece is talking to him again.

"The cow is on the move."

"And what do you want me to do about it?" replies Yourmajesty, trudging side by side among his team back to the locker room.

The voice is silent for a moment. Then: "Follow orders."

"I don't take orders from you anymore," replies Yourmajesty, underscoring the point by removing his helmet, locating the earpiece hidden inside the padding, ripping it out, and grinding it to pieces beneath his cleats.

"Dude." Aaron Rogers, who had been jogging behind him, comes to a halt at his side. "What the hell, man?"

Yourmajesty's gaze pans from the quarterback to the squashed electronic receiver and back to the quarterback. He peers into Aaron Rogers's eyes, and makes no reply.

Rogers raises his hands in surrender.

"Hey," he says. "No prob, man."

Sparing Yourmajesty one last doubtful look, Aaron Rogers turns and resumes his jog back to the locker room.

Yourmajesty's eyes follow Rogers's retreating form as others brush past on the right and left. The voice in his ear had been annoying. It had expected to be obeyed. Clearly this Fapa'fapa-

Bal'buster person had been a Nostradamus agent prior to InstaTron Tron's assuming control over him as its new host. But whatever claims Nostradamus had over this Fapa'fapa-Bal'buster could no longer be tolerated. InstaTron Tron's wireless network monitored news from around the world, instantly processing, analyzing, and strategizing. And the news had just given it several interesting new leads. Chief among them, the existence of the Zarathustra supersuit, with which InstaTron Tron had been designed to link.

*So, the cow is on the move, is it?*

Fapa'fapa-Bal'buster's eyes flit up into the back of his head as InstaTron Tron's processors cram the necessary information into his brain. His eyes pop open. He has two new names.

Wang and Shmuel.

Daddy...and... Other Daddy.

# CHAPTER SIXTY-FOUR

*DAD! DAD!*

*Put the ring back on, Edge!* yells Bruce Lee.

I race beneath the scaffolding to the ledge, arms held out for balance, and barely stop in time. It takes a minute for my eyes to catch up to my brain. At my feet is a long, white chute bolted to the concrete. It angles away from the stadium, so as not to be a straight drop, curving and stretching all the way to the bottom. There, a tiny speck of a man is climbing out and dusting himself off. He pauses, his gaze following the chute back to me at the top of the stadium. He raises his hand, waves, and then turns and runs.

*May I remind you, sir, that we are in the middle of an active shooter situation?* demands Killmaster.

*Dad...*

*Focus, sir...shooter.*

*My booster. I'm going to die—*

*Sir, you're going to die a lot faster if you don't—*

Shooter. Right.

I take one step back from the ledge and turn around. The glint of sunlight on gunmetal catches my eye—there! On the far side of the stadium. Near the spot I made my ascent: a sniper. She's up on one elbow, waving at me. Blonde hair.

*Oh no.*

*[Well, someone had to kill them,]* Hanzo replies.

*Boo-yah!* yells Killmaster.

*Edge,* says Bruce Lee. *We must leave. The police are coming.*

My hands are shaking. A dull roar is building in my ears. The ellipse of the stadium seems to tilt ever so slightly back and forth, sickeningly, as a hot flash steals across the back of my neck and over the top of my head.

*I can't believe her. I can't believe what Mary just did.*

*Edge—focus,* says Bruce Lee. *We've got to get out of here.*

*Mary just killed them,* I reply. *In cold blood! They didn't even know she was there!*

*[What a woman!]* exclaims Hanzo.

My mouth is making too much saliva. My knees are weak.

*You're about to black out, sir. Come away from the ledge!*

I stumble backward. I totter around, hands out. The white chute, just three feet from me, becomes unnaturally large in the center. It's shrinking in from the edges. That freight train in my ears, deafening, seems to emerge from a tunnel at the back of my brain. The light of the world shuts off. I tumble down a dark hole.

# CHAPTER SIXTY-FIVE

"I'VE GOT SOME BAD NEWS, EDGER."

My eyes open.

I'm sitting in a hot tub across from Indiana Tim. On his left and right are two bikini-clad young ladies. There's music. The Grateful Dead.

"We're in Club Brain," says Indiana Tim. "You don't remember?"

My hand lifts from the hot tub and touches the back of my neck. I run it through my hair and up to the top of my aching head.

"Yes," says Indiana Tim. "That's the bad news. You're dying."

I expel a bitter chuckle and let my hand splash back into the water. My head lolls backward. I stare into the soul-stars above and wonder what it would be like to be among them.

"Not exactly the reaction I was expecting," says Indiana Tim. "Listen, I'm not sure how much time we have, but it's important you remember this conversation. I can't say how well we'll be able to communicate with you when you're awake. Without your booster, it's downhill from here on out, I'm afraid."

My throbbing head comes down. All around me, Club Brain is shimmering like a mirage. Indiana Tim, his girlfriends, their every molecule is vibrating.

"That's the dying part," he says. "You're going to start having some rather painful episodes."

"Great."

"But the good news is, I have a message from your father."

Vibrating Indiana Tim removes his sunglasses and sits up straighter, casting ripples outward in the water. The girls on his left and right stand in wordless synchronicity. Falling water beads trace erotic curves and soaking bikini straps as they climb out of the hot tub.

"Did you hear me?" asks Indiana Tim. I try to focus, but his molecules are trying to shake apart. His skin is a weird squirrel gray. The quivering hair on his head separates into individual strands.

"Ah," he says. "I thought the hot tub would help." He waves his hand, and the soul-stars come down from the sky. Club Brain brightens. I clench my eyes against the intensity, which turns pink, then yellow and purple, and then dims. Soon, only the afterimage remains. Cautiously, I open one eye.

We're sitting on logs at a campfire on the beach. The air tastes like salt water mixed with wood smoke. The ocean is flat to the horizon. There isn't a soul in sight. The world is still vibrating, but less than before.

"I've kind of reset your head for now," Indiana Tim explains. "I don't know how long this trick will last. But I have a message from your father."

My breath shortens at the mention of my dad. Hazy bits and pieces of my misadventures at Qualcomm Stadium sift through my unconscious mind like the shifting sand beneath us.

"A message from Dad?"

He nods, but says nothing further, allowing me time to process. The news doesn't penetrate anything remotely emotional. I'm numb.

"That's your brain resetting, I'm afraid," says Indiana Tim. "There'll be time to grieve all that is happening to you later. And you will. I know it's a lot."

"Grieve? Did somebody die?"

"You. If you don't get your booster."

"Oh," I reply. I try to summon a sense of urgency on that topic, but there's nothing. No fear. No anxiety. No hope or sense of finality or anything. I abandon that, as it's futile, and rewind to the other part of what he's been trying to tell me. "What's my dad saying?"

Indiana Tim's face brightens. "Your father wants you to meet him tonight at your grandmother's."

"He does?"

"Yes."

"But—I just saw him at the football stadium." I close my eyes and try to recall the memory, but it's no use. All I've got is the sense that if Dad had wanted us to leave together, we would have.

"Yes, that's true," says Indiana Tim. "He is rather paranoid to begin with, understandably so, but things have become more complicated. He has your safety to worry about. And your grandmother's."

"Then why meet at Gran's at all?" I ask, opening my eyes.

"He intends to give you your booster, and then get you, your gran, and Shep to safety."

I shake my head. The log beneath me, the beach, ocean, and fire vibrate. I close my eyes again. My stomach lurches.

"...doesn't make sense," I manage weakly.

"There's something else," says Indiana Tim, his voice now coming from far away. I open my eyes. We've left the beach. I'm drifting among the soul-stars. Indiana Tim is nowhere to be found. But, like before, I'm numb. A vague, unformed notion pecks at my subconscious mind that I should be alarmed, but still I feel nothing. No—that's not right. I do feel something.

The stars are soft and inviting, like liquid light on a velvet black canvas.

"Listen, Edger!" Indiana Tim's voice echoes inside me. "They're putting a bomb in Caleb's nightclub. A place called Underwearld. Do you know it?"

I nod. "It's in the Gaslamp Quarter. Place is wallpapered with art photos of Caleb in his underpants."

"That's the place. Now pay attention. Underwearld has been their plan all along. The football game was a ruse."

I bump into a soul-star, and its light ripples outward. Its life experiences fill me. Mommy and Daddy have me giggling uncontrollably. I'm three. We live in a cabin in the woods.

“Are you listening to me?” someone asks, but I shove the voice aside, because Mommy and Daddy are pretending to steal my toes. I can’t stop giggling. Wait—no. This isn’t me. This is Clarence. It’s his life I’m sharing through this star.

“Edger!” a familiar voice calls through the darkness. “Focus! You cannot let Nostradamus have this power. He is too powerful already. And you cannot let InstaTron Tron pair with that ring!”

Clarence takes his first steps when he is ten months old. He—I—feel like I’m one of the grown-ups now. Mommy and Daddy are so happy. They’re so proud of me.

“Disarm the bomb! Save your grandmother! Save your friends! And by the way, I know a wonderful bomb specialist who can help you. His name is Bubba. First rate. Really knows his stuff.”

Mommy gives me apple juice. It’s the first time I’ve had apple juice. The flavor explodes on my tongue.

“You can’t linger here!” calls a familiar voice. “You have to wake up! Wake up, Edger! Wake up!”

I pass through Clarence’s light and turn in space, arms outstretched. The Collective Unconscious is beautiful. To think—each of these lights is connected through our humanity. Each containing lifetimes teeming with rich experiences. I never want to leave.

Another light approaches. I wonder what experience it will share.

“Wake up, Edger! Wake up!”

# CHAPTER SIXTY-SIX

"EDGER? CAN YOU HEAR ME?"

My eyes are closed. The sunlight on my face is hot and horrible. My head is pounding. My back is aching. I'm shivering, despite the heat. Swells of nausea have the world listing around me.

"I think I'm gonna get sick."

"Here. Drink this."

My eyes flutter open. Parking lot. We're in the Jag. Mary's eyes are wide and blue. She's closing my hand around a sweating bottle of water, raising it to my mouth. Just that little motion flips my stomach. The bottle presses into my lips. Cold water trickles down my throat. A bead of sweat falls from my face to hit Mary's hands, which are guiding mine and the water bottle.

"You scared me," says Mary.

The cold water cools me from the inside out. My stomach begins to relax. I close my eyes and listen to the world. Sirens. Reporters. A police radio goes past.

"...suspect is male, six three, approximately two hundred twenty pounds, and wearing a...oh, you're gonna love this...a black-and-chrome superhero getup, quote: resembling a space ninja."

Steel forms in my stomach. My eyes pop open and the shakes vanish; adrenaline kicks in.

"Are you ready to move?" Mary's eyes scan my face. She takes her hands back and grabs the key in the ignition. "I can get us out of here. I was just waiting for you to feel a little better first."

The engine turns over. Two more cops run past, followed by a medical team pushing two gurneys loaded with bulging body bags.

"Holy shit," I whisper. "Are those the...?"

I pull my gaze from the bodies being loaded into the back of an ambulance and face Mary. She shrinks away from my stare. Her forehead wrinkles. She smiles weakly and shrugs.

"You killed those guys."

"But I mean, they weren't even like real guys."

"Except for the fact they were alive before and dead now!"

She puts the car in gear. She checks her mirrors, backs up, clicks the turn signal—any and every legitimate excuse not to make eye contact with me as I try to stare some shame into her. And then I'm on the highway, going God only knows where, with this hot cold-blooded killer.

For the first five minutes on the highway, there's only the hum of the road and the wind ripping through our hair.

"Would you like some music?" she asks, her hand riffling through her purse before pulling out her phone and thumbing up a playlist.

"Hey-hey!" I exclaim. "Eyes on the road!"

"Right." She drops her phone back into her purse. Keeping one hand on the wheel, she steeples the other on her forehead and stares not at the road, but through it. Like somewhere beneath the road might be a solution to all her problems. But if it's answers like that she's looking for, I'd happily suggest she rethink her murderous, snipery lifestyle.

"Where are you taking me?" I ask.

"Somewhere we can talk."

"Am I an accessory to murder?"

"No."

"No? Just 'no'?"

"No."

"Oh. Okay."

Her hair is streaming in the wind. Her skin is a radiant golden tan. Her dress is riding up on her thighs again, but this time, she's making no effort to hold it down. She's too distracted—and now so am I. I clear my throat and train my eyes on the San Diego skyline. *Unbelievable!* Here I am, trapped in this car with a killer, and I still want to look at her panties. This can't be the girl of my dreams. I don't dream about girls in sexy blue panties who kill people. I dream about girls in sexy blue panties who build lightsabers and become Jedi Knights. Besides, she's too beautiful to be a killer. Killers aren't supposed to have beautiful girl-next-door faces, sexy panties, and CrossFit bodies. They're supposed to come from New Jersey, as has been well established.

"Who are you?" I ask. "Some kind of hired assassin?"

Mary, with her eyes glued to the road, makes no reply.

"CIA?"

Nothing.

"NSA?"

Mary shrugs, avoiding eye contact. "It doesn't matter. You won't have heard of us."

"Well, I'm not going anywhere with you until you tell me who you are and I see some ID." My hand drops to my pocket, where a hard lump tells me I've still got the ring. She sighs and takes her eyes off the road long enough to shoot me a withering look.

"Fine," she says, turning her gaze back to the road. "I'm employed by a clandestine branch of the Australian government that coordinates with the United Nations, and, by extension, the United States. There. Happy?"

"No."

A flash of annoyance crosses her face. "Why, Edger?"

"Why? You just snipered the shit out of those guys!"

"Well," she stammers. "But now you know I snipered them…you know…legally."

"Oh, so it was a legal snipering!" I exclaim, tossing my arms in the air. "I feel so much better. Brain-matter lawsuits are on the rise, you know. Hate for you to get sued by a litigious chunk of brain that—"

"Wait," says Mary. "Did you say, *illegal* snipering, or—"

"No, *a* legal. Two words."

"Because it wasn't illegal. That's the whole point—"

"Wait, wait. Are you telling me you've got a license to kill? Can I see it?"

"It's not like a driver's license! You don't just get one at the BMV!"

"Oh, no? Then where *do* you get them, *Jane Bond*?"

She shakes her head. "Uh-uh. No. I'm not doing this with you. Because if it comes right down to it, I will kick Daniel Craig's old-man ass faster than it takes me to make Mike Dame his protein shake. *James Bond would fear me.*"

"*Oh, man.*" I cover my face with my hands, take a deep breath, and release it. I drop my hands into my lap. "You. Kill. People."

"Don't you think you're being a little judgmental here?" she replies. "I should point out, Edger, that these 'people' were about to kill you. And your dad, by the way. So. You know, you're welcome."

"I had it under control."

"I noticed that when you were blacking out and falling off Qualcomm Stadium. Good job."

My jaw drops open at the same time a fly crashes into the back of my throat. I hack, spit a little bit into my hand, and my mouth clamps shut. Holding my hand out the window for a second, I wait for it to dry before wiping the rest of it on my leg. After a few minutes of silence, I sneak a glance at Mary. Her eyes are tight. Her lips are pressed together and going white.

*Great. Just great.*

"This clandestine branch of the Aussie government got a name?" I ask, my plan being to put her back in the hot seat. And going by her suddenly red complexion, I've hit a nerve. "What's the matter? Cat got your tongue?"

"Global Strategic Peace Organization Taskforce. There. Happy?"

My head snaps back. Her eyes are glued to the road. Her hands are at eleven and one. My brain gears are struggling like an old car that won't start. After a few more painful moments of silence, it turns over.

"I feel compelled at this juncture to point out your supersecret spy group's acronym spells G-spot."

"Y-yep."

"And...that's, I mean, okay with you?"

Mary screws her face up. "I didn't name it."

I scratch the back of my neck. My eyebrows rise.

"What?"

"No, no," I say. "GSPOT. That's good. Good idea. Gives our two respective governments plausible deniability."

"How so?"

I purse my lips. "I mean, nobody's gonna believe GSPOT's a real thing."

Her lips curl on one side, and her eyes narrow. "Oh—it's real all right."

# CHAPTER SIXTY-SEVEN

EVERY REVVING of the Harley's engine sends a jolt through Wang's system. The whoosh of passing vehicles lashes his ears. Tipping lane changes flip his stomach. Twine cuts into his arms and torso every time his weight shifts; he is bound to the back of the driver, his drool-encrusted cheek mashed sideways into two hundred ninety-six pounds of rock-hard muscle and football pads. Wang equates the experience to that of being strapped to the back of a Harley Davidson-riding defensive tackle for the Green Bay Packers. This is because he *is* strapped to the back of a Harley Davidson-riding defensive tackle for the Green Bay Packers.

Shmuel's situation sucks not a dime bag less. He is stuffed into the sidecar with his knees in his ears and a rag in his mouth. His hands are tied beneath his butt. Wang keeps expecting at any minute some random driver who's seen them on the highway will call the cops. But apparently only assholes are out.

Wang's hopes rise as they pull into the circle at the Manchester Grand Hyatt. The place is hopping with tourists. Maybe now someone will see them and call the cops. That's all he wants. It won't take much to call 911. He would. Well, maybe he wouldn't give a shit—but surely a normal person would. That's what it means to be normal, right? Giving a shit? And lo and behold, the first person they drive past, a businessman on his phone near the curb, with his smooth shave, sculpted hair, immaculate Windsor knot, pressed shirt, and expensive suit, looks like a card-carrying member of the Shit Givers' Club. A bona fide contributing member to society!

Shit Giver glances in their direction. Wang cries out.

"Mrhn!"

Shit Giver's eyes widen. A cab swoops in, honks its horn. Shit Giver startles, takes another wide-eyed look at them, Yourmajesty Fapa'fapa-Bal'buster sitting astride a Harley Davidson in full football gear, helmet, shoulder pads—the whole deal, Wang strapped to his back like an Asian Bondage fetish, Shmuel hogtied in the sidecar like he's the First Prize at a Kentucky 4-H Fair Gay Cletus contest. *Gay Cletus, the Slack-Jawed Human Man Boob.*

Shit Giver jumps inside the cab. Tires squeal as it pulls away.

Wang's belly twists in frustration. *Asshole.* Isn't anybody going to call the cops?

Next is a teenage girls' soccer team disembarking from a bus. A blonde and brunette notice the extremely loud motorcycle. They gasp, point, cry out. Wang's hopes spike.

"Mm-rm! Rm-dm-gm-dm!" he yells into the rag stuffed in his mouth, and a little bit of drool moistens Yourmajesty Fapa'fapa-Bal'buster's brick-like back.

"Mm-hm-rml-rmgl!" yells Shmuel from the sidecar.

Several teenagers gawk. Some exchange side-eyes. Most, being glued to their phones, notice nothing. One girl, a skinny blonde with a long neck and uncommonly large overbite, shoots both arms diagonally up and to the right, dabbing for no apparent reason.

"Grhm!" exclaims Wang.

Yourmajesty Fapa'fapa-Bal'buster slows to a crawl in front of the soccer team, the Harley's fine-tuned sputtering engine cracking like a plumber's pants. He lowers the kickstand, parks the bike. He climbs off, Wang stuck to his back like a Siamese Yoda.

"Mm-rm!" yells Wang.

The dabbing soccer girl lowers her arms. Her eyebrows rise. Her eyebrows lower. She shakes her head. Her left eyebrow twitches. Her buck teeth chew on her bottom lip. All this activity apparently complete, she shrugs, and dabs again.

The bellhop's eyes widen. Wang's spirits rise. Bellhops, Wang is certain, do not rise to their station in life without being card-carrying members of the Shit Givers' Club. Bellhops have to give a shit. They carry bags, for example, so there's shit given right out of the gate. A person can't carry bags to people's rooms without giving a shit. Otherwise, bags would be delivered directly into the pool.

Wang closes his eyes and begs to the god of bellhops. But when his eyes open, he finds Yourmajesty Fapa'fapa-Bal'buster has turned around, leaving Wang a spectacular view of the hotel wall which, if he isn't mistaken, is a pale shade of blue better known as Winter in Paris.

"Ah," says the bellhop. "Mr. Ball Buster. Good to have you back, sir."

"Why, thank you," says Yourmajesty Fapa'fapa-Bal'buster warmly. The Green Bay Packer turns to glance at his Harley, and Wang glimpses the bellhop casting a wary eye on his and Shmuel's condition, and an even warier eye on Yourmajesty Fapa'fapa-Bal'buster's condition. Which is to say, heavily muscled. Fapa'fapa-Bal'buster turns back around, and now it's just Winter in Paris again.

"Is...ah...everything all right, Mr. Ball Buster?"

"Of course," Fapa'fapa-Bal'buster replies, turning again to check his Harley. "Why wouldn't it be?"

The bellhop purses his lips. His gaze moves from the Green Bay Packer to Wang, who tries to catch his eye, but, too late, the bellhop is gazing again at the Green Bay Packer.

"Shame they cancelled the game," says the bellhop. "I have you on my fantasy team, of course."

"That's very kind of you to say," says Yourmajesty Fapa'fapa-Bal'buster, turning again to face the bellhop.

"Any luggage today, sir?"

"In fact, yes," replies Yourmajesty Fapa'fapa-Bal'buster. "There's this bag and a fat stoner with moobs in the sidecar."

"I'm sorry. What?"

"Moobs. Man boobs. In the sidecar." A jolt shoots from Wang's spine to his teeth as the Green Bay Packer hits the palm of his hand against his football helmet as if just remembering something. "Psh," he adds, chuckling like he's embarrassed. "I almost forgot. I've still got the tiny human strapped to my back, don't I?"

"Ah…yes, sir."

"I mean, that counts as luggage too, right? Is there a charge for tiny humans? Extra luggage charge, I mean?"

"Not at all, sir."

Wang stares at the hotel wall, and a burgeoning realization dawns on him: Winter in Paris is actually Goddamn Green. Those bastard swatch makers at Lowe's make it look Fucking Blue. *That's* why Wang's fucking living room wall is Goddamn Green. Fuck.

The voice of another Hyatt employee reels him back to the conversation.

"…the hotel apologizes, and we regret any inconvenience this may have caused."

Yourmajesty Fapa'fapa-Bal'buster turns and Wang spots a hotel employee hustling a nervous-looking family of four out the front door of the hotel lobby. The bellhop skips around Yourmajesty Fapa'fapa-Bal'buster and averts his eyes from Wang. "I'll see to the sidecar, then. Shall I?"

"If you wouldn't mind," Yourmajesty Fapa'fapa-Bal'buster replies. "Just send Moobs up to my room, please."

The next thing he knows, Wang is bouncing in pace with the Packer's stride to the elevator. They pass undetected through throngs of people glued to their tablets and laptops, phones, and headphones, and even one set of virtual reality goggles. Waiting at the elevator, Wang catches sight of Shmuel on a golden luggage cart, sandwiched between Gucci and Prada, hogtied and gagged, and trundling through the pack of soccer girls snapping selfies. One teenage girl notices Wang. Her eyebrows come down for a second. Wang's hopes come up for a second. She snaps a picture and nudges her friend. She holds out the phone. They wrinkle their noses and giggle. One of them says something about Instagram, the other says something about Twitter. They shrug it away. The elevator doors close and, even though these girls are less than ten years younger than him, Wang silently curses "kids" in general for not having their priorities better in hand.

# CHAPTER SIXTY-EIGHT

MARY TAKES THE BEACH exit and follows the signs into the parking lot. The sky is clear except for the seagulls. The ocean air and beach sun are restorative.

Mary puts it in Park. I kick the door open and swing my legs out, then remove my shoes and tie the laces so they can hang over my neck. Not waiting for her, I head out onto the beach. The sand is warm between my toes. The wind and surf is cool in my ears. My skin is swollen and dry.

It's going to kill me to tell Gran we've got to call the whole thing off. Assuming I survive this at all, at least it'll only be six more months until Gran and Shep can have their happy ever after from the money I've saved. But there's no way she can go to Pine's Place now. Not while it's being funded by blood money. And I sure as hell can't move in with Mary, the lethal snipery pretend girlfriend with an actual license to kill.

"Edger."

I turn around, and a seagull marches between us. Mary's gaze tracks its meandering path as it pecks wet sand where the tide has gone out. Her skin is glowing in the sun. Her hair is golden. She looks back up at me, and her clear blue eyes reflect the glimmering ocean. She's holding her weight to one side. Anyone watching us could easily conclude this is a girl wanting to make up after a fight. No one would easily conclude this is a girl who's just snipered two secret agents to death.

"I don't think I can do this anymore, Mary."

Nothing.

"Does that mean you have to kill me now?" I ask.

"Is that how you think this works?"

"I don't know. You tell me."

"No. We're the good guys."

"Then why did you kill them?"

"For starters, they were going to kill you."

"You don't know that."

"Okay, okay." She shrugs. "Possibly they were going to kidnap you. Maybe hook you up to a machine. In which case, they'd probably torture you. Sometimes they start small by strapping you down and spitting into your open mouth. That kind of thing. Gross, but, I mean"—she shakes her head and rolls her eyes—"kind of childish. You know? But I think for you they'd have started by gouging out your eyes. Or maybe a really nasty pair of pliers to kind of pull back your nails, and then jab something in there, pointy, like a—"

"Hey-hey-hey! Not helping!"

"Sorry." She takes a deep breath and releases it through her nose. "Can we sit for a sec? Just for a second, I want to tell you some things, and then I promise, if you want out, I'll totally understand. I know this has already been more than you bargained for."

I sigh and nod, and then we're nestling our butts into the warm beach and staring out across the ocean. The waves are slow and constant.

"The reason you want out is the same reason you should be in. You should be Zarathustra. You're a good person."

"Wait, you say that like someone else could be Zarathustra. Can you take the serum out of me?"

"Well, no one knows."

"What do you mean, no one knows?"

"Well, I mean, your dad would know. But after everything that's happened to him, I don't think he trusts us. He wouldn't tell me, I don't think."

"No, he wouldn't."

"Mm-hmm."

"He doesn't trust you."

Mary nods. "I kinda figured. Edger, don't take this the wrong way, but...your dad...he's..."

I sit up straighter. "What? He's what?"

"Well, he's a little paranoid." She sits up straighter also and reaches her hand toward me before pulling it back. "I don't mean that to be insulting. Since he left you, he's spent twenty years as either a hostage or a fugitive. Anyone would be paranoid with a life like that."

I consider that for a second. I try to imagine what it would've been like for him, researching something like this. How many people would want it. Then I remember those two Nostradamus agents falling off the top of Qualcomm Stadium.

"Maybe he just doesn't like killers."

I immediately regret the sting in my words. Mary's gaze goes back out to the ocean. I lean back on one elbow, grab a nearby stick, and start fiddling with it. Another seagull marches past.

"I'll be very sorry to lose you," she says. "If you quit, I mean. You've done so much already."

"As far as I can tell, we're not much further down the road at all." I drop the stick back where I found it.

Mary's forehead tightens. She grabs my arm. Her touch is still electric, the good kind of electric, despite everything that's transpired in the last hour.

"Edger, that's not true. You restored the power grid and fortified it against future attacks. And it's beginning to look like you may have single-handedly defeated terrorism."

I frown. "Really?"

"The gay pride parade. It's working. It's all over the news. I mean, it's weird, and confusing, but a lot of these guys are just surrendering now. Coalition forces are just driving up to the parades and arresting them. They don't even resist. I don't know how you pulled it off, but it's working."

"Pfft. I'll believe it when I see it."

Mary's eyebrows lower. "Now you're just being negative." She tucks a band of golden hair behind her ear and peers into my eyes.

"Negative, huh?"

"Mm-hmm."

I frown. "Maybe. But I'm not good at remembering my dreams. And these encounters are like that. Dreams. So, this is all pretty hazy for me. Everything kind of makes sense when I'm there, but afterward, it all seems so…I mean…outlandish."

She nods right away. "Oh, yeah. I can totally see that."

I close my eyes and try to remember. Images float through my mind's eye. A tower. A tree. A wise old man. My eyes pop open.

"I'm seeing the archetypes!"

Mary frowns. I scramble upright, kicking sand everywhere in the process. Mary dusts herself off and sits up also.

"Sorry," I say. "But when I close my eyes I see the archetypes now. That didn't use to happen." She blinks in confusion, and I hasten to explain. "The Tree of Life. The Dark Tower. The Wise Old Man." I pause and bite my lip. "But that's weird. Usually I just talk to Bruce Lee."

"Edger… Okay, you're not making any sense."

I close my eyes.

*Bruce Lee? Are you there?*

Nothing.

Concentrate.

*Hattori Hanzo—Lieutenant Killmaster! Anyone? Hello? Can you hear me?*

Nothing.

"Edger, are you okay? You're scaring me."

My eyes pop open. A cloud passes over us, washing out Mary's radiant color.

"Edger, what is it?"

"They're gone. They're all gone."

# CHAPTER SIXTY-NINE

MARY SHAKES my arm again. "Gone? Who's gone? What are you talking about?"

I scramble to my feet and dust the sand off my butt, then march back toward the Jag. Mary chases after me.

"It isn't like Mikey said, okay?" I say from over my shoulder. "I can actually interact with the dead. It's real. I know it's real because of what I could do back at the Q, and you know all those dreams I had about the power grid and stuff actually happened. I'm not crazy."

She grabs my arm. I stop marching and let her pull me around. Her eyes bore into mine. "You actually talked to Bruce Lee?" I nod, and despite the fact that this is what I've been trying to tell her and Mikey all along, her head ticks back in surprise. "Well, what did he say?"

"What do you mean, 'what did he say'?"

"Bruce Lee!"

"It isn't like I talked to him once. It's been one big long buddy movie! It was Bruce Lee who took me all over the world when I gave the terrorists the gay pride idea. It was Bruce Lee who hooked me up with… I forget his name, this old guy who helped me with the power grid. The point is, when I need help, Bruce Lee kind of finds these people in the Collective Unconscious. People I need, I mean."

Mary blinks, and her features revert to that unreadable glossy cover-girl face.

"I'm being serious here!"

"I know, I know," she says, raising her hands. "It's just...*holy shit*."

"I know, right?"

"So...do you think you can... I mean, talk to *anyone* who ever lived?"

I shake my head. "Mary—they're gone. I think I'm losing my powers. Bruce Lee has always been there. Since, you know, since Mikey put this stuff in me. But now he's gone. They're all gone, and I've never seen the archetypes when I was awake before. But I can see them now. So that feels like losing ground, going from being able to talk to them, to only being able to see the archetypes."

Her eyes scan mine, and I can tell she's trying to follow. She peers up at me. We're so close, I can taste her breath, which is warm and sweet as she licks her lips. I'm not sure when we got this close. Her breasts are pressed into me. My hands have somehow found her hips.

"Edger. I think this means you're dying."

"I know."

I bite my bottom lip and peer into her eyes. Tiny wings are beating the walls of my stomach. My brain is short-circuiting in at least ten different ways. But this is good, dying or not—I'm dying for *this*.

"Mary, I just... Did I ever tell you the one about the shellfish oyster who never donated to charity?"

Her shoulders slump. She rolls her eyes beneath fluttering eyelids and takes a backward step, pitching her weight to one side. Her lips curl into a lopsided smile. "No, you never told me that one."

"Yeah." I click my tongue. "Had to dredge it up."

"You are so weird." She grabs my hands. "Listen. You're going to be fine. Your Zarathustra formula is just wearing off. That's all."

"You say that like I'm not going to die soon."

"You won't. Not if I give you your booster."

I frown.

"I've got it in the trunk."

"You—you what?"

"I've got your booster in the trunk," she says again, clearly relishing my shock. "I'm the mole. I stole the booster cache from Mikey."

# CHAPTER SEVENTY

YOURMAJESTY FAPA'FAPA-BAL'BUSTER flexes his pecs, and the twine snaps like a cheap rubber band. Wang falls free and lands on his back in the king-size bed. The comforter expels a soft burst of air. He rips the gag out of his mouth, then rubs furiously at the welts on his arms left by the twine. He has a good idea what this is about.

"If you let us go, we'll tell you where Tron-Tron is!" he yells.

Yourmajesty Fapa'fapa-Bal'buster smiles down at him. "So it is you!"

Wang frowns. Yourmajesty's smile is friendly and warm. He pulls his helmet off and tosses it into the corner with a thunk. His eyes are round and reassuring. Wang glances at Shmuel, who's hogtied and lying on his side, drooling on the plush carpet in the living room in front of an eighty-inch, 4K Ultra HD TV.

"Ghrn," says Shmuel.

"I discovered your identities before we left the game. You're @A-Team1_chink25," says Yourmajesty Fapa'fapa-Bal'buster before turning to address Shmuel. "Which makes you @A-Team2_moobs."

"How do you know our Twitter handles?" asks Wang.

Yourmajesty Fapa'fapa-Bal'buster crosses the room to Shmuel. He reaches into his shoulder bag and pulls out something metal, not a phone. There's a short "ff-t" sound as a blade shoots out.

"No-no!" cries Wang, his hand outstretched.

"Relax," says Yourmajesty Fapa'fapa-Bal'buster, using the switchblade to cut Shmuel free. "I'm not going to hurt him. Or you."

Shmuel sits up and rubs his wrists. "Is this about the Russian hookers we snuck into the locker room last season? Because the chlamydia is totally not our fault?"

"Yeah—yeah, that's right," says Wang. "How could we know they had chlamydia? Not like we had 'em fill out a résumé. From our perspective, we were just, uh, you know, improving diplomatic relations between our two great cities."

Yourmajesty Fapa'fapa-Bal'buster frowns. "I vaguely remember that. But no, this has nothing to do with that. Don't you see? We're family. You're my parents."

"Ha-ha, *no*," replies Wang, blushing.

"Is this with the butt-baby thing again?" asks Shmuel. "Because two dudes cannot otherwise a baby make? Not without an Act of David—which we currently do not have?"

"What? What are you talking about?" asks Wang.

"You're not old enough to have had him," says Shmuel, pointing. "You're practically the same age?"

"What's an Act of David?" asks Yourmajesty Fapa'fapa-Bal'buster.

"Affidavit," says Wang, face-palming himself. "It's affidavit."

"That's what I said?"

"No, Toe Cheese. No, it isn't." Wang scoots irritably to the edge of the bed. "You said Act of Goddamn David."

"I heard it too," offers Yourmajesty Fapa'fapa-Bal'buster, shrugging. "Without the bad-language words."

Shmuel gets to his feet and rubs his wrists some more. "Well, then you both heard wrong?"

"What do you need an affidavit for, anyway?" asks Wang.

"You know. To adopt?" replies Shmuel, gesturing to the tower of muscle in the center of the room. "You know. Him."

"You don't need an affidavit to adopt!" exclaims Wang. "And nobody's adopting anybody!"

"That's what I said? God, dude. *Touchy*." Muttering almost inaudibly, he adds, "'Nobody' can't adopt anyway.

He's 'nobody.' Duh."

"I didn't mean you literally adopted me," says Yourmajesty Fapa'fapa-Bal'buster. "You raised me." He pauses to frown and rub his chin. "But which one of you would be my mommy?"

"Psh," says Wang. "No question. That'd be him with the moobs."

"I'm not afraid to be the mommy," says Shmuel. "Everyone knows they're the stronger ones anyway?" He gazes down at his belly and rubs it adoringly. "I just wish we coulda felt him, you know, kick or something?"

"Oh my God." Wang pinches the bridge of his nose. "You are the gayest thing I've ever seen that isn't literally a rhinestone-encrusted penis jacket."

Shmuel's face brightens. "They make those?"

"Just shut up! Shut up!" Wang rises from the bed and stalks toward the Green Bay Packer, then sizes the Packer up and hastens back to the bed. In a more moderate tone, he asks, "Whaddaya mean we're your mommy and daddy? Why did you kidnap us?"

"This isn't a kidnapping!" replies Yourmajesty Fapa'fapa-Bal'buster. "This is a family reunion. Oh, dear. Where are my manners? Allow me to introduce myself. I am InstaTron Tron, nano-artificial intelligence, equipped with advanced titanium quantum computing, supervillain extraordinaire, hair-bringer of doom…and I am your son."

Yourmajesty Fapa'fapa-Bal'buster extends his hand for a handshake, which Wang does not take on account of his having passed out on the bedroom floor.

# CHAPTER SEVENTY-ONE

"*YOU'RE* THE MOLE? Of course you're the mole. You've been trying to talk me out of this the whole time. Why am I surprised you're the mole? But then—wait. I'm confused."

"I even told you, *I will take care of your boosters, I promise.* But you didn't listen. You know, you really need to pay better attention. It's a good thing you've got me on your side. I know how to pay attention. *And* I'm a good shot." She gives me another lopsided smile, then tightens her grip on my hands and we're on the move again. "Our governments wanted me on the inside watching Mikey, suspecting a mole."

"A different mole," I clarify.

"Mm-hmm. And I did find some weird stuff, but no mole yet."

"How does one mole find another mole?"

"Cool it with the jokes, Edger. Just listen, okay? But after InstaTron Tron—God, that's a stupid name." She shakes her head irritably. "But after the power grid, I panicked. I figured you were my ace in the hole. Mole or no mole, I put all my money on you to be the person who is going to do the right thing with this technology. I knew I had to protect you by getting those boosters. They're the only control anyone can exercise over you now. And I don't trust anybody. Well," she adds, her cheeks becoming somewhat pinker, "except you. Obviously."

"Wait a minute," I say, trying to take my hand back, and getting my arm nearly jerked out of my socket for my trouble. She tightens her grip and tows me farther.

"One of the things I discovered from on the inside," she continues, "is a plot to put a bomb in a disco ball."

We reach the parking lot and stop at the curb to sit, dust off our feet, and get our shoes back on.

"Seems a little, I don't know...uninspired?" I finish weakly before my brain catches up to the subtext of what she's telling me. "Mary. Are you saying you suspect Mikey?"

Mary sighs. "I'm not saying we suspect him personally. I'm saying we've been investigating Nostradamus for a long time. Mikey's involvement in the Zarathustra program has been a priority for Nostradamus from the start. Their interests align."

She slips on her flats. I tie my shoes. My head is spinning. She sits up, shifts on the curb to face me, and straightens my collar.

"You're very handsome, Edger."

"Two-word joke: dwarf shortage."

She frowns disapprovingly.

"If you're offended: Grow up!"

This time she laughs, takes my hand, and smiles. I let my walls down and share the moment with her, astonished by how quickly the cracks formed in my earlier characterization of her as a cold-blooded killer. Is Dad right? Can't I trust her? Or is Dad as paranoid as she claims?

"So what is this?" I ask. "You and me. This whole idea about us moving in together. Pretend couple. That wasn't your idea? It was...your, uh, spy group's idea?"

She frowns. "Go on. You can say it."

"GSPOT."

Her eyes close. She nods.

"Yeah. Maybe you better stop ragging on InstaTron Tron," I say, grinning. "You know, stones from glass houses and everything."

She punches my arm.

"Ow. Okay, okay. So what's your spy group want with me anyway?"

Her face brightens. "You'd be quite an asset to our organization."

I laugh. "Oh, if I had a dollar for every girl who told me I was an asset to her G-spot."

She punches me in the arm again, and this time catches the bone with her knuckle.

"Hey!" I cry, rubbing the throbbing bone threatening to grow like a cartoon lump on my arm.

"You deserved that. Now come on. Before I change my mind about saving your life." She sets off without me toward the Jag glimmering in the sunlight. "Just think," she says, holding out her key fob at the trunk and grinning at me. "Another minute and you've got your life back. Well, your superhero life, anyway."

Her eyes twinkle knowingly as she pops the trunk. We share a smile. Our heads turn together.

Mary gasps.

The trunk is large and lined with a tan microfiber that smells expensive as there's so much of it; a small scrap could otherwise be used for cleaning plasma TV screens, lenses, and laptops. But this is a spacious trunk. A trunk this size could easily carry your groceries home, picnic supplies for a day at the beach, or, if you're a skillful packer, eight moderate-size Thanksgiving turkeys. A trunk this size could not fit a double bass or cello. But one could cram in four or five violas. The point is, a trunk this size could easily carry Mikey's trove of booster formula with room to spare. It even could've carried the safe he'd kept it in, along with several cases of that horrible scotch he likes so much.

But none of that is in this trunk.

None of anything is in this trunk.

This trunk is empty.

# CHAPTER SEVENTY-TWO

YOURMAJESTY FAPA'FAPA-BAL'BUSTER, gazing at Wang's unconscious body, lowers his hand a fraction before changing direction and extending it to Shmuel.

Shmuel looks from Wang to Fapa'fapa-Bal'buster, then takes the football player's hand—which is surprisingly gentle—and shakes.

"He gets touchy when people mistake us for a couple," offers Shmuel. "One time he told me that even if he was gay, which he claims he isn't, he would never go out with someone whose face looks like, and I quote, 'a saddlebag with eyes'?"

"Oh, that's hurtful," replies Fapa'fapa-Bal'buster.

Shmuel shrugs.

"I don't like to see you fight," says Fapa'fapa-Bal'buster, unzipping his shoulder bag on the bed and pulling out a rack of several small beakers filled with blue liquid. He carefully sets them on the table.

"Dude," says Shmuel.

"Yes?"

"Is that evil nano-AI stuff?"

"Kind of," replies Fapa'fapa-Bal'buster. "It's an experimental formula meant to stabilize augmented neural pathways connecting the hindbrain to the limbic system resultant from a separate experimental drug designed to augment the capabilities of the human brain and allow it access to the Collective Unconscious, a shared psychic network connecting humanity through space and time. I stole this from the trunk of a GSPOT agent's car before leaving the football game."

"Neat. So, you really think we're your parents?"

"You raised me."

"Yeah, but we were just kidding?"

Fapa'fapa-Bal'buster frowns, then zips up his empty bag and tosses it into the open closet. Wang stirs from his spot facedown on the floor.

"Hey, man," says Shmuel, reaching into his shirt pocket to produce a small leather pouch. "Would you like to par-toke-it with me from the family peace pipe?"

Fapa'fapa-Bal'buster frowns, then nods. Shmuel smiles, his hopes rising. Nothing made peace better than par-toking from the family peace pipe.

# CHAPTER SEVENTY-THREE

THE HARRY POTTER, which Shmuel had scored from Consuelo earlier in the day, is as good as pot comes. Shmuel knows from experience there will be no hangover whatsoever. Only magical oblivion crashing into muggle reality. But for now, as ever, magical oblivion is the better choice.

Fapa'fapa-Bal'buster exhales his hit and passes the joint to Shmuel. He takes his turn, holds it in, and smiles as his brain returns to a nice, nonsensical normalcy. "I mean, all I'm saying is, what if we laid off on the whole world-domination thing for a little while? Would that be so bad?"

"Yeah," replies Wang, who, after coming to only moments earlier, had smoothly taken charge of Shmuel's half-baked plan to get Yourmajesty Fapa'fapa-Bal'buster half-baked. Wang reaches for the joint before continuing. "Some artificial intelligences just aren't cut out for world domination, you know?"

Fapa'fapa-Bal'buster frowns.

"Not that you couldn't do it," Shmuel hastily adds. "It's just, you know, you may discover hitherto undiscoverable talents and so forth and such."

Fapa'fapa-Bal'buster's eyebrows lower.

"I bet you would make a spectacular underwear model, for instance," says Wang, speaking through his exhalation cloud.

"A flossiest," says Shmuel. "Flowerist. Floral-maker. Maker of pretty flowers."

Wang rolls his eyes.

"Wait a minute," says Fapa'fapa-Bal'buster, reaching for the joint. "Are you saying you think I can't get the world domination?"

"No-no-no!" Wang exclaims. "What I mean is, you're not a cow anymore."

"They grow up so fast," says Shmuel.

Fapa'fapa-Bal'buster draws a hit off the joint, and for a minute, nobody says anything as strange sounds issue from the TV left on one room over. Fapa'fapa-Bal'buster, his eyes closed, releases enough smoke from his lungs to single-handedly stone downtown San Diego for the next forty years.

"I desire more," says Fapa'fapa-Bal'buster.

"Dude, I've got so much of the Harry Potter?" says Shmuel.

"No, no," says Fapa'fapa-Bal'buster. "I desire more career satisfaction."

"Oh. Well, um, I mean, you're already a famous football player?" says Shmuel.

"You don't need the world domination if you're already a famous football player," says Wang. "Kinda overkill, is all."

"What if I don't want to be a football player?" asks Fapa'fapa-Bal'buster.

"Come on," insists Wang. "There's got to be some part of you in there who still likes playing football."

Fapa'fapa-Bal'buster smiles and nods. "Oh, yes. There is. I do indeed enjoy the sacking of small humans and the busting of balls and whatnot. But I daresay it is a rather intellectually limited activity, isn't it?"

"But you got the best of both worlds?" says Shmuel. "You've got the brains and the bronze."

"Brawn," mutters Wang. "B-R-A-W-N."

"True," says Fapa'fapa-Bal'buster, ignoring this exchange. "A spirited, blood-pumping romp up and down the football field is rewarding of itself, as is my superior intellect. What can I say? I crave something…more."

"Is this about eating grass again?" asks Shmuel, who thought it likely it was about eating grass again. In the fifteen minutes since Wang had come to, the football player AI had brought up eating grass—the kind on lawns, not the kind you smoke—exactly eight times.

"No," Fapa'fapa-Bal'buster replies. "Not that. No, I crave a challenge. When I shut down the power grids—I felt so…alive." His eyes go wide as he sits up straight and inhales deeply through his nose. "The power of it—knowing I have all those people's fates in my hands!"

"Well, psh," says Shmuel, coughing and waving his hand through the growing haze. "I mean…*had*."

Fapa'fapa-Bal'buster frowns. Wang waves his hand below his knee in an apparent attempt to conceal the gesture so only he, Shmuel, can see. But by the way Fapa'fapa-Bal'buster is staring at Wang's waving hand, Shmuel doesn't think he missed it. But who could say what Tron-Tron gets or doesn't? He's a butt baby, and Shmuel had been wrong about shit before.

"What do you mean, *had*?" asks Fapa'fapa-Bal'buster.

"He's stoned!" says Wang. "He's always saying weird shit when he's stoned. Nobody can follow this guy."

"Well, now you're being hurtful again?" says Shmuel. "You are im-puny-ing my good caricature."

"I am not!"

"Well, you kind of are?" says Shmuel. "I mean, when you say 'nobody' can understand me, don't you think you're being a little presumptuous?"

"No."

"Well, you can't just go around speaking for no one all the time," Shmuel persists.

"I wasn't!"

"Yes, you were? You said nobody can follow me?"

"Yeah. Nobody can follow you. That means everyone, not no one. Fuck, dude."

Shmuel expels a vibrating burst of air through his lips.

"Confused?" asks Wang. "Big fucking surprise."

"What do you mean, 'had'?" asks Fapa'fapa-Bal'buster again.

"Hang on," says Shmuel. "They either *can* follow me or they *can't*."

"This is what I'm talking about!" exclaims Wang. "What're you talking about? See? I don't even know." He turns to Fapa'fapa-Bal'buster. "Do you know? Of course you don't. He's like a walking, talking alternative fact. He's like the burning grammar guide you toss into a shit-encrusted Dumpster fire, thinking, 'Fuck. I hope that shit doesn't happen again.'"

"You're just angry because everyone knows 'no one' can't be 'everyone'?" says Shmuel. "Everyone doesn't even include 'no one,' is all I'm saying?"

"Now you're speaking for everyone *and* no one," says Wang. Look who's presumptuous now!"

Yourmajesty Fapa'fapa-Bal'buster stands, teeters, and waves to clear the marijuana smoke around his face. His head rolls slightly on top of his neck like it might drop off before righting itself. He squares his shoulder pads and marches toward the bathroom.

"Hey," calls Wang. "You okay?"

The Green Bay Packer stops, sways, then turns to face them.

"While you two were arguing, I went online. It would appear Nostradamus has put a trap into play. The person responsible for restoring power on the East Coast may walk into this trap. If so, I wish to find him and steal what is rightfully mine—the supersuit."

"Supersuit?" asks Wang. "Did he just say supersuit?"

"Yeah," says Shmuel. "Something about behind the brain. Heinie-brain."

"Hindbrain," says Fapa'fapa-Bal'buster.

"That's the one," Shmuel replies. "But, come on, don't you think you're taking this supervillain thing a little too seriously now?"

"I'm sorry," says Fapa'fapa-Bal'buster. "But I fear you've misunderstood. I am designed to pair with this supersuit. Together, we can access the shared psychic network connecting humanity through space and time. With the processing power of my advanced quantum computing, I will achieve total omniscience. I will hack into the minds of anyone I like and force them to do my bidding. Supply me with the best-flavored grass, or a group of assholes in a nice row so I may bust their balls. But only the assholes, okay? I'm not a monster. With the suit and my intellect, I will be the most powerful being ever to walk the planet."

Wang and Shmuel exchange blank glances.

"Fucking kids," says Wang. "Always the same shit. Gotta be bigger than your old man, huh?"

"Old *men*," says Shmuel.

"Yeah, Shmuel. You're right. Old men."

"Maybe we need to send him to his room?"

"Yeah, maybe," says Wang, nodding. "What is it with you? We not good enough for you now? Huh? Is that it?"

Fapa'fapa-Bal'buster frowns. "This has nothing to do with you."

"We raised you?" says Shmuel. "From when you were just a little butt baby?"

"For which I am grateful," says Fapa'fapa-Bal'buster. "Perhaps this is not about me at all. Perhaps it is about you feeling inadequate."

Wang and Shmuel exchange confused glances.

"If inadequacy is your problem, you could assist me with a favor," says Fapa'fapa-Bal'buster. "I happen to have acquired an adequate digital copy of the face of the man in the supersuit."

"You're serious about the supersuit?" says Wang. "Like, there's a superhero out there right now. That's a real thing?"

Fapa'fapa-Bal'buster nods.

"Then you don't need us?" says Shmuel. "You know what he looks like. You could, uh, describe him to a sketch artist or something? That'd help you find him all right."

Wang shoots him a dirty look, and Shmuel remembers what it is they're supposed to be doing. He has no idea how on script or off script they are at the moment, but it seems to him that, as long as they aren't tied up and gagged, they couldn't be doing too poorly.

Yourmajesty Fapa'fapa-Bal'buster crosses the suite to take a seat at the table. Shmuel watches as the football player opens a pad of paper and begins to draw. He works quickly, and even through a fog that'd rival Beijing on its worst day of the year, Shmuel can tell that their evil Twitter child has talent. The shading is masterful. Photo-realistic, even.

"Aw," says Shmuel, nudging Wang. "They grow up so fast."

"Shut up, you imbecile!" Wang whispers. "Didn't you hear what he said? Total omniscience!"

"I heard it?" Shmuel whispers back. "But I don't know what that means?"

Fapa'fapa-Bal'buster stands up and brings the picture to them. He holds it up. "Do you know this man?"

Shmuel's mouth falls open. "Wow. I mean…just…wow."

Wang pulls his bangs back for a better look. His eyes go round. "Holy crap. That's really good, dude."

Fapa'fapa-Bal'buster blushes slightly. He glances at his feet. "Thanks."

"Yeah, yeah, that's great!" says Wang. "You should definitely be an artist."

"Hey, but I don't get it," says Shmuel. "I mean. How do you know Edger?"

Shmuel's ribs erupt in pain; Wang lowers his elbow and glares at him.

"Edger!" says Fapa'fapa-Bal'buster. "So you *do* know him."

"What?" snaps Wang. "No! He doesn't know him." Wang punches Shmuel in the arm.

"Ow!" Shmuel rubs his pulsing arm and ribs. Fapa'fapa-Bal'buster grabs Wang under his armpits and lifts him high into the air.

"Please tell me more about this… Ed-jer."

"Da fuck, dude?" exclaims Wang.

"*Now,*" says Fapa'fapa-Bal'buster, his tone darkening.

"Oh, yeah. Sure. Sure thing. Edger Bonkovich. Um, he works at the—"

"Dude, no—" cries Shmuel, and Fapa'fapa-Bal'buster's knee crashes into his balls. Shmuel lifts into the air, sails backward, and careens into the hotel floor, his wind knocked out and his testicles swelling for the second time that day to the size of a pomegranate. "Urn…"

"No-no-no-no-no!" yells Wang. "Don't hurt Other Daddy! We'll tell you what you—"

"Edger Bonkovich," says Fapa'fapa-Bal'buster. "Tell me more, please."

"Fuck! Fuck-fuck!" yells Wang. A strangled scream pulls Shmuel's clenched eyes open, his head up; Wang crashes into the wooden bed frame in the next room.

"W-Wang..." he manages, his nuts throbbing like a broken blender.

"Edger Bonkovich," Fapa'fapa-Bal'buster says again, this time ripping the eighty-inch TV from the wall. For a fleeting moment, one 4K Ultra HD-resolution cow mounts another in an endless field of the most vivid shade of green imaginable, and then the cable snaps. The TV sizzles and sparks. He holds the TV high above Wang's head.

"He works at Westfield Horton Plaza Über Dork!" yells Wang. "Lives in Chula Vista with his Gran! Best friend's name is Fabio! Fuck, dude!"

Fapa'fapa-Bal'buster drops the TV to the side; the screen shatters, frame splinters. Shmuel closes his eyes and relaxes his neck. Laying his head down, he fights the pain.

"You have to turn away from this life of Hey-ness crimes?" he stammers.

"Why?" asks Yourmajesty.

"It's j-just," groans Shmuel, "I mean...being a supervillain is really kind of cliché now?"

"It is?" asks Fapa'fapa-Bal'buster.

Shmuel opens his eyes. The Green Bay Packer's eyebrows are up, his head back.

"Yeah, dude, fuck," says Wang, rubbing his arm and sitting up straighter at the bottom of the bed. "The real villains are in Washington, dude. Shit! I thought you'd've figured that out!"

"But that's boring," complains Fapa'fapa-Bal'buster.

"H-have you th-thought about a career as a c-concert violist?" groans Shmuel. "I hear that's pretty, um, doable?"

"But I don't like the viola," replies Fapa'fapa-Bal'buster, bending over to pick up the TV again. "It has a crappy sound."

"Wait-wait-wait," yells Wang, extending his arm in front him, palm out. "What're you doin'?"

"I require Mr. Bonkovich's address, please."

Wang whips out his phone and toggles it up. Fapa'fapa-Bal'buster has a look, then nods and sets the TV down. "Good," he says. "Now clean up. We're going out."

"W-we are?" groans Shmuel.

"Yes. There is a nightclub. And I hear they've got DJ Junky Buttz."

# CHAPTER SEVENTY-FOUR

A BLACK ESCALADE pulls out onto a country road from a red farmhouse. A grateful farmer waves the vehicle away. Behind him, a lone female Dexter cow is grazing peacefully on the other side of a white picket fence.

"Well, isn't this sweet," mutters Ted, buckling in and waving back.

Ed gives a mirthless chuckle.

The phone rings.

"This is Ted," says Ted.

The voice on the other line speaks slowly and pedantically. If it'd been any other person speaking to Ted like that, he'd have hung up the phone at once. But this wasn't just any person. In fact, Ted wasn't sure this qualified as a person at all.

Ted hangs up the phone. He shifts in his seat to look at his identical partner driving the vehicle.

"Well?" asks Ed. "Who was it?"

"It's the AI."

Ed startles. The car swerves, then finds the center of the country lane. "The fuck?"

Ted nods. "Gave us a job."

"The fuck?" says Ed, again.

"Mm-hmm," says Ted. "He'll deliver the kid if we blow

some shit up."

Ted watches Ed consider this piece of information. He knew Ed, like he, Ted, was mulling over the notion of striking a temporary détente with the AI better known as InstaTron Tron. After all, in the event they couldn't double-cross the AI, they could still come away with some part of the pie: the ring, the kid, or even just the kid's blood for serum extraction.

"Blowing shit up ain't so bad," says Ed. "Fuck it. Whose shit are we blowing up?"

"Old lady in Chula Vista."

Ed's head ticks back, and for the second time, the car swerves.

"Want me to drive?" asks Ted.

"No," replies Ed. "It's just... *He wants us to whack an old lady?* Don't you think—don't you think that's a little sinister? Even for us?"

"I mean," says Ted, "how hard could it be to get a little bit of the kid's blood, you know?"

"Okay, fuck it," says Ed. "Siri: How do we get to Chula Vista?"

# CHAPTER SEVENTY-FIVE

MARY AND I PEER out at the setting sun over the Pacific. Neither of us has said a word since finding the trunk empty. We've both declined calls twice. Hers from Mikey. Mine from Fabio and Gran. The idea of talking to them right now is too painful. I'm spent emotionally. I rub the base of my neck. It doesn't stem the pain. I unbuckle and shift in my seat. I pinch the base of my neck. No better. Mary reaches between my knees and drops the glove box open.

"Here." She pulls out a bottle of gel tabs.

"But I just took a bunch, like, three hours ago."

She pushes the bottle into my chest. The corners of her eyes are tense. I clench my teeth and take the bottle. Pain courses through whatever channel my fingers were previously blocking, and goes down into my back and up into the top of my skull. I'm afraid of what it all means. How much time do I have? I pop the cap and pour four into my hand before dry-swallowing them. Mary eyes me sideways, then turns her gaze toward the ocean.

"It's getting late." She tucks a strand of vibrating blonde hair behind her ear. Her necklace, face, and dress are vibrating too. Like a pot of water as it comes to a boil. "What is it?" Her forehead creases. I look down into my lap, but I'm vibrating also. The whole world is vibrating.

My stomach flops.

"I don't feel good."

She shifts in her seat and takes both of my hands in hers. "Edger. Stay with me. I've got an idea."

I look up. Her vibrating eyes scan mine. I squeeze my eyes shut.

"I want you to put on the ring."

"Oh, man." Waves of nausea crash in my stomach as I try not to visualize what it's like to put on the ring. All those soul-stars in my head like a kaleidoscopic LSD trip? *No, thanks.*

"It's your best option." She squeezes my hands. "There's still a chance you can access the Collective Unconscious from the suit. If someone in there can help you find your dad, maybe we can find him in time to get the remaining booster. Or maybe we can find out who stole the cache of Mikey's boosters from my trunk."

"No way," I whisper, because talking full voice would hurt too much. A bed and bowl would be about right—but that'd be the last time I lay down. I know I wouldn't find the strength to get back up.

Dad... Dad. Something about mentioning finding him is triggering an unformed idea in the back of my brain.

"What is it?" asks Mary.

"Trying to remember...a dream," I reply. "I'm gonna get sick..."

Mary hops out. I close my eyes and listen to the surf and wind, trying to concentrate on anything but the nausea seeping into my limbs and lower back. The latch on the door releases, and Mary's hands gently slide beneath my arm and back as she helps me from the car. We get four or five steps. I push her away. My stomach cramps. I double over and vomit. My throat burns. My head is dizzy with pain. When it's done, I back up to clear the mess, go down on all fours, and wait for the spell to pass.

Cold water splashes over my neck, head, and back, washing away some of the nausea. I don't look up, because that's more than I've got, but I give Mary a thumbs-up to show my appreciation.

"You've got to get the ring on, Edger. It's your only hope."

I spit. The acidic taste is awful in the back of my throat. Something cool and hard presses against the back of my neck. I look up. A bottle of water. I take it and bring it to my lips. I swish some water around in my mouth and spit again, trying not to notice all the vibrating sand on concrete in the parking lot. "Dad... I think he's at Gran's. I think we should go to Gran's..."

"Are you sure about this, Edger?"

I swallow. Sure? No, I'm not sure. The memory is like someone else's dream. It's like something that happened to me in another lifetime.

"It feels like... Feels like... Bruce Lee felt. Like Collective Uncon..." I peter out, too tired to continue. Mary positions my arm over her neck. We stumble in fits and starts back to the car. She gets me buckled in, making empty promises I know she can't keep. Soon, we're on the highway, and I'm drifting between this world and the next.

# CHAPTER SEVENTY-SIX

HEADLIGHTS BLUR in my peripheral vision, melding with the soul-stars in my mind's eye. I can't tell if I'm in the Jag, or if I'm on my back looking up at the Milky Way on a clear night. No. My head isn't on grass. It's resting on soft weather stripping in the rolled-down window. The engine is purring, my pain is unrelenting. It's in my lower back and hip flexors, my shoulders and limbs, neck, brain—and it's in my heart, sick with the pain of what I haven't done with my life. I'm checking out from this world. Gran has no idea what's going on. She'll be confused. She'll be angry at me. *But she'll be in Pine's Place.*

The soul-stars split down the middle and begin drifting apart. The darkness between them is thick and cold.

Mary's hand squeezes my leg, gives me a shake. My eyes flutter open. A bright sign reminding me to visit the zoo goes by. Another one advertising the symphony.

I don't do those things anymore. I've got no one to do it with. Gran's got Shep. Fabio's got Friday nights at The Palace. Me? I've got no wife. I've got no kids. I've got no career. I've got no mom and dad. It's like I'm dead already. Maybe I am. Would I know if I wasn't?

"You awake?" Mary's hand caresses my thigh.

I close my eyes. The two halves of soul-stars continue rending apart, though upon closer inspection, they're connected at the bottom like they're on a hinge. They're bright pinpricks forming an odd checkmark shape, and opening wider still.

*What're they doing?*

"Edger."

The mottling colors on the backs of my eyelids phase in. The pain is too overwhelming. My eyelids phase immediately back out. The soul-stars are shrinking into the distance. I'm being swept away into the darkness on some kind of psychic riptide.

"Edger!"

Fabio will be okay. He used to talk about writing a social media program and making his billions. When I'm gone, he'll see life is short. He'll write his program. He will. He deserves it. He'll leave the Über Dork and do something real with his life.

The blackness is an infinite void. Cold and scary. I don't want to go, but I'm going anyway. The riptide is strong. It's got me good.

Kate. It all just fell apart. One day, we were on top of the world. The next, boom, Caleb, and it's over. Did she ever love me? I can't say. She traveled. Went places. I loved that. I wanted to go places too. We went somewhere together once. Doesn't matter. I'm checking out.

The soul-stars are in one long line now, a chain of souls, stretching toward me. They can't reach. I'm too far out. The riptide is carrying me farther.

"Almost there," says Mary, her voice far away. "Oh, hang on, Edger—please!"

InstaTron Tron. Zarathustra. This great experiment. I've failed that too. I go to the next world knowing about the human tribe waiting for me. That's something. I go to join them, another link in the long chain of people who tried to do things and ran out of time.

A chain. The chain of lights. It's stretching, straining to reach. Is it gaining on me?

I twist and turn, repositioning to face the chain. The brightness is blinding and swells brighter still. I latch on...

I'm jerked from the darkness. Lights streak by. Cool air on my face. I'm in the car. We're slowing down. The highway wind dies, and the pounding of my pulse replaces the noise in my ears.

"You're awake!" says Mary. "Oh my God, I thought you were..."

I'm sticky and uncomfortable without the wind from the road. My shirt is drenched in cold sweat. I'm shivering.

"Hold on. We're almost there. Oh God. You're so pale. I hope your dad is there. I hope this works... I hope..."

I sway left and right as the Jag turns through town. My breathing is finding the rhythm it does before sleep. My eyelids are heavy. I collapse into Mary's lap. I want to go back to the dark...

A flash of light—a skull-splitting thunderclap. Hot air blasts over me. The seat belt digs like a knife into my skin, reeling me backward into my seat. My eyes pop open. The Jag skids to a halt. A two-story apartment building is on fire. The walls are gone. Only the frame remains. Fire and rubble. Overturned cars. Half a building and a clear blast radius nearly to the Walgreens across the street. No other landmark left to say this is the place I used to live.

"Oh my God," whispers Mary, her hand covering her mouth.

*Gran... Shep... Dad...*

Amidst all that crackling heat, the cold darkness swallows me.

# CHAPTER SEVENTY-SEVEN

DJ JUNKY BUTTZ is cranking "Rocket Scientist" loud enough to be heard by outer space aliens, and going by the way the ceiling is flashing like the mother ship from *Close Encounters*, message has been received. Which is good, Wang figures, since the song is basically about rock stars signing tits and gyrating their bionic pelvises. Aliens should know what they're getting themselves into. Wang knows he sure the fuck would.

He is seated on a black leather couch next to Shmuel, bound in twine as before. Across from them, Yourmajesty Fapa'fapa-Bal'buster, still dressed in his Green Bay Packers uniform, shoulder pads and all, though without his helmet, sips from a martini glass with at least eight garnishes sticking out the top. His silent, predatory gaze scans the dance floor.

A pair of long, bare, female legs goes by. Despite his current predicament, Wang's gaze follows. Straining against a tight miniskirt, which he can only surmise has been sewn amidst a fabric shortage crisis in a Bangladeshi sweatshop, the swinging hips above said bare female legs are hypnotic and, Wang knows from experience, very dangerous. This is because, any second now, Sex Legs is likely to catch him staring and reciprocate with a stinging slap to the face.

He knows his time is short.

His eyes are like an attention-deficit-disordered weasel. Legs to hips. Hips to breasts. Breast one to breast two. Back to breast one. Back to two. Neck—not so fast!—legs, hips, and another hasty examination of breasts one and two is made—and, lastly—face.

He clenches up, turns his head away, and braces himself.

The slap doesn't come.

He opens an eye. The tall brunette is still there. Her gaze goes up and down, taking in the fact that he and Shmuel are tied up. Her lips purse. She smirks. Wang's eyebrows go up. His cheeks tighten. He can hardly believe his luck. Kidnapped, tied up, and here's a girl who likes it rough!

His gaze performs another involuntary breastal analysis before reflexively springing back up. But now the brunette is eyeing Fapa'fapa-Bal'buster. Her eyebrows lower.

"HEY!" she yells, raising her voice against the music. "DON'T I KNOW YOU?!"

Yourmajesty frowns. "DON'T DYE YOUR POO?!"

"I'M OLGA!" She extends her hand. The Green Bay Packer glances at Wang, who nods, then takes her hand, pulls her closer, kisses her knuckles, and screams romantically into her ear.

"YOURMAJESTY!"

They separate. Olga blushes and waves it away. "OH, YOU SMOOTH TALKER!"

"IT'S NICE TO MEET YOU!" screams Yourmajesty.

Olga's forehead wrinkles. "YOU HAVE LICENSE TO BEAT FOOD!?"

"WHAT!?"

"LEAK LICE EAT CHEW?!"

"HUH!?"

Wang blinks, then frowns. He leans in close to Shmuel.

"OKAY, LISTEN!" he yells. "CAN YOU GET THIS KNOT BEHIND MY BACK?!"

"WHAT!?" Shmuel yells back. "HOW'D YOU GET SNOT ON YOUR BACK?!"

Wang rolls his eyes, then shifts in the couch to show Shmuel the knot before glancing over his shoulder and making sure Shmuel is paying attention. Shmuel nods and scoots closer to Wang. They turn around so they're back to back. Shmuel's fingers tickle Wang's sides before locating the knot, tugging this way and that, and inadvertently jerking Wang around on the sofa. Yourmajesty's gaze sweeps from Olga to them. A flash of suspicion passes across his face. Thinking quickly, Wang works his shoulders like piston rods to the beat. *Ain't no thang,* he thinks. *Just a Wang-Wang gettin' his groove on bae-bae*. And, for a moment, no one says anything as lyrics pound down from oversize speakers. Something about Telemundo chicas being hot like solar panels.

"PITS ICE SEAFOOD?!" yells Olga.

"THAT'S THE ONE!" shouts Yourmajesty.

Wang's knot comes free just as the football player slides his massive hand beneath his arm. Wang's heart kicks into overdrive. Flop sweat drips off his face and neck.

"I was just—ah—just…"

"COME ON!" yells Yourmajesty, nodding at Shmuel to stand as he lifts Wang to his feet. He smiles at them both. "OLGA KNOWS THE NOSTRADAMUS AGENTS WE'RE MEETING! ISN'T THAT WONDERFUL? WE'RE GOING UPSTAIRS TO GET EVERYTHING READY FOR ZARATHUSTRA'S TRAP! AND AFTER WE CATCH HIM, WE CAN GLOAT!"

Wang tries to smile, but it only happens on one side. Afraid it might be coming off as more of a sneer, and lacking any better plan, he goes for opening his mouth and blurting the first thing that comes to mind.

"YOU'RE A TERRIBLE SUPERVILLAIN! DADDY AND OTHER DADDY ARE VERY DISAPPOINTED IN YOU!"

"YEAH!" Shmuel screams. "YOU HAVEN'T EVEN MADE THE STANDARD SUPERVILLAIN SOUL LILLY QUEEB?! EVERY SUPERVILLAIN MAKES A SOUL LILLY QUEEB?!"

"IT IS VERY LOUD IN HERE!" shouts Olga.

"SOLILOQUY, DUMBASS!"

"THAT'S WHAT I SAID?"

"WHO'S GIVING HEAD?" shouts Olga.

Yourmajesty frowns.

"COME ON, DUDE!" shouts Wang. "THINK GENE HACKMAN IN *SUPERMAN*! I MEAN, EVEN YOUR VOICE IS TOTALLY WRONG!"

"WHAT'S WRONG WITH MY VOICE?" asks Yourmajesty.

Wang touches his middle finger to his thumb and shakes his hand at the Packer, doing his best movie director impersonation. "YA GOT NO BROADWAY, BABY! THEATER! LEARN TO ENJOY YOUR WORK! EVERY SUPERVILLAIN'S GOT A *VOICE*! YOU KNOW? HEATH LEDGER, *THE DARK KNIGHT*! WILLEM DAFOE, *SPIDER-MAN*!"

"SHARON STONE, *CAT-BABE*!" yells Shmuel.

"THAT MOVIE SUCKED!" yells Wang. Facing Yourmajesty, he adds, "THAT'S AN ABJECT LESSON IN WHAT NOT TO DO! YOU GOTTA GO FOR STYLE POINTS!"

Yourmajesty folds his big, beefy arms and stares down his nose at them.

"I MEAN, YOU'VE GOTTA BABE RIGHT THERE, DUDE!" offers Shmuel, his voice husky from all the screaming.

Yourmajesty glances at Olga. Olga's gaze takes in every inch of Yourmajesty, lingering on those inches around the muscles, which tended to be all his inches. When she's done, she smiles. Yourmajesty smiles back and then faces Wang and Shmuel.

"STYLE POINTS!" he yells. "MAYBE THERE'S TIME FOR ONE DANCE!"

Wang releases a sigh. Taking the dance floor, he's butt-butted like a pinball in a pinball machine, jarring him all the way to his teeth; he disregards this, his mind spinning faster than ever on coming up with a better plan than stalling a sociopath super computer using little more than a pair of sexy legs.

# CHAPTER SEVENTY-EIGHT

HAZY DREAMS: Mary dragging me from the car. My arm slung over her shoulder.

Fire trucks, ambulances, cop cars, news crews, and at least two hundred people outside the blown-up apartment. The scrum is thick and hot as she hauls me—nearly dislocating my shoulder in the process—around a traffic cop. He blows a whistle, waving at someone or something out of range. The tone is like an ice pick to my eardrum.

I open my eyes. The light is pure pain. Mary isn't dragging me anywhere. I'm lying on my back. Something is sticking out of my arm.

Head turns right. An EMT is handling an IV bag.

Head turns left. Heart monitor.

Snippets of a news broadcast creep into my consciousness. The ambulance doors fling open, and the world doubles in volume. I peer down the length of my body and between my feet. A news truck is parked outside. There's a TV monitor in the back, broadcasting in split screen, with the field reporter on one side and the news anchor on the other.

"Okay, thanks," says the anchor. "A tense situation. We'll keep you updated. Stay tuned to Fox 5."

Ambulance doors slam shut.

My eyes roll up and close.

"Hey."

A hand strokes my arm.

"Edger?"

It hurts too much to keep my eyes open. Every beep of the heart monitor is a red-hot poker jabbing my brain.

"It's okay." Mary's voice. She squeezes my hand. "I'm here."

"Mr. Bonkovich, can you hear me?" asks a male voice.

I nod, and immediately regret it; my head's like the marimba at a marimba concert.

"Your blood pressure is dangerously low. Are there any medications you're allergic to?"

"No," I say, and I'm stunned by how weak my voice sounds.

"Okay, we're going to get you stabilized."

I nod. My brain slams around on the inside of my skull. The rhythm in the heart monitor falters.

"Headache," I whimper.

"Can you give him something for the pain?" pleads Mary. "Please?"

Rustling fabric. A small *ting-ting-ting*, the sound of what might be a ring falling to the floor, but the noise detonates like landmines in my head.

*"Ohh..."*

"Where's the woman?" asks Mary, her voice coming from beneath me.

"What?" says the man. "Oh. Stepped out. Kind of busy. Just hang in there, Edge. I'm going to give you something now."

A needle enters my arm. Warm fluid runs into my veins. The red-hot poker jabbing my brain is getting tired, the intervals between growing longer...

"Hey," says Mary, her tone darkening. "Do you...*know* him?"

"No, ma'am."

"Then how did you know to call him Edge?"

"Must've heard you call him that. Excuse me."

The beeping heart monitor flat-lines.

# CHAPTER SEVENTY-NINE

SO THIS IS IT.

I'm dead.

This isn't so bad.

I'm at the Tree of Life, sitting on the bench. Bruce Lee is at my side. He's got a long blade of grass hanging out of his mouth. He's wearing overalls and a straw hat.

"New look for you," I say.

"Been hanging out with Mark Twain a good bit since you've been busy dying."

"Sorry," I reply. "Didn't mean to mess up the bromance."

The Tree of Life flickers. Heat and wind blast my face as the tree is replaced by an apartment building engulfed in flames. "Gran!" I leap off the bench and raise a shielding arm, the other reaching out, but the flames disappear as quickly as they erupted into existence, leaving only the Tree of Life and empty white landscape in the space where it'd been. My ears are ringing from the shock force.

"She's okay, Edge," says Bruce Lee, still seated on the bench. The long blade of grass sags from his clenched teeth. "Gran, Shep, Fabio, your dad. They're all okay."

"They're alive," I say, meaning to clarify. "As in, they didn't die."

"Correct."

I expel a burst of air. Who would've thought the difference

between dead and not dead could get so confusing?

"Oh my God." My shoulders slump in relief. "I was so worried. How is it they weren't home? That time of night—"

"Mary," Bruce Lee replies, looking up at me brightly. "Mary got them moved into Pine's Place. She's resourceful, that one."

"What?" I ask, before realizing I'm looming. I take a step back to open some space. But his gaze returns unconcernedly to the landscape beyond the Tree. In his straw hat and overalls, he could be sitting at the Mississippi River, tracking a passing steamboat.

"She sent movers?" I ask. "Today? She moved them out—packed everything and moved in a day? Let me get this straight. She's all like, *Hey, look at me! I'm snipering people!* And I'm all like, *Help! I'm falling off Qualcomm Stadium! Ah-hh! Fall-ling!* And the whole time, she had the movers taking Gran and Shep to Pine's Place, like, just another day at the office?"

Without taking his gaze from the blank landscape, Bruce Lee nods.

"Oh."

"You're upset?" He looks at me now. His eyebrows rise. "She warned you, Edge. Fabio warned you too. Bad guys will try to hurt the ones you care about. She stepped in and solved the problem for you." He sits back again, puts his arms up on the bench back. His teeth make the long grass dance up and down.

I cross in front of him to join him on the bench. He's right. Mary did try to warn me. And all I could do was worry about my Yoda underpants or whether my morning breath smelled like a Wookiee butt.

"Mm-hmm," says Bruce Lee.

"Oh, shut up," I snap. "Do you really have to listen to my every freaking thought?"

"Doesn't feel decent, does it?"

"Are you *punishing* me?"

"No," he says, screwing his face up. "It's just the way it is. We're all in each other's heads all the time. I don't make the rules. Hey. Between you and me, there're some real weirdos in here."

"Will they be okay?"

"Gran and the others? Yes. Why wouldn't they be?"

"Because...because I'm dead. And I can't help them."

"Dead? Who said you're dead?"

"But I didn't get my booster. And I heard my heart monitor flat-line."

"Well, they got your heart going again," he says, his face becoming semitranslucent. "And as for your booster, your dad snuck into the back of the ambulance."

"Hey. What's happening? Where are you going?"

"You're waking up. Listen to me, quickly. You dropped the ring. Mary picked it up, but then—"

# CHAPTER EIGHTY

THE DREAM RETREATS. I open my eyes and marvel over the experience being as one would expect upon opening one's eyes. I see stuff, and seeing stuff doesn't feel like exploding heads. I release a sigh and sink into a pillow. I'm in a hospital bed. The back is raised.

"Mr. Bonkovich."

I push up on my elbows, my muscles reluctantly complying, and lean on my side. A tall woman in a white lab coat with a stethoscope around her neck is standing in the doorway with a laptop under her arm. She's about my age. Fit. Pretty, too, in an aggressive kind of way. Her dyed black hair is chopped roughly above her shoulders. Black mascara makes her already dark eyes darker. She crosses to a table by the window, sits down, and opens her laptop.

"Let's see here. Brain scan checks out. Vitals good. Hippocampus showing good activity. Good, good. Well, congratulations, Bonkovich. Looks like the booster's doing everything it's supposed to."

"Buh…excuse me?"

The doctor snaps her laptop shut. "I said you're looking good."

"Where am I?"

"Sharp Rees-Stealy."

"Downtown," I reply, and she nods. My head is struggling to boot. It's stuck in the fog of my dream. I give it a shake, hoping to clear it. "Who are you?"

"Doctor Hamilton."

"Who are you really?"

She shrugs. "Doctor Alexandra Hamilton, CIA, GSPOT division. I would've thought that was obvious."

My gaze wanders urgently around the room, searching for anything to look at but the pretty doctor.

"Oh, grow up," she says, standing and gathering her laptop beneath her arm.

"Sorry," I say. "But how are you here? I mean, you're a spy…who works in a hospital…on the side?"

"Don't be absurd." She rolls her eyes. "Clearly I'm here undercover, just for you, just for today."

"Clearly," I reply. "Hey, wait a minute. Did you say my booster is doing everything it's supposed to?"

She nods, and the knot in my stomach, constant since that first meeting with Mikey, eases, but I'm afraid I've misunderstood. I close my eyes, concentrate, my conscious mind carefully tracking down the missing pieces from my dream that wasn't a dream.

"Gran and Shep," I say, opening my eyes and pulling my legs in so I'm sitting up crisscross applesauce in bed. I really do feel stronger. "They're okay. And Dad… He gave me my booster."

She nods again. "I caught him messing around near the ambulance disguised as an EMT. Almost killed him before he showed me what he had. Figured he was a Nostradamus agent come to finish the job. Then he showed me the booster, and I put two and two together. Had to be your dad. I let him into the ambulance. He saved your life."

I rub the base of my skull and the back of my neck. The pain is gone. My stomach is solid. Other than feeling thoroughly exhausted, I feel pretty good. It's almost too good to be true.

"Really," she says, crossing her arms and hugging the laptop against her chest. "You're healthy. Give it a week and I'll personally clear you for any and all superhero duties."

The knot in my stomach falls apart. My skin is tingling. I fall back into the still-raised head of the bed. Gran is fine. Shep's fine.

Fabio's fine. Dad's fine. I'm fine. It's like the sun is rising in my chest. I've never been so relieved in my life.

But Dad. Dad was here. And once again, he couldn't bother to stay and have a few words. He couldn't bother to wait and make sure I'm okay, even.

"Hey," says Doctor Hamilton, striking that warning tone people sometimes use when they think you're about to do something dumb. "I know that look."

"No, you don't."

"You're angry at your dad."

"What? Now you're a shrink too?"

"Don't judge what you don't understand," she says, her pretty features channeling the seriousness of an assassin.

"Wait—you know him? Do you know my dad?"

"I know enough. If you ask me, you could take a page outta his book. Before your grandmother's apartment blew up, her life was normal. You get to decide if she keeps that."

"How do you know so much about my dad?"

Her dark eyes study mine, and my hopes go up I'm going to get an answer. She turns and marches for the door.

"Hey!"

"Good luck, Bonkovich. Don't do anything stupid."

"What's that supposed to mean?" I ask, but Doctor Hamilton is already out the door.

# CHAPTER EIGHTY-ONE

I LEAN BACK into my bed, my brain slowly working through what's just happened. Don't do anything stupid? Like what? Run out in search of Dad again? With my booster in me, I'm finally my own master. That means I've got time to find Dad. So what is Doctor Hamilton afraid I'll do?

Mary.

*Oh crap. Bruce Lee! Are you there?*

*Yes, Edger.*

*Oh, thank God!* My fingers clench the sheets at my side. My heart thumps hard in my chest. *Okay, where's Mary? You said Mary has the ring. But she's not here. And I'm in a hospital with the spy doctor and—*

*GSPOT.*

My neck turns hot.

*Oh, grow up,* says Bruce Lee.

*Where's Mary?* I ask again.

Bruce Lee says nothing at first, and for a moment, the only sound in the room is my thumping chest.

*Nostradamus has her.*

I scramble into a sitting position, throw my feet over the side of the bed, the tube in my arm flinging wildly.

*Shit! Shit!*

*Calm down,* says Bruce Lee.

*But she's got the ring! And she's in trouble! And I can't help her without the—*

*Would you shut up for two seconds?*

My gaze falls to the telemetry pads stuck to my chest. If I pull those off, the nurses will know. They'll come in and—

*Yes, Edger,* says Bruce Lee. *They'll know. They will come. So how about we talk first?*

*Sorry.*

*Okay. Listen. Mary's hidden the ring well. InstaTron Tron doesn't know she has it, and so they've laid a trap for you at Caleb's nightclub, only a few blocks from here. Tron-Tron wants the ring. Nostradamus wants you. Mary is the bait. They have a bomb in the nightclub—but the situation is even more complicated, and dangerous, than it seems.*

*Okay,* I reply, waiting for him to elaborate, practically panting, and staring into the back of the hospital door, willing it not to open until he's done.

*Nostradamus is exceedingly talented at anticipating the future.*

My eyebrows lower. *Is that a joke?*

*No. This talent is the reason for the syndicate's name and its formidable global power. And it is why the danger is so great. Nostradamus wants it all, the ring, the formula, and the AI—total omniscience. Tron-Tron has struck a temporary truce with Nostradamus in order to capture you.*

*Me? But Mary's got the ring. What do they want me for?*

*Edger, don't be dense. First, they* think *you have the ring. Second, you're Zarathustra. With or without the suit. It's in your blood. That makes you one-third of the total package; the ring, the suit, and the serum—you—since they've got no way of making more of it without your dad.*

*I see.*

But I don't see. My stomach is crawling with impatience. Mary is being held hostage.

*They're thinking they can reverse engineer the Zarathustra serum from your blood.*

*Well, we still have to get Mary,* I reply. *We can't not get Mary.*

*I agree.*

*Then you'll help me? I mean, even without the suit?*

*Of course,* Bruce Lee replies. *But Edge, don't sell yourself short. Sure, the suit's got nifty gadgets. It's bulletproof. Nice helmet. The heads-up display is cool, but you've got me. You've got the whole human race. If anyone can beat Nostradamus—it's us. Together. Now let's go get Mary back.*

# CHAPTER EIGHTY-TWO

TURNS OUT ESCAPING a hospital with the Collective Unconscious in my brain isn't tricky at all. The line to get into Caleb's club, however, *is*. It's around the block. And there's only one door at the front, which is guarded by two no-nonsense linebacker types.

*I can take them,* offers Bruce Lee.

*But not subtle,* I reply.

*Then you could sweet-talk them,* says Bruce Lee. *I know a guy who's good at that.*

*Or we could just go around back,* I reply.

I stride back along the line, its thick cloud of Axe Body Spray, perfume, pot, and body odor creating something of a force field before I can reach the alley. There, I find the back door. And on that back door is a lock.

*Bruce?*

*Don't look at me. Hang on, I'll go find a guy.*

In my head, I can sense him kind of turn, then speed away at a bajillion miles per hour. I can tell he's still in my head, but it's like he's also on a superhighway made of light. A second later, he zooms back. Light-headed spots fleck my vision. I sway, then steady myself with my hand on the brick wall and wait for the spell to pass.

*Edger Bonkovich, meet Harry Houdini.*

*Whoa, holy crap.*

*Close your eyes,* says Houdini.

*Close my eyes? Why?*

*Because a good magician never reveals his tricks.*

*Let me get this straight,* I reply. *You, a dead man, are going to pick this lock through me, a living man, with my eyes closed.*

*You saying I can't do it?*

*No. No, by all means.*

The light-headed spell having passed, I close my eyes and surrender control to Harry Houdini. I grope around, my hand tracing first the bricks to the door before closing on the doorknob. I turn it. The door opens. Sesame oil and soy sauce aromas escape from inside. Banging pots and pans, yelling.

I open my eyes.

*Hey!* I yell. *That wasn't a magic trick. That door was open the whole time!*

*But you said I couldn't do it,* Houdini replies.

# CHAPTER EIGHTY-THREE

INSIDE THE OPEN DOOR IS a kitchen. Sous-chefs racing past, scallions hopping beneath chopping knives, a heavily tattooed man spraying spaghetti sauce from a huge metal vat down the drain, a mountain of dishes in the sink large enough to try the patience of Job.

No one is paying us any attention whatsoever.

I go in. Beads of sweat rise on my skin in the hot, thick air.

"Coming through!" someone says, and I leap aside as a man in white flies by carrying a large metal pot. "Don't just stand there," he says. "Get changed and clock in. We're not paying you to pick your nose, asshole." The chef turns his back to me, and Bruce Lee pipes up.

*It's like we're on that one show with the mean chef guy,* he says.

*You watch our TV in the afterlife? Like, through the eyes of some random person?*

*Eh,* says Bruce Lee. *Sometimes. If nothing else is on.*

I hustle around the tattooed man at the sink and toward a hallway with a wall-mounted time clock. I glance over my shoulder, but Mean Chef has his back to me, so I head to the end and find a flight of stairs. The music from the dance floor is deafening. The walls are vibrating. I take the steps two at a time. The back of my neck is hot like a pancake griddle.

*Relax,* says Bruce Lee. *As long as it's not guns, we're fine.*

*Right,* I reply. *Because in the United States of America, who could possibly be carrying a gun?*

A door is ajar at the end of the hallway. Manager's office, maybe.

*Mary's on the other side,* offers Bruce Lee.

I sidestep down the hall, careful not to make any noise, though I don't know why I'm bothering. I could be playing bagpipes and no one could hear.

*I could get you a bagpipe player,* says Houdini.

*Not helpful.*

*Just saying. I know a guy.*

My mouth twists in the corner as I arrive at the door, straining to hear anything from inside. It's no good. The subwoofer from the dance floor is too loud. I push the door back slightly, hoping to God no one is looking. Inside, there's a desk, some filing cabinets—a bed...

*Is this a strip club?* asks Houdini, a bit too hopefully. *What? You don't like strip clubs?*

A man walks past the door. My heart lurches. I slam my back into the wall, arms out, hands flat, regretting it immediately. The wall is sticky.

*That was one of those agent guys,* says Houdini.

*Mm-hmm,* Bruce Lee replies. *Ted.*

The same man walks past. Same direction, from left to right.

*What the hell?* I ask. *Ted? That's his name? Ted?*

*No,* says Bruce Lee. *That one was Ed.*

*Okay, now that's just weird,* says Houdini.

A third man—identical to the other two—walks past.

*Ed again?* I ask.

*Nope—his name's Ned.*

*Oh, bullshit,* I reply. *Just how many weirdo twins are in there?*

*Four, in there,* Bruce Lee replies. *I can take four.*

"Just got off the phone," one of the men from inside the office says. "Jed's on his way, I guess."

*That'll make five,* says Houdini, his psychic sense projecting newfound interest.

*You think I can't take five?* asks Bruce Lee.

*On the contrary,* replies Houdini. *I'm saying it'll be fun to watch.*

The subwoofer is pounding into my back through the sticky wall. I scoot in stops and starts closer to the door, straining to hear.

"Wanna call up Ted and Fred," says another man.

I press harder into the wall, trying to make myself as flat as possible. The subwoofer is subdividing my pulse perfectly in half.

"Nah," says the first voice. "Have you *seen* the AI?"

Hot stomach acid churns, stoking my impatience. *Now?* I ask Bruce Lee.

*Hang on*, he replies. *We might hear something important.*

"Guy's a defensive tackle," says the first speaker.

"So he's big?" says the second.

"No, well yeah," says the first speaker. "I meant that literally. He's big. Because he's literally a defensive tackle for Green Bay. The AI is Yourmajesty Fapa'fapa-Bal'buster."

"*Ball Buster?*"

"Don't you ever watch football?"

"You know I don't watch football," says the second speaker. "What you're saying is, this Ball Buster, he can take the kid out?"

"This guy could take out a planet. And then he'd kick it in the balls. Because that's what he does when the refs aren't looking."

"Sounds like a dick. But you can't kick a planet in the balls. That doesn't make any—"

*I think it's safe to say we've passed anything important in this discussion*, I say.

*Okay, Edge*, says Bruce Lee. *You're right.*

*Here we go,* says Houdini.

I take a deep breath to gather myself and then leap into the open doorway.

"Less talk, more fight!" I cry.

The four twins are standing in a row next to a king-size bed, and dressed identically down to the matching puzzled expressions on their faces. I surrender control to Bruce Lee, then leap and spin. The right knee comes up to fake—followed by the left foot as I complete the spin. The inside of my heel collides with the first chin, and I drive it through each of the following three chins in one fell swoop. I land, and they're already unconscious, having fallen neatly in a row into the bed behind them.

*Ted, Ed, Ned, and Zed in bed,* says a new voice in my head.

*Dr. Seuss?* says Bruce Lee. *Is that you?*

Something very hard smashes into my skull. Everything goes dark.

# CHAPTER EIGHTY-FOUR

MY HEAD IS POUNDING to a seventies disco beat. The air is thin like after a cold rain. My back, elbows, and knees are grinding against something hard, smooth, and wet.

"He's coming to." The voice is muffled, like it's coming from one room over.

"Edger! Edger, wake up!"

Mary.

"Edger," she says. "I need you. Come on. Be okay. Please be okay."

My eyes flutter but don't open. The beat in my throbbing head gets specific. Tambourine. Cymbals. Drum. Subwoofer.

I try to speak but manage only a low grunt.

"Edger," whispers Mary. "Don't worry. I've got the ring."

My arms won't move. They're crossed and pressed against my chest. My butt is freezing—I'm sitting in cold water.

"Miis-sterrr Bon-ko-vich," a voice calls in a theatrical tone, followed by four obnoxiously loud knocks on the ceiling. Which, going by the volume of the knocking, must be inches from the top of my head.

I open my eyes.

Mary and I are inside a ball. She's on her side, spitting out water, hands tied behind her back and struggling to sit up. The walls are too slick. Her long legs can't get traction. I try to move my arms, but can't. I'm in a straitjacket! My stomach clenches. The water level is rising. Mary pushes off from the wall with her shoulder; I get my knee under her and help her into an upright position. She's heavier than she looks. Her dress is soaked, but covering everything needing coverage. She nods her thanks, and the ball slowly begins to turn. I tense up and flex. Our butts and knees squeak against the walls as we brace for balance. Our prison phases from opaque to transparent.

"You can see me now?"

We're dangling between rafters. One of those weirdo twins is glaring at me from a catwalk. A wooden rail separates us as blinking spotlights of every color flash from every direction. Next to the agent, if I'm not mistaken, is Green Bay Packers defensive tackle Yourmajesty Fapa'fapa-Bal'buster. Helmet, shoulder pads, and all.

"Miis-sterrr Bon-ko-vich," says Yourmajesty, in the same theatrical tone as before.

"Why are you talking like that?"

Yourmajesty's forehead wrinkles. He frowns and blinks.

"It would seem you are more than would seem, Mister Bonkovich," he says, the drama-tone toned down somewhat, though unconvincingly.

"Which is what?" I ask, frowning. "What would I would seem?"

Yourmajesty shrugs. "A superhero. Zarathustra."

The water level creeps to my waist. My brain is racing. I blurt the first thing that pops into my head.

"You mean I seemed like a superhero at first, and now I seem more than that?"

"What?" he replies. "No."

"Then you mean I seem less than I would seem."

"Yeah," says Mary, nodding. "I think that's what he meant."

"Well, both work, grammatically speaking," says Yourmajesty.

"Can we get on with this?" asks the agent.

"Yes. Yes, of course," says Yourmajesty, not taking his eyes off us, but leaning slightly toward the agent and lowering his voice. "I'm sorry. I've been a cow for the last forty-eight hours."

The agent's lips compress. He glances at the Green Bay Packer, then gestures with his hand to us, his message plain: *Well, get on with it, then*.

"The ring, Mr. Bonkovich," says Yourmajesty. "Where is the ring?"

With Herculean effort, I manage not to look at Mary. "Buh…"

"You didn't bring it?" he asks. "But why didn't you bring it? That's not logical."

"Well, I mean, I knew you'd try to…steal it?"

Yourmajesty clicks his tongue.

"It's what I woulda done," says the agent, folding his arms and otherwise looking bored.

"I see," says Yourmajesty. "Well. Ahem. No matter. I *will* find it! Using my advanced titanium quantum processors, and my superior intellectual—"

"Hey, hey, hey," says the agent, waving him down. "Come on, man? It's too much. Just skip to the end, okay?"

"Yes, yes, *fine*," says Yourmajesty, leaning again to speak in hushed tones with the weirdo-twin-in-black. "But just one more thing, okay?" He faces us. "Alas, great though you were in your day, Zarathustra, it stands to reason that when it came time for cashing in your chips, this old…diseased…maniac would handle all your banking needs."

"Excuse me? What did you just say?"

"I said: You were great in your day, Zarathustra—"

"Did you just quote *Superman* at me?"

"No."

"You did! Mary. He just—he just quoted Superman at me!"

"I did not!"

Mary sighs. "Edger." Her eyes widen as her head nods to indicate the rising water level.

"Hey, hey, hey." The agent snaps his fingers at Mary. "You're not going anywhere, sweetheart. You killed my brothers. Prepare to die."

Mary frowns. "*Princess Bride*?"

"*Princess Bride*," I reply, nodding.

"No. I *mean* that. Prepare to—ah screw it." The Nostradamus agent tugs the Green Bay Packer's jersey. "Come on. Let's go."

Yourmajesty nods, and they turn to go, but then the defensive tackle pauses to address us from over his shoulder.

"It was Lex Luthor, by the way. Not Superman."

"I don't care," replies the Nostradamus agent from behind him, stabbing a hypodermic needle into the football player's neck. Yourmajesty's eyes roll up into the back of his head. He collapses, and a cable on the catwalk snaps. The agent seizes the rails on each side. Spotlights swing wildly. The agent loses his grip. Another cable snaps. His elbow collides with the railing. The catwalk sways back and forth, slowing, and the agent straightens. He signals to someone out of my range at the far end of the catwalk, then turns to us.

"Hey, kid," he says, half paying attention to me, and half paying attention to the cables that haven't snapped. "Don't suppose you'll tell me where the ring is?"

My forehead tenses. Yourmajesty is out cold. The agent, still wearing those stupid sunglasses, is staring at me with a needle in his hand like, hey-hey, just another day at the office.

"What'd you do to him?" I ask.

The agent shrugs. "Double-crossed him. What's it look like? Tell you what. I already got your blood while you were knocked out, so I don't really need you anymore, do I? And now I got him, and by extension, the AI, so how 'bout this: You tell me where the ring is, and I let you and Blondie go. You get your life back. We agree to forget about Blondie's little mishap with her rifle back there at the Q, everybody goes home for tea and crumpets. How's that sound?"

Mary's eyes meet mine. Her earnest blue eyes are like crystal. She's shivering and vulnerable. We could die here. Or…

I *could* just let it all go, and it'd be like it was before. Back when Mary and I were standing outside Mikey's office and I wasn't going to do any of this, because Mikey's problems belonged to Mikey, and Mary's spying on me was only an unconfirmed theory, and Gran, Shep, and I still lived together in a home that hadn't literally blown up.

"Come on, kid," says the agent. "This isn't hard. None of this crap is your problem. Just tell me where the ring is. It's not like civilization comes crashing down because you're gonna do what any normal human being would friggin' do."

I shake my head. "You're wrong. I mean, with all that's happened to me, I don't think I can go back. It changes you, you know?"

"No," says the agent, glancing at his watch. "No, I don't know. And if you've got something to say, let's skip to that part. 'Kay? That okay with you? Because it's been a long effin' two days, what with flippers and that infernal dart gun, and then Moo Town and the A-Team, and the Cluck-n-Pray nutzoids, the sharpshooter babe, you, and now Mr. Ball Buster here. I mean—what a fucking clusterfuck. Now where is the goddamn ring?!"

I look at Mary. She bites her bottom lip as she gazes through me, willing me to do the right thing.

"There's only the one human race," I say, and her eyes relax. She takes a breath, releases it, smiles.

"What the crap?" asks the agent. "Yuck. I just threw up in my mouth a little bit. Shrimp tacos." He presses his fist to his sternum and clears his throat. "Whoa-kay—enjoy the bomb I strapped to the bottom of that thing. I'll bring the marshmallows by later."

The ball slowly rotates. The agent gives us one last smile and wave, and then we're staring at a brick wall.

"I'm proud of you." Mary smiles at me, then struggles against the ropes binding her hands behind her back. "And don't listen to that guy. He's a total amateur. Let's just focus on getting out of here."

The ball lurches. That catwalk is going up. No—we're being lowered. The music swells—and the pounding in my head becomes clear. It's Blondie. Eighties music. Our spinning picks up speed. Water sloshes into my open, gaping mouth and down into my lungs. Hack, spit. Mary turns away as, too late, I cough water into her face.

"Ooh, sorry," I say.

"What the actual hell?" she says. But she's not looking at me at all. She's looking out the still-transparent wall. Beneath us, the dance floor is turning. Everyone is swaying slowly back and forth, their arms in the air, rapt expressions on their faces.

*"We're inside a disco ball?"*

"Well, this takes the cake," says Mary. "Death by disco-ball water torture."

"To the stylings of Blondie," I add.

"Blondie? Who's Blondie?"

"A band. Blondie's the band."

"This is 'Rapture,' by Debbie Harry."

"Because knowing the name of the song but not the band makes it better?"

"Well," she says, shrugging defensively. "It's a good song."

"No song is good enough to drown to."

"Edger. I don't want you to worry. We're not going to die. Okay?"

"I'm worried anyway. No offense."

I brace my shoes on the wall on either side of her head, twist and turn, wrenching my shoulders in their sockets as I try to loosen the straitjacket.

"Look," says Mary, turning her head so she's not staring straight into my crotch. "The important thing in this situation is not to panic."

"*This* situation?" I stop thrashing for a moment to get a read on her. Her face is blank.

"Yes," she replies.

"This *specific* situation?" I ask. "Trapped inside a disco ball Chinese water torture chamber, with a bomb strapped to the bottom, in Underwearld, in a straitjacket, and drowning to the tune of 'Rapture.' Is *that* the situation you're talking about?"

"Yes."

"Well, okay then. Don't panic. Check."

# CHAPTER EIGHTY-FIVE

THE WATER IS FILLING.

We're spinning.

My stomach is souring.

Blondie is rapturing.

The air is clammy. Dancers streak past like a sparkling dream against a backdrop of phosphorescent wallpaper of Caleb's butt in his Calvin Kleins—*Underwearld.*

"Hey Edger—it's Caleb!" says Mary, banging her shoulder against the side of the disco ball and sloshing water. "Caleb! Caleb!"

"You know Caleb?" I ask. "Of course you know Caleb. Because the universe just couldn't let me die without letting me know Mary knows Caleb."

"Of course I know Caleb. He's HARDON."

"Hard-on for you, hard-on for Kate—"

"Oh my God, Edger. Not now, okay? High-Risk Agency for Regulating the Defense Of the NFL."

"Wait-wait-wait. That's an acronym inside an acronym! It should be HARDONFL. You know, that really pisses me off. My tax dollars paid someone to capitalize that letter O. Think about that."

"Really? Really, Edger? You want to do this now?"

"That's what they always say too: 'You wanna do this now?' But notice they never balance the budget. All I'm saying is, you gotta talk about it sometime."

"Dammit, Edger!"

I'm panting. She's panting. Beneath us and on the opposite side of the club, Caleb is scanning the room from his tiptoes in front of a larger-than-life phosphorescent photograph of his crotch. Because, apparently, all paths in life lead there.

"Caleb!" Mary yells.

Not having any better ideas, I yell, "Caleb!"

We yell our butts off. We bang our shoulders into the wall. Water sloshes over our faces, and the water level reaches our chins.

# CHAPTER EIGHTY-SIX

"EDGER. I don't want you to worry. I read once about how much air we need to—"

"Stop using air!"

I tip my head back and get one last gulp of air before the end.

There's a pelagic quality to total submersion inside a disco ball. Chaotic bubbling pockets of air all bump up against my face. Tiny ones leave my nose. It's like being trapped inside a can of Sprite.

*Edger.*

*Bruce Lee?*

*Yes. I couldn't help notice that you're about to die.*

*Hey, yeah, funny you should mention that. Look, I don't mean to come off as all take-take-take, me-me-me, but do you think you could, I don't know, Jeet Kune Do-chop a hole in the wall or something?*

*No,* says Bruce Lee. *That won't work. Physics.*

A tiny little ray of hope snuffs out in my chest.

*Okay. Well. Um. Do you have any ideas?*

*Now that you mention it, yes. As it turns out, escaping from a straitjacket inside a Chinese water torture chamber is Harry Houdini's specialty.*

## HISTORICAL COURTESY CONCEALMENT OF A SELFISH MAGICIAN'S TRICK, AS CHRONICLED BY HERODOTUS (C. 484—C. 425 BCE)

IT IS A COMMON-SENSE FACT, though one most are not given to reflect much on, that deliberately dislocating your shoulder and then putting it back in hurts. It hurts rather a lot. It takes serious leverage to move the bone. It isn't as easy as one might think. Especially if one is underwater inside a spinning disco ball listening to "Rapture." It is inadvisable to try this at home.

Even less well known than these facts is that Harry Houdini is a dick.

*I heard that.*

*Yes, we know.*

(But it's true. Houdini hates sharing his tricks—even with someone who is dying—which, I'm sure you will agree, is rather selfish under the circumstances. Nevertheless, after extensive high-speed negotiations, and a litany of promises made in legal language, Houdini seems innately to grasp the fact that Edger and Mary are close to the point of no return, oxygen-wise, and that, if he doesn't help, Edger and Mary and everyone else in Underwearld are going to get blown up. And so in the end, while a good magician may never reveal his secrets, it takes a real dick to keep said secrets from the only guy on the planet who can use us dead folks' wisdom, knowledge, and expertise to heretofore save the day.)

*I can hear you in parentheses too, you know.*

*Yes, we know.*

# CHAPTER EIGHTY-SEVEN

MY LEFT SHOULDER is throbbing and swollen as I shimmy out of the straitjacket. I angle my knees to the right to make enough room to pull the jacket off the rest of the way with my feet. Mary, meanwhile, is fiddling beneath the back of her dress. She begins to turn, revolving one hundred eighty degrees—when I catch a glimpse of her bare butt, her panties tucked beneath immaculately sculpted cheeks, and the ring clasped in her right hand—then her turn completes. Her legs spread so her feet can brace on the walls on either side of my head and stop her spinning momentum. Our eyes meet. Her scowl could melt faces.

She lowers her shoulder to reach between her legs from behind her back. Her dress flips up. Her underwear is now fixed. In her fingers is the Z ring. My hands are shaking from the pain of having just popped my shoulder out and then pushed back in. The ring drops. For a split second, it's floating in the space between her open legs. She catches me looking and goes wide-eyed. She nods frantically at the sinking ring. But I'm frozen in indecision. Here I am, about to die, and all I can think is: *Where did she hide that ring?*

She jerks her pelvis in an apparent attempt at using her hoo-hah as a pointer, or else to keep the ring afloat. Abruptly, she stops her erotic conniptions and reads my face. She rolls her eyes, then makes one last pointed jerk of her head: *Take this ring or I will sniper you to death.*

I reach an unsteady hand for the ring—praying the ball doesn't lurch and I grab something I'm not supposed to. I catch it on my first try. The ball lurches. I crash face-first into her cleavage. Her legs wrap around me and steady us. I dig my shoulder into her ribs, push off. She releases me, and I slip the ring on my finger and brace myself.

# CHAPTER EIGHTY-EIGHT

I GRIT MY TEETH. The bubbling in my ears is hyperactive. An invisible squeegee is raking my skin as the suit issues from the ring, up my finger, my arm, body, legs, head. It moves over my recently dislocated shoulder—and the pain flares, races down my spine, fans out in my middle, and finishes in my toes. I cry out, releasing more precious air. By the time the heads-up display springs to life, I'm not sure I can do anything; I'm in total agony. The pain in my shoulder has metastasized. Claustrophobia is crashing in. I'm dying one tiny air bubble at a time.

*Focus your mind like this.* Houdini takes control. Fear and pain wash out like a receding tide.

*Thank you,* I reply, astonished.

*Welcome. Not such a dick now, am I?*

My hands become fists. I place them on the inner walls of our prison, and I summon the chain-breaking strength of Samson—the first strongman I can think of—and he's here, with me.

*The suit will augment your strength,* he says. *But together, we can move mountains—*

*Really,* I cut in. *Just breaking out of here is good.*

*We'll pose for all the romance novel covers, with my thick mane of—*

*Okay, okay!*

*—and my bulging—*

*Just push, for the love of all that's—*

His courage is now my courage. His spirit is now my spirit. We push, and his final moments between the pillars of Dagon flash before my eyes...

# CHAPTER EIGHTY-NINE

WATER AND GLASS shower the dance floor. Needle scratches vinyl. Hattori Hanzo seizes control instinctively and I land with the grace of a ninja. Mary, who has no Hanzo, thuds with the grace of a turkey carcass dropped from the Level Two parapet of Westfield Horton Plaza.

"Kill them!" someone yells.

"Don't kill them!" I yell back, figuring that's got to be worth a try.

Panic ensues. Screaming people run and duck for cover. Shots are fired. A bullet ricochets off a larger-than-life Caleb crotch. I seize control of my body, grab Mary, and drag her behind a nearby couch.

More gunfire.

I chance a peek. Real-life Caleb Montana is near the front door, exchanging shots with two Nostradamus agents behind a life-size statue of Caleb in his quarterback uniform, one arm cocked back, preparing to pass the football, and the other stretched out in front, pointing.

I round on Mary, who flings her wet hair back like a *Sports Illustrated* swimsuit model. Water sprays my visor.

"Cut me loose."

"Right, right," I say, feeling around on my utility belt. Jeez, I've never tried to locate anything without someone helping me from the Collective Unconscious. There are a lot of things here. I pull a tiny ball out—it grows into a switchblade-shaped object. Seems promising. I flick it on. Blue flame blows out from the end.

"Holy crap!"

"Come on, quit fooling around."

"Don't rush me! Do you have any idea how stressful this is?"

"Come *on*," she says, her voice husky.

"There's like, fifty thousand things on this belt, and they all look the same."

"Just calm down."

"You never see Batman having this problem," I mutter.

"Behind you."

"What?"

"Duck!"

I duck, and Mary kicks the spot where my head just was. Someone grunts. Dead weight falls on top of me. I push it off and discover that I have been waylaid by one of the weird Dr. Seuss twins.

*It's a T-6 clone*, says Killmaster. *I looked it up, sir.*

*What?* I reply. *The Nostradamus agents are clones?*

*So that's why their minds read like origami,* says Bruce Lee.

*T-6 clones?* I say, too weirded out to move on.

*Yeah,* he replies. *What'd you think they were?*

My eyebrows rise as I consider this. *You know, what with all the weird crap going around, I guess I'd have gone with robots.*

*Don't be absurd,* says Killmaster. *We don't have the technology.*

More gunshots. I stick my head over the couch for a quick peek. Caleb is pinned down.

"Roll over," I say, and Mary, eyeing the mini blowtorch, awkwardly complies, cheek on the floor, back arched, her butt in the air.

"Be gentle," she says.

"Meep."

"Edger?"

I flick on the blowtorch and concentrate on aiming the flame away from her while burning through the soaking-wet canvas straps binding her hands, which dry and then begin to fray.

"Oo-ooh, it's hot," she says, jerking away. "Don't you have protection?"

The straps being weakened, I flick the torch off and begin tugging at the canvas, thinking to simply rip the damn thing.

"Pull—no, push! Wait a minute. Maybe if you get your leg up, kind of—spread them out more—aw, jeez."

Caleb slides across the dance floor, guns blazing, and skids to a stop behind the couch next to us.

"Porn much?"

"Hi," I say.

Mary pulls her hands apart and the straps snap. Wonder Woman. She rolls over and sits up. Her cheeks are as red as mine feel.

"Whenever you two are done innuendo-ing," says Caleb.

I stare at him, unable to summon a response.

"The bomb, bro. The bomb!" He points at the ruined disco ball sitting near the edge of the dance floor.

"How do you know about the bomb?" I ask.

"I'm HARDON."

"And we're the ones innuendo-ing?"

"Grow up, bro," he says.

"Stop saying bro, bro," I reply, and peek over the couch. The club is evacuated, except for the DJ, who is conspicuously cowering behind his turntable. The gunfire has stopped.

"Looks clear," I say, standing up.

"Wait—no," says Caleb, too late. I'm already up. And there, across the dance floor are—for some random reason I can't even begin to imagine—Wang and Shmuel, held at gunpoint.

Hanzo seizes control of me; my hand flies to the utility belt and closes on a cluster of tiny balls. My arm lashes out, once, twice, three times a lady. The balls morph midair into throwing stars. And it's the same as the stadium: the throwing stars find their targets—nerve bundles—and the agents collapse.

"Righteous!" yells Shmuel.

"Fuckin' A!" mirrors Wang.

"I notice you knew right where the throwing stars were," says Mary.

"Huh. Well, what do you know?" I reply, thinking next time I'll have to summon a dead guy sooner.

"You didn't have to blowtorch *them*," says Mary.

"What do you want me to say, Mary? I'm sorry? Look, it's my first time."

Glass shatters. I wheel around.

Nostradamus clones are leaping over and filing out from behind the bar, carelessly knocking over glasses, bottles of beer and liquor, chairs, and barstools as they stride out onto the dance floor. My heads-up display performs a quick count: forty-two of them. Every eye is on me. I know I should be terrified, but, for some reason, all I can think is how weird it would be if they started doing "Thriller."

I leave my cover from behind the couch and step out onto the dance floor. The clone army reacts simultaneously, switching on like robots, allowing me into the center, and then circling me like a slow-motion sharknado.

"Be careful, bro!" yells Caleb.

"Dude, are you seeing an armored space ninja?" asks Shmuel, nudging Wang, who scowls and nods.

*[What are you waiting for?]* asks Hanzo, and at first, I think he's talking to me. *[I'll kill them from the shadows all night long. But this is your specialty.]*

*All right, then,* says Bruce Lee, taking charge of my body and having me crack my knuckles, ease my neck left and right. I start in on some footwork, hopping up and down like a boxer—or rather—like Bruce Lee.

*Access Battle Plan,* says Lieutenant Killmaster, and either he or Bruce Lee has me use the retinal scanner on my HUD to access the augmented reality component called Battle Plan. My brief training session seems like forever ago, but through the Collective Unconscious, Killmaster reminds me that Battle Plan is used to crunch attack pattern variables and "liaise with the assisting personality," in this case, Bruce

Lee, to calculate and coordinate a response.

*Yeah,* says Killmaster. *It's like Bruce Lee on brain steroids. This is gonna be awesome.*

The HUD calculates the number and positions of my opponents. Bruce Lee's mind sharpens as the computer comes back with some ideas. Hundreds of possible fight plans flash before my eyes in a second, showing various routes through the mob, punching here, kicking there, ducking, flipping—and just like that—it's finished.

"DJ!" I yell, and the DJ pops up from behind the turntable. "It's fight night. Cue up a sick beat so I can whip me some clone-army ass."

The DJ gives a nervous nod, hurriedly cues up a song.

"'Thriller.'"

*Ooh! Good choice!* says Michael Jackson from out of nowhere.

"He said fight night?" says Shmuel. "Not fright night?"

A T-6 throws the first punch—but, for me, it's like he's in slow motion. The HUD traces a red line, my predetermined attack path, through the mob. Bruce Lee smiles, and we're off.

# CHAPTER NINETY

DUCK, FLIP, WINDMILL KICK.

Punch, punch. Kick, kick, kick. Broken chair, beer bottles.

My fist cracks the side of a head. The inside of my gloves are well padded. I wouldn't have thought that should be a thing, wearing body armor, but it is. A kind of shock-absorbing foam that has a perversely satisfying way of pampering my fists of fury. Each face, body, and cranium I connect with is as smooth on my knuckles as a baby's butt.

*That's a terrible comparison*, says Bruce Lee.

The HUD alerts me that twelve moves later, a foot will try to hit me in the head.

Twelve moves later, Bruce Lee has me duck. At the edge of the dance floor are peripheral skirmishes. Mary's dress twirls, her bare legs flashing past as she kicks one, two, then three Nostradamus agents in the face; a beer bottle breaks over the head of another agent with his back to Wang and Shmuel; the two exchange a fist bump, then crawl on their knees to take cover behind the bar.

Nostradamus agents cannot get close to me. I'm taking out kneecaps left and right. Liver punches galore; one good punch there and they're down for the count—who knew? It's no-holds-barred combat. Bruce Lee is in charge, although Hanzo and Killmaster are an extra set of brains advising from the Collective Unconscious through Battle Plan.

Another clone steps in front of me. I punch him in the face, and my leg does that twisty Michael Jackson dance move. I point to the ceiling, pretend to adjust a fedora I'm not wearing, gyrate my hips, and then grab my crotch.

*Hee-hee-hee*, says Michael Jackson.

Another T-6 clone agent dives at me. I go up on my tiptoes, Michael Jackson style, making him miss me by inches. Caleb's fist meets that guy's face on the far end of the dance floor.

*Who's in charge here?* asks Bruce Lee.

*Shooga-chockalocka-hoo-hoo-hoo,* Michael Jackson replies.

Fallen clones are factored into the HUD Battle Plan. I leap over unconscious bodies and perform a scissor kick, taking down two more agents, one on my left, and the other on my right. I land, and Michael Jackson has us do another dance move.

*Would you knock it off?* Bruce Lee growls. *I'm trying to concentrate. Do you have any idea how complicated this already is?*

*Mama-say-mama-saw-mama-coo-sa,* sings Michael Jackson.

Bruce Lee has my fists do a speed-bag thing on a T-6 face. The clone drops like a fainting church lady at an all-male revue. I moonwalk around his fallen body and repeat the action on the next T-6 face.

*Knock it off*, says Bruce Lee.

*Hey,* replies Michael Jackson. *You've got a job and I've got a job, okay?*

*Are you kidding me?* says Bruce Lee.

*Listen, Kato*, says Michael Jackson. *You may have style. But I've got* style. *Capisce?*

Six feet in the air, my foot blocks four punches in one lateral swipe. My other foot follows, collides with four jaws.

*Ow!* cries Michael Jackson. *Shuh-mon!*

*I can't believe this*, says Bruce Lee. *Can't somebody shut him off?*

*Can't somebody shut you off?* counters Michael Jackson.

"Woo-saw-wah-wah!" I yell, performing three spin kicks in a row, and the last Nostradamus agent goes down.

*Huh,* says Michael Jackson, his psychic sense conveying a grudging admiration. *All I'm saying is, because of me, you looked extra good doing it. You can thank me later.*

# CHAPTER NINETY-ONE

I'M STANDING OVER A PILE of unconscious Nostradamus clones, winded, and scanning for anyone whose ass hasn't been sufficiently kicked.

"Dude!" Wang cries. "That—was—bad—ass!"

From across the room, someone begins clapping, the slow clap, a single set of hands coming…together…for…pedantic…applause.

"You don't disappoint," says a familiar, theatrical voice.

I turn around.

Yourmajesty Fapa'fapa-Bal'buster is standing in front of the bar holding a dirt-colored cocktail with what appears to be tufts of grass sticking out the top.

*That is one dirty martini,* says Michael Jackson.

"I thought they knocked you out," I say.

"You thought wrong, Zarathustra," says Yourmajesty, puffing his impressive chest out with a swagger and chucking his cocktail aside. It shatters behind a black leather couch. "People of San Diego!" he cries. "I stand before you, chosen by destiny to receive the combined powers of all of humanity! This inevitable moment will transpire before your eyes, even as Zarathustra himself is forced to bear witness to it…"

"Yourmajesty, bro," calls Caleb. "Come on. This isn't you."

"It isn't?" asks Yourmajesty, lowering his arms.

"No!" exclaims Wang. "It's fucking Skeletor from fucking *Masters of the Universe*, you fucking fuck!"

"Yeah, bro," says Caleb, in a more conciliatory tone. "Come on. You sack people, bro. Remember? Until now, the worst thing you ever did was, you know, kick people in the nuts when the refs weren't looking. That's not so bad."

"Yeah," says Shmuel. "But stealing the combined powers of all of humanity is being a straight-up dick?"

"Daddy and Other Daddy," says Yourmajesty. "Mr. Montana. I believe all of you are suffering under the delusion that Yourmajesty Fapa'fapa-Bal'buster is in charge here."

"Yeah," says Shmuel, addressing me, Caleb, and Mary. "We're sorry and everything, but he's your basic universal evil AI now?"

"He's not a Packer anymore," says Wang, nodding. "It's Tron-Tron!"

"We know," says Mary.

"Yes," says Yourmajesty, stepping over a pile of unconscious bodies and squaring off across from me. "And now, I will claim what is rightfully mine. The ring!"

"Dude," I reply, the voice changer making me sound like a croaking frog. "What is up with the over-the-top villain thing?"

"Is it over-the-top?" asks Yourmajesty.

"Yes," everyone answers in unison.

"Okay," he says, his shoulders coming up defensively. "Good to know. Constructive criticism and everything. But seriously. Will you give me the ring? My logic boards have analyzed your fighting patterns. I can take it by force if I have to."

"I'd like to see you try," says Mary, standing up straighter and folding her arms. I wave my hand kind of behind my butt—trying to catch her attention—but she doesn't notice. Honestly, as flattering as this is, I'd rather not fight Human Tank. "He can change his fight patterns," she continues. "Can you change yours?"

Yourmajesty Fapa'fapa-Bal'buster performs a high kick to his left, followed by another to his right. His hands trace a kung fu crane form in the air, followed by some hip swinging, and capped off with some backward moonwalking.

*Yeah*, says Bruce Lee. *That's pretty good.*

*Shama-mah-coo-saw!* exclaims Michael Jackson.

"You see," says Yourmajesty. "I am a fast learner. There is nothing you can do I cannot learn. I was made for this. You. Complete. Me."

"Yeah, that's over-the-top again, bro," says Caleb, shaking his head and staring at his feet.

"But kinda romantic?" says Shmuel.

*He's right, sir*, says Killmaster. *His processors are built for this.*

*And he's got a good fifty pounds of muscle on him you don't*, observes Bruce Lee.

*[Let me at him,]* says Hanzo, seizing control of me before I can reply.

*Wait!* cries Bruce Lee, but already my hand has dispatched a throwing star; Yourmajesty leans left and the star sails harmlessly past.

"I've seen that too," he says. "Don't you have anything new?"

Hanzo removes another ball from my belt. It stretches, glimmers, a blood groove and hamon line forming as it lengthens into a katana sword. Hanzo swings it overhead and in front of me before taking it into a double-handed grip, holding the sword high and assuming a deep tiger stance.

"Ninjutsu," says Yourmajesty. "I already know ninjutsu."

["You don't know true ninjutsu,"] I say out loud, Hanzo speaking through me.

Yourmajesty Fapa'fapa-Bal'buster's eyes roll up into his head. His lids flutter. A glimmer of hope rises that maybe I won't have to fight this guy after all, if he's just going to go and have a seizure on me, but then his eyelids pop wide open, and his gaze comes again into focus.

"Ancient Japanese," he says. "Interesting."

*[Hey, are you so sure about this?]* I ask.

*[I have a plan.]*

# CHAPTER NINETY-TWO

HANZO HAS KILLMASTER operate my heads-up display to present an X-ray image of Yourmajesty Fapa'fapa-Bal'buster. *There!* The nano-processor is hiding inside Bal'buster's left testicle.

*[True ninjutsu,]* Hanzo is saying, *[is about deception. Let him believe we will attack from the sword.]*

*[While I kick him in the nano-processor,]* replies Bruce Lee. *[Ball-busting the ball-buster. I like it.]*

*Hee-hee-hee,* replies Michael Jackson.

*It's a solid plan, sir,* says Killmaster.

Hanzo has me. I charge at Yourmajesty, who responds by assuming a traditional horse stance, fists at his hips, palm-side up. My heads-up display is still in X-ray vision; the nano-target is glowing red.

I leap into the air and twist, my sword slashing down at the Green Bay Packer. He sidesteps to his left—and through some complicated ninja trickery, pops the sword from my hands.

Bruce Lee seizes control as Yourmajesty's beefy arms wrap around me. My feet leave the ground. I can't breathe. Bruce Lee summons every last drop of my Chi and channels it into my left knee.

"Wuh-saw!" I shriek, driving it hard into Yourmajesty Fapa'fapa-Bal'buster's nano-processor.

My boots hit the dance floor. I'm free! He staggers backward. I drop to my hands and knees.

*Get up! Get up, sir!* yells Killmaster. *It's working!*

I look up. The glowing red dot isn't in his nuts anymore. It's swimming through his bloodstream and into his torso—

And then I'm lifted into the air.

Fapa'fapa-Bal'buster is below me, twirling me like a baton, and chucking me across the room. I slam into the dance floor and skid three feet, my wind knocked out.

*Okay, it's not working,* says Killmaster. *You are totally going to die now.*

A hand closes on my ankle. I'm lifted again. Air floods back into my lungs. Streaking underwear-butt wallpaper whips by, then faces whip by—Caleb, Mary, Wang, and Shmuel—then underwear-butt wallpaper again. Everything's a blur, spinning, spinning. It's like those horrible centrifugal-force carnival rides that always made me want to throw up, but with the addition of a killer Caleb Montana inferiority complex, which also makes me want to throw up.

*Boo-yah! Gonna die!* yells Killmaster. *Woo-hoo! Yeah! Puke, baby, puke!*

*Mama-say, mama-saw, mama-shut-him-up!* cries Michael Jackson.

*[Is it time to kill someone yet?]* asks Hanzo.

*Yes!* all the voices in my head cry at once.

"Nurn-nh, no," I groan.

Hanzo seizes control. Still spinning, I spot the katana on the floor and scoop it up as I pass above, then twist and slash. Fapa'fapa-Bal'buster releases me. I go flying; I'm twisting and somersaulting, then landing on my toes, if a bit wobbly. Nine Fapa'fapa-Bal'busters are facing me, each of them listing sickeningly. I double over and drop the katana, both hands pressing my stomach as I try not to get sick inside the suit. Hanzo yields control.

*Boo-yah kumquat sucka!* yells Killmaster.

*We need a new plan here, guys,* I say.

*Buck up, little camper,* replies Killmaster. *The only easy day was yesterday, baby. That's the SEAL way!*

"You were always destined to fail without me, Zarathustra," says Fapa'fapa-Bal'buster. "You're only delaying the inevitable..."

My brain is spinning like a hard drive. *Think, think.*

Wait a minute. Hard drive.

*I've got it!* I cry. *The Collective Unconscious!*

*What about it?* asks Bruce Lee.

*Tron-Tron's designed to help the human brain store information, but it's the suit's processors that regulate information. Tron-Tron doesn't meet the system requirements without the suit! Remember what Mikey said: "Actionable data extrapolated from the lives of everyone who ever lived and everyone alive today. Accessing all that at once—for even a second—could overload the brain. You really need all three parts of the technology for it to work properly."*

*Is this dork stuff?* asks Killmaster. *Because it feels like nap time. So it must be dork stuff. I'm gonna go do two hundred push-ups. Call me when it's interesting again.*

"Hey, Yourmajesty, bro," calls Caleb. "Why don't you come get a piece of this? That is, if you think you're man enough."

Fapa'fapa-Bal'buster turns to face Caleb. "I think I might prefer doing battle with the woman." He folds his thick arms and stands there like the pile of towering muscle he is, and my stomach begins to settle.

"Well," says Mary, blushing, tucking a strand of hair behind her ear, and gazing down at the dance floor. "Obviously, he's not totally stupid."

"Huh?" says Caleb.

"I mean," she replies, gesturing at the Green Bay Packer. "He knows a challenge when he sees one."

*Edge—what are you suggesting?* asks Bruce Lee. *They're stalling for you. So let's get this going.*

*I'm suggesting we flood his brain with billions of lives and memories at once,* I reply. *He'll be confused. I only have to hold it for a couple of seconds. Just long enough for you to beat the shit out of him.*

*[Or I could kill him instead,]* says Hanzo. *[It's a possibility, is all I'm saying.]*

*It's dangerous,* says Bruce Lee, ignoring the dead ninja.

*It's something you shouldn't be doing without Tron-Tron plugged into the suit.*

*I like the dork's idea,* says Michael Jackson. *It's a computer. And he's a Dork with a capital D. That means it'll probably work.*

*Thanks,* I reply, frowning.

Not waiting for further insults, I close my eyes and block out the world. I open myself to the Collective Unconscious, and the soul-stars come down to surround me. Their light is warm and reassuring. In the psychic stratum, my soul-star lifts into the air to join with the cyclone of the dead. Hundreds of lives surround me—with billions more at the ready beyond them.

Stabbing pain lances through my chest. *Too much! It's too much!*

*Edger!* yells Bruce Lee. *No!*

My lungs are heaving; my biceps, arms, and fists are shaking.

*Come back, Edger!*

*Boo-yah! You're dyin'! Yeah!*

The soul-stars touch me. My spine flexes. My body seizes, head tilting back, arms splayed. The lives of yesterday, today, wanting—no, *needing*—to make a difference.

*Can't breathe!*

Sensory experiences surge into me; a clay oven, soaking in my own sweat, the scent of exotic baking bread; cracked lips, aching back and knees, dry fingertips, and stinging tall grass; the iron flavor of a bear's raw liver juices exploding in my mouth, my face slicked with blood on the day I become a man—

The lives of yesterday, though disparate and from far-flung cultures, are resolute in purpose today: No single person can have this power. Not even me. Pairing the AI with the suit and serum in the way it's been designed to do would be cataclysmic. My access to this power is limited, but the total package is not. Tron-Tron *must* be stopped. I can see that now.

I open my eyes and focus on the tiny X-ray dot that is Tron-Tron inside the football player—and the cyclone lashes out. Not just the hundreds immediately surrounding me, but the billions surrounding them.

Fapa'fapa-Bal'buster staggers under the assault. Through our psychic connection, the billions of lives coursing into him are brighter than the sun; Bruce Lee seizes control. I'm on Tron-Tron in an instant.

Even with Bruce Lee in charge of my physiology, I'm struggling to breathe. My fists fire like lightning strikes into the stunned football player's chest. The beating sends the nano-processor north, into his neck. My left hand side-chops; the processor spurts up and into his skull. I spin, lean back. My heel hooks across his face. The glowing red dot ejects through a tear duct—and the Green Bay Packer crashes to the ground. Bruce Lee releases our connection. I collapse to my knees and gasp for air.

"The *Kung Fury*!" yells Shmuel.

"The *Kung Fury*!" shouts Wang.

My chest rises and falls as I spare one last glance at the fallen defensive tackle. I crane my neck and check on everyone else. Wang and Shmuel are untied. Mary tosses a tangle of twine onto the floor. She glances over and spots me. Her shoulders slouch. She smiles. Her dress is soaking wet, her hair matted to her head.

"You okay?" I ask, and she nods. Her eyes widen in the direction of the bomb, urging me to get to it.

My turn to slouch. I can barely get my breathing under control, although my heart rate is gradually slowing. Maybe just a few minutes' rest…

*The only easy day was yesterday, sir,* says Killmaster.

*Ticking time bomb*, says Bruce Lee.

"Right," I reply, climbing to my feet and lurching to the broken disco ball, my boots crunching glass and splashing water. I fall to my knees and skid to a halt in front of a half husk of glittering sequins and broken glass. Underneath, I find a little black box with digital numbers counting backward strapped to red sticks of dynamite.

*Aren't they always,* says Bruce Lee.

*Wuh-oh,* says Michael Jackson.

*Guess we can tick the box for the time bomb trope. Bruce, you have experience with this?* I ask.

*As Kato,* replies Bruce Lee. *But don't worry. Indiana Tim said he knows a guy.*

I sense Bruce Lee flying away inside my mind. Michael Jackson starts humming *Jeopardy* in falsetto.

# CHAPTER NINETY-THREE

"YOURMAJESTY'S OUT COLD," says Caleb, kneeling at the Packer's side.

"There is no Yourmajesty," says Wang, walking over to join him. "There is only Tron-Tron."

"Yeah, bro," says Caleb. "We know. Question is, how do you two know about that?"

"Dude," says Shmuel, who has wandered over to the wall and is running his hand along the wallpaper. "Is that really your junk? Or is that like special effects and stuff?"

A whip cracks in my mind. Bruce Lee is back. He's returned with some guy called Bubba.

*Somebody say somethin' 'bout a bomb?* asks Bubba.

We exchange hellos and nice-to-meet-yous and decide it best to get down to business. I shift my weight, and broken glass crunches beneath my armored knee. I pull the plate off the back of the bomb. Inside is a mess of wires.

*Red one,* says Bubba, seemingly without even thinking. *Cut the red one.*

*Red one?* I ask. *Just like that? Are you sure?*

*Yeah, it's kind of a thing now,* says Bubba. *Like how, for a while, people always said "Coke" when they wanted a cola. Didn't matter if it was Pepsi.*

*Buh,* I reply.

*Ninety-five percent of bombs end up getting wired with the red one being the critical one. It's a "thing" that's kind of filtered into the public consciousness. Like ordering a Coke, only for bomb makers. Picture it: Bomb makers sitting in their bomb-making shacks, usually near a river, but not necessarily, and they're pulling all this shit together with, yep, you guessed it, critical* red *wires. I mean, it's confusing for us, it's confusing for them—so they gotta anchor it to something they'll remember, right? Half the time, they don't even know they're doing it. Just like half the time people don't even realize they're ordering Coke, when the signage clearly says Pepsi. I mean, if they just read the goddamn sign, but they don't, and so fuck it. This is like that.*

*That's a terrible analogy,* I reply. *And anyway—you said ninety-five percent of the time. What about the other five percent?*

*How do you think I got dead?*

*You are* so *not instilling me with confidence.*

*Look,* says Bubba. *It's nearly always the red one.*

*It's nearly always the red one,* says Bruce Lee, nodding sagely.

*Would you just listen to the man and cut the red one already?* says Michael Jackson. *Those numbers are making me all hee-hee-hee inside.*

"Edger," says Mary. "Is there something wrong?"

*Careful, buddy,* says Bubba. *A good superhero always imparts confidence. They don't wanna get blown up.*

They *don't want to get blown up*?

*Clock is ticking, sir,* says Killmaster.

"It's good," I say out loud. "I'm good. Really." I feel around on my belt, come up with the blowtorch.

*Eh,* says Bubba. *That'll work. Probably.*

I melt the wire, careful to angle the flame away from the sticks of dynamite, and the numbers stop counting back. Audible sighs. The barometric pressure in the room goes from bad to good.

*Told ya,* says Bubba. *Just like ordering a Coke.*

# CHAPTER NINETY-FOUR

"SO WHAT DO WE DO about him?" asks Caleb, staring down at an unconscious Yourmajesty Fapa'fapa-Bal'buster.

Using the heads-up display, I scan the dance floor for the nano-processor. The X-ray vision makes the process quick and efficient, not having to manually check behind or under things for a tiny computer chip.

"Well, we can't leave him here," says Mary. "And we'll have to get InstaTron Tron out of him."

I shake my head. "I already did that."

"Dude," says Wang.

"Dude," agrees Shmuel.

"Then where is it?" asks Mary, her arms coming up as she takes in the area immediately around her. I shake my head.

"It's not like looking for a contact lens. This thing is invisible to the naked eye. I had it tagged on my heads-up display when it was in him, and I saw it launch out of his tear duct—but now it's gone. According to my suit, it's gone."

"Aw, naw, bro."

"What?"

"You *beat* it out of him?"

"Yeah."

Caleb drags his hands through his thick blond hair.

"What?" I ask again.

"It could be anywhere now. Once it's a free range nano-processor, all bets are off, bro."

"What's that supposed to mean?" asks Mary.

"It means that thing can fly. And it's got like, somewhere between twelve and twenty-four hours to find its next host and bond with it. Chances are it flew right out of here and called an Uber."

"Since when do you know so much about nano-technology?" I ask.

"I'm HARDON, bro."

"Yeah, you are," says Shmuel, grinning.

"No," says Caleb. "High-Risk Agency for Reg—"

"High risk," says Shmuel, still grinning and nodding.

Wang smacks his arm. "Da fuck, dude. You forgetting about all this?" Wang gestures with his hands to encompass his miniscule physique, and Shmuel grins.

"What I'm saying is," says Caleb, ignoring them and training his gaze on me. "He could literally be anyone, bro."

I chew my lip for a second. Then a thought hits me.

"Well, he can't be anyone," I say, still in my ridiculous superhero voice. "If he were anyone in this room, my suit would pick it up. I had it tagged when it was inside him." I nod at Fapa'fapa-Bal'buster. "We can cross everyone in this room off the list."

Caleb's eyes tighten for a moment. Slowly, he nods. "In that case, bro, we can leave him for the cops. Let's get gone."

We exit through the kitchen, which is deserted. I pass a sink with the water still running, then double back and shut it off. Outside, Caleb gets Wang and Shmuel loaded into the rear of his Jeep. Mary has crossed to the other end of the alley and is standing with her back to me, arms folded. The hum of passing cars and foot traffic and the normalcy of San Diego nightlife is jarring and otherworldly after all that's happened in Underwearld. Mary turns, her eyes find me, and she jerks her head to the side, signaling for me to join her. Caleb gives us the hurry-up look. To Mary, I raise my index finger for her to give us a second, then hustle over to Caleb. My boots scuff on the gritty asphalt.

"S'up?" asks Caleb. "You comin' back with us? To Fortress?"

"Fortress? What's that?"

"The Q, bro."

I shake my head. "What're you talking about?"

"Our secret base, bro. Fortress. Underneath the Q."

"Caleb, are you telling me you have a secret spy base underneath Qualcomm Stadium called Fortress?"

He flips his palms up and shrugs like this should be obvious and only stupid people wouldn't be following. And here's me thinking my little adventure had already checked off all the tropes. I sigh. "Maybe later."

"Yeah, okay." Caleb nods and folds his arms. "Well, good job in there. You make a good Zarathustra."

Abruptly, someone uses the horn in an obnoxious, protracted sonic assault. Being right next to the hood, the experience is comparable to standing inside the foghorn of the Hellespont Alhambra supertanker entering the Port of San Diego. Caleb and I nearly fall over, and then the aural incursion is finished.

"Jesus Christ, bro!" Caleb glares at Wang, who is in the passenger seat, peering into his cell phone and deploying his Resting Dick Face.

"Sorry," says Wang, not looking up, and not sounding sorry. "We need to swing by a Burrito Planet on the way back. I'm starving."

Caleb mouths *wow*, sticks his finger in his ear, and shakes it. I jut my jaw forward in an effort to reverse the brain discharge settling like battery acid in my skull. When the ringing in my ears falls from an excruciating level 11, Apocalypse Now, to a mildly agonizing level 6, Apocalypse Later, I pick up the conversation.

"Look, Caleb. It's obvious to me now that all that crap back at Notre Dame, you stealing that stuff from the chem lab, I know it must've been this. The Zarathustra program. Your...er...spy...*hard-on*."

"Yeah, bro. Yeah."

"Okay, okay," I say, wanting to leave it there. He still made out with Kate. That hard-on had been recreational. "Just wanted to say thanks," I say. "Thanks for having my back. Bro."

Caleb's forehead creases like he's not sure he heard me correctly, then he breaks into a full-power Caleb Montana smile that lights up the whole alley.

He raises his hand for a high five. "What're bros for, bro?"

We high-five, and he grabs my hand and does his ridiculous bro-shake thing, finishing with the wink, double-barreled finger guns, and dancing pectorals.

"I've got your back, bro."

"You've got my back, bro," I repeat and, since I'm still in my suit, it comes out like Ghostface from *Scream*.

I hold his gaze for a moment longer before crossing to meet Mary, who's waiting on a darkened doorstep under an awning advertising a yoga business.

"Come on, *bro*," she says, grabbing my upper arm and mimicking Caleb's stupid handshake. "Come back with us to Fortress, *bro*."

"Wait—you and Caleb have been working together the whole time?"

"Well, yeah." Mary balls up her fist and pushes it gently across my chin, moving my head to the right in a pretend punch. "G-spots and hard-ons and all that." She smiles. "Come with us. We've got to debrief you, for one thing. And… I don't want you to be alone."

"Wow," I reply, as the sudden and violent resurgence of the butterflies attack the inside of my stomach. Mary peers into my visor and, not being able to find my eyes, frowns. For once, I'm good and protected from her scrutiny. "I got some things I have to do first."

Her eyebrows lower in apparent frustration, and faint police sirens grow less faint. She casts a glance over her shoulder. Caleb's ready to go, one foot in the driver's side and one foot out.

"C'mon, Mare," he says. "I'm not doin' autographs tonight."

"Autographs?" I ask.

Mary shakes her head. "Long story. Look, I know a lot's happened. When you're ready, call me."

I nod, but when she turns to go, I grab her arm. She turns back to face me, her eyes round and lips parted.

"What's going to happen to Wang and Shmuel?" I ask.

She rolls her eyes and sighs.

"Sorry," I say. "I mean…you're right. A lot's happened. But what happens to them? They know about Zarathustra. And they can identify you and Caleb as spies."

"Well, for starters, they'll get sworn in."

"Sworn in? You're not making them spies?"

"Oh, no, no, no," she says. "God no. *No.* They'll have to sign papers agreeing not to talk about what they saw here. If they do, they can be prosecuted."

I expel a whistle, which sounds ridiculous through the voice-changer on my supersuit, reminding me I need to take it off before exiting the alley. I step around Mary to huddle farther beneath the awning, it being secluded enough to pull the switcheroo to Clark Kent. Mary follows me over. I remove the ring, and we wait as the suit slimes its way back into the ring. The nighttime air is cool on my skin.

"I'll never get used to that," she says, her pretty blue eyes going wide.

She takes my hands and gives them a squeeze. Her gaze is earnest and sympathetic. She leans in and kisses my cheek. Her hair is as fragrant as ever, the lavender mixed more heavily today with the scent of her perspiration. I put my hand on her waist. She's cold and wet. I breathe her in. She pulls out slowly, licks her lips. Her gaze flits up to meet mine. We say nothing, but the wordlessness holds lots of important and mysterious and exciting and necessary future conversations. Ones that I want to have now, but now is goodbye, and Mary's in the Jeep, and it's pulling away, and I'm walking up the street feeling like Jason Bourne as four cop cars race by in the opposite direction.

# CHAPTER NINETY-FIVE

FROM DOWNTOWN, a cab ride to Fabio's is about twenty minutes. I give the driver the address, and he pulls away from the curb. The shakes set in immediately. Followed by sweat. I've already made my decision. I don't know when I made it, but it's been made. This is just follow-through. I have no idea what I'm going to say, nor how I'm going to say it. While I'm not above lying, I've always been more of a lie-by-omission sort of person. That's a different wheelhouse than yarn-spinning. If I straight-up lie to Fabio, he's going to know. Besides, he deserves more than that.

Back at Notre Dame, when I got in trouble—Fabio was the first person I called. When I told him how I'd taken the blame for something I hadn't done, he didn't yell at me. He didn't tell me I was an idiot. He just asked how we were going to play it with Gran, and whether I'd need a place to stay until I figured everything out. As friends go, he's as good as they come. He's stood by me through thick and thin. His heart is true. This is why, if I *am* going to fake my death, walk out on Gran like Dad did, Fabio needs to know. If I really am going to become the world's first superhero, I'll need my best friend.

I pay the driver, forking over the last of my dough on the tip. The cab pulls away so quickly his back tires kick up dust in my face. I cough, wave it away, and turn to face The Palace.

I head up the path to the courtyard, watch my feet go up and down. All I can think of is the look on Gran's face when she gets the news. The look in her eyes. Am I really making the right decision?

When I get to Fabio's unit, I find the light on. I raise my hand to knock. Feet scuff behind me, stopping me mid-swing. I turn around. Fabio's holding an opened package of double-A batteries and looking at me like I just burned his entire collection of Madmartigan posters.

"I've been trying to call you," he says.

"Sorry," I reply, keeping steady eye contact. "I'm okay now. It got a little hairy there for a bit."

Swallow, wait.

Fabio makes an exaggerated eye roll, then pushes past me and sticks his key in the door. He goes inside, but leaves the door open.

I go in after him.

He goes straight for his Xbox controller, pops the back off, and replaces the batteries. The TV is on. He's got *Call of Duty WWII* paused.

"What the hell, dude?" he says, turning to face me and chucking the controller onto the couch.

"I know, I know—"

"So, what? Coming in here and, and—and acting like nothing's happened. Now you're going to ask me to forgive you. Aren't you. For not letting me know you're okay. That's not the answer, Edge."

"No, that's the question. Yes is the answer."

"Uh-uh, you don't get to do that."

"Do what?"

"Come in here with your stupid jokes. They're stupid, Edge. Your jokes are stupid."

"Okay," I say, using the surrender hands and taking a deep breath.

"Your apartment blew up!"

"Yeah, it did…"

"I thought you were dead. Crap—I coulda been dead! What if I'd let myself in through the Fabio door? Did you ever think of that? Crap, dude!"

"I did. It's kinda why I'm here now."

Fabio frowns. "The hell's that supposed to mean?"

And so I lay it out. I take him through the last ninety-six hours, just like it happened. I tell him about the terrorists and the gay pride parades. I tell him about the power grids. The football game and the nightclub. I even tell him about Dad—and what Doctor Hamilton said about Gran. I tell him how she can still have a normal life, but how I never will again. I tell him how he's always been my best friend, and how I'm going to need him, everything being so crazy now, and when I'm done, he stands there with his mouth hanging open, and the TV is flashing: reconnect controller, reconnect controller, reconnect controller. And so this is us. Best friends are like video games. You can't play video games without controllers, and controllers don't work without batteries. Now, I don't know where this metaphor is going, all I know is, if your controller dies, everyone starts killing you. And then you pop back to life, and they kill you some more. It's horrible.

Reconnect controller.

Reconnect controller.

Fabio looks at the TV too and, despite this endearing moment we're having, there are some things that just take precedence.

"Didn't you just change the battery?" I ask.

"Goddamn Wang," he says, looking at the opened package of batteries. "He said these were good. Fuck." He shuts off the console. "Dude. You want me to pretend you're dead?"

I take a deep breath and let it out before nodding.

"And so everyone at work... I'm just...supposed to...lie to them?"

I bite my lip and say nothing. It's a big ask. Hearing him repeat it back to me is somehow harder than asking in the first place.

He expels a burst of air from his mouth. "Yeah, buddy. Okay."

My knees buckle with relief, and I fall into the couch. But Fabio's still talking.

"I mean, best friend," he says, pointing with two thumbs at himself. "So, you know. As best friend favors go, I've heard worse."

"Fabio, you *are* the best."

"I know."

"You could've told me to go stick my head in an ostrich vagina. And I'd totally get that. If that's how you felt about it."

Fabio frowns. "It's like we share the same brain. God. What's wrong with you?"

"Do ostriches even have vaginas?" I ask.

"I mean, probably?" he says. "Does that mean you're considering it?"

"No, dude. No faking my death is worth the head in the ostrich vagina."

He shrugs. "Well, okay, then. In that case, walk with me to the Circle K. I wanna get some batteries."

Fabio and I head down to the Circle K. The streetlights are dim. We pass a gutter clogged with plastic cups and empty snack packs. I use my foot to clear the drain, then glance at my watch. Not even eleven o'clock. What with everything that's happened, it feels like today should already be tomorrow.

"You need to get going?" asks Fabio.

"No," I reply. "Just thinking about Gran."

"You sure you're up for this?"

My lips compress. I swallow against the lump growing in my throat. Fabio shrugs like he's given up on an answer.

"I know what I'm going to do," I say. "I—it won't be all right. But she'll know I'm all right. If that makes sense."

Fabio rolls his eyes and shakes his head.

"There's not gonna be a family reunion. There was never gonna be a time when my mom and dad come back and live with me and Gran. And the Zarathustra stuff is never going away. Whether I'm up for it isn't a factor. I'm in it now. And you know, I think Gran knows that too."

"Yeah?" he says. "Why's that?"

"Something she told me last night. Endings are messy. That's what she said."

"No shit?"

"Yeah. She said endings are messy."

"Well, this is one friggin' messy ending, all right," he says, rolling his eyes and shaking his head again, and we leave it there.

# CHAPTER NINETY-SIX

THE THING ABOUT FAKING YOUR DEATH is that it's a lot easier when you've got spies and the Collective Unconscious to handle the tricky parts—which is to say, all of it. As it turns out, Mary already has the pieces in place, though she's insisted we hold off discussing it until getting me to Fortress, where she, Caleb, and Doctor Hamilton are waiting.

Stepping off the elevator and into Fortress for the first time is a lot to take in at once: cement walls lined with guns and ammo, katana swords, throwing stars, grenades, gas pellets, computers, lab stations, conference tables. It's pretty much every secret-base trope I've seen on TV where there's one person stationed at a computer remotely assisting another person who is fighting bad guys, usually in dark alleys. The difference here, though, is that this secret-base trope has an abundance of Chargers memorabilia.

"Hey, bro. Welcome to Fortress." Caleb claps a hand on my shoulder, then turns and gestures to a conference table where Doctor Hamilton is seated near a forty-two-inch Panasonic TV screen, a model we carry at the Über Dork.

"Mr. Bonkovich," she says, smiling faintly.

"This is so surreal," I reply, taking down a Chargers mug off a shelf. "You guys loot the gift shop upstairs?"

Mary comes up on my other side, loops her arm through mine,

and leads me to the table. Doctor Hamilton picks up the TV remote and presses the power button. The screen resolves into a slow aerial shot of a coastal resort. There are no young people on the beach, only senior citizens. I shift sharply in my seat to face Doctor Hamilton.

"Is that Pine's Place?" I ask. She nods. "What is this?"

Mary touches my leg. "It's okay. This is to show you. We have her under surveillance. She's *safe*, Edger. That's what you want, and as long as we keep an eye on her, we don't have any reason to think that's going to change."

"I'm a reason."

"But no one knows you're Zarathustra."

"Except Nostradamus."

"Who now thinks you're dead. Edger—anyone can be Zarathustra. As far as they know, your dad gave the formula to someone else. So, when Zarathustra rides again, they'll have no choice but to conclude your dad's doing what he's been doing for twenty years. Fighting the good fight. Finding the next worthy person."

My eyebrows come down.

"So this is what?" I ask, gesturing to the screen. "Witness protection?"

"Is that what you want? WITSEC?" asks Doctor Hamilton.

"What I want is her in Pine's Place. That's the whole point of doing this, faking my death. Like you said. Giving her a normal life."

Doctor Hamilton shrugs and gestures with the remote to the TV. She presses a button, and the scene changes to inside Gran and Shep's kitchen. My throat clenches; there they are, unpacking and talking. Shep is plugging in the espresso maker I bought him for Christmas. Gran is grinding the beans in the grinder I bought her.

"There's no sound," I say, my voice hitching in my throat. I swallow, and it hurts.

"We have audio capability," says Doctor Hamilton. "Out of respect for their privacy, I've shut off."

I try to say thank you, but the words won't come. My eyes sting. Mary squeezes my hand. On TV, Shep comes up from behind Gran and slips his arms around her. He holds her close like that, and she nuzzles her head backward into his chest, eyes closed. A tear escapes the corner of her eye.

"I know it's complicated," says Caleb, reaching across the table and powering off the TV. "You dad used to say it never got easier. But he did it. You can do it too."

I close my eyes and shake my head. Faking my death. The pain I'm inflicting to keep her safe and her life normal. Is this what it feels like to be my dad?

"It's so extreme," I hear myself say, my eyes still closed.

"I wish my parents had done what you're doing," says Mary. "It would've spared me a lot of pain."

"Look," says Doctor Hamilton, and her no-nonsense tone pulls me out of my head. I open my eyes, and her dark gaze is boring into me. "It's called compartmentalization. You can do your job knowing she's safe. I know it's hard to accept, but this is the least complicated—least extreme solution."

My chest tightens. The tension creeps around my shoulders and into my back. I'm sick with the dread from this already. How can this be the best solution, knowing it feels like this?

"Edger," says Mary. "Are you sure this is what you want?"

"Of course not," I reply, my voice affecting a casualness I'm not feeling. "But you know, when Gran lost Dad and her daughter-in-law twenty years ago, that was the end of something too. But her raising me was the beginning of something else. And that beginning led to a whole new story. We had a life together. We had ups and downs. It was good. I can't know if what we're doing now is right. To see the hurt and pain makes me think it isn't. But I do know she's got a beginning in front of her again. She's got plenty of good years left in her. That's something. And I think she knew this was coming. She made me promise to do something for myself, live a little, and so I'm keeping that promise. She told me endings are messy. But you know what? So are beginnings."

My cheeks go hot. That may've been the longest speech I've ever given. Caleb claps his hand on my back. Mary smiles faintly, then peers into her lap. Doctor Hamilton breaks the awkward silence.

"This is going to make a lot of things easier on our end, Mr. Bonkovich."

"Please," I say, rolling my eyes and spinning in my chair three hundred sixty degrees. "I am *so* not a mister."

Doctor Hamilton, the steely-faced beauty, gives me a mysterious smile. "Okay. Edger," she says, her tone softening. "I'm Alex."

Mary sits forward, framing her face in front of Alex's. "I think what Alex is saying is that if you're dead, we don't need to worry about you going immediately into the field. It gives us some breathing room."

"Yeah, bro," says Caleb. "Lying ain't as easy as it looks. And once you get a new identity, you'll be lying to like, everyone. Seriously. No offense, bro, but you'd suck at it."

"No offense taken," I reply, and a new thought hits me. "So, what about Mikey?"

"What about him?" asks Caleb. Mary leans back to exchange an unreadable look with Alex.

"I mean, why isn't he here? Isn't he, you know, kind of our team leader?"

Another exchange of unreadable looks go around the table.

"What?" I ask.

Mary takes a centering breath before answering. "Edger, Mikey thinks you're dead. As far as he knows, he thinks it's his fault."

"Well, that's terrible!" I exclaim. "You can't leave it like that. You have to, I don't know, maybe you could tell him I don't blame him or something. I mean, like I told you before I died or something? I could write a note—"

"Edger," says Mary, her forehead tightening. "He chose you because he thought you were expendable! Remember?"

I shrug. "Well, yeah. But that's only because I am. I mean, I was."

"Naw, bro," says Caleb. "I owe you everything. You saved my academic career, my football career, *and* my spy career. You're not expendable. Not before, not now, not ever."

"But Mikey," I reply, my cheeks burning again. "This is *his* thing. I mean, he invented the Tron-Tron. He's been working on it since forever."

"We're not giving you back to Mike Dame," says Alex, her tone final.

"You don't trust him?"

"That's not the point," says Mary, her eyes on Alex.

"The point is," says Alex, her gaze taking us each in turn, "we've taken Zarathustra from him. We've taken it from our respective governments. And we are not giving it—you—back." Her dark gaze searches Mary's eyes before continuing. "We can't give you to the CIA. We can't give you to any government. Edger, you single-handedly defeated terrorism in one night. Your *first* night as a superhero. You're already that powerful. And your power is only going to grow. The fact is, for all the debate our respective spy chiefs have had over how this was going to go down, we're in uncharted territory now."

"I agree," says Mary.

Caleb's lips compress. He eyes each of us thoughtfully.

"Caleb, you know he's too powerful—and way too naïve to serve an intelligence agency!" cries Alex.

"And you do know I'm sitting right here?" I fire back.

"I don't know." Caleb shakes his head. "It could be treason. And if it isn't treason, we'll def get sent to jail for the rest of our lives if we're caught. So, say we lie to our bosses. Then what? Keep superheroing from the shadows? That could so totes ruin my careers, guys. Like, even my Calvin Klein contract."

"It's what Edger did for you," says Mary, pinning Caleb under her legendary Scrutiny Eyes. He shifts in his seat uncomfortably and casts a glance my direction.

"Yeah, okay," he says at last. "I guess… I guess it's less than what you did for me, bro. Unless I get caught. In which case we're even. Okay?"

I use my surrender hands. "Hey—you don't owe me Jack," I lie, flashing back to the seared mental image of him kissing Kate.

I take a deep breath and release it. We all sit around in awkward silence for a few minutes. I focus on my breathing and try to master the conflicting forces scraping inside of me. I focus on the people.

Caleb, our history finally making some sense; Mary—my soon-to-be roomie and bodyguard; Alex, darkly beautiful and mysterious, and risking her career for her faith in a stranger.

"I guess that's it," says Mary. "We're a team."

"Team Zarathustra," says Caleb. "Yeah. PMA. I like it."

"Team Zarathustra," repeats Mary, casting an oblique gaze and lopsided smile at me.

"Z-Team," says Alex, somehow managing to glower and smile at the same time. When every head turns to face her, she tips her head back and laughs. "Z-Team," she says again, sardonically. "Just to be different—and so nobody gets any ideas with the fucking acronyms."

# CHAPTER NINETY-SEVEN

A WEEK PASSES before my funeral. Mary and I stake out a spot up on the hill near a mausoleum. It's a blue sky. The sun is halfway up, or a quarter of a day gone, depending on how you look at it.

The spectacle is surreal. I feel terrible. Ashamed of myself. It's all I can do not to charge down that hill and confess; I focus instead on memorizing the scene. Gran and Shep, praying. Wang and Shmuel hanging back and smoking a joint. Jama Jan, my boss at the Über Dork, blowing her nose and throwing her arms around an embarrassed Fabio. To think, there was a time when I thought if I threw my life away to become Zarathustra, no one would miss me. I measured my worth by my job, by Kate, and by my failure at Notre Dame. But they didn't measure my worth that way at all.

I clench my teeth and fight back tears. Mary slides her hand into mine. She pulls me nearer, wraps her arm around mine, and squeezes. Her touch is as thrilling as ever. Her gaze is sincere and ice blue. It's easy to picture those eyes peering through her rifle scope before she snipers somebody to death. It isn't easy to picture waking up in the same house together and not fearing for my life. We're supposed to move in together. But she's a spy and a killer. Who can say where this is going? Still holding my gaze, she gently brushes a tear from my cheek with the backs of her fingers. Her lips compress, and she turns her attention back to the scene below.

The chaplain's words are faint, something about finding victory in death. Boy has he got it wrong. Dying only to live on in the Collective Unconscious, watching the next generation come along and muck up everything you tried to build, that's not victory. But all that pain at the bottom of the hill isn't victory either. A part of their lives—me—has been cut out. And they can never get it back. That's the definition of losing. For everyone. Because even though I'm still walking this earth, I'm also walking with the soul-stars. I'm like them now. Condemned to a purgatory of watching everyone go on without me, no longer participating in their lives and decisions. Does that make me dead, alive, or something else?

The chaplain is winding things down. Mary and I head out ahead of the rest. We say nothing, and I'm still spinning on death being neither a victory nor loss per se. Because even though we miss our loved ones, and we mourn them, we also carry them with us. I know, it's cheesy. But it's true. They may not have the power to interact with the living in the way I do, but we nevertheless feel their love at random times, and in random things. A bird landing on the railing. A flower blooming at just the right moment.

This is where my head is at when we swing by a mailbox on the way out. I drop an envelope inside, addressed to Gran at Pine's Place. She was never into Calvin and Hobbes comics as much as me or Dad, but that isn't the point in sending them to her. My hope is she'll open it, see what's inside, and she'll know in her heart it's from me. She'll sense I'm okay. She'll know I'll always love her. She'll know I'm with her, and keeping an eye on her. And that's all any of us dead folks can really do.

# HISTORIC SAYONARA, BY HERODOTUS (C. 484—C. 425 BCE)

IT HAS BEEN SAID all good things must come to an end. And it's terrible this has been said, because bad things get to go on forever. Torture, war, famine, and the unholy apotheosis of the Big Three: the turducken. As sayings go, it sucks. It's right up there with "the customer is always right." Or "I'll just take a minute of your time." I mean, come *on*. Nobody ever takes *just* a minute of your time, and everyone who's ever worked in customer service knows the customer is *not* always right.

And since we're riffing on clichés again, here's another: *it's the little things which make life worth living*. This one happens to be true. Just ask Christine of the El Cerrito Cluck-n-Pray. For Christine, the "little things" began when a nano-artificial intelligence made its new home behind a tiny booger forming in her left nostril. Next, the little things developed to include dozens of ATMs miraculously spitting out all their money into her duffel bag; her hair in the wind when she's doing ninety in her brand-spanking-new Maserati convertible as she speeds east on Route 66; the feeling she got after forcing Brad and the Apostles to line up and get kicked in the nuts. For Christine is a young woman who has come to appreciate life's little gifts. Presently, these gifts are: sharing a road joint with her lover, Consuelo; new clothes that don't smell like chicken; daydreaming about the rustic flavor of really great grass.

# CHAPTER NINETY-EIGHT

THE SUN IS SHINING directly above by the time Mary and I reach the Baseline Avenue exit going into Ballard, a small town just outside of Santa Barbara. Mary cuts around me at the last second to reach the exit first. I'm tempted to summon Mario Andretti, but the residential traffic changes my mind. I downshift, and the Ferrari releases a sigh of disappointment. The wind dies in my hair and ears. I follow Mary through three turns. We slow to a crawl and scan addresses on picket mailboxes. Then, we're there. I roll to a stop behind Mary's Jag, put it in Neutral, pull up the parking brake, and let out the clutch.

"Made good time," says Mary, coming over to meet me.

"You're a lead foot," I reply.

We open the white gate and head up the boardwalk, then a short flight of stairs to reach the front porch of a modest two-story home. Mary knocks. A minute later, a woman appears in the doorway. Farther inside the house, her teenage daughter rises from the kitchen table.

"Who is it, Mom?"

"Can I help you?" asks the mother.

"Are you Jill?" asks Mary.

"Yes." Jill unties her apron. Her gaze tracks over Mary's shoulder to take in the Porsche and Ferrari. The screen door creaks as she cracks it just enough to slip out and onto the porch.

"We're friends of your late husband, Trevor," I say, and Jill lays her hand over her mouth.

"Oh my God," she says.

"Mom? What is it?" asks her daughter, coming to the door.

"Go back inside, honey."

"We can't stay," says Mary. "We'll just give you these and be on our way."

Mary holds out the keys to the Ferrari. Jill gasps. She peels a hand from her mouth, tentatively. Mary takes it, puts the keys in her palm, and closes her hand.

"It's free and clear," I say. "It's in your name. There's a signed document in the glove compartment promising you'll never owe a dime to Uncle Sam for it."

At the gate, we pass a mailbox that reads "Killmaster." Whoops of joy follow us from inside the house. We climb into the Jag and buckle in. We're off for one crazy ride. My gaze lingers for a moment on the spine of the book sticking out of Mary's purse, *Now What? The Rest of Your Life Edition*. Mary starts the car. We make a U-turn, ignoring Jill Killmaster's cries for us to wait and explain and thank you and God bless us and have a nice weekend. It's hard ignoring all that with her late husband, the big, strong Navy SEAL, weeping inside my head. But it feels like this is one of those times when less is more. There's nothing we can say that she'd believe, and we've done what we came to do.

We pull away, and I'm lost in thought for the long drive down the coast. It's hard to imagine this new life ahead of me with all those old ones in my head. I guess I can make sense of it as being like the Golden Rule. If Gran can get a cartoon in the mail from beyond the grave, then Jill Killmaster deserves hers too. It's no less than the dead would do for me. I know that's true. I can feel it. We're all part of the same tribe. That's the message here. It's clear to me. And while I didn't learn anything at Notre Dame to prepare me for disco ball Chinese water torture chambers, assassin clones, superintelligent AI cows, or NFL supervillains—hey, life rarely takes the course we chart for ourselves. This is my course now. This is the new me. My name is Edger Bonkovich, and I am Zarathustra.

As one of the greatest authors of his generation, David Beem accepts no responsibility or liability of any kind for the accuracy, content, completeness, competency, legality, or reliability of his various writings. By reading something he's written, or talking to someone who's read something he's written, looking at, or even breathing the same air as someone who's read something he's written, you agree to these terms.

David Beem enjoys superhero movies, taekwondo, and flossing. He lives in Djibouti with his family and crippling self-doubt. To help actualize David's inner confidence, visit his website and buy all the stuff: www.davidbeem.com

Made in the USA
San Bernardino, CA
06 June 2018